Written in Blood

Stephen Puleston

ABOUT THE AUTHOR

Stephen Puleston was born and educated in Anglesey, North Wales. He graduated in theology before training as a lawyer. A Time to Kill is his fifth novel in the Inspector Drake series

www.stephenpuleston.co.uk
Facebook:stephenpulestoncrimewriter

OTHER NOVELS

Inspector Drake Mysteries

Brass in Pocket ✗
Worse than Dead ✗
Against the Tide ✗
Dead on your Feet ✗
A Time to Kill ✗
Prequel Novella– Ebook only - Devil's Kitchen

Inspector Marco Novels

Speechless ✗
Another Good Killing ✗
Somebody Told Me
Prequel Novella– Ebook only -Dead Smart

ISBN-13:9781728662664

In memory of my mother
Gwenno Puleston

Background

In England and Wales the legal profession is divided into solicitors and barristers. The term 'lawyer' can be used generically for both. Solicitors make up the largest profession and barristers generally specialise in court work. Barristers are based in 'chambers' in the larger towns and cities, whereas solicitors have offices open to the public.

A circuit judge hears the majority of criminal cases in the Crown courts and is usually appointed from the ranks of the barrister profession. The role is prestigious and carries the title His/Her Honour Judge.

Chapter 1

Nicholas Wixley poured the last mouthful of the Taittinger 96 into a cut-glass champagne flute. The last time he had savoured the same vintage was in the company of Mandy, and she had been just as energetic tonight as she had been that evening. He walked over to the picture window and watched as the last of the milky moon slipped behind a bank of dark cloud. It had been a good day, a good few weeks. Now he looked forward to a week of sailing on the waters of Cardigan Bay, which stretched out below him. A friend described the sport as a great leveller among men, but Nicholas Wixley thought differently. It was a sport he had to push to its limits; he challenged himself to win every race, stretching the sail until the wind squeezed every last knot of speed from it.

He smiled as he reminded himself that every eventuality had developed exactly as he had anticipated. Now he planned to enjoy the rewards. The prestige, and the investment plans carefully nurtured over the years would maximise his income, his wealth and status.

A ripple of moonshine crossed the surface of the water reminding him of the salt on his lips and the sea air on his face that afternoon. Sailing for a few hours had been the tonic he needed after three testing weeks in the Manchester Crown Court. During one case, he had even gently corrected the judge about a point of law although he had no idea why he did so – the old fool was retiring very soon. Then things would change.

He moved his gaze across the long beach below the headland and noticed torchlight and a fire – youngsters having a late-night barbecue. He sipped on the expensive champagne; the fizz had gone but the taste of luxury remained. He grinned to himself, he would sleep well tonight.

He'd shower before bed, allow the remains of the evening's exertions to be washed away. In the morning, he'd open the windows and clear the place of the smell of sex and perspiration. It could be thick in the air, especially in a house that had been closed for most of the winter. He turned back to face the room. Mandy's pink gilet lay on the sofa. Tomorrow he'd discard it in a bin near the marina.

Deciding a decent slug of a twenty-year-old malt whisky would be his nightcap, he ambled through into the kitchen where he poured himself a generous measure. Leaving the kitchen, he stopped and stood in the hallway on hearing the sound of movement outside the front door.

Mandy must have returned for her gilet.

She had left only a few minutes ago.

He opened the door. His face darkened.

Chapter 2

Monday 25th March
9.34 am

Ian Drake pressed the top of a coffee flask and watched as a hot liquid dribbled into the heavy china cup he had collected from a table near the entrance of the training suite. Since the creation of the Wales Police Service after the amalgamation of the four previous forces, more all-Wales events took place. That day's session for young aspiring detectives, on being part of a major crime squad, was no different. Drake picked up accents from numerous places, including Cardiff – the voice of one female officer reminded him so much of Annie they could have passed for sisters.

Lisa Robinson from HR and another civilian fussed around, making certain there were adequate pads of paper and bottles of water on each table before turning their attention to the PowerPoint presentation. An inspector from Wrexham was going to lead the first session. Drake's hour-slot wasn't due to start until eleven and he idly wondered whether anyone would have noticed his absence had he not arrived first thing. He could have stayed in bed with Annie for another hour. The prospect made him smile to himself. She was working from home that morning – lecturing at Bangor University's history department certainly had its perks, Drake thought.

Later that week the group of probationers would be visiting an outward bound centre – a converted farmhouse in the mountains – for a full day's activities. Gareth Winder and Luned Thomas, the constables on

7

his team, had both recently participated, tramping through the mud and gorse. Paintballing would probably have been a lot more effective and a lot more fun, Winder had announced when they'd returned to headquarters.

'Good morning, boss,' Sara said, arriving by his side without him realising she was in the room. Drake turned to face her and she smiled. Her auburn hair looked neatly trimmed, and her navy jacket with a cream blouse underneath made it very clear to the young probationers that she was a detective sergeant.

'What was the traffic like this morning?' Drake said.

Asking about the traffic was almost as popular as asking about the weather, particularly as the roadworks on the A55, the main route along the north Wales coast, affected everyone working in Northern Division; it could dominate conversations.

Sara gave a world-weary shrug as though there was nothing new she could say. 'Did you travel over this morning?'

Sara probably knew that he hadn't. Once she had discovered Annie was on the scene Drake had felt a distinct change in her attitude towards him. Sara seemed more relaxed now in his company and working alongside him. He shook his head. 'I stayed over.' It was all he needed to say.

'Do you think this is a valuable use of our time?' Sara said.

Drake took a sip of the bitter coffee and smarted, feeling the acrid taste clinging to the side of his mouth.

'I can think of better things we could be doing this morning.' Drake's mind drifted to the series of robberies in some of the isolated villages on the island of Anglesey. A man brandishing what looked like a replica handgun had threatened shopkeepers demanding the contents of their tills. 'Have you made any progress with the photofits for those robberies?'

'All of the shopkeepers have got a different version. I'm not certain we'll ever make headway without CCTV.'

Drake nodded as Lisa Robinson jerked her head towards the front of the room. Two tables and chairs had been set out facing the rows of seats reserved for the probationers.

'Time to begin,' Drake said.

He left his coffee, depositing the cup and saucer on the table next to a plate of custard creams and a plastic mug full of dirty teaspoons. Sara followed him, and they sat down.

Drake and Sara listened to Lisa Robinson explaining what would happen that day. She nodded at Drake and Sara when she mentioned their names as the two officers leading on 'complex murder investigations'.

Two-dozen enthusiastic pairs of eyes gazed over at Drake and Sara. As unlikely as it seemed, looking at them now, these are the detectives of the future, Drake thought. Some of these young officers would go on to become inspectors, superintendents, maybe even higher up the chain of command. Others, from his own experience, would leave the force, unable to handle the stress, having their ambitions thwarted by office politics, or seeing less able colleagues promoted ahead of them.

Drake gave Robinson a serious nod of

acknowledgement.

She turned to the other inspector who was about to begin his presentation.

A uniformed sergeant entered the training suite and walked purposefully down the side of the room, and Drake realised he was heading towards him. Robinson gave him an inquisitive, almost troubled, glare as though she were personally offended he was interrupting.

The sergeant leaned down and whispered in Drake's ear. 'Superintendent Price wants you to call him. It's urgent.'

As Drake stood up Sara nodded her understanding that he had to leave.

The sergeant led Drake into an office warmed by banks of computers and monitors. A whiteboard on one wall had weekly rosters of officers pinned to it. 'Use one of these phones.' He pointed to an empty desk.

Drake drew up a chair and punched in the right number.

'I tried your mobile earlier.'

'I'm in this training session, sir.'

'Of course, of course,' Price sounded flustered as though he were annoyed with himself that he had forgotten.

'There's a report of a body in a house near Pwllheli. And it's the worst possible morning for something like this to happen. Detective Inspector Hawkins should have taken it but he's on holiday in Turkey and it's impossible to get hold of him.' It sounded as though Price had contemplated the possibility of getting Hawkins back from Turkey to be in charge of a murder inquiry on the Llŷn Peninsula.

'I'll need to notify Lisa Robinson.' His mind accelerated. 'Are there officers at the scene?'

'Get on with it, Ian. I'll tell the people from HR what's happening. I want you and Detective Sergeant Morgan en route within five minutes. I'll get operational support to contact you with all the details.'

The line went dead.

Drake got to his feet. The night before, he had practised the PowerPoint presentation several times, absorbing Annie's suggestions – she had called it 'constructive criticism' – and that morning he had been rehearsing the comments he intended to make. Part of him was disappointed that he couldn't actually share his experience with the recruits.

It lasted a fraction of a second.

There was a murder scene to get to.

Drake hurried back to the training suite and gestured at Sara to join him.

He motioned for Robinson to leave with Sara, and the frown on her face deepened. The Wrexham inspector's voice droning on became a muffled sound as Drake made for reception.

Sara was the first to arrive.

'We are leaving now. A body's been found in a house near Pwllheli.'

Robinson joined them. She opened her mouth to say something, but Drake cut across her. 'We have to leave. Superintendent Price wants to speak to you.'

Drake and Sara jogged to his Mondeo parked in the police station's secure car park. He swiped his security pass and sped out of the industrial estate towards the main road out of Caernarfon.

'Call area control.' Drake snapped.

As they reached the outskirts of the town, the traffic slowed their progress and he cursed that he wasn't in a car equipped with blue flashing lights and a siren loud enough to sweep all vehicles to one side. Getting to the crime scene was a priority, even though there was a dead body that was going nowhere except the mortuary. It reminded Drake that high on his list for sharing with the trainees that morning was the importance of the first twenty-four hours after the discovery of a corpse. Eyewitnesses would have to be traced, house-to-house enquiries commenced, recollections were at their best in that period. Impatience clawed at his chest as he watched a slow queue of traffic dawdling its way over the roundabout at Bontnewydd. There had been talk of a bypass for years and Drake had even visited an exhibition in the village with his mother but in an age of austerity and tight budgets, the plans had been shelved.

Sara was on the phone. She nodded occasionally, and asked for a postcode and details of names, and the anticipated arrival time of a forensic team. When she finished, she turned to Drake.

'Victim is a man called Nicholas Wixley. His cleaner found him this morning – his throat had been cut and his body mutilated.'

'Any more details? Family?'

'That's all I got, boss. Operational support is going to send us the postcode.' Before Sara could continue, her mobile phone buzzed. She glanced at the screen and punched the details into the satnav.

'Thirty-five minutes,' she said.

In the rear-view mirror, Drake saw the traffic backing up behind him. He tried to think of an alternative route that would get them there more quickly. Going left at the roundabout would take them back around Caernarfon, and he dismissed the possibility of going via Beddgelert and Porthmadog, guessing it would add ten miles to their journey at least.

Gradually the traffic moved on through the roundabout.

'Find out about the CSIs.' Drake hovered his hand over the car horn ready to blast the vehicle in front, which appeared to be slowing to turn right across the slow-moving traffic approaching them.

'Mike Foulds and his team are behind us,' Sara said, referring to the crime scene manager.

The team would have come from headquarters. Drake could well imagine that Superintendent Price would have organised a high-speed escort, lights flashing and siren blaring, to cut through the inevitable delays.

After Bontnewydd the traffic thinned as the roundabouts and junctions gave way to clear stretches of road. It pleased Drake when the traffic in front of him took the left-hand slip road by a roundabout for Porthmadog. He followed the directions for Pwllheli and the Llŷn peninsula. After another collection of houses lining the road he floored the accelerator but it was a single-lane carriageway and soon he saw a van and two cars in the lane ahead of him. 'Why the hell do we have all these Sunday drivers on a Monday morning?'

Sara didn't bother responding.

Despite the initial delays to their journey, they made good time and within twenty-five minutes they were slowing down as they neared their destination.

The satnav instructed Drake to follow a narrow, gravelled road up towards a headland. To his left were two timber-framed properties under construction. Further on to his right were detached bungalows overlooking the sea.

In the distance a uniformed officer stood by a gate to a house.

After parking, Drake walked over and introduced himself. 'I am glad to see you, sir. Constable Tony Roberts; I'm based in Pwllheli.'

Drake glanced over the young officer's shoulder. The property was an older style with large windows, its immaculate Welsh-slate-clad roof broken by two dormers. A Mercedes S Class, its plates less than two years old, sat outside a garage with old oak doors.

'This way,' Roberts said as he turned on his heels, nodding at the same time to the inside of the building. 'The cleaner found his body a little after nine-thirty this morning.'

'Is this a holiday home?' Drake said.

Roberts nodded. 'Apparently she's worked for the family for twenty years.'

Roberts turned a brass knob on the dark-blue front door and they made their way inside. The property felt modern, with white walls and ceilings, stripped-down and minimalist. Alcoves displayed small sculptures, and artworks hung from the walls in carefully curated groups. The owners wanted to broadcast that they had lots of money.

Drake glanced at Sara, knowing she had an interest in antiques and art. 'Anything you recognise?'

Sara shook her head but seconds later she spoke. 'Any sign of a break-in? Anything missing?'

'The cleaner is in a pretty bad way. We haven't been able to get much out of her. We've got the contact telephone number for Mrs Wixley and we've given all the details to area control.'

Drake nodded. He could hear activity in what he assumed was the kitchen to the left of the hallway, but he followed Roberts through to the right. The property felt larger on the inside than it looked from the outside. At the far end of a passageway a door was ajar.

'He's in there.' Roberts stopped a few feet short of the doorway itself, his face a sickly grey.

Drake turned to Sara. They exchanged an encouraging glance, not knowing what to expect.

Drake snapped on a pair of latex gloves. Sara did the same and followed Drake inside until he stopped and stood, looking down at the body of a middle-aged man, naked apart from a pair of red football socks.

'Christ Almighty,' Sara exclaimed, pressing a hand to her mouth.

The letter E had been stencilled into Wixley's stomach. His neck had been severed, which meant there was blood. Lots: on his body, on the white sheets of the bed, on the headboard, on the pillows and presumably all over the killer.

Drake slowly took in everything about the room. A glass tumbler and a half-filled champagne flute stood on a bedside table. A killer had been there hours earlier.

'He'll be covered in blood.' Sara turned her back to the man on the bed.

'It could have been a woman.'

'You should take a look at this, boss.' Sara was looking at a makeshift corkboard nailed to one wall with protruding six-inch nails. On it were cuttings from various newspapers reporting the outcome of court proceedings – 'child killer gets life', 'prosecutor describes life of depravity'. The name of the prosecutor stood out – Nicholas Wixley. Looking at the headlines, it struck Drake that their immediate suspect could well be in the pot of criminals Wixley had prosecuted. But how many of them would go to the trouble of staging such a scene?

A few feet from the base of the bed, five dining chairs were set out neatly. A funeral directors' order of service lay on each seat cushion. Drake picked up the first. 'This is for a Jason Pownall from Stockport,' Drake said. He opened the cover and recoiled when he saw blood. He turned to Sara. 'The letter D has been daubed inside.'

He replaced the first and picked up another from the second chair and discovered the letter E written in blood on the inside. Sara opened the third carefully. She turned to Drake. 'It has the letter A.'

Then Sara opened the final two. 'Two more letters, T and H.'

'Death,' Drake said. 'What sort of sick bastard...?'

Why had the order of service from five different funerals been left at a murder scene in a holiday home in north Wales?

Drake surveyed the rest of the room. A fifty-five-inch television dominated one wall. Drake flicked through a collection of DVDs on top of a cupboard, including the Jason Bourne trilogy and the latest James Bond films. Behind him, Drake heard Sara opening the contents of a bedside cabinet.

'You won't believe this, boss.'

Drake turned and saw her holding up a bag of

white powder.

'That doesn't look like talcum powder to me,' Drake said, raising an eyebrow.

The sound of vehicles arriving drifted into the house: engines being switched off, car doors being opened and discussions taking place with Constable Roberts. Drake recognised the voice of Mike Foulds. This would be his crime scene now.

'Let's go and talk to the woman who found the body,' Drake said.

He reached the door into the hallway when his mobile rang – Superintendent Price's name appeared on the screen. It put Drake on edge that Price had called so quickly for an update.

'Is it Nicholas Wixley, the barrister from Manchester?' Price said.

Drake cast a sideways glance back into the bedroom. 'Yes, sir.'

'Jesus. His wife is Laura Wixley.'

The name meant nothing to Drake, so he wasn't certain how to react. His silence must have irked Price, who raised his voice. 'That's Deputy Chief Constable Laura Wixley.'

Chapter 3

Monday 25th March
12.30 pm

A white-suited Mike Foulds whistled under his breath when he entered the bedroom. The crime scene manager had seen some horrific examples of human depravity and his reaction encouraged Drake to believe that he could still be shocked.

'Somebody's been busy.' Foulds glanced at Drake and Sara standing in the doorway. Behind them a team of investigators lugged bags of equipment into the hallway.

'Do you need identification?' Foulds studied the body and the bed slowly.

'Nicholas Wixley,' Drake said. 'He's a hotshot barrister from Manchester and this was his holiday home.'

'Lawyer?' Foulds said, as though the very word explained everything, offering up a whole world of suspects with genuine motives. 'We'd better get to work then.'

Drake and Sara walked through to the kitchen where PC Roberts stood by an ancient Belfast sink. He straightened when Drake entered and introduced his colleague, sitting at a large pine table in the middle of the room, as Nia Jones. She got up, but Drake motioned for her to sit back down alongside a woman in her late forties. 'This is Gillian Evans, sir. She was the first on the scene this morning.'

Drake pulled up a chair and leaned over and looked at Evans. Her hair had been tied back severely; a streak of blood discoloured the top half of her housecoat and for a moment Drake contemplated the possibility that she had been the killer. Her eyes were swollen, and she played aimlessly with a small handkerchief.

'It is important you tell us as much as you can remember. What time did you arrive?'

Gillian Evans gazed at Drake as though he had spoken a foreign language.

'I don't remember.' Evans had a strong Welsh accent.

Drake lowered his voice, and spoke a few words in Welsh, *cymerwch eich amser*, telling her to take her time, hoping he could put her at ease.

'It would have been my usual time.' Evans gave Drake another helpless look. 'I usually leave home about eight-thirty, so I would have been here before nine.' Her chin wobbled, tears filling her eyes.

'Did you see anybody else when you arrived?'

Evans shook her head.

'Did you see any other vehicles parked on the road? Anything unusual?'

Evans gave Drake a pained look.

'It was just the same as every other day I come here. Until I went into the bedroom, that is…' She slumped back in her chair, snorting into the handkerchief. Sara's glance at Drake told him she didn't think there was anything further they could achieve.

'Did you move anything when you came into the house?'

Again she shook her head.

'How long had you been here before you found the body?'

'Not long. I thought it was odd that he wasn't around. So, I called out.' She shivered. 'I knocked on the bedroom door a few times before I went in.'

She put a hand to her mouth and choked back a sob.

'We may need to speak to you again.' Drake gave Evans a weak smile. He explained they would need her fingerprints, and terror creased her face.

'It's to eliminate you from the inquiry.' Sara's voice was soft.

Drake nodded at Tony Roberts, who took his cue to organise Gillian Evans' departure.

Once the two uniformed officers had left with the cleaner, Drake looked around the kitchen. A range cooker was tucked neatly into an old chimney breast, and glass-fronted wall cupboards filled with wineglasses and crockery dominated one wall. A half-empty bottle of a twenty-five-year-old whisky stood in one corner of the butchers-block worktops, its top loosened. Sara absent-mindedly opened some of the drawers.

Drake announced, 'I'm going into the other rooms.'

Sara nodded.

In the hallway, Drake paused. The sound of activity in the bedroom drifted down the passageway. In front of him were frosted glazed doors but before them were two other doors, and Drake opened the first to find a small bathroom with ancient fittings, which doubled up as a closet for coats, judging from the hooks and boxes overflowing with woolly hats, gloves and scarves.

A study opened out from the door opposite the

bathroom. Neat shelves of books lined one wall while various watercolours in ornate carved frames covered another. Drake fingered some of the papers on a mahogany desk: they related to a case listed in the Knutsford Crown Court.

Retreating back into the hall, Drake opened the frosted double doors into a sitting room that stretched out over the headland. Instantly the view took his attention and he walked over to the wide bay windows that were lined with a padded bench. He could imagine Nicholas Wixley and his wife entertaining their inner-city friends here, marvelling at the wonderful scenery. A bank of swirling clouds drifted overhead and on the long beach beneath the headland, dogs raced after balls thrown by their enthusiastic owners.

'Wow, that's a spectacular view.' Sara joined Drake and continued to gaze out over the headland and bay.

As Drake turned to take in the rest of the room, he noticed items of clothing draped on the back of a sofa. He strode over, reached down and moved a pink gilet. A heady, perfume filled his nostrils.

'That looks expensive,' Sara said, as she moved alongside him.

Drake read the label inside – Michael Jason.

'It looks like a size ten,' Sara said wistfully.

Drake set it out carefully against one of the seat cushions. 'I wonder if Mrs Wixley is a size ten?'

'Nicholas Wixley looks to be in his mid-fifties. So, unless Mrs Wixley is a gym bunny, I think it's unlikely.'

A man's crumpled boxer shorts lay on the sofa alongside a white shirt with double cuffs. A navy tie with a red stripe had fallen onto the floor. Drake noticed the glistening links of a watch bracelet and he kneeled down, gently easing the casing out from underneath the sofa. It was a heavy Breitling chronograph. It only confirmed for Drake that he wasn't dealing with a burglary.

'We'd better leave all this for the CSIs.'

'It looks like Nicholas Wixley got undressed in a hurry.' A touch of cynicism crept into Sara's voice.

Drake took in again the view from the windows of the sitting room. The house wasn't overlooked. None of the adjacent properties could peer in. Nicholas Wixley could have done anything in that sitting room and nobody would have seen him.

'I'll do a search later for the name of the gilet's brand,' Sara said.

'The CSI team will need to get a forensic analysis done.' Drake made for the door, Sara following behind. After telling Foulds about the gilet they left the house.

It was the Easter weekend in a few days and the warm spring temperatures had already arrived. The uniformed officers standing by the gate nodded an acknowledgement at Drake and Sara as they stepped over towards the Mercedes. Drake peered in. The leather upholstery was pristine, no plastic coffee mugs stuffed into cupholders; even the compartments in the doors were empty. A folded copy of the *Financial Times* sat on the back seat.

A gate fixed to the wall of the garage opened easily and Drake and Sara took a footpath between the garage and the property. The earlier grey clouds had thinned although the wind picked up as they sauntered down over the rough lawn of the headland.

He was still enjoying the view when he heard his name being called.

Drake turned and saw Superintendent Wyndham Price striding down the footpath towards them. Reaching the rank of superintendent meant being chained to a desk. Only exceptional circumstances required the presence of the senior officer at a crime scene.

Wyndham Price's shaved head glistened and for a moment Drake thought the superintendent appeared a little tanned, from the distinctly orangey hue to his skin. Perhaps a sunbed had found its way to the Price household.

'I want to see the crime scene, Ian, for myself. Please accompany me.' Price turned on his heels and Drake hurried after him, Sara following in his slipstream.

In the hallway, Drake nodded down the passageway. 'He's in the master bedroom.'

'We've been trying to contact DCC Wixley since we realised who was involved,' Price said.

'Do you know her, sir?'

'Only by reputation.'

Drake wanted to ask *and that reputation is?* but thought better of it. Price continued in any event. 'She's the chair of various committees for the Association of Chief Police Officers. She's very vocal, very ambitious and doesn't suffer fools gladly.'

'The woman who found the body does have a contact number for her, if you would like me to speak to her?' Drake asked.

Price snapped. 'I'll speak to DCC Wixley.'

'Yes, sir.'

One of the CSIs emerged from the bedroom and walked down the passageway towards them. The investigator tipped his head at Drake and Price.

'Follow me, sir,' Drake said.

Horror and disgust crossed Price's face as he gazed down at the body of Nicholas Wixley.

'The whole thing is staged,' Drake continued, before drawing Price's attention to the dining chairs a few feet away and to the board nailed to the wall. 'We're looking for a determined killer. This wasn't a burglary gone wrong.'

Price continued to grimace as he surveyed the room, the CSIs huddled together in the far corner of the room, having temporarily suspended their work.

'We're looking for one sad loser,' Price said, before leaving the room abruptly.

Drake nodded for the CSIs to continue. Back in the hallway Price turned to Drake, standing with Sara by his side. He gave them both an intense stare.

'We need to inform the next of kin,' Drake said.

'I'll be talking to DCC Wixley *personally*. I want to be kept fully informed about everything in relation to this investigation.'

Drake nodded his understanding of Price's insistence. The wife of the victim being such a senior police officer meant plenty of scrutiny to come. Plenty more senior officers looking over his shoulders. It meant he would have to check and recheck everything. It would make everything about this case that bit more challenging.

Price's Jaguar sped away.

Drake stood by the gate casting his gaze around the other properties. The cars parked in the driveways were all expensive, Range Rovers, Audis and the occasional BMW. The Easter weekend was coming up and Drake guessed that most of the holiday home owners would arrive on Thursday evening: it was the first weekend of the season. In due course everyone would be interviewed, exact movements established for the day before.

'Somebody must have seen something,' Drake said without expecting Sara to reply.

A man wearing red cords and a rugby jersey approached them, a puzzled frown intensifying as he neared Drake and Sara. He wore sunglasses, the sort popularised by Tom Cruise decades previously.

'I've come to see Nick. What the hell is going on?'

'And who are you?' Drake produced his warrant card. 'Detective Inspector Ian Drake and this is Detective Sergeant Sara Morgan.'

'Colin Horton,' Horton craned over Drake's shoulder. 'Is Nick all right?'

'When did you see Mr Wixley last?'

'Now look here – tell me what happened. Do you *know* who he is?'

Drake stiffened. 'I'm afraid I will need your full name and your address.'

'And, more importantly, do know who *Mrs Wixley* is?' Horton continued.

Drake took two steps towards the man and squinted into his face. 'Mr Wixley is dead. There are suspicious circumstances. The property is now a crime scene. I need you to tell me exactly the nature of your relationship with Nicholas Wixley. Now.'

'Christ,' Horton ran a hand over his mouth as he paled. 'Dead? We were sailing together yesterday. We were going to meet up this morning...' Horton glanced over his shoulder again.

'Mr Wixley has a boat?'

Horton nodded. 'He was looking forward to this week. His chambers had organised some big dinner at the weekend. And he was going to take part in the regatta. He had everything planned.'

'How well do you know him?'

Horton looked through Drake. 'I've known him for years ... I mean, this is awful.'

'Where do you live?'

Horton jerked his head behind him and mispronounced Bodlondeb as the name of his house.

'We'll need to get some details from you, Mr Horton.'

'Yes, of course.'

'Go home and wait for us.'

Horton turned on his heels and marched away.

Drake fished out his mobile from his jacket and called Price. 'I've spoken to a neighbour and I've told him about Nicholas Wixley. Have you tracked down Mrs Wixley yet, sir?'

'We don't know where the hell she is,' Price said. 'She's on a week's holiday somewhere, and apparently her assistant doesn't know where. Her force mobile is turned off. She has a personal mobile that's also turned off. I mean, who the bloody hell turns both their mobile telephones off?'

'I'm going to interview the neighbour.'

'If we can't find her then we can't find her. Damn it.'

The line went dead and Drake glanced at Sara. 'No sign of her?' she said.

Drake shook his head. 'We'll have to hope nobody she knows contacts her before the super.'

Drake took in the other nearby properties as he walked over to Bodlondeb with Sara. He hoped that Horton hadn't rang around all his friends and neighbours announcing the murder of Nicholas Wixley. Being unable to reach Mrs Wixley could be embarrassing if someone else reached her first.

Horton's house was of the same vintage as Wixley's with a generous drive and well- maintained garden. Three cars parked on the drive suggested Horton had company and Drake worried again that Price wouldn't be able to reach Mrs Wixley before someone else told her about her husband. Through the open rear door he shouted a greeting and voices down the corridor confirmed his fears. Horton appeared at the end of the hallway and gestured for Drake and Sara to join him.

An ancient kettle stood on top of an Aga. Two men sat by the table nursing bottles of lager. They turned to face Drake and Sara.

'This is Tom Levine and Marcus Abbott.'

Pleasantries exchanged, Horton continued. 'Do you want tea or something?' He glanced at the beer bottles on the table. 'I know it's early. But in the circumstances…'

'No, thanks,' Drake said.

Horton slouched into a chair and waved a hand for Drake and Sara to do likewise.

'When did you see Mr Wixley last?' Drake said.

Levine answered as Horton swigged on his beer.

'We all saw him yesterday in the sailing club. There was a race and Nicholas had put his boat into the water on Saturday, so he was dead keen.'

Abbott nodded. 'It was the first real race of the season and there were lots of yachts out on the water. Nicholas didn't win, which really annoyed him.'

'Nicholas was extremely competitive and hated to lose. He always thought he'd win every race,' Horton added as both Abbott and Levine nodded. 'We had a meal together and a couple of pints in the sailing club afterwards.'

'Did Mr Wixley mention that he was seeing someone last night?'

All three men shared a conspiratorial glance.

Horton was the first to reply. 'He said he had some work to do. Some papers to read.' Abbot and Levine had their eyes firmly fixed on the wooden table top.

'Did he mention seeing anyone?'

Three heads shook in unison.

Horton cleared his throat. 'Nick had an argument yesterday with a local contractor. They'd fallen out about a bill.'

'We'll need the details.' Sara already had her notebook in hand.

Levine rested one elbow on the table in front of them and let out a long breath. 'Like we said, we had been sailing. *PI* had just been put back into the water. There—'

'PI?'

'*Presumed Innocent* – the name of his yacht. The engine failed when he needed it. It had recently been refurbished by one of the local contractors.'

'Who was that?'

'John Speakman. Apparently, he's employed some new mechanic who was supposed to be excellent.'

'And where was this argument?'

Horton paused again. 'Nick was furious. Blind with rage, he kept going on and on about having spent ten grand on refurbishing the engine. Soon as we got back into the marina he spotted a young kid – Jamie something or other. He was working on some other yacht and Nick rushed over to him. They began pushing and shoving. Nick smacked him a couple of times before the young lad got a length of rope and threatened to horsewhip Nicholas. That's when things got really out of hand.'

Horton shared a glance with Drake and Sara.

'Jamie charged at him and they both finished up in the drink. The lad's head was cracked open – there was blood all over the place.'

'Did someone call the police?' Sara asked, as she continued to make notes in her pocketbook.

Horton shook his head.

Before he could ask any more questions, Drake's mobile telephone rang with a number he didn't recognise.

'Detective Inspector Drake.'

'It's Tony Roberts, sir, at the Wixley house. It's just that ... Mrs Wixley has arrived.'

Chapter 4
Monday 25th March
3.23 pm

Deputy Chief Constable Wixley stood on the drive by the Mercedes and glared at Drake, before staring at his warrant card. She ignored Sara.

'Do you have some identification?' Drake asked.

It earned him a sharpened glare, her eyes darkening. Wixley scrambled through her handbag before producing her City of Manchester police force warrant card and thrusting it at him for a brief second. 'Satisfied? I demand to be told what's happening.'

'Has Superintendent Wyndham Price spoken to you?' Drake said.

'And who the hell is he?'

'He's my divisional commanding officer.' Drake added. 'Ma'am.' Hoping his deference would be rewarded.

'This is my home. These officers...' She tipped her head towards Roberts and Jones. 'Have prevented my lawful right to enter.'

Drake took a deep breath. 'Superintendent Price has been trying to get hold of you all morning. I'm afraid we have some bad news. Your husband has been killed.'

Laura Wixley didn't move for a moment. She blinked rapidly, and her mouth fell open slightly. 'I ...' Drake reached a hand towards her arm, but she waved him off. Would she explain where she had been that morning and why she had been out of contact? 'Can I see him?'

Any police officer would know that visiting the

crime scene was out of the question until the forensic team had finished. But it wasn't a police officer asking; it was the widow of a man brutally killed in his own home.

'The forensic investigation is still ongoing.'

'I need a glass of water,' Wixley said.

Drake led Laura Wixley inside to the kitchen and pulled a chair from underneath the table. She sat down heavily. Laura's gaze followed Sara around the room as though she was surprised Sara knew where to find things. Sara filled a glass and set it down in front of Wixley.

'When did you receive the first call?' Wixley asked after her first mouthful of water.

'Your cleaner discovered the body when she arrived this morning.'

Wixley dragged a loose strand of her thin brown hair back over her ear. She had bloodless narrow lips and a strong nose, and rimless glasses couldn't hide the crow's feet around her small, dark-blue, piercing eyes. Her cheeks were make-up free, but a diamond-shaped earring hung from each lobe. Drake also noticed that Sara had been right; there was zero chance Laura Wixley was a size ten: more like sixteen.

'Gill,' Wixley replied flatly.

'Do you know anything about your husband's movements yesterday?'

Wixley adjusted her position on the chair. 'Very little. I believe he was due to be sailing in the afternoon with Colin Horton. It's a regular thing.'

'Where were you yesterday?'

Wixley squeezed her lips together into a sharp thin line. 'I thought you wanted to establish what my husband was doing?'

'It will give us a complete picture.'

'I think your job is to find my husband's killer.' Wixley gave Drake a challenging glare.

Establishing her whereabouts would have to wait. She had been out of contact that day and now she refused to explain where she had been the day before, which only made Drake suspicious. A quick glance at Sara told him she shared his misgivings.

'When did your husband leave home?'

Wixley ran a finger down the glass in front of her. 'He left on Saturday morning. He was going to travel here and get the yacht ready for the racing on Sunday morning. I had a text message from him Saturday confirming he had arrived.'

'You didn't speak to him?'

'No.'

Drake turned to Sara. 'Check with Mike Foulds to see if he has recovered a mobile telephone.' Her chair scraped on the quarry-tiled floor as she stood up.

Wixley gave Drake a look he couldn't read. Was it defiance, resilience?

'Was he expecting anyone?'

'What do you mean?'

Drake averted his gaze. He could count on one hand the number of occasions he had spoken with a deputy chief constable – one rank below chief constable. Now he was interviewing the deputy chief constable of the City of Manchester police, a force three times the size of the Wales Police Service, and the uncomfortable sense she was hiding something surfaced in his mind.

But he was the senior investigating officer and she

had no jurisdiction in Wales. Even so, he could feel the presence of Superintendent Price in the room, looking over his shoulder, questioning every thought process.

'Do you know anybody that he would be entertaining?'

Not even Deputy Chief Constable Wixley could infer anything from such an innocuous question, Drake hoped.

'He didn't tell me about any of his plans. I suppose some of his sailing pals could have been here over the weekend.'

'Did your husband ever complain that he felt unsafe?'

Wixley shook her head.

Sara returned clutching a plastic evidence pouch. 'Is this Mr Wixley's mobile telephone, ma'am.'

'How can I possibly tell?' Laura Wixley raised her voice before glaring at it. 'It looks like it but they all look alike.'

She reached down into her bag, found her own telephone and made a call. The bagged mobile rang. 'There, you have your answer.'

'Does your husband have any enemies?' Drake said.

Wixley groaned. 'Every successful person has enemies, Detective Inspector.'

'Your husband was a barrister, so he must have prosecuted a lot of criminal cases. Did he also act for defendants facing justice?'

'Recently he specialised almost exclusively on prosecuting. He enjoyed it.'

Every successful barrister had to be terrier-like in their attention to detail and utterly determined, but

Laura Wixley made it sound like a blood sport.

'Were there any particular cases in the past few years where your husband might have made enemies?'

Wixley shrugged.

Drake heard the thud of a car door and an exchange of words between the two officers on duty outside. A louder voice approached the front door and Drake recognised Wyndham Price's tone. It occurred to Drake that Price's driver must have turned around as soon as he knew Mrs Wixley had arrived.

Drake stood up and met Price as he entered the house.

'Where is she?'

Drake nodded to the kitchen door. 'In there.'

Price barged past Drake, who followed him into the kitchen. Price reached out a hand. 'I am most terribly sorry for your loss, ma'am.'

Her handshake looked limp and lifeless. Drake hadn't attempted such a step; perhaps reaching superintendent rank made it permissible.

'Your inspector has refused to allow me to see my husband's body.' Venom laced her voice and Drake pitied any of her junior officers.

Price gave Drake a troubled glance.

'As a serving police officer who, incidentally, outranks you all, there's nothing to prevent you allowing me into the crime scene.'

Drake folded his arms. He had made his decision. Price could indulge Laura Wixley if he wanted to. It avoided any flak for breach of protocols being levelled at Drake. Drake and Sara looked over at Price, who had been fixed by one of Laura Wixley's javelin-tipped stares. He had no real option. A pang of sympathy for

Price pricked Drake's mind.

'Follow me.'

When Laura Wixley reached the door of the bedroom, Drake sensed her hesitation. She dipped her head, paused. Superintendent Price did not notice; he was already in the room talking to Mike Foulds, warning them to clear out of the way.

Laura Wixley composed herself and entered the room. She averted her eyes until she reached the bottom of the bed. Then she turned and drew her arms tight to her chest before giving out a brief whimper. There were no tears, no hysterics. She took in the rest of the room, ignoring the crime scene investigators as she did so. Nearing the newspaper cuttings on the board, she frowned and squinted.

'These clippings are all about cases where your husband was involved,' Price said.

Wixley didn't react, didn't nod confirmation or raise an eyebrow.

Turning her gaze to her dead husband's body, she raised a finger and pointed in his direction. 'Is that the letter "e"?'

Foulds cleared his throat. 'That is certainly what we believe.'

Wixley glanced at the crime scene manager and then at Price.

'Does that mean anything to you?' Price said.

She blinked away tears before making straight for the door without a word to Price, who followed her out. Drake caught up with them in the kitchen as she drank another glass of water.

'There was a case years ago called the alphabet murders. A letter from the alphabet was tattooed into each victim's chest. The killer had reached the letter D before he was caught. He was sentenced to life imprisonment.'

'And is there a connection with your husband?' Drake said.

Wixley nodded slowly. 'He was the prosecuting barrister.'

Drake breathed out heavily. This information meant they had their first realistic thread. He hoped that forensics would give them enough to move the inquiry forward. 'We'll need all the details about the case.'

'You need to talk to some of the other barristers involved. One of the defence barristers, Justin Selston, I believe, was from the same chambers as Nicholas.'

'Presumably chambers can provide a record of all your husband's past and current cases.'

Wixley lifted her gaze from her feet and looked over at Wyndham Price. 'I suggest your detective inspector should talk to them today. Some of the members of chambers and staff are staying at the Portmeirion Hotel. Chambers are celebrating fifty years and there is a big dinner this weekend. It was going to be a special occasion for Nicholas as well.'

'What do you mean?' Price asked.

'He had recently been appointed as a circuit judge.'

Chapter 5

Monday 25th March
5.05 pm

'What did you make of her, boss?' Sara sipped on a thin plastic cup containing a thick brown builders' tea. One look at the mobile food kiosk on the outskirts of Pwllheli persuaded Drake to opt for a soft drink. At least the Coke was cold.

'It's odd she was so secretive about her whereabouts.'

'I agree.' Sara nodded enthusiastically.

Price's words still rang in his ears. *'Keep me informed about every step.'* He had reacted with exasperation mixed with annoyance when Drake had explained that Mrs Wixley had refused to provide any explanation for her whereabouts that day or for the previous day. Mrs Wixley's circumstances had to be investigated: he had been sorely tempted to remind Price that most murders are committed by someone already known to the victim.

A judge had been killed and his wife, a deputy chief constable, could well be a suspect. At the very least Drake could see they had to treat her as a person of interest. Police officers were meant to be upstanding and above reproach. Wixley's murder challenged the assumptions of a civilised society: that the judiciary was a fundamental part of the system and alongside police officers made for a law-abiding world.

Drake started the engine. 'Digging into the life of Nicholas Wixley will inevitably mean including her too.' A few minutes later Drake indicated for the entrance to the Portmeirion Hotel.

Drake slowed to a halt in front of the barrier restricting his access. Non-guests had to pay a fee for visiting the hotel and its grounds with the famous Italianate village. Drake had promised himself to visit with his daughters but had never got around to it.

He produced his warrant card for the staff member who approached the car. 'This is official police business.'

The man gave Drake a startled look and allowed him through.

'I've never been here,' Sara said. 'Although friends of mine are going to book for the No.6 Festival this year.'

Drake negotiated the road down to the hotel at a sedate pace.

'A drama series in the 1960s was filmed here,' Drake said. *The Prisoner.*'

'Never heard of it.'

Leaving the car, they skirted around a low wall overlooking a shallow bay. It was a calm night; the early spring sunset cast a warm glow over the sea and Drake saw the impressive array of property scattered over the hillside above him. Discreet lighting lit up the red and yellow surfaces of the gables and exterior elevations, creating a magical quality.

'It's spectacular,' Sara said.

Dozens of guests bustled on the patio outside the entrance enjoying the view over the estuary. Inside, the reception had a comfortable, prosperous feel. Drake identified himself to a receptionist whose face turned from a standard warm customer greeting to stiff and serious. She led them to a bay window where two men sat, grim-faced.

'Mr Selston?' Drake reminded himself of the name of the barrister Laura Wixley had mentioned.

Both men stood up. The taller one, the same height as Drake, reached out a hand. He had a carefully trimmed short back-and-sides, a developing paunch and a mouth fixed in an emotionless weak smirk.

'Justin Selston.'

They shook hands before Selston turned to his colleague. 'This is Michael Kennedy, the chief clerk of our chambers.'

Both men shared an expensive tailor judging from the quality of their suits. The prominent chalk line on Kennedy's three-piece pinstripe complemented his baldness, although a smattering of white hair clung to the back of his head.

Kennedy's hand was surprisingly damp when Drake shook it.

'Do sit down, Detective Inspector,' Selston said, beckoning over a waiter. 'Can we get you a drink?'

A lonely piece of sliced lemon sat at the bottom of the cut-glass tumblers on the table in front of both men.

'Sparkling water, thank you,' Drake said. Sara ordered the same and Selston motioned for the waiter to refresh their glasses.

'This is the most frightful business,' Selston said.

'I've spoken with Mrs Laura Wixley this afternoon.'

'Poor darling must be devastated. I can't imagine what she must be going through.'

The waiter returned, depositing the drinks on the table. Kennedy and Selston took a decent mouthful of each.

'How is she?' Selston leaned forward slightly, his lips barely moving as he spoke.

There was a clear pecking order in the relationship between the men. Selston was the barrister, an accomplished lawyer, Kennedy merely the hired help.

'She's gone to stay with some friends locally. Has there been anything to suggest Nicholas Wixley was a target for a disgruntled criminal or client? Any threatening letters?'

Selston again. 'Nicholas was a very successful member of chambers. He prosecuted some extremely high-profile cases. He was exceptionally able at what he did.'

Drake looked over at Kennedy. 'Any problems at work?'

Selston gave Kennedy a sharp look.

'He was well liked by all the members of staff. We have an administration team that runs the day-to-day operation of chambers.' Kennedy's flat northern accent contrasted sharply with Selston's cultured, rounded vowels.

Both men emptied the other half of their glasses.

'We shall need to visit chambers in due course and speak to the staff as well as removing any personal items that belonged to Mr Wixley. Someone from my team will be in contact about the necessary arrangements.'

'Of course, of course. We shall do everything to cooperate with your inquiry,' Selston said.

'Quite a few of the members of chambers are already here.' Kennedy said. 'They've taken the opportunity to take some holiday before the dinner on

Saturday night.'

Selston butted in. 'We thought you might want to talk to the members of chambers who were here last night. So, I've asked them to gather in one of the dining rooms.'

Another grain of suspicion developed in Drake's mind. He hated being manipulated but it was always sensible to start identifying the killer from those nearest to the victim. Colleagues, family members and Mrs Wixley were all in that group. Was everything as rosy in Nicholas Wixley's chambers as Kennedy made out?

'That might be helpful, thank you.'

Michael Kennedy left, announcing he would corral everyone together. Drake turned to Selston. 'Are you familiar with the alphabet killer?'

Selston's mouth barely quivered but he squinted, obviously surprised. 'Is there some connection?'

'I can't discuss the details but Mrs Wixley suggested you were involved in that case.'

Selston fingered the rim of his glass. In one smooth movement he waved the waiter over with a confident jerk of his hand. 'We'll have two more G&Ts, thanks.' He tipped an inquiring head towards Drake and Sara, who both turned down his offer.

'I was the defence counsel on that case. Zavier Cornwell was convicted of four murders. He had tattooed onto the chest of the first victim the letter A and onto the second victim the letter B and so forth. The random nature of his serial killings was bizarre. They were all celebrities in different ways, having featured in various magazines, none of which, I hasten to add, I had ever read before taking on the case.'

Selston's gin and tonic arrived, at least his third

drink by Drake's reckoning, but it could have been more. Drake couldn't judge from his demeanour whether the alcohol was having any effect on him.

'The killer had erected a makeshift board in each crime scene with newspaper clippings and magazine articles relating to the victim.' Selston shivered and took another mouthful of his drink. Now he opened his eyes wide. 'He was the most evil man I have ever encountered. Utterly devoid of emotion.'

A spasm of cold fear ran up Drake's back at the possibility they had the wrong man behind bars or that a copycat killer was at large. He and the team would need to work fast. 'How long ago was the case?' Drake nodded at Sara and she reached for her pocketbook.

Selston turned the glass through his fingers before replying. 'Four years.'

'And what happened?'

'Four life sentences, of course, with a minimum term of twenty-five years.'

'Any doubt about his guilt?'

'None whatever. The evidence was overwhelming and utterly unchallengeable.'

Kennedy appeared before Drake could ask any further questions. 'We're ready.'

Drake and Sara followed the two men through reception into a small private dining room. A quick headcount told Drake that fifteen members of chambers were present, all young with open, healthy-looking faces.

'This must be one of the saddest days for our chambers,' Selston said, continuing in the same vein for a few minutes as though he were practising the eulogy for Nicholas Wixley's commemoration service. There shouldn't have been a dry eye in the house, but there were only hard, determined faces staring at Selston. Perhaps this was another hallmark of a successful barrister, Drake thought.

'Detective Inspector Drake and Detective Sergeant Morgan are leading the inquiry into Nicholas's murder. If any of you have anything that might assist, then no doubt both officers will be available to discuss any details with you.'

Drake sensed the gaze of the young lawyers and became increasingly uncomfortable as Selston and Kennedy introduced him and Sara to more senior-looking members of the group. This wasn't a social event – he was investigating a murder.

'Is it true that his body was mutilated?' An ardent-looking woman with dank, lifeless hair addressed Drake. The conversation of the barristers by their side stopped abruptly and their eyes turned to interrogate Drake. It was like being cross-examined.

'The crime scene investigators are still at the house.' What else could these barristers expect, Drake thought.

He drifted out into reception with Sara, reading the time on his watch, realising he needed to update Price, and that he anticipated an early start in the Incident Room the following morning with the rest of his team. He had already texted Annie, telling her he was going back to his own apartment that evening. He hoped a time would come when he could give up the flat in Colwyn Bay and move in with her permanently. His plans for her to meet Megan and Helen again over the Easter holiday were something he wasn't going to change, no matter what. Even so, an irritating grain of doubt worked its way relentlessly into his mind. A murder inquiry always took priority over his private life and he had let police work ruin his marriage to Sian. Annie was different, more tolerant and forgiving of the demands on his time but, even so, he wasn't going to let work ruin his chance of things working out with her.

Justin Selston and Michael Kennedy, both in conversation with one of the barristers he had noticed earlier, caught his attention and he joined them, Sara by his side.

'This is Pamela Farley, Michael's wife,' Selston said.

Pamela reached out a hand. She had a strong and forceful grip. Drake had Michael Kennedy as being in his early fifties, but his wife was younger. Pale blue eyes looked at Drake and then at Sara. She maintained the detached, imperious stance barristers nurtured.

'Did you find the murder weapon? It must have been an awful scene.'

Drake didn't reply directly. 'Officers will be calling tomorrow to take statements and contact details.'

Selston and Kennedy nodded, before Pamela added, 'Do please reach out if we can be of any help at all.'

Drake and Sara made their way outside, pausing for a moment to watch the incoming tide flooding over the sandbanks. Two other guests jostled their way past Drake, and one of the younger barristers from the dining room earlier came up to him. 'Glorious view isn't?'

He felt a hand in his jacket pocket. It was there for a moment and he glanced at the blonde-haired lawyer.

She gave him a conspiratorial look before glancing briefly at his pocket. A second later, she hurried away.

Drake dipped a hand inside and fingered a business card.

He walked over to Sara. Standing by her side, he eased the card out.

'What's that?' Sara said.

On one side of the card was the name Holly Thatcher, Barrister-at-Law, with her contact details. On the other side, she had written, 'Call me.'

Chapter 6

Monday 25th March
10.05 pm

After dropping Sara at Caernarfon police station Drake decided he had time to see Annie. He called her on his mobile.

'I'm in Caernarfon.'

'You've only just finished? You must be exhausted.'

'I was going to call in to see you on my way back to Colwyn Bay, if it's not too late?'

He had almost said 'home' instead of 'Colwyn Bay', but Annie's house on the Menai Strait felt more like home each time he stayed there.

'Of course not. I'll make you something to eat.'

It was a short journey to her house and after she opened the door Drake pulled her close. As they kissed in a long, intense embrace it felt longer than breakfast time since he had last seen her, as though the activity of several days had been packed into a few short hours.

'You look tired.' She drew a gentle hand over his face, her welcoming smile matching the warmth of her voice on the telephone.

'I know I said I wouldn't call but…' She put two fingers on his mouth to stop him continuing.

'I don't mind. It's lovely to see you.'

She pulled away, but Drake drew her back. He enjoyed the simple pleasure of sensing her body close to his. 'I'll make you something to eat.' She tore away from him and busied herself in the kitchen while Drake walked over to the window that overlooked the Strait. A yacht cruised by, its sails furled, a rib lashed to the tiller bobbing around on its wash.

After slumping on the sofa, he reached for the television remote and flicked through the channels before he found the local news. A reporter standing outside Northern Division headquarters shared with the world that a 'famous barrister' had been murdered in his holiday home on the Llŷn Peninsula and that his widow was a deputy chief constable in Manchester. Annie sat down beside him, putting a plate with a sandwich and a cold drink on the coffee table in front of him. He hadn't realised how hungry he was until he started eating.

'Is that your case?' Annie said.

'Yes. A barrister called Nicholas Wixley.'

'And his wife is a chief constable?'

'*Deputy* chief constable.'

'Is she a suspect?' Annie said. 'Aren't a lot of murders committed by loved ones?'

Laura Wixley's reaction had hardly been that of the loving widow. But he couldn't share that thought with Annie. 'We're pursuing our normal line of inquiries.'

Annie giggled but then turned serious. 'We were supposed to take Helen and Megan out on Friday.'

His mind sagged as the prospect of having to explain to Sian, his ex-wife, that he'd have to postpone taking his daughters out for the day. Anticipating when he'd next have a day off was like divining for water.

Although he had known Annie for only a few weeks, he treasured their relationship, hoping it would develop, and was pleased that she had accepted the demands of his job.

He finished the sandwich and reluctantly got up to

leave, knowing he had an early start in the morning. Annie held his face with both hands as he stood on the threshold before heading for his car.

Tuesday 26th March
8.05 am

Calling Sian first thing in the morning wasn't the best timing. Breakfasted and caffeinated, Drake felt fuelled up for the conversation, however brief it might be.

'Good morning.'

'You know this is a bad time, Ian. I don't know why you do it.'

'I've got a busy day and it's impossible to speak to you at work.'

The receptionist at Sian's GP surgery saw to that.

'What do you want? The girls are getting ready for school. Why don't you call them tonight?'

'I'm the SIO on the murder case on the Llŷn Peninsula.'

Sian said nothing, but Drake heard her breathing. And he sensed the tension down the telephone. She had heard this excuse for his non-attendance at weekend activities and school plays and ruined holiday plans many times before.

'I suppose...' she started, with a heavy voice. 'That means you won't be able to take the girls on Friday.'

'You know what it's like, Sian.'

'Yes, Ian. I *know* what it's like. I had made plans too, you know.' She slammed the telephone down.

Great start to the day, Drake thought as he left the apartment for his car.

He toured around the car park at the hospital,

getting more and more annoyed at the lack of a parking space near the mortuary. Someone should have had the foresight when they built the place to realise a multistorey was crucial. He crawled around in first gear, deciding eventually to mount the kerb and park on ground already churned up by car tyres. He fumbled in the glove compartment and found an official bilingual laminated sheet – 'On Police Business/Heddlu – Swyddogol' – which he stuffed above the dashboard.

A young slim girl with blonde hair in curls cascading over her shoulders was having a profoundly positive effect on the usually hostile and rude mortuary assistant, who actually smiled at Drake. 'Good morning, Inspector. This is Sharon, she's on work experience for a week.'

Sharon beamed at Drake, her courtesy and warmth displayed in the mortuary unsettling him. He scribbled his name on the relevant forms the assistant pushed over the table towards him. A door led into a long corridor where he heard symbols clashing and an orchestra thundering its way through a famous piece of music that sounded familiar.

'What's this?' Drake raised his voice as he joined Dr Lee Kings by the slab with a white sheet covering what Drake assumed were the mortal remains of Nicholas Wixley.

'Beethoven's 9th Symphony. Please tell me you recognise it,' Kings said as he fiddled with a remote control. The noise subsided to a quiet background rhythm. Drake could hear himself think.

Kings got to work after removing the white sheet with a flourish. It always amazed Drake that a pathologist could look so pleased about carving up a corpse. The shape of the wound disfiguring Wixley's chest seemed more pronounced now that the blood had congealed. Drake tried to imagine the lacerations the killer must have made – presumably it would have been the vertical downward slash followed by the three legs of the letter E. A ruler carefully positioned by Kings would record the precise measurements of each wound.

'Have you established if there's a significance to the letter E?' Kings enquired, without looking at Drake.

'It could be a copycat related to a serial killer from Manchester several years ago, where Wixley prosecuted the case.'

Kings gradually moved his attention towards Wixley's face. After a few minutes he used a pair of well-used stainless steel forceps to extract something from Wixley's mouth. He repeated this delicate manoeuvre half a dozen more times. And each time, the evidence removed was placed in a kidney dish gleaming brightly under the theatre-style lights.

'Anything interesting?' Drake said

Kings raised an eyebrow and looked over at Drake. 'It looks like pubic hair.'

'In his mouth?' Drake thought about the pink gilet and its wearer – the likely owner of the pubic hair.

Kings worked meticulously around Wixley's head, swabbing his nose and eyes. At one stage he squinted to examine particles at the end of a cotton bud extracted from Wixley's nose.

'We'll need to get some toxicology tests done but I wouldn't mind betting he was snorting cocaine before he died.'

Drake nodded. 'A bag from the scene is with forensics at the moment but preliminary tests suggest it could be cocaine.' He folded his arms, wondering what else was likely to be uncovered. He had been a detective long enough to know that cocaine had no social barriers and it meant that Wixley had a supplier somewhere who had a dealer and that meant the criminal underworld. Not the usual company for an aspiring judge.

A deep 'Y' incision opened Wixley's body. Drake was convinced Kings took pleasure in this final act of removing any semblance of dignity from the body. The heart and lungs and other organs were removed, weighed and inspected before being taken, in turn, to the counter for slicing and further examination. Once Kings had finished, he stood back, a contented look on his face. 'I would say death was caused by haemorrhagic shock – massive blood loss in other words. There's no indication he was bound or restrained in any way and no defensive wounds, all of which suggests he was drugged or incapacitated somehow before the killer was able to do his work. The toxicology test should help us.'

Drake stood patiently as Kings scraped what little material existed under Wixley's fingernails, taking care to study his fingers and hands. Occasionally he made some comment about the condition of the body. It all suggested Nicholas Wixley had been healthy, well fed, perhaps too well fed from the mass of flesh forming his double chin. Drake grimaced as Kings started on Wixley's genitalia.

The forceps were hard at work again. Kings gestured for Drake to join him as he inspected the contents of two kidney dishes. Minute particles of hair lay at the bottom of each.

Kings pointed to the first. 'This is the pubic hair I removed from his mouth and as you can see...' He tapped the second tray. 'There is a similar sample from his genitalia. I'll send the samples off for DNA analysis.'

'And it's likely he'd been snorting cocaine the evening before he died.'

Kings turned to face Drake. 'He certainly made his last night on earth one to remember.'

Drake made moves to leave the post-mortem room as soon as Kings started suturing the 'Y' incision he'd made earlier, which looked like a large zip. Before he was able to escape, Kings sermonised on the dangers of cocaine, everything from heart attacks to a disintegrating nose. It was enough to bring on a nagging headache.

From the window of his office Wyndham Price followed the team of gardeners busy around the parkland surrounding Northern Division headquarters. Next week there would be an hour of extra daylight and it made him realise that winter was behind him. He could look forward to longer days and warmer temperatures. But lurking at the back of his mind was a recent email from the human resources department at Wales Police Service headquarters in Cardiff, who wanted to 'discuss his retirement planning'. It meant that soon enough one of the assistant chief constables would call him and sound affable and friendly as they sought his agreement to a date.

Retirement loomed in Wyndham Price's mind like a storm-laden cloud heading towards the shore. He knew it would happen but somehow hoped to avoid its consequences. The prospect of not working filled him with irrational terror. Whenever he did take time off he pined for the routine of work. Breakfast at six-thirty, arriving at headquarters at seven, and leaving only after twelve hours had passed. He would miss the paperwork, the reports to read, the decisions to be taken.

His wife had dropped hints that she wanted to go on holiday more often and brochures for cruises had recently appeared at home. Sticking needles in his eyes would be preferable to being stuck on a ship with strangers, Price thought. His wife's interest in holidaying came as a surprise as throughout their married life her aversion to people and social events and all of his immediate family had meant a lonely existence.

Putting off the decision wasn't going to work long term but the death of Nicholas Wixley and the fact that his widow was a deputy chief constable gave him the perfect reason to ignore HR, at least for now. Had he been right to let Inspector Drake be the senior investigating officer on the case? Perhaps he should have taken the role himself. It focused his mind on Drake's past. Price pondered if Drake really had got over a previous case in which two officers had been killed. The counselling that followed helped Drake, but Price knew that Drake's determination could be a hindrance when the OCD he suffered from overwhelmed him. Price chided himself for doubting Drake's ability, reminding himself that recently he had appeared more relaxed; the divorce was behind him and office gossip told Price he had a new girlfriend. Even so, Drake could be annoying and pedantic and sometimes a bit charmless.

The Wixley murder inquiry gave Price the perfect reason to be more hands-on with Drake and his team. He reached for his telephone and called Drake.

'Where are you?'

'In reception,' Drake said. 'I've been at Wixley's post-mortem.'

'Bring me up to date.'

Drake arrived a few minutes later and Price noticed his navy suit and double-cuffed shirt. The red spotted silk tie was perfectly knotted; Drake always looked the part, Price thought.

'Sit down.' Price waved to one of the visitor chairs. 'Did the pathologist have anything interesting?'

Drake chose his words with care as he settled himself in the chair. 'He might have discovered pubic hairs in Wixley's mouth and his genitalia.'

Price grimaced.

'And Kings thought he removed the remains of cocaine from his nose.'

Price reached a hand to his shaved head and gave the back a good scratch. 'That's all we need. I hope the press don't get hold of any of this.'

'When I initially spoke to Mrs Wixley, she couldn't offer us any explanation for her movements yesterday or Saturday.'

Price squinted over at Drake as though the mere act of doing so was painful. 'You're not suggesting?'

'If Nicholas Wixley had an *interesting* private life—'

'Interesting.' Price snorted.

'We need to know what Laura Wixley knew about her husband and what she thought about it.'

'This could turn out to be really messy. She's a deputy chief constable.'

'Everything about her reaction felt distant, wrong somehow.'

'That doesn't make her a killer,'

'I know but—'

'No buts about it, Ian. The crime scene suggests it's a copycat killing inspired by the alphabet murders. Any inkling that Zavier Cornwell was innocent?'

Drake shook his head, recalling the horror on Justin Selston's face at the mere suggestion Cornwell wasn't the alphabet killer. We need to give this top priority.' Price paused. 'He was a judge for Christ's sake. The chief constable and both assistant chief constables in Cardiff have emailed me asking to be kept in the loop.'

Price watched as Drake buttoned his jacket and left.

Gareth Winder and Luned Thomas both jumped to their feet when Drake entered the Incident Room. Drake shared a 'good morning' with his team, and Sara nodded a greeting. A grainy photograph of Nicholas Wixley had been pinned to the board.

Winder said, 'I printed it from an image on the barristers' chambers' website.'

Drake made his way over. Nicholas Wixley's eyes suggested he really did know better than anybody else. He had full lips and a healthy-looking complexion. It was a world away from the decaying mass of flesh Drake had seen that morning. It was almost difficult to believe the face in front of him belonged to the same person.

He turned to face the team.

'The pathologist believes there is evidence to suggest he was entertaining at least one other person last night – let's assume for the time being it was a woman. She's the focus of the inquiry.' Drake tipped his head at Luned and Winder. 'I want both of you over in Pwllheli as soon as we've finished. Get the house-to-house organised and talk to Horton and any of Wixley's sailing pals. Try and find out if they knew anyone he was seeing. And we need to trace the man who fought with Wixley – Jamie someone – he works for a John Speakman. There was an argument between Wixley and Jamie the day before he was killed.' Winder and Luned barely moved, clearly understanding this was going to be a high-profile inquiry.

Drake drew himself up to his full height. 'Superintendent Price is taking a personal interest in this case, but we treat it like every other murder inquiry. What makes this case different is that Wixley was a newly appointed judge and his wife is a senior police officer. So, if you get anybody from the press making contact with you, I want to know immediately.'

Three serious pairs of eyes registered their understanding of what Drake told them.

The main door, banging against the wall as Mike Foulds barged in, broke the silence in the room. 'I need a word, Ian.'

Chapter 7

Tuesday 26th March
11.08 am

'You wouldn't believe the pressure I've had from Superintendent Price.'

Mike Foulds sat in one of the visitor chairs in Drake's office, and put the laptop on the desk and a plastic evidence bag carefully on top. It had been three days since Drake had last sat in his room. It meant he needed to check the position of his daughter's photographs, make certain the columns of Post-it notes were in the correct order. He even surreptitiously gave the bin at his feet a checking glance. He hoped his rituals went unnoticed by Mike Foulds, who clearly had the recent hassle and aggravation from Price prominent in his mind.

'Nicholas Wixley had recently been appointed as a judge. And—'

'I know all that. It's all this implied criticism that we're not going to do a decent job I don't like. And he wanted everything to be done in double-quick time. All my spare investigators worked late last night. And they were back first thing this morning. Some of them have only had five hours' sleep.'

Drake wondered why Foulds wasn't there with them. The crime scene manager continued. 'I was in early finalising work on this laptop and mobile we recovered from Wixley's house.'

A delay of a day or two was normal in getting electronics cleared for his team to examine so it impressed Drake that the forensics department had released the computer so quickly.

Foulds continued. 'I'm going to report to *you* on this. You're the SIO. You can deal with Price.' Foulds adjusted his position and leaned on the desk with one elbow. 'The white powder we found has proved positive as cocaine. And it was enough for substantial personal use.'

'We need to trace his dealer,' Drake said, thinking aloud.

'I'm going to expedite an analysis but the preliminary testing I did this morning suggests it's of reasonable quality.'

'The pathologist thought he had recovered cocaine from Wixley's nose.'

Foulds nodded. 'And we discovered semen on the bedding. I should have the DNA results very quickly.' Foulds stood up and glanced at his watch. 'I had better get back there now. Was Wixley from Rotherham by any chance?'

Drake looked puzzled. 'No. Why do you ask?'

'He was wearing Rotherham United socks. The name of the club is sewn vertically on the back.'

Once Foulds had left, Drake scooped up the bag with Wixley's mobile and walked out into the Incident Room and over to Sara's desk. 'The CSIs found a quantity of cocaine at Wixley's house.'

Sara raised an eyebrow. 'Do we interview Mrs Wixley in relation to a possible possession charge?'

The same thing had briefly occurred to Drake, but she was the wife of a murder victim and she wasn't in possession even if it had been in her home. 'The best we could consider would be to report it to the City of Manchester Professional Standards Department but as

DCC Wixley is the head of that department it might be tricky.'

He placed the mobile telephone on her desk. 'You get started on his mobile contacts while I work on his laptop.'

Before returning to his office, Drake detoured to the kitchen and organised coffee. After spooning the correct proportion of ground coffee into a cafetière, he waited for the kettle to boil and cool, for the required minute and a half. Walking back, brewing coffee in one hand and a china mug in another, he was reminded of how Annie pulled his leg about the way he fussed over making coffee. Her gentle ribbing had been far different from the critical comments of his ex-wife Sian.

Drake booted up the laptop easily enough. Most of the icons he recognised as familiar – Excel spreadsheets and Word documents. Navigating his way to the Documents section, he found various folders, and clicked open one entitled 'financial planning'. More yellow icons for each of the past eight years suggested Nicholas Wixley was fastidious. Opening the oldest folder, Drake noticed several more with titles relating to investments and savings accounts. Even eight years ago, Nicholas Wixley's income had exceeded Drake's ten times over. The tax Wixley paid made a substantial contribution to reducing the national debt, Drake thought. Becoming a circuit judge clearly wasn't going to benefit him financially – it was likely to mean a pay cut – but the appointment meant he became 'His Honour Judge Wixley', a status he must have coveted. Drake moved onto the most recent year, when the investment strategy Wixley adopted had paid healthy dividends. Any reduction in income as a result of his elevation to a judge would have been softened by the several million pounds he had already saved.

Drake jotted down the details of Wixley's bank accounts, and put in hand all the usual protocols for a full financial search. He made a mental note to delegate Luned to complete that task; she had a more thorough mindset than Gareth Winder, even though he was her senior.

Drake turned to some of the other personal files in the Documents section. One was called genealogy and it piqued Drake's interest. Other folders emerged after he'd clicked it open. Another was entitled *clippings*, and Drake pored over a selection of newspaper articles about a Neil Thorpe. He was a prominent rugby league player in the Wigan squad, who had played for Great Britain in the last Rugby League World Cup. Others related to more Thorpe family members and went back several years. There appeared to be no obvious connection between Thorpe and Wixley. Why had Nicholas Wixley assembled this collection of cuttings?

By midday Drake's stomach and headache reminded him he had eaten very little. He had one more folder to read before lunch – the title 'Betting Shops' intrigued him, as did the mass of files and spreadsheets inside. Each had an address and in the first he read down the list of names to discover if Wixley was on the list. He wasn't; although there were lots of 'Williams'. He mulled over its significance as he heard Sara in the Incident Room answering a call.

Sara raised her voice. 'Were on our way.' Moments later she appeared on the threshold of his door. 'We've got an eyewitness, boss.'

Chapter 8

Tuesday 26th March
2.45 pm

Drake hammered the car along the A55. Sara didn't bother with the satnav; they both knew the route back to the Llŷn Peninsula. She had spent the morning working her way through Nicholas Wixley's mobile telephone, identifying texts and calls: several to Colin Horton, Wixley's sailing companion, and other individuals she'd have to identify. Sara assumed a WhatsApp group called PI referred to his boat and its crew. She would call each member in turn. On Saturday Wixley had texted his wife three times but not at all on Sunday. It was difficult to make out the tone from a message with few words, but they struck Sara as cold, businesslike, and not a digital kiss in sight. Sara scolded herself – she wasn't dealing with a teenager, but a barrister recently appointed a judge.

'What did Mike Foulds have to say?' Sara said as they approached the Penmaenmawr tunnel.

'He confirmed the white powder we found was cocaine, which ties in with the pathologist's comments about a white substance he removed from Wixley's nose at the post-mortem.'

It didn't surprise Sara that a senior member of the legal profession had a recreational drug habit. Cocaine was now the drug of choice for the intelligentsia.

'I've emailed the company that distributes the Michael Jason clothing brand. Hopefully we should have details of all the retailers quickly,' Sara said. 'The pink gilet cost over a hundred and fifty pounds on the high street so it's not a run-of-the-mill item.'

'We'll need to work on the contacts in his mobile over the next few days.'

That was exactly what Sara feared. The vacation she had booked to Ireland with a group of friends over the Easter bank holiday would be impossible now. Sometimes she just hated being a detective. On occasions like this she rued her decision not to train as a teacher or a lawyer.

They reached the road leading to the Wixley property and Sara noticed a scientific support vehicle parked in the drive – a yellow crime scene perimeter tape flickered gently in the early afternoon breeze. Sara guessed it would be several more days before the investigators had finished their painstaking work. On the opposite side, two men in their sixties stood gossiping. One had a brightly coloured check shirt and red cord trousers. His companion wore a pair of Bermuda shorts.

'You can always spot the tourists,' Drake said, nodding at the man's bare legs. 'They wear their shorts whatever the weather.'

They left the car and Sara took in the surrounding properties. On their first visit, she hadn't paid them much attention. Now she took in the collection of old bungalows with dormer windows, suggesting bedrooms in converted attics, others with newly slated roofs. Paved drives and neat gardens meant owners with money to spend on the upkeep of their properties.

'We need to speak to a Mrs McAllister and the name of her property is Haul a Gwynt.' Drake tipped his head towards a small bungalow tucked between two large extended older houses.

Sara reached the gate and registered the paint peeling around the window frames, weeds punching their way through a slate-waste strewn drive. The property appeared out of place, as did the ten-year-old Fiesta parked in front of a rusting garage door.

Mrs McAllister opened the door and invited Drake and Sara inside. It was like walking back in time. She matched her home and car perfectly. Sara paused for a moment, enjoying the view over the sea and headland.

'Can I make you a pot of tea? McAllister said. She was in her late seventies, no more than five foot four, and her Crimplene skirt reminded Sara of her grandmother.

'Thank you,' Drake said.

He even smiled. When Sara first worked with him he would have declined the offer of tea and definitely refused coffee, and she put his new human face down to his relationship with Annie. Sara had yet to meet this mysterious new girlfriend, but she was convinced Annie was having a positive impact on Drake's interpersonal skills.

The room had a warm, lived-in feel, Sara thought, even if it could do with a good coat of paint. Tassels dangled from the bottom of a sofa covered with highly patterned scatter cushions.

Mrs McAllister returned with a pot of tea and three cups and saucers. She fussed about, announcing that the tea had to brew properly, and sat down on the chair opposite Drake and Sara.

'I understand you spoke with one of the uniformed police officers about what you saw on the night Nicholas Wixley was killed.'

'I've known Mr Wixley and his wife since they

bought the house. My Bill used to do some gardening for them. He never did have much of a pension, so the extra income was a help.'

She got up and poured tea. 'I must say I preferred Mrs Wixley. I thought that he was a bit of a cold fish.'

'How long have you lived here Mrs McAllister?' Sara took the initiative, fearing Drake would get straight into asking what she had seen rather than asking some preliminary questions. Mrs McAllister struck her as a lonely old woman, so spending a few moments passing the time of day with her might be time well spent.

'Bill inherited the house from his father who was a local farmer. We moved here after Bill left the merchant navy.'

Mrs McAllister gazed off into the distance towards the horizon through the windows of the sitting room. 'I don't know what'll happen to the place after I've gone. My Jennifer wouldn't be interested.'

'Is that your daughter?'

Mrs McAllister gave her a wistful glance. 'Jennifer lives in Brisbane. I haven't seen her for...'

'Were you at home last weekend when Mr Wixley was killed?' Drake interrupted their chat, clearly eager to get the interview under way. Mrs McAllister put her cup and saucer down on a small table by her side and nodded seriously.

'Can you tell us what you remember?'

'I saw him arriving on his own on Saturday afternoon. He pulled a suitcase and a briefcase out of the boot of his car.' It sounded like Mrs McAllister had been keeping a very careful eye on her neighbour. 'He passed me later in the car when I was going out for a walk. He completely ignored me. He didn't even raise his hand. Some people have got no manners.'

'Did you see anybody visiting the property?' Drake said.

'Oh, yes.' Mrs McAllister paused theatrically and took another sip of tea. 'It was on Sunday evening. A red car arrived and a woman … young woman … a girl really, got out. I was sitting in my favourite chair.' She tipped her head towards a recliner in the window. 'And it must have been nine o'clock. There's a street light outside the house. I saw him making certain the car was parked right out of the way as though he wanted it hidden.'

'Can you describe the woman?'

'She was tall and thin and wore high heels.' Mrs McAllister struck a prudish note.

'And did you notice the registration number of this red car?'

Mrs McAllister shook her head.

'And have you seen the woman here before?' Drake said.

Another shake of the head mixed with a look of disgust.

Sara asked. 'Did you see what clothes she was wearing?'

Mrs McAllister paused before shaking her head once more. Sara finished scribbling notes in her pocketbook while Drake continued, establishing that none of the other neighbours had visitors and that the road had been quiet that evening.

'If you remember anything else then do please contact us.'

Sara complimented Mrs McAllister on some of the

china exhibited in a glass cupboard in the hallway as they left, and the older woman smiled at Sara when she admired her pictures of Pwllheli and Cardigan Bay. Walking down the path, Drake and Sara stood by the corner of the property looking over at Nicholas Wixley's home.

There was an unobstructed view towards his driveway. Was Mrs McAllister more than a nosy neighbour?

'How reliable do you think she is, boss?'

'She was quite clear about what she saw. And we have the gilet the woman possibly left behind. Now we need to find her.'

'Why are we meeting down here?' Sara asked as Drake negotiated through the village of Llithfaen towards Nant Gwrtheyrn, a collection of refurbished terraced properties abandoned a century earlier but now a thriving wedding and conference centre.

'I don't know.'

The three peaks of Yr Eifl loomed in front of the car. Drake recalled walking with his father to the middle peak and enjoying the view down towards Aberystwyth over Cardigan Bay and then up the Menai Strait. An Iron Age hill fort clung to the third of the three peaks, the first nearest the sea and inaccessible, its summit home to an electricity substation.

Holly Thatcher, the barrister who had slipped her business card into Drake's suit the previous evening, had insisted they meet at Nant Gwrtheyrn, a few miles from Portmeirion. As Drake negotiated the narrow switchback road down into the valley in low gears and slow speed, he guessed the place's privacy appealed to her.

Sara looked out of the windscreen, enjoying the view. Drake focused all his attention on making certain he was driving carefully.

'I never knew this was here,' Sara said. 'It's so beautiful.'

Drake parked. To his right were two terraces of refurbished properties with a square of recently mown grass in front. The sheer valley sides rose behind the houses, giving the place a warm stillness. Dark Welsh slate covered the roof of the single-storey café, and floor-to-ceiling windows curtained the building. Sara followed Drake inside and he cast his gaze around looking for Holly Thatcher without success.

'Let's see if she's outside,' Drake said.

They toured around the wide decking that skirted the exterior but found no one they recognised. The azure sea glistened, the thinning clouds giving way to a crisp blue sky. It was the reason tourists flocked to the Llŷn Peninsula.

'Maybe we should wait inside,' Sara said.

Drake nodded, and they retraced their steps. In a far corner, Drake heard snippets of conversation from Welsh learners occasionally struggling to find the right word with an encouraging tutor. He ordered a double shot Americano, and a latte for Sara.

They found a table by the window and sat down.

'I hope this isn't a wild goose chase.'

'Did Holly Thatcher tell you what she wants to discuss?' Sara asked.

'It was all a bit James Bond and then she gave me a sort of secret agent type look.'

Their drinks arrived, and Drake took his first sip, thinking the coffee was strong, just as he liked it, when Holly Thatcher breezed in. She made straight to their table.

'I'm sorry to keep you waiting. I wanted to be sure nobody from chambers was going to be here.'

'Isn't this a bit cloak and dagger?' Drake said.

'You won't believe what it's like.'

Thatcher ordered a cappuccino from a waitress before sitting down opposite Drake and Sara. 'I love this place,' she said. 'I came here to do a course learning Welsh. My boyfriend is from Cardiff and he's a Welsh speaker.'

'What did you want to see us about?' Drake said.

Thatcher drew her chair nearer to the table and lowered her voice. 'I suppose you've been told that everything in chambers is hunky-dory.'

'I have spoken with Michael Kennedy and Justin Selston, as you know.'

The waitress arrived with Thatcher's drink and she said nothing until the young girl was well out of earshot. 'I'm leaving soon. I'm starting in a new chambers in Cardiff. And I cannot wait. The atmosphere at the moment is poisonous.'

Drake wouldn't have to cajole Thatcher for more details.

'Nicholas Wixley was the most obnoxious man I have ever met. A brilliant mind, a great barrister, but as a person he had few, if any, redeeming features. He was manipulative and devious with wandering hands.'

'Did he ever...?' Sara said.

Thatcher shook her head. 'I never allowed myself to be in the same room as him unaccompanied. I heard from some of the other young barristers that he would come onto them. And I mean *really* come onto them, all the time.'

'Didn't the other members of chambers do something about Wixley?' Sara struck an exasperated tone.

Thatcher sipped on her coffee. 'Julia Griffiths, the head of chambers, is an unprincipled woman with no moral scruples.'

'I thought Justin Selston was head of chambers?' Drake said, realising Selston's status hadn't been made clear.

'Selston is a strange character. He was so certain he was going to be elevated to the bench he didn't bother standing for election to be head of chambers. It devastated him when Wixley was appointed. He hosts the annual chambers party at his holiday home on Bank Holiday Monday when *everyone* is supposed to attend.'

'Was the appointment between Selston and Wixley?'

Thatcher nodded.

'That must have caused tension between both men?'

'They were hardly friends.'

Drake continued. 'So, will Selston be appointed now in Wixley's place? How does the system work?'

'I have no idea. I suppose the judicial appointment board will make a decision.'

Drake decided a call to the civil servant in charge might be sensible.

Sara butted in. 'What does Michael Kennedy do?'

Thatcher drew a spoon around the creamy froth caught on the side of her cup. 'Nicholas Wixley treated him like a piece of shit. Although apparently Wixley had an affair with Pamela, Kennedy's wife.' Thatcher continued to stir her coffee. 'He's the chief clerk. He runs the place, makes sure all the bills are paid. So, the career of every barrister depends on being on good terms with Kennedy.'

Thatcher finished her coffee and gave Drake and Sara an unvarnished account of her two years at chambers. It didn't make for happy listening. 'There's one other young barrister I get on with reasonably well but everybody else hates the place. The only reason most are staying is for the money. They don't see any alternative. God knows how Nicholas Wixley would have treated the barristers from his chambers if they appeared in his court.' Thatcher shivered. 'I'm glad I'm out of it. I never thought working as a barrister would have meant such appalling conditions.'

'Is there anybody else you could suggest we talk to?'

Thatcher gave him a puzzled look. 'What do you mean?'

'From what you say, Nicholas Wixley had enemies.'

Thatcher nodded energetically.

'Who would have wished him dead?'

Thatcher whispered. 'They all did.'

Chapter 9
Wednesday 27th March
8.12 am

Driving on the A55 Sara listened to Drake's one-sided conversation as he barked out instructions for Winder and Luned to get a full background check on the convicted alphabet killer, Zavier Cornwell, including identifying his visitors in prison and the prisoners who shared a cell with him. Sara pictured the exasperation on Winder's face as Drake also insisted he and Luned start searching for possible CCTV footage to trace the red car; the task of discovering where the pink gilet had been sold would be easy by comparison.

The traffic on the M56 into Manchester slowed to a crawl. Sara was barely out of first gear before she'd had to slow and brake. Commuting into a major city was something she had never done, and based on the progress they were making that morning it was something she didn't want to experience regularly.

After their prearranged meeting with Detective Inspector Ramsbottom of the City of Manchester police force they'd visit Britannia Chambers and DCC Wixley. It would be another long day.

'I hope you've nothing planned this weekend,' Drake said.

'As a matter-of-fact, I was going to Ireland with some friends.'

'You'll have to cancel.' It sounded like the old-fashioned Drake, brusque, verging on rudeness. 'I was due to be taking Helen and Megan out on Friday. Sian wasn't too pleased when I cancelled.' Drake peered out of the window, his tone suggesting he didn't want to discuss it.

Sara had been looking forward to her long weekend for weeks. She would lose the deposit at the very least and she'd have to call her friends and break the news.

Another thirty minutes elapsed until they reached the headquarters of the City of Manchester police force: an enormous high-rise building in the suburbs. The car heaved and bumped its way to the second floor of the multistorey car park and Sara slowed to a crawl, worried she might scratch the side panels against the concrete pillars. After parking they found the main reception where Drake spoke to a woman behind a long counter who gave him a brief smile of acknowledgement. After finding the right contact, she spoke briefly into her mouthpiece and then turned to Drake and Sara. 'Please take a seat. He'll be with you shortly.'

After a wait of twenty minutes Drake became restless and Sara expected him to make some critical remark when a man in his mid-fifties, with a tired-looking face, ageing clothes and scuffed shoes approached them. Ramsbottom introduced himself, and Sara and Drake did likewise. 'Follow me.' Once they were through security it took them another ten minutes to reach the tenth floor and Ramsbottom's small, stuffy office.

He fluttered a hand over two visitor chairs. 'I understand you want to see the file on the alphabet killer.'

'You were the SIO on the case?' Drake said.

'For my sins.' Ramsbottom sighed.

'What can you tell us?'

Ramsbottom settled back into his chair. His paunch strained at the buttons of his shirt. 'The first victim had the letter A stencilled onto her chest. Her throat had been cut, and scattered like confetti all around the room were snippets of newspaper articles about the woman. And the letter A had been written in the victim's blood over one wall. She was a prominent campaigner for LGBT rights. Her girlfriend found her when she came home after working away in London for a couple of days.'

'She was never a suspect?'

Ramsbottom shook his head. 'We treated her as a person of interest of course but her alibi panned out. And she was so distressed you could never fake it. The CSIs spent days in the flat, but we didn't find any DNA we could use to identify the killer. Absolutely zero.'

'Was there any chance of it being a hate crime?' Sara said.

Ramsbottom threaded the fingers of both hands together and rested them behind his head. 'That's what we thought at the start, love.'

Sara smarted. She wasn't his love and if he said it again...

'Inspector.' Sara emphasised his rank. 'How far did your investigation get with establishing a possible relationship to homophobic criminality?'

By the tired look in his eyes Sara guessed Ramsbottom would probably trot out a critique of political correctness. Instead, he moved on.

'Let me tell you about the second murder. Trevor Hopkins was a successful DJ. He got his name in the newspaper all the time about these gigs he ran in nightclubs. He'd go over to the Costa Brava and other places in the Med. He made a fortune, so he helped set up this charity for disadvantaged kids. Too good to be true. He had a penthouse apartment in one of the swanky blocks in Salford.'

Ramsbottom pulled himself back near the table and laid his hands flat on the desktop. He gave Drake and Sara an inquisitive look as though he'd only just remembered something. 'Would you like some coffee or something?'

'Thanks,' Drake said.

Ramsbottom dictated their choices down the telephone and settled back into his chair.

'Where was I? Trevor Hopkins didn't stand a chance. He was having a quiet night in and he'd ordered an Indian takeaway. Apparently, he liked red-hot vindaloos. A man whacks the delivery driver and leaves him unconscious by his scooter. He takes Hopkins' curry up to his apartment and whacks him too: probably using a baseball bat.

'Hopkins is bound and gagged, and the killer slices open the arteries of his arms all the way up to his elbows. Not across the wrists like the self-harmers. It was like something out of a hard-core gangster movie. There was blood everywhere. It must have pumped out of his body. Our man sat there watching Hopkins' life ebb away.'

Ramsbottom paused and gathered his thoughts. 'The letter B was carved into his chest post mortem.'

'Any newspaper cuttings?' Sara said.

Ramsbottom nodded. 'There were copies of Hopkins' Facebook page scattered over his flat. Pictures of Trevor Hopkins hobnobbing with the great and the good, you know, lots of stupid, grinning inane pictures when people take selfies.'

'It sounds as though you didn't like Hopkins, Inspector,' Sara said, measuring her tone.

Ramsbottom continued unaffected. 'What can I say? He was a murder victim. Doesn't matter what I thought of him.'

'When did you become convinced you had a serial killer?'

A young civilian entered with a tray of steaming mugs. Ramsbottom ladled two teaspoons of sugar into his tea and Drake gave his coffee an inquisitive look. Sara sipped her drink.

'We ran the investigation with an open mind. We were looking for a killer. There was nothing to suggest definitively it was the same until the third.'

Ramsbottom took a mouthful of his drink. Sara sensed his reluctance to relive the inquiry, which surprised her coming from a detective clearly nearing retirement with a jaded attitude to match.

'The third was a lawyer. One of these do-gooders who wanted to get his name in the newspaper. He championed every bleeding-heart cause he could in Manchester. He came from a family rich enough to be able to let him indulge his career. He would be on the local radio and local television whenever they wanted somebody to make a clever comment about some minority's rights being oppressed.'

'How did he die?' Drake said.

Ramsbottom took another slug of his drink and wiped the back of his hand over his mouth.

'The killer took nine-inch nails and crucified the man to a piece of chipboard.' Ramsbottom allowed the enormity of his comments to sink in. 'Then he sliced open his neck.' Drake and Sara sat without moving. She forced back a knot of bile, wanting to blot out the image created by Ramsbottom's description.

'He somehow propped him against a wall and carved the letter C into the man's chest. It was the only time he used nails and a board.'

'And the fourth?' Drake said.

'A councillor, again someone who got his name in the newspapers a lot. This time the letter D was carved in his chest. Before I forget, there were other things that linked all the murders. Cornwell left funeral orders of service at each crime scene. Inside each he had written in the victim's blood the letters of the word "death". And at each scene he dressed each victim in a pair of Rotherham football club socks. I mean, who supports Rotherham, for Christ's sake?'

Nobody said anything for a few chilling seconds.

'Do you think Cornwell had an accomplice?' Drake asked.

Sara could see exactly where Drake was heading. Only one man had been convicted of the alphabet killings, so there could be another murderer still out there. 'We could never prove it, but I always thought that one man couldn't have done everything,' Ramsbottom said.

'Did you ever make any progress?' Drake said.

Sara hadn't seen anyone shake their head quite so mournfully.

'You've got to understand, Zavier Cornwell is a complete psychopath. I've never seen anyone so evil. I had to take a month off work after the case ended. I've seen some shit things in my time, but Zavier Cornwell is as bad as they come.'

Drake sympathised with Ramsbottom. He knew well enough how cases could affect detectives. They dealt with sick, depraved individuals and sometimes it wasn't easy to switch off and go home to normality. A case, years before, had meant Drake had received counselling and the prospect of being unable to cope with the demands of a case still daunted him.

Ramsbottom continued. 'We looked at everything, all his known associates, his family, his friends. And we couldn't get any leads. I suspected he was in some group of sad weirdos he'd met on the internet. We even thought he was communicating with someone using encrypted messaging. But his phone was clear of any trace of texts.'

'How did you catch him in the end?'

'He got careless. He left a beanie hat in the house of his last victim.'

'Did you manage to get some DNA from a hair sample on the beanie?'

Ramsbottom nodded as he finished the last of his coffee. 'We reacted quickly; surveillance of his house was authorised and an armed response unit deployed to break in and arrest him. I conducted the interview. I'm not much of a religious man, but I really did feel he was like the devil. I could sense all this evil coming out of him. Like a hand reaching up to me and slowly squeezing my throat.'

'What did he say in interview?'

'Not a lot. You can listen to the tapes yourself.' He stood up. 'You can collect the files from storage. And if it is Cornwell's accomplice, be very careful.'

Chapter 10
Wednesday 27th March
1.34 pm

Neatly folded copies of the morning's *Financial Times*, *Daily Telegraph* and *The Times* sat on a table in reception at Britannia Chambers. Their uncreased appearance suggested nobody had read them. Drake admired the neat precision of the column of magazines nearby, including *Investors Chronicle*, the *Economist* and editions of a Sunday supplement several months old.

'What did you make of Detective Inspector Ramsbottom?' Sara made herself comfortable on a sumptuous leather sofa.

Drake thought of the hours of work needed to read the papers in the ten boxes they'd manhandled to the car. 'We'll have to make the alphabet killer a person of interest.'

'It could be a copycat, of course.'

Drake drew a hand over the arm of the sofa that matched Sara's; it felt sticky as though it had recently been cleaned.

'We can't ignore the possibility there was an accomplice.'

A request for additional manpower would be on the top of the list for his next meeting with Superintendent Price.

Michael Kennedy walked into the room and reached out a hand to Drake and Sara. 'Good afternoon. I am sorry to keep you waiting.' He wore a dark navy suit with a white handkerchief jutting a couple of centimetres from its lapel pocket. It gave him a dandy air Drake hadn't noticed when he had met him on Monday evening. 'Do follow me.'

Luxurious carpeting covered the staircase and landings of the building. Expensive-looking watercolours hung along the wide hallway, and at the end Michael Kennedy pushed open the door and let Drake and Sara in first.

A tall thin woman, with a sharp jaw and fine white hair cut so severely she didn't need to tuck any stray hairs behind an ear, approached Drake. She gave him and Sara a staccato handshake before waving them to a dust-free table surrounded by plush conference chairs.

'Julia Griffiths, head of chambers.'

'Detective Inspector Drake and this is Detective Sergeant Sara Morgan.'

Everyone sat down and Griffiths weighed in. 'I want you to understand that in my capacity as head of chambers we shall do everything in our power to assist you with your investigation. No stone must be left unturned. We all want to find out who was responsible for this ghastly crime.'

It was difficult to make out her accent. Educated and cultured certainly, honed by appearances in courts where English with rounded vowels was expected.

'How can we help you, Detective Inspector?' Griffiths said.

'We'll need a full list of all Mr Wixley's cases in the last five years. And we need to interview his colleagues and staff.'

Griffiths nodded. 'Of course, of course.' She glanced at Kennedy. 'Michael will organise a conference room for you to use. All the support staff have been told to expect you to question them.'

And prepped with the right things to say, Drake thought, taking a dislike to Griffiths' headmistress-like voice.

She stood up. 'I'll let Michael take charge. If there's anything else you need from us then please do not hesitate to contact me.' She handed Drake a business card. 'It has my personal email address on it.' Her tone suggested it shouldn't be used on pain of death.

'Thank you, Mrs Griffiths.'

She returned to her desk, a model of tidy, precise paperwork that Drake grudgingly admired. They left with Kennedy and followed him until he stopped outside a room with Nicholas Wixley written on a brass plaque screwed to the glistening white paint. Kennedy fumbled with the keys from his jacket and unlocked the room.

It felt cold inside. Drake made for the desk and Kennedy flicked on the central light, which illuminated a green shaded desktop lamp at the same time. The place exuded a well-ordered professional air. A large, modern, abstract painting was the only thing out of place.

'Mr Wixley doesn't have any of his personal possessions here,' Kennedy said. 'I've already printed out for you a list of his cases in the past five years with the names of the solicitors who instructed him and the Crown Prosecution Service lawyers who coordinated the cases where he prosecuted.'

Drake ran a finger along the edge of the desk. 'How did you get on with Mr Wixley?'

'I always thought he was fair employer. My job is to look after the administration of chambers. We let the barristers get on with all the legal stuff and we make certain their professional lives run smoothly.'

Kennedy stood for a moment until Drake turned to him. 'We'll let you know once we've finished.'

Kennedy hesitated. 'Of course. I'll be in my office on the ground floor.'

The door closed with a reassuringly expensive-sounding thud and Drake sat at Wixley's chair. In one corner, a shelving unit that held piles of papers secured by pink ribbon caught Sara's attention. There was little of interest in the desk, Drake decided after rummaging through the contents of most of the drawers – pens, pencils and the normal stuff of a working office.

'Anything interesting?' Drake said.

'I suppose all these cases will be on the list of his current and past work,' Sara said. 'It could be like searching for a needle in a haystack.'

Drake got up. Behind him were bookcases with old volumes of legal reports and textbooks on procedure. He imagined Wixley poring over the papers for the prosecution of the alphabet killer. The details of that case would have been thrashed out in this room, and if everything he had been told about Wixley was correct, his sharp mind made certain that Zavier Cornwell spent the rest of his days behind bars.

'Let's interview the staff,' Drake said.

Sara followed him downstairs.

Kennedy joined them in the conference room, clutching a pile of paperwork. 'I've printed a list of all the barristers and support staff,' Kennedy said. 'As well as details of Nicholas Wixley's past and current cases.'

In the background, an air conditioning unit hummed quietly.

'Thank you,' Drake said as a young woman entered with a tray of china cups and saucers. Drake and Sara both opted for coffee and the woman promised to return shortly. There was even a plate of fancy biscuits. Sara gave them a hungry glance.

Drake scanned the list. 'Let's get started.'

For the next two hours Drake and Sara sat listening to complaints of varying intensity. Some of the older barristers were unwilling to criticise or praise Wixley. Younger employees were less reticent: one woman in her mid-thirties appeared particularly reluctant to speak her mind, allowing her fingers to play together nervously as she chewed her lower lip. Eventually Drake teased out of her that she was doing everything possible to leave chambers and unless she found a job soon she would be giving her notice without somewhere to go. 'Why are you leaving?' Drake said.

'I hate it here.' She looked over helplessly to Drake and Sara. 'I can't stand them.' Abruptly she got up and left. Sara, encouraged by Drake's raised eyebrow, underlined the woman's name.

A tall, gaunt man in his sixties with the air of a ham actor well past his sell-by date was the only barrister unafraid to speak his mind. 'I'm retiring next month,' Alan Lees said, folding himself into a chair. 'I suppose you believe that someone at chambers might have a motive to kill Wixley.' He paused, waiting for Drake to reply, but seeing Drake's frown he continued. 'It's all a bit Miss Marple, don't you think? I can imagine the title of an Agatha Christie novel – *Murder at Britannia Chambers*. The truth is, Inspector Drake, that Nicholas Wixley was thoroughly hated by us all. Every single one of us; but nobody will tell you that of course. But because his reputation brought in lots of cases and we all prospered and, well ... you know ... earning a living is important, isn't it?'

Did Lees have anything to gain by Wixley's death? He sounded jaded and tired of the professional intrigue of life as a barrister. But he didn't sound like a killer. How indiscreet might Lees be if pushed?

'Are there any members of chambers that you think might have a motive to kill Nicholas Wixley?'

Lees drew a hand slowly over his thinning hair as he composed his face for a serious reply. 'How Michael Kennedy ever put up with his insults I shall never know, and he treated everyone with contempt, especially younger females.'

'Anyone in particular?'

'Holly Thatcher was the most recent to leave. Many good lawyers left because of him. But she wasn't the first.'

Lees continued sharing his recollections and opinions about Wixley. No one could accuse Lees of not playing to the audience, Drake decided.

'He should have retired years ago,' Drake said once they were alone.

Sara nodded. 'He was really sanctimonious.'

Pamela Kennedy was the final barrister who traipsed into the conference room. She tucked her legs under the table and smiled at Drake, ignoring Sara.

'How did you get on with Mr Wixley?' Drake said.

'He was fair-minded and an excellent lawyer.'

This echoed what Michael Kennedy had said. Drake concluded that Pamela and her husband had interests in common and that protecting his job and her status in chambers was predictable. Perhaps it was nothing more than what he should expect from an ambitious lawyer.

'And what was your relationship like with Mr Wixley?' Drake searched for any awkwardness on her face, but she kept an inscrutable appearance.

'Professional. I'm sure you'll forgive my prying – professional curiosity – but do you have any evidence from the scene?'

'We're pursuing a number of lines of inquiry.'

'Of course, I understand.' She gave Drake an intense smile.

'Were you aware of how other members of chambers felt about Nicholas Wixley?'

'I don't pay office gossip much attention.'

'How did he treat other women barristers?'

'Again, I don't listen to idle chatter, Inspector.'

After finishing with Pamela, they spent the rest of the afternoon with the administration team. One of the final members of staff was a man in his mid-forties whose role was Crown Court coordinator. He had a broad London accent and a silver-grey goatee beard.

'I don't know there's anything I can do to help,' Richard Murdoch said, unprompted. 'I just get on with my job.'

'What did you think of Nicholas Wixley?'

'As a man – I couldn't abide him. I thought he was obnoxious. He treated everybody like a piece of something he'd picked up on his shoes.'

'What was he like with you?'

'I always did my job and never gave him cause to complain. The Crown Court staff used to tell me Wixley got all the best cases recently because Michael was looking after him, despite the way Wixley treated him. It made Wixley a fortune. And he gave up being head of chambers because he wanted to become a judge. And that's another thing – he and Justin Selston hated each other. They couldn't stand being in the same room as one another. When Selston heard that Wixley had been appointed as a judge he puked his ring in the toilets. And I mean gut-wrenching stuff.'

'So he was disappointed at not being appointed himself?'

Murdoch guffawed. 'You could say that.'

Although Drake's mobile was on silent, its vibration alerted him and he saw the London number he had telephoned earlier that morning. He looked at Sara. 'I need to take this call.'

He glanced around the corridor, making certain no one could hear.

'Detective Inspector Drake, Wales Police Service.'

'It's Rufus Dixon from the judicial appointments board. We spoke earlier this morning. I wanted to confirm that only two candidates were interviewed for the vacancy filled by Nicholas Wixley. The other was Justin Selston. Is this the information you needed?'

Drake stood for a moment mulling over the reply. Was it a real possibility that Justin Selston had killed Nicholas Wixley because he had defeated him for appointment as a circuit judge? It certainly meant Selston required far more of their time.

'Will Justin Selston now be appointed as a judge?'

'I couldn't comment but I daresay he'll be considered sympathetically when the appointment process is reopened.'

Chapter 11

Wednesday 27th March
6.27 pm

'You don't really think Justin Selston could be the killer?' Sara said.

Drake sat in the passenger seat turning a bottle of water through his fingers. It was difficult to imagine the placid barrister slitting the throat of his colleague and then scratching the letter E onto his chest. But Drake had seen some unlikely murderers, human beings that had appalled him with their hate and the depths of their depravity.

'Nicholas Wixley was universally disliked. I wonder what Justin Selston thought about him. If he was driven mad by jealousy I suppose it's possible. And he knows about the alphabet murders case and all its gory details. So perhaps he tries to create the impression that a copycat or the mysterious associate of Zavier Cornwell is responsible.'

Sara had parked a little distance from Mrs Wixley's home. Stripes ran along the narrow lengths of lawns that lined the neat verges dotted with carefully trimmed ash and sycamores. Expensive Mercedes and Jaguars glided past.

'Let's go and talk to the grieving widow.'

'Not so much of the grieving.' Sara reached for the door handle.

They left the car and walked over to the gate where Drake pressed the buzzer on the intercom. A crackly voice emerged. Drake leaned forward. 'Detective

Inspector Drake and Detective Sergeant Morgan.'

The gate ahead of them clicked open. Ahead of them a navy Range Rover Sport was parked in front of a garage with old-fashioned oak doors. The house was an old Edwardian mansion. Money had been regularly spent to maintain its upkeep – the windows look spotless, even the guttering glistened, and Drake noticed the discreetly placed CCTV cameras.

Deputy Chief Constable Laura Wixley stood in the open doorway as Drake approached.

'I was expecting you earlier.' Wixley fixed Drake with a reproachful stare.

'It has taken us rather longer than expected to complete the interviews with the staff at Britannia Chambers.'

Drake read a glimmer of disdain on Wixley's face. Or was it simply her default position? She led them into a hallway where tables groaned with vases filled with cut flowers. The sound of activity down a corridor drifted towards them and a thin woman in her twenties, with high cheekbones and a prominent jaw, emerged from the room, a clothes iron in hand. She retreated as soon as she saw Drake and Sara. All the domestic chores continued unchanged, Drake thought.

'When we spoke on Tuesday I should have mentioned that family liaison officers from the Wales Police Service are available. And—'

Wixley raised a disdainful eyebrow and folded her arms.

'Do you have immediate family?' Drake determined that not even a deputy chief constable would deflect him from following the right protocols.

'You needn't trouble yourself about my wellbeing.'

Her reply dumbfounded Drake. Most normal grieving widows would have offered details about a supportive sibling or a heartbroken mother. Wixley glared back at him.

'Do you have any children?'

'No, Inspector. Nicholas and myself never had any children.'

'Did Mr Wixley have any immediate family?'

'He was an only child and both his parents died when he was a teenager.'

'Did he have any other relatives?'

'None.'

Her reply included a prohibition against further questions. Drake got the message but he sensed something out of place – the world of DCC Laura Wixley wasn't the calm ordered version she wanted them to accept. Killing Nicholas Wixley had seen to that.

'I'll take you to his study.'

Drake looked over at Sara as Wixley turned her back on them and headed down the corridor. Sara frowned. Drake guessed she was as troubled as he was about the reaction from Laura Wixley.

At the end a door led into a ground-floor room with large French windows looking out over a long garden where two men worked on various shrubs in the borders.

'The gardening contractors were booked weeks ago – Nicholas always liked the place to look pristine. He kept his personal papers in the desk.' Wixley pointed at a substantial knee hole desk positioned in the middle of the room, allowing the user an unrestricted view down the lawn. Embossed invitation cards lined the mantelpiece of the fire surround. 'That awful man Kennedy from his chambers has already been to collect any legal papers Nicholas was working on.'

'Who do you think might have killed your husband?' Drake said.

Somewhere in her past Laura Wixley had been a detective barking out orders to officers like him, so Drake felt justified in asking her opinion. Surely it would have surprised her had he not. He could imagine her complaining about him to Price, or even one of the assistant chief constables in Cardiff, that he hadn't asked even the basic questions a good detective should ask.

'I think it must have been linked to one of his cases.'

'Do you think it could be the suspected accomplice in the alphabet killings?'

Wixley nodded. 'Or a copycat. So many of these serial killer stories are published in the newspapers. It's so easy to access all the details about the case. He prosecuted a lot of important murder cases so he made enemies.'

'It's unusual for defendants in cases to have a grudge against the lawyers involved; police officers, maybe.'

Wixley shrugged. 'I suggest you focus your inquiry on his past cases. There's bound to be someone that fits the profile of the person you want.'

Wixley made for the door.

Sara made her first contribution. 'Can we see his personal items too, ma'am.'

Respecting Wixley's rank didn't spare Sara from an angry retort. 'Whatever for?'

Sara didn't immediately reply, but Drake seized the initiative. 'I'm sure you appreciate that it's only part of building a complete picture of your late husband's life.'

Wixley swung her glare at Drake and barely lessened its intensity.

Drake wasn't going to be intimidated by Wixley baring her teeth.

'Once you've finished. I'll show you his bedroom.'

Wixley left Drake and Sara, who stood looking at each other. 'Do you think she's hiding something?' Sara whispered.

'At least she relented about his personal stuff.'

'She said she'd show us his bedroom, so they must have slept apart,' Sara said.

Drake nodded. Discreet lighting illuminated several canvases of modern art. Sara squinted at one appreciatively. Drake couldn't make out the mass of colour and shapes. Against one of the walls was a glass-fronted display cupboard with fountain pens and ballpoints and propelling pencils in their original boxes.

'It looks like he was a bit of a collector,' Sara said.

Drake walked over to the desk as Sara started on a filing cabinet in one corner. He ran a finger along the surface and collected a film of polish. He wondered if Mrs Wixley had been through the contents carefully already. More fountain pens occupied the top drawer. A simple ballpoint from the local supermarket satisfied Drake.

Legal pads and Post-it notes in neat and tidy order filled the second drawer. By the time he reached the bottom Drake realised Wixley had been a fastidious individual, which he approved of. Turning his attention to the drawers in the right-hand side, he dispelled a feeling he had missed something or at the very least that he should have found something that wasn't there.

The arms of the office chair were sumptuous leather. Wixley struck Drake as a man vain enough to have the chair specially made.

Getting up, he spotted speakers built into the shelving units of the bookcase lining one wall. Sara dumped a selection of buff-coloured photographs, suspended filing pockets and lever arch files on a table before continuing to delve through the cabinet.

From the bookcase Drake found a stack of boxes and placed them onto the desk.

Envelopes and stamps filled the first. In the second he fished out old maps of Lancashire and the Peak District as well as a battered copy of the historic county of Caernarfonshire that included the Llŷn Peninsula and Pwllheli.

A nagging feeling they were wasting time circled the edge of his mind.

'He was loaded,' Sara announced.

Drake turned to face her.

She nodded at the pile on the table.

'He must have millions in various investments. And there are share certificates relating to private companies.'

'We'll take it all back with us. And I'll requisition a full search of his finances.'

Drake turned his attention to the third box. A motley bunch of electronic gadgets was stored inside: an old dictating machine and cameras and chargers, but at the back Drake found a mobile telephone. It looked reasonably new and he switched it on, surprised no password was needed. He returned to the desk. If Mrs

Wixley had already been through her husband's belongings, she had missed this. He sank again into the chair, propped his elbows on the desk and scrolled through the numbers.

Drake read the first girl's name – Veronique. It sounded foreign. The second name on the screen was Mandy and the third Kelly. Which one owned the size ten gilet?

Drake put down the mobile, covering it with his hand as Laura Wixley entered the room, reading the time on her watch as she did so. It had a substantial silver metal bracelet. At a guess Drake thought Rolex and expensive. The recently applied blusher gave her face more colour and there was a faint odour of perfume.

'Are you going to be much longer? Some friends have invited me out this evening and...'

'Of course.'

'If you haven't finished then you could always come back.' She sounded unwelcoming.

Half an hour later Drake and Sara had finished a rapid search of Nicholas Wixley's bedroom and wardrobe and sat in the car outside the house. Drake had recognised some of the designer labels on the suits – they made some of the German design labels in his own wardrobe seem like cheap off-the-shelf versions.

'And not even a cup of tea,' Sara said.

Drake reached for the mobile he had found. 'We've got calls to make.'

Chapter 12
Thursday 28th March
7.49 am

Drake woke from a dreamless sleep, struggling to remember which day it was. Then he remembered his conversation with Annie the night before. Thank goodness for Skype, Drake thought, as the image of her warm smile filled his thoughts. He still hoped he could take at least one day off that weekend. Meeting her parents had been planned for weeks and he knew how much it meant to her.

Cancelling his arrangement to see Helen and Megan tomorrow only reopened harsh memories of holidays and family events he had cancelled because of work, and the old feelings of guilt resurfaced. How could he protect Annie from his life as a police officer?

A message from Annie reached his mobile and focused his attention. *Did you sleep ok? x.* Last night he'd arrived home exhausted, feeling like he had worked two days in one. He sat on the edge of the bed and smiled – he always did when she messaged him. He tapped out a reply. *Slept like a log. Talk later x*

Drake only left the apartment once satisfied the kitchen was neat and tidy. He wore a fresh set of clothes, the shirt and suit from yesterday discarded to a pile for dry cleaning. Although his black brogues had been polished the previous weekend, he gave each shoe a cursory polish with a brush before leaving the flat.

On the way to headquarters, Drake bought his regular broadsheet and focused on the Sudoku. He drove off after managing five numbers quickly, feeling pleased with himself.

By the time he'd parked, his mind had turned to Deputy Chief Constable Wixley. Even successful professionals were allowed to be emotional when a partner died, Drake thought. A sallow complexion or evidence of tears would have been expected, but she had appeared unaffected. Walking over to the main reception, Drake reminded himself about the initial comments by Kennedy and Selston, suggesting Wixley was respected and well liked.

Those comments couldn't be further from the truth, and either they were lying or they had no idea what he was really like. The first explanation made more sense.

Drake reached his office and stood by his desk. The columns of Post-it notes were undisturbed and the bin was empty. He adjusted the photographs of his daughters near the telephone and, satisfied everything appeared to be in apple-pie order, he booted up his computer as Sara and the rest of his team arrived.

Usual morning greetings filled the Incident Room outside his office.

He extracted the photograph of Zavier Cornwell from the file and noticed the lifeless eyes and blank expression – it looked like any other mugshot Drake had seen over the years. He left his room and walked over to the board, past Winder and Luned.

'How did you get on yesterday, sir?' Luned spoke first.

Drake nodded at the boxes of files on a nearby table. 'That's the alphabet killer's file from the major crime team in Manchester.'

Sara didn't look at them; she had supervised the team of civilians that had transported them from her car late the previous evening.

'Detective Inspector Ramsbottom was in charge of the investigation.' Drake reached the board and pinned onto it the photograph in his hand, turning to face his team. 'We start looking for a link to Zavier Cornwell.'

'Ramsbottom always thought there was an accomplice, but they never traced anyone,' Sara said.

Drake added, 'If it is an accomplice then there may be other intended victims at risk. I want everyone directly linked to the original prosecution listed and contacted. Today.' He paused to scan the faces of his team. 'There could be lives at risk. Speak to Ramsbottom and by this afternoon I need that list finished.'

'It's going to be difficult to get hold of people over the holiday weekend.' Winder said. Typical, Drake thought; the detective constable would always look for difficulties, but this time he had a point. They couldn't afford to lose four days because of the extended Easter break, otherwise the impact on the case would prey on his mind.

'Get telephone numbers and call them tomorrow and over the weekend if needs be. This is an important inquiry. Bank holidays will have to wait. And I need background on Justin Selston. Apparently, he was devastated when Wixley was appointed a judge instead of him.'

'He might be a target too,' Sara said.

'We'll arrange to speak to him again in due course.'

Drake searched for defiance in the faces of his team. He thought he saw disappointment in Winder's eyes and resignation in Luned's. Detective work meant round-the-clock attention in the first few days of a case.

Drake read the time on his watch, reminding himself of Superintendent Price's email asking for a briefing at ten-thirty.

'Let's make progress today.' Drake went back to his office, gathered up his papers and threaded his way to the senior management suite.

'Good morning, Ian,' Hannah said. 'They're waiting for you.'

Drake gave a puzzled look, inviting her to explain the 'they' but the superintendent's secretary was already announcing his arrival down the telephone. This was a routine briefing, and unexpected attendees always unnerved Drake.

Entering Price's room, he stopped dead in his tracks when he saw Chief Constable Riskin.

'Good morning, Ian.' Riskin offered a hand that Drake shook. Riskin was only a few years older than Drake but his ambition and drive spilled out of the lean and well-toned officer. He looked just as athletic as Drake remembered.

'I wasn't expecting... sir.'

'My plans weren't finalised until last night.'

Riskin glanced at Price as if silently instructing him to get on with the meeting. This was no normal briefing, nor was Price in charge.

Riskin sat next to Price at the conference table and tension gripped Drake's chest. Had he missed a notification from Price in all the activity over the past two days?

'I flew up on the shuttle this morning.' Riskin struck an amiable tone. 'It's so much easier than spending hours in the car.'

Drake nodded. He wasn't even certain the

comment had been addressed to him.

Hannah interrupted with a cafetière of coffee and Northern Division's finest china cups and saucers.

'Bring us up to date with the Wixley inquiry.' Riskin gave Drake a long, calculated stare.

'We recovered the file of papers from the major crime team in the City of Manchester force that handled the original alphabet killing. I've already got my officers working on them.'

Riskin nodded. Price gripped an orange Lamy fountain pen tightly.

'I assume you think they are linked?' Riskin said.

Addressing Price was one thing but having Riskin there daunted Drake. His pulse pounded in both ears and his lips suddenly felt chalk-like.

'Wixley prosecuted Zavier Cornwell. The DI in charge of the inquiry thought Cornwell was a psychopath, and he strongly suspected he had an accomplice.'

Riskin nodded as though he already knew everything Drake was sharing.

'But they never traced him.'

'Or it's a copycat,' said Riskin.

'Yes, sir.'

'And a copycat who has murdered a Crown Court judge.' Riskin let the last sentence hang in the air. 'And his wife is a senior police officer. It is an attack on the very fabric of our legal system.' Riskin tapped the file of papers on the table in front of him.

'We'll need to interview Zavier Cornwell in due course.' Drake paused. 'And we're searching for a woman in a red car seen at Wixley's home the night he was killed. Tracing her is a priority.'

'Cornwell is in HMP Marchfield,' Riskin announced in a sombre tone, emphasising the name of one of the securest prisons in England and Wales, housing only the most dangerous offenders.

'We also visited Britannia Chambers. None of the admin staff liked Wixley. And he was despised by the majority of his colleagues too. A Justin Selston, one of the senior barristers, may well be a person of interest.'

Riskin squinted at Drake. 'How so?'

'Wixley beat him to the appointment as a circuit judge. One witness told us Selston took his defeat badly.'

'Good, you've been making progress.' Riskin gave a brief, noncommittal smile.

Drake glanced at the file under the chief constable's hand. There has to be more to this visit, Drake thought.

'We visited the home of Nicholas Wixley and Mrs Wixley yesterday.'

'DCC Wixley,' Riskin corrected him.

'Yes, sir.'

'Which brings us to the DCC indeed.'

He faced Drake. 'DCC Wixley applied for the chief constableship of the WPS when I was appointed. She was shortlisted at the time and interviewed. On paper, she was an outstanding candidate and an exceptional police officer. She has dedicated her whole life to her career. Her rise was meteoric through the ranks. She took a master's degree in criminology in her own time and eventually it led to her appointment to the City of Manchester force.'

Riskin drew breath. 'She'd spent part of her early career in Cardiff, which made her the favoured candidate.'

Drake glanced over at Price, his gaze firmly on Riskin.

'The chairman of the appointments panel made contact with me yesterday. He made me aware of a background briefing they had received on Mrs Wixley. There were concerns about Mr Wixley's contacts with certain members of organised crime groups in Manchester, which might have made her appointment *problematic*.'

Drake could barely believe what he heard. 'Are you suggesting we treat Mrs Wixley as a person of interest?'

Riskin made an odd sound as he sucked air into his mouth. This was difficult for him.

'We want her eliminated from the inquiry as soon as possible.'

Presumption of innocence from the start then, Drake thought. 'Is her promotion being formally blocked?'

Riskin shook his head. 'She has made several unsuccessful applications.'

'So you think she could be blaming her husband. And that without him around she might stand a better chance of a chief constable appointment.' Drake's moment of clarity was met with stony silence.

'We need to make certain that because DCC Wixley is such a high-ranking police officer she should not be automatically excluded as a person of interest.'

Two faces with resigned inevitability looked over at Drake.

Riskin continued. 'I know Laura Wixley from various committees and I cannot imagine her being a killer.' It pained Riskin even to contemplate the possibility. Drake felt like a small cog in a large wheel that he couldn't see turning. Was the chief constable asking him to seriously investigate Laura Wixley or merely go through the motions?

Riskin pushed over the folder.

'There are contact names and telephone numbers in the file. And I'm organising to get the minutes of the appointment panel made available for you. I'm sure I can rely on the complete discretion of your team?'

Chapter 13

Thursday 28th March
11.34 am

Winder jumped to his feet when Drake entered the Incident Room. 'Boss, the chief's here apparently. He flew up this morning. The traffic escort from the airport got caught in the roadworks on the A55.'

'I've just been in a briefing with him.' Drake reached the board and stood to face the team, all wide-eyed in astonishment. Drake drew breath. 'We need to treat Deputy Chief Constable Laura Wixley as a person of interest, if only to dismiss her from the inquiry.'

Sara uttered the words on everyone's minds. 'On what basis – does she have a motive?'

'There's intelligence to suggest her promotion has been hampered by her husband's reputation. And without him around her path to a chief constableship is easier.'

Sara nodded. Winder looked stunned, as though such a possibility was unthinkable. Luned sat heavy-faced, ruminating.

'And she wouldn't disclose where she had been on the morning Wixley's body had been found, nor indeed for the day before.'

'We don't have any evidence ...' Luned said.

Sara added, 'I suppose the chief doesn't want anyone to say we ignored her as a possible person of interest because she's a deputy chief constable.'

Drake nodded. 'Our focus will be on the alphabet killer and finding the woman who was with Wixley the night he died.' And as an afterthought. 'And tracing that Jamie character who argued with Wixley.'

'It's Jamie Eaton, boss. I spoke to Speakman's Engineering,' Winder said.

'Good.'

'The wholesalers sent me a list of the shops that stock the pink gilet in the northwest of England. None in north Wales,' Luned announced.

'Contact them all,' Drake said. 'And any progress tracking the red car on CCTV?'

'Slow,' Winder replied. 'It could take hours. How far do you want us to go? I mean, it would take days to check all the footage from garage forecourt CCTV around north Wales.'

'You know the drill.' Drake sounded sharp. 'Identify every CCTV on the roads from Wixley's house. She must have stopped for petrol or diesel or something to eat. It was the middle of the night so that should narrow it down.'

Winder gave a brief, sullen look at the admonishment.

'But our main priority…' Drake looked over at the box from the City of Manchester police force. 'Everyone involved with the original alphabet case needs to be listed. There could be other intended targets. We need to identify anyone at risk.' He registered the shock on the faces in front of him, the enormity sinking in.

Back in his room he tried to prioritise, but a briefing on a murder inquiry with the chief constable was a rare event and he disliked the niggle in his mind that suggested he wasn't being told something.

He found the contact details for HMP Marchfield and emailed a formal request to see Zavier Cornwell.

Reaching for Wixley's second mobile telephone, he copied the numbers down from the screen and requisitioned a search against each, guessing they'd be pay-as-you-go and untraceable, before calling each in turn. The same voice he had heard the previous evening invited him to leave a message. He didn't bother, and he pushed the mobile to the far corner of his desk.

Drake digested reports from house-to-house inquiries, reread the pathologist's report and picked up the preliminary toxicology conclusions that confirmed no trace of any poison in Wixley's body apart from the cocaine.

His stomach grumbled by lunchtime and he texted Annie, hoping he could talk to her.

Despite being a successful barrister, nobody had a good word to say for Wixley. Even his widow seemed unaffected by his death. The CV on Britannia Chambers' website had details of his school and it reminded Drake that he had read the name before, when he'd scanned the cuttings on Wixley's computer for Neil Thorpe. On Wixley's laptop he found images of a smiling Thorpe, with children and teachers all beaming at the camera. Wixley didn't strike Drake as someone to keep random reports about a former pupil of the same school he attended.

Making contact with the school would be the next step, but before he could get started his mobile rang and he recognised Annie's name. Lightness filled his chest and he smiled to himself.

'Sorry I couldn't talk earlier,' Annie said. 'I had a tutorial.'

'I won't be able to make it over tonight and it looks like I'll be working tomorrow.'

'Oh … I can come over to Colwyn Bay. I'd love to see you.'

The prospect of seeing Annie that evening washed over him. 'That'll be lovely.'

A Google search brought up the contact telephone number for the Moreton-Pritchard High School. He'd be lucky to track down anyone in the office at this hour in the middle of the school holidays, and he steeled himself for the inevitable answer machine, surprised when his call was answered.

'Moreton-Pritchard High School.'

'I'm trying to trace the family background of a former student.'

'Let me put you through to the bursar.'

The line went dead and Drake hoped the call had gone through. A tired voice responded. Drake made the introductions and the man's voice perked up once he realised he was assisting in a police investigation.

'Wixley, you say?'

'He probably left the school in the early 1980s.'

'That shouldn't be a problem,' the man said, sounding distracted as though his attention was focused elsewhere. 'We computerised all our records years ago and I think we should be able to find what you need. You're lucky to catch me here. I'm working late as I am going on holiday next week and there's a pile of paperwork to complete.'

'Is there anyone working at the school who might remember pupils from that time?'

'That would be going some.' Another pause. 'I'm into the main database now.'

Drake heard the faint sound of a mouse being clicked.

'Sorry, I can't find any record.'

'Are you sure?'

The voice sounded irritated. 'I'll check again but …'

'Can you search by Christian name?'

'There are bound to be many boys with the name Nicholas, Inspector.'

'It would help with our inquiry.' The usual standard reply and Drake sensed that he sounded unconvincing.

'The records might be wrong, and I don't have the time to do a full search now. One of the admin assistants has been here a long time and she might remember who you're looking for. She was in earlier – I'll ask her to call you.'

Drake gave the man his contact details and rang off.

Sara stood in his doorway and rapped two knuckles on the door. 'I've done some preliminary work on the alphabet killings.'

Drake gestured her in.

She sat in one of his visitor chairs. 'How do you want us to prioritise? Dozens of police officers were involved and then several lawyers at the Crown Prosecution Service as well as the jury and the judge. And, of course, the press that covered the whole trial.'

Sara was right. The prospect of prioritising possible targets for an accomplice of a psychopathic killer would be daunting.

'If Zavier Cornwell's victims were random then we haven't got a hope of establishing who might be the next victim.'

For a moment, Drake stared at Sara as they both

realised the consequences of what she had said.

The telephone rang and interrupted them.

'DI Drake.'

'My name's Iris. Mr Jacobs at the Moreton-Pritchard High School asked me to contact you.'

Sara made to leave but Drake waved a hand for her to stay.

'Iris, thanks for calling. Do you remember a Nicholas Wixley at school?'

'Oh yes. He was a nasty piece of goods even then. He was one of the most selfish and unpleasant boys I have ever met.'

Drake scribbled on his notepad.

'But he wasn't called Wixley back then.'

Drake stopped writing. 'What do you mean?'

'He changed his name. He didn't want anything to do with his family after he left. Mind you, they were an odd pair who hated mixing with people.'

'Was he related in any way to Neil Thorpe, the rugby player?'

'Maybe … There were two or three Thorpe brothers and I think Nicholas was the son of one of them.'

Drake sounded a sympathetic tone. 'It must have been difficult for Nicholas when he lost his parents as a boy.'

'Come again?'

Drake heard the incredulous edge to her voice.

'They are still alive. I saw Mr Thorpe in Tesco's last week. He was walking with a stick, mind. So I don't know where you've got the idea they were dead.'

'My mistake,' Drake said. 'Do you know where they live?'

She reeled off the name of a suburb but no street or house number. 'They're probably in the phonebook.'

'Thanks for your help.'

Drake finished the call and flopped back in his chair. 'Wixley's parents are still alive.'

'Really?'

'It means a trip tomorrow to Manchester.'

'At least we've found *someone* who loved him.'

Chapter 14
Good Friday 29th March
8.34 am

Annie's perfume hung in the air like an early-morning mist on a warm summer's day.

A dreamless sleep followed their lovemaking the previous evening and Drake woke that morning with his passion renewed. He leaned over and ran a hand over her naked shoulder. She warmed to his touch, turning under the duvet to face him.

She scratched the stubble on his chin.

'Good morning,' Drake said.

Annie smiled and reached a hand to squeeze him tightly and grinned. 'Do we have time?'

Afterwards, they showered together. Drake pulled Annie close, allowing the hot water to run down their bodies. Using a sponge, he lathered her shoulders and each breast in turn, thinking she was the most beautiful person he had seen.

Breakfast in the small kitchen of his apartment had a quiet, relaxed, holiday feel. Annie drank tea with a bowl of fresh fruit while Drake enjoyed two cups of Americano. Working that Easter bank holiday was the last thing Drake wanted. But Annie seemed content to share him with the inquiry and his work.

'When do you leave?' Annie said.

'Sara is collecting me in an hour.'

'What's she like?'

Drake gave a noncommittal shrug. 'She's been with me for less than a year. It's taken a bit of time to get into the swing of working with her. She can be aloof, but she is clever and dedicated.'

'It makes me feel quite jealous.' She managed a light tone before reaching over and squeezing his hand. 'We should invite her over one evening. What time will you be back tonight?'

'Hopefully it won't be too late. Sara cancelled a weekend away with some friends in Dublin.'

Annie rolled her eyes as she finished the last of her tea. 'I think you're all very dedicated.' She got up, moved over to the sink and rinsed the dishes.

'Will you still be okay for Monday?' Annie turned to Drake.

Drake stood and walked over to Annie. He threaded an arm around her waist and she turned to face him. 'I'm looking forward to meeting them. But don't book anything just in case.'

Annie nodded. Her father's recent ill-health must have had an impact on her and he hadn't wanted to interrogate her too much about the prognosis but her reticence suggested she feared the worst.

She left soon afterwards, and Drake returned to the kitchen, fussing about, making certain the dishcloths hung at exactly the same length from the oven handle and stacking the dishes away carefully. Surely Annie had noticed his obsessions? But having her around always made him more relaxed.

Bang on time, a text reached his mobile from Sara telling him she was outside. He left the apartment after finding his jacket, staring in the mirror, adjusting his tie a few millimetres and dragging a comb through his hair.

'Good morning, boss.' Sara stood by her car in the warm spring sunshine and she tilted her face skyward. 'At least it's a nice day.'

Drake punched the postcode into the satnav and

Sara navigated to the A55 and then east. When the M56 turned into the Manchester inner ring road the satnav bleeped and the disembodied voice directed them through various junctions.

Sara slowed as the voice took them to a park near a school. Its gates were locked, the building deserted. And then Fox Lane started, a well-maintained terrace with small front gardens. At the end they reached their destination and Sara parked the car at the kerbside opposite Thorpe's Emporium. The woodwork badly needed painting, and the special offers advertised in the window were neglected and ancient. A large 'closed' sign hung in the middle of the door.

Drake walked over to a gate that led to a rear yard. He joined Sara by the front door and pressed the bell on the door frame. A few moments passed before the door creaked open. A woman in her Sunday best stood looking at Drake and Sara as though they weren't expected.

'Mrs Thorpe? I'm Detective Inspector Drake. And this is Detective Sergeant Sara Morgan of the Wales Police Service.' The previous evening a text from the civilian support staff notified Drake that Mr and Mrs Thorpe would expect him and Sara. 'Somebody from our headquarters made contact with you yesterday.'

'Of course, dear, come in.'

Drake tried to guess Mrs Thorpe's age. She was thin, her face lined and her hair scraggy, unhealthy and greying. Drake guessed late seventies, based largely on assuming she had been a mother in her late twenties, knowing Nicholas Wixley was in his early fifties.

Sara closed the door behind them and they trooped through a cold corridor towards a room at the rear of the building. A man with sunken cheeks and penetrating eyes stood by a fire, its weak heat only barely taking the edge off the chill in the room. A jet-black tie had been knotted up to the collar of a ragged white shirt.

'This is my husband, Jack,' Mrs Thorpe said.

Mr Thorpe was a couple of inches shorter than Drake when he got up, and he gave a lifeless handshake with bony fingers.

'I wanted to extend my condolences on your loss,' Drake said, uncertain exactly how to react to Mr and Mrs Thorpe. He would be able to gauge their reaction once he learned more about the family.

'Thank you. I've just got back from mass.' The cheeriness in Mrs Thorpe's voice felt oddly out of place. 'I'll go and make tea.'

'You had better sit down.' Thorpe pointed to two armchairs. 'You can say your piece once the missus is back.'

Drake shared a glance with Sara and from the frown on her face she shared his unease. They sat in silence for a few minutes listening to the clinking of china cups and an electric kettle boiling water.

Mrs Thorpe bustled in with a tray that she plonked on the dining table in one corner.

'Have you driven all the way from north Wales today?'

'It's not far, Mrs Thorpe,' Sara said. 'The satnav is handy for directions.'

'I don't understand any of this modern technology.' Mrs Thorpe handed Drake a cup and saucer. He gratefully accepted the chance of stirring sugars into the milky tea he was offered.

'I know this is a difficult time for you,' Drake said once Mrs Thorpe sat down next to her husband. 'But we need to learn more about your son Nicholas. You're aware that we're investigating his murder.'

Drake searched for a reaction, an awkward swallow, eyes blinking, but Mrs Thorpe gazed towards the meagre fire while her husband stared at Drake.

'How often did you see him?'

Drake addressed both Mr and Mrs Thorpe, anticipating one or another would fill in the family background. Mrs Thorpe cleared her throat.

'Nicholas was always an independent lad. Once he was at school, we knew he was too clever for us, that he would want to leave us behind. We were always proud of his achievements. I've got a scrapbook. I can show you about all the cases he was involved with.'

Drake wondered why she'd avoided answering his question. 'Why did he change his name?'

'He wanted a fresh start. We all knew he'd be a big success,' Mrs Thorpe said again.

She ran out of steam, as though finding excuses was difficult, and moved uncomfortably on the sofa, giving Drake an insincere smile.

'He didn't want anything to do with us,' Jack Thorpe continued. 'He was so busy. He had such an important job.'

Drake allowed a pause to develop.

'That's why he changed his name. And he told us he was going to marry this woman who wanted to lead a private life; she wanted nothing to do with us either.'

Drake thought he noticed the cup and saucer in Mrs Thorpe's hand start to shake. 'I've got photograph albums I can show you.' She stood up and rushed over to the table, placing the crockery on the tray before it fell from her grasp.

'Did you ever meet Nicholas's wife?' Drake said. If Laura Wixley had lied to them there had to be a reason, a motive, and this strange family set-up troubled Drake.

Jack shook his head. A fisted hand and a tight jaw suggested a hatred and tension Drake found hard to understand.

'Mrs Wixley is a senior police officer in the City of Manchester force.' Drake made it sound like a statement and a question. Jack Thorpe nodded knowingly; he probably knew all about his son's wife.

'He told us she was dead quiet and that she couldn't deal with other people, had no social skills.' He nodded towards the door. '*She* believed him of course. But they had this big fancy wedding. You can't keep much private these days.'

Either Laura Wixley had lied, or her husband had lied to her. Drake favoured the latter as he looked over at Jack Thorpe. It would have been absurd for Laura Wixley to have lied, Drake concluded. An officer of her seniority would know that basic police work would uncover the truth eventually. But people did lie, even clever people, when they couldn't confront the truth.

Mrs Thorpe bustled in with several photograph albums in her arms and resumed her seat, flicking through them as though she were partaking in the familiar activity of a normal family sharing photographs of everyday domestic events. The physical act of opening the albums reassured her, calmed her.

'I have an album here of cuttings from the newspapers; some of them were the national newspapers that covered Nicholas's cases.' Mrs Thorpe showed Drake and Sara the faded newspaper extracts about various murder and rape charges her son had prosecuted and defended. Drake made courteous, polite comments and Sara did likewise until they passed them back to Mrs Thorpe.

Jack Thorpe looked on, unimpressed, saying nothing, a darkness settling over his presence.

Mrs Thorpe went through each photograph album in turn, the tone of her voice oscillating between admiration for her son's achievements at school, disappointment they had little contact with him and boasting of his eminence as a barrister. Sadness tinged everything she said, imbued every word.

'This last one is about his time at university.' Mrs Thorpe forced enthusiasm into her voice. She pushed it over at Drake, who sensed she could well be on the verge of tears.

'He had lots of friends when he was at university.'

'He was still Thorpe back then,' Jack Thorpe interjected.

Mrs Thorpe ignored him. 'We were so pleased when he got a place to read law at university. We've only ever run this shop and nobody from our families has ever been to university or done anything of note so we were so proud of him.'

'He could be bloody difficult.' Jack Thorpe stopped her in her tracks. 'He didn't like people very much. Unless you were useful to him.'

Drake flicked through the images in the album on his lap. One caught his attention – Nicholas Wixley and his parents smiled at the camera in a park outside a stately home. They were ordinary family holiday snaps.

Sara engaged Mrs Wixley with conversation about Nicholas's childhood, and it pleased her to recount his achievements at school.

Drake reached the photographs of Wixley at university and recognised the distinctive features of a much younger Justin Selston.

'This is Justin Selston; was he friendly with Nicholas at university?'

'Is he some lawyer?' Jack Thorpe didn't wait for a reply. 'Nicholas never brought any of his friends home. He always went to visit them.'

'Do you know the others in this photograph?'

'Look on the back, dear,' Mrs Thorpe said. 'I wrote the names of everybody on every photograph. Just in case.'

His interest piqued, Drake studied the names on the back. As he did so he recalled his own university days when friends would camp in tents on his father's fields and his mother would make enormous fried breakfasts before they'd go trooping off into the hills of Snowdonia. Drake glanced at Mr and Mrs Thorpe, wanting to share their pain that their son wanted nothing to do with them.

'Can I take some of these photographs?' Drake said.

Mrs Thorpe nodded briskly. 'We will get them back, won't we?'

'Of course.' Drake smiled.

After another hour Drake had established that Neil Thorpe was a rugby league player and was Jack Thorpe's great-nephew. The old man brightened as he discussed his great-nephew's sporting career, telling Drake that there was a good chance he would be picked for the Great Britain test squad. Neil lived nearby, with a wife and three children, all of whom pitched into family events. It was as though Jack Thorpe were pining, Drake concluded.

As Drake and Sara left, Mrs Thorpe showed them their shop. Pride filled every word when she described the strength of the local community and how they had enjoyed running the place for fifty years. Things were different now, of course – fewer customers, and most people went to the supermarkets instead of corner shops.

Drake and Sara thanked Mrs Thorpe, who closed the door firmly behind them. Sitting in the car, Sara turned to Drake. 'That was the saddest thing I have seen in a long time.'

'I agree. Nicholas Wixley must have been a monster to cut his family from his life. We'll need to speak to Laura Wixley again though.'

Chapter 15

Good Friday 29th March
10.17 am

It was likely to be a very bad day, Winder thought. After he'd broken the news to his girlfriend that he couldn't take her on the train to the summit of Snowdon, she had sulked. Not one of her flouncy, half-hearted versions but the full silent treatment for the past two days. It made him feel thoroughly miserable, but he consoled himself that the rest of the team had to work too.

He arrived at the Incident Room later than normal, giving Luned, already clutching a mug of herbal tea, a noncommittal nod before dumping a bag of his favourite Danish pastries on the table and heading for the kitchen in search of his first coffee.

After the first sugar rush from a raisin swirl, Winder washed it down with a mouthful of his drink and gathered his thoughts. 'It's going to take hours.' Although it was a statement, he was looking for a response from Luned. She gave him a weak smile that barely troubled her cheeks. Although he had no inkling what Luned had planned for the holiday, her taciturn mood suggested her disappointment. It wasn't the same working with a woman, Winder thought, reminiscing about Saturdays with Dave Howick. Things had been easier with two men on Drake's team.

'You know the boss wants us to make progress today.' Luned didn't even look up as she reproached Winder.

He took another slurp of his coffee before booting

up his computer as his mind focused on the unfinished work from yesterday. It had been late the previous evening when Inspector Drake had finally been happy with the list of possible targets and prioritising the tasks needed.

Sir Ivan Banks, the high court judge who sentenced Zavier Cornwell, was at the top of the list. Winder followed Drake's instructions and made contact with the Metropolitan Police force in London where he lived. He spoke to a detective inspector who agreed in a languid cockney drawl to send some officers to the judge's home.

Next Winder turned his attention to the prosecutors.

Wixley's junior barrister and several lawyers had been prominent in the Crown Prosecution team. A database of mobile telephone numbers helped the task and by mid-morning over half had been called. All expressed surprise and shock that he should be contacting them.

'Please make certain you take your personal security seriously,' Winder announced in a serious tone as he finished conversations. 'And contact your local police force if you suspect anything suspicious.'

Winder returned from the kitchen with a coffee when his telephone rang, almost spilling his drink as he reached his desk. 'DC Winder.'

'We spoke earlier about Sir Ivan Banks, the high court judge.' Winder recognised the voice of the inspector from the Met. 'We can't find him.'

Winder's lips dried. 'What do you mean?'

'Just that. He wasn't at home and his neighbours don't know where he might be.'

'Does he have family?'

'No, single. The next-door neighbour thought he had a brother in Vancouver.'

'Might he be there?'

'Look, constable. This isn't my case. I've done what I can. I can give you the contact numbers for the neighbours. After that it's up to you.'

Winder scribbled down the details and flopped back in his chair, knowing now he had calls to make. By lunchtime he had spoken with several of Sir Ivan's neighbours but had learned nothing new.

The judge was a bachelor, and occasionally spoke to his neighbours who he invited into his home at Christmas for sherry and mince pies, but they knew little about him apart from a mention of a brother Winder already knew about. Winder tracked down the name of a civil servant on duty that morning in the Ministry of Justice government department responsible for the courts, resolving they were likely to be able to reach Sir Ivan Banks. But Wanda Preece's number rang out.

He wasn't going to work through his lunch hour and with his girlfriend having announced at breakfast in a staccato monotone that she was going to spend the day shopping with her mother, it left him contemplating a lunch with Luned.

'Do you want to get a bite to eat?' Winder said, loudly enough for Luned to hear him.

Luned looked over. Was she amused or surprised? 'Thanks.' She got up and they wandered through headquarters to the canteen where Winder ordered a sandwich and a plate of stale chips. He gave Luned's chicken salad a mournful glare. She picked her way through it as Winder gave her a summary of his activity that morning.

'Are you making progress?' Winder said.

'I've tracked down the names of all the officers on the case and I've spoken to half of them. I've got the rest to do this afternoon and then the defence team.'

'Justin Selston was the defence barrister.'

Luned nodded. 'The boss spoke to him in Portmeirion. I've been working on his background.'

After forty minutes Luned made a move to return to the Incident Room. Normally Winder would have felt short-changed; after all, it should be an hour for lunch, but the urgency in locating the original judge weighed on his mind.

The early afternoon dip in his concentration forced Winder to repeatedly stifle a yawn, hoping Luned wouldn't notice. He rang Wanda Preece again and this time got through. She reluctantly agreed to make contact with the judge on the mobile telephone number the department held. It meant waiting. And that unsettled him.

He turned his attention to the emails in his inbox and discovered an overlooked report from the prison service with Zavier Cornwell's incarceration history. He read probation reports, and updates from the officers on the prison wings where Cornwell was housed, but it was the prisoners who shared a cell with the alphabet killer that took his attention.

Lunch with Winder had been bearable. Sometimes he acted like a spoiled child and often Luned felt like telling him to grow up. Working with someone like

Gareth Winder wasn't what she had hoped for in CID so she'd wait a year, maybe eighteen months, before requesting a transfer.

At least he had asked about her plans for the weekend. She shared his frustration that their bank holiday, the first after the three months of winter, had been ruined by the demands of the inquiry into Nicholas Wixley's death. But she hadn't booked a vacation, like Sara, and her arrangements to see her parents could be changed to dinner one evening.

It took her an hour to reach the rest of the investigation team from the City of Manchester police force before she turned her attention to the defence lawyers. By mid-afternoon all the calls had been completed so she started on building a picture of Selston's background.

Selston hailed from an eminent legal family. His grandfather had been a circuit judge in Liverpool and his father had also been appointed as a judge in the Manchester area. Luned's research even turned up a Wikipedia entry for a distant cousin who was a Member of Parliament. She unearthed grainy images of archived photographs from various local newspapers of his father and grandfather in their robes and fineries, smiling with other dignitaries. The pictures of his father and grandfather reminded her that, for a family like the Selstons, status was invaluable. Did he crave it enough to kill Wixley?

Selston's curriculum vitae included references to his education at a well-known public school. Did Selston believe he had a preordained right to be elevated to the bench? If he did then Nicholas Wixley had ruined his plans.

A quick internet search told Luned that Selston's detached property, where he lived alone in a leafy suburb of Manchester, was valued at at least £1 million.

She recalled Drake's comment that a member of staff at Britannia Chambers had seen Selston violently sick when he'd heard the news of Wixley's appointment. Both men must have been rivals, competing for the best cases; making complimentary sounds to the judges who might put in a good word with the judicial appointments board.

It was late in the afternoon by the time she finished all her checks on Selston. She glanced over at Winder; he appeared more animated, and Luned guessed he had made progress too.

Drake stood by the board in the Incident Room, both hands pressed against his lower back. Spending four hours in the car on Good Friday wasn't his idea of the best way to spend a bank holiday. He felt stiff and uncomfortable, and, more than anything, grimy and dirty, which meant a long shower when he returned home. A spasm of loneliness struck his thoughts as he realised Annie wouldn't be there. He would call her, they could talk on Skype, but it wouldn't be the same.

He glanced over at Winder and from his wide-eyed enthusiastic expression, assumed the young officer had something on his mind.

Sara returned with coffee that he hoped wouldn't be the cheap, instant variety they kept in the kitchen. The cream glaze on the surface of the black liquid encouraged him to give Sara a grateful nod. 'Thanks.'

She sat down and he nodded at Winder. 'What's on

your mind, Gareth?'

'Zavier Cornwell shared a cell with a David Eaton.'

Drake frowned. 'Eaton? Is he related to the Jamie Eaton who assaulted Wixley?'

Winder nodded energetically. 'Jamie Eaton is his son.'

'Good,' Drake said. 'Have you been able to trace Jamie yet?'

'The lads in Pwllheli are still looking for him.'

'What do we know about Eaton?'

'David Eaton has a violent temper – he assaulted three guys outside a nightclub in Manchester city centre. One of them died and the other two were badly beaten. He was lucky to get a minimum sentence of eight years for manslaughter. I've requisitioned the file from the Manchester police as well as the CPS and the prison service. And he was released last month.'

Drake paused when Winder finished. 'Eaton could be our man. Cornwell shares his secrets with him as they fritter away the hours in their cell talking about his modus operandi and when he's released, well, it's.... We need to find Eaton – senior and junior. And have we heard from the prison about visiting Cornwell?'

Winder shook his head. 'Nothing yet, boss.'

'Bring me up to date with the list of possible targets.'

'The original trial judge, Sir Ivan Banks cannot be traced,' Winder announced.

'And I've drawn a blank with the defence lawyers,' Luned added.

'Maybe they're on holiday,' Sara said.

'They all need to be contacted. Send me the

updated list. Contact the relevant civil servant in the Ministry of Justice and ask for contact numbers for other judges who might be friends with Sir Ivan.'

Luned made her first contribution. 'How did you get on this morning, sir?'

'We spoke to Mr and Mrs Thorpe.' Drake took a mouthful of his drink. 'It was a bit odd.'

'It was more than that, boss. It was extremely sad,' Sara said.

Winder and Luned listened intently as Drake explained how Nicholas Wixley had disowned his parents. 'Mrs Thorpe seemed too cheery, as though she were forcing herself to sound normal.'

Sara butted in. 'They run a convenience store in the backstreets of Manchester. A world away from the fancy life of a barrister and a senior police officer.'

'It can't have been easy,' Drake said. 'Knowing your only child wanted nothing to do with you.'

Drake paused and allowed a beat to pass. Winder and Luned looked away, their thoughts elsewhere. He found the faded image of Wixley and Selston as young students from the folder on the desk and pinned it to the board.

Behind him, Luned said. 'So, did Laura Wixley lie about not knowing his family?'

Drake's attention moved to the official City of Manchester police force photograph of Laura Wixley. They certainly needed an answer. He turned back to face his team and replied. 'I want to know more about Laura Wixley first. And in the meantime, we need to build a clear picture about Selston and Nicholas Wixley's relationship.' Drake tipped his head back towards the board.

'Are we going to interview Justin Selston?' Sara said.

'Tomorrow, he'll be at his holiday home.'

Chapter 16

Easter Saturday 30th March
7.45 am

The sultry voice of Alys Williams filled the Mondeo's cabin as she sang her opening line of 'Llwytha'r Gwn' by Candelas, a Welsh-language rock band Annie had encouraged Drake to experience. Connecting a Bluetooth device to his car radio had been annoying and he regretted now buying the cheapest version on the internet. Downloading the band's album to his smartphone had been easy by comparison.

But he wasn't listening to the music. He read the headline of the newspaper, the latest vitriol about 'fake news', and it struck him that finding the journalists who had covered the alphabet killing was something he hadn't contemplated. Sensationalised coverage might well make them a target.

He discarded the paper onto the rear seat before he even started the Sudoku and drove to headquarters.

In the Incident Room he ticked off mentally a to-do list. Trawling through hours of CCTV footage would be the only way to identify the red car and the missing woman unless they could trace the pink gilet. The risk that the alphabet killer's accomplice or a copycat might strike again filled him with dread as he looked at the blank, expressionless face of Zavier Cornwell.

Sitting by his desk, the columns of different coloured Post-it note reminders helped clear his mind. He studied the most recent notes he'd jotted down – CCTV, pink gilet, woman, red car, Wixley's enemies. Someone had a motive to kill Wixley, something about

Britannia Chambers warranted more investigation, and he contemplated what exactly Justin Selston might say later that morning.

Until then Drake had a Google search to carry out.

Every national newspaper had carried details of the case and Drake hoped for something new but the articles all repeated the same message: 'sadistic killer jailed for life'.

The list of newspapers and the names of the journalists involved filled a sheet in his legal pad. It would be another task for Winder and Luned. He reached the top of the third page in the Google search results, and a reference to a YouTube video took his attention. He clicked it open and watched a freelance journalist pontificating about the alphabet killer and how society had failed and that the death sentence needed to be restored immediately. Drake half expected the man to offer to be the hangman himself such was the intensity of his jaded bigotry.

A door banging against a wall and raised voices announced that Winder and Luned had arrived. Both officers stood by the threshold of his office after he called their names.

'We need to warn these journalists.' Drake lifted the sheet of paper in one hand. 'They covered the trial.' Luned and Winder nodded. 'And trace a Hector Murren. He's posted several times on YouTube and he clearly hates Zavier Cornwell.'

'Yes, boss,' They both replied in unison.

Sara arrived moments later but Drake was already searching for the number of the first of the high court judges who might know where Sir Ivan Banks might be. How did he address a high court judge? It was Your

Honour for a circuit judge, but high court judges were knighted by the Queen when they took office so he favoured 'Sir ...' instead of 'My Lord'. As the SIO he decided he had to make the calls and not any other member of the team.

The first number rang out.

Sir Jonathan Meeks was the second and when his mobile rang Drake cleared his throat.

'May I speak to Sir Jonathan Meeks?'

'Who is this? This is my private number.' The deep, baritone, cultured voice sounded urbane and relaxed. It was the weekend after all.

'My name is Detective Inspector Ian Drake of the Wales Police Service. I am the senior investigating officer in relation to the murder of His Honour Judge Nicholas Wixley.'

'I see.'

'The Ministry of Justice gave me your number, Sir Jonathan.'

Drake explained how he hoped Sir Jonathan could help. When he finished, the reply was succinct.

'I cannot help, I am afraid. I haven't seen Ivan for some time – perhaps two weeks. I've been tied up on one long case. And I have no idea where he could be. Do you think he might be in danger?'

Drake paused. No point prevaricating. 'We are warning everyone connected to the alphabet killings to take their personal security very seriously.'

'Of course. If I think of anything I shall call you. Thank you, Inspector.'

Drake dialled the first number again and a sleepy woman's voice answered. She fumbled the handset as she passed it to Sir John Fountain. The conversation was as unhelpful as the previous one and foreboding made itself an unwelcome visitor in Drake's mind. Sir Ivan needed to be found.

He read the time on his watch; unless he left soon he might be late. He strode into the Incident Room. 'I've spoken to both the high court judges we thought might know Sir Ivan's whereabouts, but they couldn't help. Find his clerk or someone who knows him. A high court judge can't just disappear.'

Winder and Luned gave him nods of acknowledgement.

He turned to Sara. 'Let's go.'

Trem y Mor stood alone on a promontory looking out over Cardigan Bay, a few miles from the home of Nicholas Wixley. The translation meant Sea View but the Welsh name for the substantial house sounded more attractive. Everything about the property was gloomy and depressing. Green algae tinged the edges of the Welsh slates; large slabs of dressed stone had been used for its construction giving the place a gothic feel.

'It looks a bit spooky,' Sara said as they drove down a narrow track towards the gated entrance. Drake couldn't avoid the puddles that a shower of rain the night before had created. To his right he noticed three sailors gathered with their kit bags on a jetty that reached its way into the bay.

Parked outside the wooden doors of a single garage was a glistening Mercedes E Class. Drake drew up alongside, and once he left the car he felt the uneven surface of the fine gravel on the soles of his brogues. He reached for his jacket, carefully folded on the rear seat. The Easter bank holiday brought the first visitors of the year to the Llŷn Peninsula. The weather always changed at Easter as though the previous three months were a cold and miserable afterthought.

Sara joined Drake as he left the car. A substantial set of steps led up to the front door, and at the top Drake rapped with the heavy, cast-iron, oak-shaped handle.

He half expected a butler in formal morning clothes to appear, but Justin Selston opened the door. A yellow cravat folded neatly at his neck and his immaculate short back-and-sides gave him an austere appearance. Selston wore a pinstripe suit with a waistcoat and a gown and a wig for most of his working day so he probably had little time for current fashion, Drake thought.

'Good morning, Inspector.' Selston glanced over Drake's shoulder towards the sea. 'It's a fine morning, don't you think?'

'Good morning, Mr Selston,' Drake said. Selston gave Sara a brief nod of acknowledgement. He ushered them both into the house and closed the door behind them. He led them along a corridor. 'Let me show you to the morning room. We can speak there.'

Mahogany wooden panels lined the walls into the main part of the building and after a few more steps led into a generous hallway. Sunshine poured in through a roof light over an enormous staircase.

A woman, mid-fifties, wearing a housecoat, appeared from a door and looked over at Selston. 'Mildred will organise coffee,' Selston announced.

Mildred looked at Drake, her face blank and expressionless. Drake and Sara expressed a preference and Mildred gave them a nod before scuttling off. Selston stood by the window where Sara and Drake joined him. There was a faded elegance to the room. The curtains were old and thinning, and the sofas and armchairs were from an era when people invested in furniture that they hoped would last a lifetime.

For the second time in the investigation, Drake stood at a window looking out over Cardigan Bay. In the distance, sails fluttered from a flotilla of yachts already underway in a regatta.

'Do you sail, Mr Selston?' Drake said.

'I did some as a boy with my father. He was quite a keen dinghy sailor. The family keep a rib at the jetty you passed.'

'Has the house been in your family for very long?' Drake asked. Holiday homes like Trem y Mor passed through the generations, providing a retreat from the bustle of the cities of northern England.

'My grandfather had the property built between the war years. I share its use with my cousins and their family, although the younger generation much prefer to fly off to Spain than come to this draughty old place.'

Mildred reappeared and deposited a tray with a cafetière and three china cups and saucers on a coffee table.

'Thanks awfully, Mildred,' Selston said, without looking at her. He waved a hand as though directing Drake and Sara to sit down.

'Now, do tell me how much progress you're making with your inquiry,' Selston said. Sara helped herself to coffee and she handed a cup and saucer to Drake – it gave him time to gather his thoughts. Selston had given his voice an authoritarian ring as though

Drake were in the witness box being cross-examined.

Drake took the first sip of his coffee – it was strong and clean, just as he liked it.

'We were hoping you might be able to help us with more background about Nicholas Wixley.'

If Justin Selston didn't like his question being ignored, he didn't let on. He was a man who had seen people lie on oath, cross-examined witnesses, read the expression on the face of an accused and interpreted the body language of a defendant squirming to hide the truth. And now Drake was doing exactly the same. How far would Selston go to conceal what he was really feeling?

'We were colleagues.'

It was true, of course: a simple statement of fact. Drake would have to work at his questions to get more detail out of Selston.

'What was your relationship with him like?' Sara sounded warm and inquisitive.

Selston gave her the beginnings of a sneer that he quickly checked into a condescending smile.

'Cordial and businesslike, of course. We often crossed swords in the courtroom but that's what barristers do.'

'When did you last see him?'

Selston hesitated. 'Some time in the week before his death. I cannot be certain.'

'Did you socialise with him?'

'Good heavens no.'

'Have you been in the same chambers with him for many years?' Drake butted in as Sara drank her coffee.

'Yes, we practised at Britannia Chambers for a number of years.'

Drake expected a little more detail, more background and perhaps a tinge of emotion.

'So what was he like as a colleague?' Drake persevered. 'There must have been business meetings all the barristers attended. How would you describe the atmosphere in chambers?'

Drake reminded himself of the comments made by Kennedy, the chief clerk of chambers, praising Wixley, which contrasted so sharply with the working environment described by Holly Thatcher.

'What are you implying?' Selston lowered his head and frowned at the same time. Drake having to contend with lawyers when he was interviewing suspects was one thing, but actually interviewing a lawyer was different. Resolving that Selston wasn't going to intimidate him, Drake continued.

'I am not implying anything, Mr Selston,' Drake said. 'I'm investigating the murder of your colleague Nicholas Wixley. As I am sure you are aware, we need to build a complete picture of his life.' The mild rebuke worked; Selston's body language mellowed as he reached for his cup and saucer and sat back in the sofa.

'Things were always very cordial between us.'

Obfuscation wasn't going to help, Drake concluded. Was Selston hiding something?

'So there were never any arguments or disagreements about the running of chambers, hiring and firing of staff, finances etc.?'

Selston replaced the cup and saucer on the table before giving Drake a withering glare. 'If you have heard something about the *atmosphere* in chambers that you want to put to me then now is the time to do so, Inspector.'

Drake took a moment, but he kept eye contact with Selston. Perhaps 'atmosphere' hadn't been the best choice of word. The barrister's face gave nothing away, but his answers suggested Drake had far more to discover.

'Were you friends with Nicholas Wixley at university?'

Selston averted his gaze first. Drake wondered if he was calculating what they knew already. How far would this man go to colour the truth?

'The law faculty had many students when Nicholas and I were undergraduates. Our paths rarely crossed, and we couldn't be described as close friends. I was focused on my degree; there was never any doubt in my mind I wanted to practise as a barrister.'

Drake had resolved earlier to ask Selston about the photograph from the home of Mr and Mrs Thorpe. On the surface, it had been a picture of *close friends* but something made Drake hesitate. Something about Selston's replies made him suspicious. 'Did Nicholas Wixley ever mention his family to you?'

A thoughtful expression creased Selston's face. 'I don't believe he ever did. I seem to recall his parents died when he was a teenager. I'm sure that Laura Wixley can give you more details.'

'Yes, of course.'

Sara stopped making notes for a second and turned to Selston. 'Do you have any immediate family, Mr Selston?'

'I've never married. I have several cousins.'

'I understand you come from a family of highly respected lawyers and judges.'

Selston gave her a grudging nod of approval.

Drake glanced over at Sara, wondering if she had finished. He had one more line of questioning, probably the last one Selston would tolerate.

'When Nicholas Wixley was appointed as a circuit judge you were a candidate as well.'

Selston did exactly as Drake thought he might: a chill invaded his face, and the realisation that two police officers were in his holiday home scratching into his intimate professional life would be intolerable.

'You are very well informed.'

'As your father and grandfather were both on the bench, it might seem that being a judge was natural for you, almost dynastic.'

The chill turned into an arctic freeze.

Selston said nothing.

Drake continued. 'How did you feel when Nicholas Wixley was appointed to the bench?'

Selston pressed his lips together very tightly.

Drake kept his eye contact. 'Were you disappointed?'

Selston cracked. 'How dare you!' He stood up, put his hands on his hips. 'Come here and suggest I could in some way be implicated Nicholas's murder. It is preposterous. Get out now.'

Drake glanced at Sara, who had closed her notebook. Their coffees were unfinished. They had nothing further to ask Selston, for now. Drake got to his feet, slowly buttoning his jacket. 'We'll see ourselves out, Mr Selston but if there is anything else you'd like to tell us, you know where to find me.'

Selston sneered, as though making contact with Drake would be the last thing he'd contemplate.

Drake's brogues echoed against the wooden

flooring as they made for the front door.

'Pompous oaf,' Sara said. Even her choice of words matched Selston's personality and his depressing morbid property. 'Do you think he is involved?'

'He is hiding something: whether it's how he really feels about Nicholas Wixley or something altogether more serious is what we need to discover.'

Drake crunched the car into reverse gear before negotiating his way out of the property and back to the main road. His mobile, sitting in a cradle, rang as he indicated right. Sara took the call. 'DS Morgan – D I Drake is driving.'

Drake changed down through the gears.

'What!' Sara said. 'You better give me the postcode.'

She finished the call. 'One of Wixley's friends we met with, Tom Levine, has been killed. Someone discovered his body on his yacht.'

Chapter 17

Easter Saturday 30th March
12.04 pm

When Drake neared the outskirts of Pwllheli, tension clawed at his chest. He wanted to scream at the cars dawdling in front of him. He reached a roundabout and prayed the traffic causing the delay would stream away to the right or left so that he could travel straight ahead.

'Yes,' Drake exclaimed, unable to hide his relief as he covered a few yards towards the next small roundabout. After the railway station he took a left and powered along the edge of the inner harbour. Banks of sand and mud lay exposed by low tide. In the distance, Drake spotted the marina.

He parked by the entrance of the old sailing club building and saw a uniformed officer standing next to the security gate by the ramp leading down to the pontoons. A group of half a dozen men in sailing trousers and beanie caps stared over at them as they neared the officer.

'Gareth Hawkins, sir. It's a yacht called *Terra Firma.*' Hawkins dictated directions. 'Griff is down there making sure the scene isn't contaminated.'

'Have you been told when to expect the CSI team?'

Hawkins shook his head.

'Just make certain nobody gets down this ramp.'

Hawkins tapped a code into a security pad and the gate swung open.

Sara joined Drake as he jogged down towards the first pontoon. It swayed gently under their footfall.

Terra Firma was a handsome, substantial yacht

tied up alongside a pontoon at the far end of the marina. The word *Sigma* was stencilled onto the side of the hull and Drake made a mental note to google the details. A pleased look creased the face of Griff Jones, the second uniformed officer, when Drake and Sara reached him.

'He was supposed to be racing this afternoon,' Griff said. 'One of the crew members found him when he arrived to prepare this morning.' The officer nodded at the yacht. 'He's in one of the cabins. It's a bit of a mess.'

'Who was it who found him?' Sara asked.

'A guy called Peter Duncan. He's in the clubhouse, waiting to talk to you.'

Drake snapped on a pair of latex gloves, and Sara did likewise. He wasn't going to wait for the CSIs before examining the crime scene. It would be cramped inside, and he could imagine they'd take hours to finish the examination. He didn't have time to waste. Reaching up, he grabbed hold of the railing surrounding the deck area. Then he placed his right foot on the deck and clambered up and over the thin metal wire.

Looking down into the cabin Drake realised the board discarded by his feet was the makeshift entrance door. The security was minimal; presumably nothing of value was ever kept on a yacht apart from the equipment, which would have been difficult to dismantle and steal.

Drake turned and lowered himself down three steps into the main cabin area.

A bottle of single malt whisky stood on a table in the galley area with a glass by its side.

'He must have been drinking early,' Sara said once she had negotiated the steps.

'He could have been here all night,' Drake said, glancing over at the sailing jacket discarded on a bench seat.

'There's probably CCTV covering the entrance ramp.'

Drake nodded: it was to be expected, and doubtless one of the things the owners paid for as part of their mooring fees.

A bank of equipment dominated one corner. Drake looked down towards the cabins at the bow of the yacht. He said to Sara. 'I'll go first.'

Drake made as little contact as possible with the handrails, conscious he shouldn't contaminate the scene. He could imagine Mike Foulds' irritation if he did so.

Two cabins led off left and right at the bottom. Each had a small single bunk against the hull. At the end of the short corridor was a door that Drake gently nudged open with his shoe.

Tom Levine was spread-eagled on a bunk. Drake looked for signs of a struggle, but none was apparent. His throat had been cut like Wixley's. There was no sign of a murder weapon, but the blood covered the sheets, drenching his clothes. And he wore an identical pair of socks to Nicholas Wixley.

'It's the same MO, sir,' Sara said under her breath, gazing at Levine's legs and feet.

Had both been killed by the same man? Drake turned around as Sara joined him in the small space and noticed the letter F written in blood on the bulkhead near the door.

Soon it felt claustrophobic and Drake couldn't imagine how the CSIs might feel having to work in such a confined area. The cabin had no personal effects. Levine wore a pair of denims, and a blue chambray shirt under an expensive-looking half-zip sweater.

'I didn't see any blood anywhere else in the yacht,' Sara said. 'It suggests he was killed here. But why was he down here?' Sara sounded perplexed. 'If he was expecting somebody wouldn't there be two glasses on the table?'

Drake nodded. 'Perhaps he knew his killer, but didn't like him enough to offer him a drink. Let's go back outside. There's nothing more we can do here.'

Drake and Sara clambered off the yacht, avoiding falling flat onto the pontoon by accepting Griff's offer of help. They retraced their steps back towards the entrance ramp and spotted Hawkins talking with two anxious-looking women in their thirties.

'This is absurd,' one of them said to Drake after the gate snapped shut behind him and Sara. 'You can't possibly prevent us from going to our yachts. There's a full calendar of racing today, for goodness sake.'

Drake glanced at Hawkins, who gave him a pathetic what-can-I-do stare.

'A man has been killed.' Drake glared at the woman. He wasn't in the mood to be patient. 'The marina will stay out of bounds for as long as I decide.'

Everyone's attention was taken by a team of crime scene investigators marching towards them with boxes of equipment.

Drake turned to the woman again. 'I suggest you leave now.'

He joined Mike Foulds and the investigators with him. Drake and Sara led them down the ramp and then on to *Terra Firma* as Drake outlined the crime scene.

Their footfall clattered over the deserted pontoons. Griff looked pleased to see them, and Foulds put him to work helping the investigators. 'Get back to me with your report as soon as,' Drake said.

Drake and Sara returned to the ramp. Both women were gone and Hawkins had relaxed. Half an hour later Drake and Sara were sitting in their car having interviewed Peter Duncan, who'd discovered Tom Levine's body. He was in his early thirties, and lived locally, having answered an advertisement in the sailing club to join Levine's crew for the season. Usual inquiries would have to be made into his background, but he seemed to be genuinely shocked.

'Let's go and see the widow,' Drake said after they'd finished with Duncan.

Breaking the news of a death was something Drake hated, and he was pleased that a family liaison officer had already arrived at Dorothy Levine's home. It was a comfortable bungalow in Abersoch. The sort of property that sold within a day to the moneyed elite from Cheshire. Drake sympathised with a distant aunt who lived nearby who complained vociferously that locals had been priced out of buying a home in the village. The Levines' bungalow would have been affordable anywhere else on the Llŷn Peninsula.

The large panes of glass in the wooden-framed windows suggested the place had been built at a time when conserving energy wasn't a priority. An Audi 4x4 was parked in the drive alongside a Ford Fiesta.

A family liaison officer Drake knew from a previous case opened the door. She moved to one side and nodded towards the rear. 'Mrs Levine's in the kitchen.'

The room had a busy, bustling feel. A glazed extension provided for a generous kitchen with granite worktops and a dining table large enough to seat a dozen people. Behind it, bifold doors led onto a patio where Drake noticed an enormous gas barbecue. A door led to what Drake assumed was the garage.

At one end of the table a woman, drawn and pale, her auburn hair lifeless and unbrushed, sat nursing an oversized goblet of white wine.

Drake stepped over. 'My name is Detective Inspector Ian Drake of the Wales Police Service. I am most sorry for your loss. This is Detective Sergeant Morgan.'

Levine took a substantial mouthful of wine. Uninvited, Drake and Sara sat down. The family liaison officer stood in the kitchen area.

'I told him to be careful.' Levine struggled not to slur. 'I never liked the business Tom was doing. He could be really stupid. And he had some nasty friends. All those *bastards* in the sailing club.'

She emptied more of the wineglass.

'Do you know where your husband was last night?' Drake asked, allowing the woman to talk.

She looked up at Drake. 'He was at the sailing club. We all were – some fancy do for the start of the season. I couldn't abide the place.'

'When did your husband leave? Were you expecting him home last night?'

'Not particularly. He often stays on *Terra Firma* if he's had a skinful.'

'Do you do a lot of sailing, Mrs Levine?' Sara said.

She guffawed. 'I hate it. I can't even swim. I was only here because Tom wanted to keep up with his mates. He thought it would be handy for business.' Dot Levine looked over at Sara. 'I hate this fucking place.' Then she reached for the wine bottle and emptied its contents into her glass.

Chapter 18

Saturday 30th March
3.19 pm

Taking time for a hurried lunch invigorated Sara, even if it was the middle of the afternoon. She finished her coffee as Drake pushed the remains of his uneaten sandwich to the corner of his plate. He beckoned over a waitress, mimicking the writing of a bill. A couple of Sara's friends had texted yesterday telling her how much they were missing her on their Guinness-fuelled trip around the pubs of Dublin. She hadn't replied, but that morning she had responded only to find her message box filled with more pithy remarks and photographs of smiling faces raising glasses at the camera.

'Anything interesting?' Drake joined Sara outside the café after paying.

'Nothing, just friends' stuff.' It might sound like sour grapes to complain that she had missed her holiday when all the team were working that weekend.

A short drive took them back to the marina where more uniformed officers guarded the entrance ramp to the pontoons. A crime scene perimeter tape flickered across the pontoon leading to *Terra Firma*.

Sara followed Drake into the marina building. The sound of a crackling radio drifted down the stairs and voices filtered out of various rooms. On the first floor they entered a room with 'Control Centre' embossed on a brass plate underneath a glass section.

The room provided a perfect view over the harbour entrance and marina.

Tides, wind speeds and expected arrivals were marked up on a whiteboard. Two men sat by tables browsing images from CCTV footage.

'Which one of you is the harbour master?' Drake said.

The older man, his bald head glistening in the artificial light, stood up and reached out a hand. 'Mervyn Phillips.'

Phillips glanced briefly at Drake's warrant card before they shook hands. 'I'm Detective Inspector Drake and this is Detective Sergeant Sara Morgan.'

Phillips turned to his companion. 'This is Joe; he was on duty this morning.'

Drake tipped his head towards the equipment. 'Do you have CCTV footage of visitors to the marina?'

'Everybody who needs access to the pontoons has to go through the security gate. There's always somebody here and the footage is kept for a month before it's erased automatically.'

'Is there a record of Tom Levine arriving?'

'It was last night,' Joe said. 'He looked to be pissed up to the eyeballs. He couldn't walk straight, and he had trouble punching in the code.'

'Show us,' Drake said.

Joe fiddled with the controls on the desk before the screen filled with the grainy images of the night before. They watched in silence as Tom Levine staggered to the entrance gate. After negotiating the security code, he wandered down the ramp, banging into the sides occasionally. Somebody had visited Tom Levine and he had been killed as he slept, Sara guessed.

'Can we see the footage from this morning?' Drake said.

'I can send you it all,' Phillips said.

Joe fussed over the computer again and leaned back once the screen came to life. At seven o'clock a group of three men with tools and equipment, who arrived at the security gate, took Sara's attention. She squinted at the images on the monitor. One of them looked familiar. Where had she seen his face before? She moved nearer the desk and studied the footage. 'Can you stop it there?'

Joe did as he was told. He froze the image as one of the men turned his face towards the camera.

'That's Jamie Eaton,' Sara announced.

Drake joined Sara. 'We've been looking for this guy.'

'You won't have to look far,' Joe said.

Drake and Sara turned towards him.

'He was in the bar at Plas Heli next door an hour ago.'

Drake scribbled an email address on a card and thrust it at Phillips before rushing for the door. They took the stairs down to the ground floor two at a time. They jogged over towards Plas Heli, the sailing centre built several years previously, and threaded their way through the car park.

Dozens of youngsters with small dinghies and adults fussing over them filled the main hall. Sara searched the faces; Drake did likewise.

'The bar must be upstairs, boss.'

They turned on their heels and hurried to the staircase.

At the top Drake pushed open a door. The bar area heaved with customers standing at the bar, others sitting at tables finishing their meals. The smell of chip fat hung in the air. Outside on a balcony more of the sailing fraternity mingled in the spring sunshine. Eaton could have left of course, Sara thought as she searched the faces of the diners.

Drake made his way through the drinkers mingling at the bar, checking every man who appeared to be the right age. Sara followed him, wanting to make certain he didn't miss anyone. He showed the photograph of Eaton to one of the staff, who nodded towards the glass doors from the restaurant area to the terrace they'd seen earlier. Muscling their way back through the crowd proved heavy going. The occasional profanity assaulted her ears as she and Drake caused beer to be spilled onto clothes and shoes.

The spring air was cool on Sara's cheeks as they left the warmth of the bar.

On the open terrace she was almost tempted to interrupt couples where she couldn't get a proper look at a husband or boyfriend. As they neared a larger group of younger men, Sara noticed one of the waitresses surreptitiously glancing over at her. And then a moment later a figure rushed away from the group. Sara dragged at Drake's coat. 'He's done a runner, boss.'

They set off in pursuit, reaching a staircase that Sara almost fell down in her haste. She made for the car park while Drake sprinted round to the front of the building. Where the hell had he gone? She peered into cars and SUVs but they were all high-end models and she decided it was unlikely that Eaton drove anything that expensive, so she sprinted out into the road. Drake joined her and had to stop, his breathing heavy and laboured.

'Have you seen him?' Drake gasped.

The sound of a car engine failing to start took her attention, and she noticed a blue Volkswagen Golf, its paint faded, the number plate hanging off.

'There he is, boss.'

They started running but Eaton set off in a cloud of dust and gravel as he shot out of the car park.

Drake stopped. 'Let's get back to the car.'

By the time Sara reached Drake's Mondeo she was sticky and breathless, and her pulse pounded in her head.

'Did you get the registration number?' Drake sounded hoarse.

'Yes.' Sara was already calling operational support on her mobile.

Sara switched on the satnav as Drake accelerated towards the junction Eaton had taken. She finished her call, knowing that every police officer, community support officer and even the road traffic officers would be looking for a blue Golf. Drake flashed his lights and blasted the horn at two vehicles in his way, who veered to one side. Sara fiddled with the satnav screen until the map of the surrounding area appeared.

'There are a number of junctions off this main road he could have taken,' Sara said, noticing the minor roads that led back into the countryside and the lanes to the right that led towards the coast.

After a roundabout near Afon Wen, Sara spotted the Golf stuck behind an enormous tractor pulling a trailer piled high with topsoil. Eaton was dodging in and out of the opposite lane trying to get a clear passage to overtake but there was a regular stream of oncoming traffic.

'There he is,' Sara called out.

Drake pressed on and when the tractor slowed into a layby he floored the accelerator. Ahead, a puff of smoke left the Volkswagen's exhaust as it hurtled towards the village of Llanystymdwy. Sara could see from the satnav that at this speed they would be in Criccieth shortly. Surely he would slow down as he travelled through the town, where there'd be pedestrians, children and lots of traffic. But he barely slowed. The main street was straight and Sara could hear Eaton blasting his horn as he charged on. Sara glanced over, reading the worry on Drake's face.

Her mobile rang, and she yanked the handset from her jacket, realising it was area control. 'One of the traffic cars from western area division will be in Porthmadog within three minutes. And there are two vehicles from Caernarfon travelling south that will be with you in fifteen minutes.'

Eaton had disappeared from view as the road meandered inland around Moel y Gest, its twists and turns following the contours of the land. They passed under a bridge that carried the Cambrian Coast railway line and in the distance they saw Eaton overtaking three vehicles, an oncoming bus flashing him furiously. He cut back in with inches to spare. The traffic slowed towards a junction, but Drake couldn't overtake, and he slammed his hand against the steering wheel. There was no sign of Eaton when they reached the outskirts of Porthmadog.

'See if you can find the patrol car,' Drake said, negotiating the main roundabout in the middle of the town before sedately travelling past shops and cafés. Sara's mobile rang again.

'We have a positive identification on your Volkswagen.' She didn't recognise the voice of the road traffic officer. 'It's down by the port area.'

Sara gave Drake the details.

Drake nodded as he drove down to the bottom of the main street and indicated right where they joined the patrol car with its lights flashing, two officers wearing high-visibility jackets standing next to a discarded blue Volkswagen.

'Any sign of him?' Drake said once they joined the officers.

Both shook their heads.

'Why the hell did he come here?'

Northern Division headquarters was eerily quiet when Drake and Sara returned that evening.

Winder and Luned sat at their usual desks and Drake joined them in the Incident Room. Sara returned from the kitchen with a coffee for them both. He tried and failed to remember when he had last eaten anything.

'Are we going to organise house-to-house enquiries in Porthmadog?' Winder said.

Underlining the question was the clear hope that the rest of the young officer's weekend wasn't going to be ruined by the inquiry.

Drake nodded. 'We've also organised for the sailing club to request as many of their members who were present on Friday evening when Levine was at the sailing club to gather tomorrow morning before they start their Sunday morning regatta. We'll get names, addresses and as much detail as we can.'

'Anything yet from the forensics?' Luned said.

'The MO looks exactly the same as the Nicholas Wixley murder scene. Even down to the Rotherham United football club socks,' Sara said.

Drake looked over at Winder. 'We need to contact the Rotherham United football club shop. They might have a record of people who have bought socks in the last few months.'

Winder scribbled a reminder to himself.

'Any luck in tracking down the journalists?' Drake asked Luned.

'I'm still waiting to hear about Hector Murren but I've spoken to all the rest. And I've narrowed the likely source of the pink gilet to half dozen shops. I called one today and I'll contact the rest at the beginning of the week.'

There was a tired, despairing edge to Winder's voice. 'There's hours of CCTV footage, boss, from garage forecourts along the coast. And I haven't started tracking down possible footage from any other route she might have taken through Porthmadog or Blaenau Ffestiniog or Bala so it could be days before we have anything helpful.'

Drake took a mouthful of the coffee. It was hot and wet and at that moment in time he didn't care that it tasted awful. 'There's nothing more we can do tonight. Go home. We've got the house-to-house in Porthmadog tomorrow morning.'

Drake could see the despondency on their faces at the prospect of working the entire weekend.

Luned's number rang as they finished up for the evening. Drake saw the serious look on her face crease to a troubled frown. She finished the call and turned to face him. 'That was Hector Murren's partner. He was expected home this afternoon and he hasn't arrived.'

Chapter 19

Sunday 31st March
9.09 am

Porthmadog had a sombre, Sunday morning Welsh Puritan feel. None of the shops were open yet. Not Bible black but stillness Drake welcomed.

Winder and Luned had travelled separately to join Drake and Sara at the quayside in the centre of the town. Winder's journey from Colwyn Bay had been significantly longer than Luned's, who lived in a village on the north coast of the Llŷn Peninsula. Drake struggled to unfurl a large-scale plan of the town over the bonnet of his car. Terraces fanned out from the middle – getting the house-to-house inquiries completed was a priority. He could see the buds of resentment on the faces around him, so making certain they could all have Bank Holiday Monday away from the inquiry was a priority too.

That morning they had to find Jamie Eaton.

'Do we have any idea if he has a connection to Porthmadog?' Winder said.

'None that we know of,' Drake said.

A main road divided Porthmadog neatly into two halves, and Drake allocated a team of uniformed officers to Winder and Luned.

Drake and Sara left and retraced their steps from the night before back to Pwllheli. The car park at Plas Heli bustled with activity as sailors arrived for the morning's race. On the first floor Drake recognised Wixley's sailing friends, Marcus Abbott and Colin Horton. A woman of the same age accompanied both men, and Drake guessed they must have been their respective spouses. Michael Kennedy sat with a group of three other people.

A tall man with a brusque manner and a loud voice walked over to Drake, announcing he was the club secretary. 'Do you want to make an announcement or something? There's a lot of racing today and everyone is keen to get out onto the water.'

'Yes, thank you.'

He turned and proceeded to call for everyone's attention, and conversations muted to a silence. 'Detective Inspector Ian Drake wants to say a few words.'

Drake cleared his throat and then raised his voice a couple of decibels. 'We need details of who was present on Friday evening at the party Tom Levine attended. Detective Sergeant Morgan and myself will take full details from everybody.'

Drake and Sara found a table each and jotted down the basic details of every party-goer's name, date of birth, home address and mobile telephone details. That morning only confirmation of whether Tom Levine had been seen leaving the sailing club in his drunken state was needed. Any eyewitness would be interviewed in more detail later.

An hour passed before Marcus Abbott and his wife Jessica sat in front of Drake. 'This is dreadful,' Abbott announced. 'I feel sick.' His thin, waxy complexion left Drake in no doubt that the brutal killing of two of his friends had affected him.

'Is there any danger? I mean, there must be a serial killer out there.' Jessica Abbott cast a glance over her shoulder but her whispered comments couldn't have been heard by anyone.

'Did either of you see Tom Levine on Friday evening?' Drake managed a kindly tone.

Abbott nodded although his wife looked frightened. Drake scribbled down as much as Abbott could recall while confessing to have drunk far too much himself. Neither of them had seen Levine leaving the party and he hadn't been missed.

'How is Dot?' Jessica leaned over the table, an earnest look on her face. 'I haven't been able to ... work up the courage to visit her yet.' She bowed her head in embarrassment.

'Mrs Levine is obviously very distressed. If we need to contact you again, officers from my team will be in touch.'

Selston arrived mid-morning and bustled his way to Drake's table. 'I was at the party briefly and I had nothing to do with Tom Levine. A cousin of mine is a keen sailor and he and his family were here. I felt a duty to attend.'

'I thought you didn't sail,' Drake replied.

Selston ignored him, got to his feet, and glared at Drake and Sara. Then he left.

Another half a dozen guests gave similar accounts to Drake before Michael and Pamela Kennedy sat down.

Michael Kennedy interrupted. 'I'm sure you appreciate this is a difficult time for everyone. Tom Levine was at the party, but we didn't see him leave the club that evening. As I recall he'd been drinking quite heavily.'

'How well did you know him?'

Kennedy avoided Drake's gaze. Pamela fixed him

with an intense glare.

'Not that well,' Kennedy said.

'We're all part of the sailing set. We don't mix much with the locals,' Pamela added.

Sara appeared at Drake's table as he mulled over whether Michael and Pamela Kennedy might need to be spoken to again. 'Sorry to interrupt, boss.'

Drake turned to Kennedy. 'We'll be in touch again.'

Sara sat down by Drake's side once they had left. 'Colin Huxley Horton is convinced someone spiked Levine's drinks.'

Drake glanced over at Horton who gave him a brief conspiratorial nod. He walked over and whispered to Drake what he had told Sara already from the way she nodded. 'He got very drunk quickly.'

'I'll get one of my team to speak to you again,' Drake said.

By lunchtime Drake and Sara had a list of guests and details of another dozen who had left Pwllheli to return to their homes in northern England. And Drake knew the names of all the bar and the waiting staff working the evening Levine was killed. Each would need to be interviewed, memories jogged.

Drake bought a sandwich each for Sara and himself and they sat on the balcony looking out over Cardigan Bay. 'Everyone drank far too much that Friday evening,' Sara said.

Drake nodded. 'Nobody saw Tom Levine leave or even missed him when he had gone.' A frustrating morning of interviews had given them nothing tangible and he hoped the afternoon would be more productive. Drake scrunched up the food packaging. 'Let's get back to Porthmadog.'

He left and walked to his car, texting Mike Foulds as he did so, requesting a toxicology test on Levine.

Drake stared down at the map open on the bonnet of his car as Winder explained the morning's activities. Inquiries on one side of the town had been finished. The team would cover the northerly section that afternoon as well as the isolated properties on the outskirts. Drake noticed the white oblong shapes representing chalets and static caravans dotted around the area behind the beach to the south. Morfa Bychan was a wide, flat and safe beach a short distance from Porthmadog and he let his gaze drift along the coastline, remembering his visits there as a child with his mother and sister. Had it been thirty years since he'd visited? A spasm of guilt announced itself, challenging Drake to answer why he hadn't taken his own children there.

This summer, he resolved to take Helen and Megan with Annie. They could go swimming, have a barbecue. The sound of two marked police cars arriving interrupted his train of thought. Car doors creaked open, radios crackled, greetings exchanged as the officers joined his group.

'That must be a big holiday camp at Morfa Bychan,' Drake said tapping the map. 'Sara and I will go over there.' He glanced at his watch. 'We'll do as much as we can today. Tomorrow is a rest day.'

Sitting in his car he fumbled in the glove compartment for a CD – 'This Is My Truth Tell Me Yours', pleased that it was where he recalled. He passed the case to Sara.

'The cover photograph is the band standing on Morfa Bychan.'

She gave the Manic Street Preachers CD a cursory glance but said nothing. She had shown little interest in his taste in music, but it was a short drive, so he decided she would have to tolerate rock music for the journey.

The route took Drake out of the town and up over Moel y Gest and then down for the holiday park and the beach beyond it. Drake recalled warmly his father driving onto the sand and producing a windbreak from the boot of the car before settling into a family day at the seaside. A sign welcomed visitors to Morfa Bychan Holiday Park. He slotted the car into a parking space. Checking that Sara had a photograph of Jamie Eaton, they left the Mondeo and made for the entrance building next to a gate with a horizontal bar. A CCTV camera was discreetly positioned under the eaves.

A woman in her sixties with thinning hair gave him a weak smile. She was sorting paperwork and looked up at them from behind a counter.

'We are fully booked I am afraid.'

She gawped wide-eyed at the warrant cards Drake and Sara produced.

'Do you have a list of the people who own the chalets?' Drake said.

'Yes ... but, I don't know if I can give them to you.'

Drake leaned on the countertop. 'This is a murder inquiry. I'm sure you want to help.'

The woman nodded. 'The boss isn't here right now.' She glanced over at a clock hanging on the wall. 'He won't be long. Perhaps you could wait.'

Waiting for the owner to materialise on a Sunday

morning was the last thing Drake would tolerate. 'I need the names now.' He lowered his voice. 'It really is important that you cooperate.'

Colour faded from the woman's face. 'Give me a minute.' She grabbed a mouse on the table and clicked frantically as she peered at the monitor on her desk. Soon the printer behind her purred into life as it spewed out various sheets.

She pushed them over the counter at Drake. 'This is a list of people who own the chalets.' She fumbled to reach for a book on her desk. 'These are the names of people staying as guests.'

Drake started reading. Sara showed the woman a photograph of Jamie Eaton. 'Have you seen this man?'

'No ... I don't think so.' she squinted at the picture. 'There are lots of people that come and go. And sometimes guests don't sign in. They are supposed to, I know, and the boss gets really angry if they don't. He says it's all to do with health and safety.'

The park had over two hundred chalets and each owner listed alphabetically according to the zone in which the chalets were located. Drake recognised a name – Michael Kennedy.

'Do you know this Michael Kennedy?' Drake wondered if it was the Michael Kennedy he had seen that morning.

'He inherited a chalet after his father. Michael works in some fancy legal firm in Manchester.'

Drake nodded.

'Michael is really nice; he's taken my son sailing and he does a lot with the kids on the park when he's here. He's got a boat in Porthmadog.'

Drake read the name 'Eaton' on the owners'

register and blanked out the woman's high-pitched voice as he saw he was registered as a chalet owner.

Drake shared a glance with Sara as he showed her the list.

'Do you have a key to the Eaton chalet?' Sara said.

The woman shook her head.

'You'll need to tell us where their chalet is located.'

Drake and Sara hastened back to their car. The entrance barrier was already in the upright position as Drake approached, but the speed bumps meant it was impossible to do more than five miles per hour. Visitors sat on makeshift balconies looking out over the beach and the sea beyond as they ate breakfast, enjoying the spring sunshine.

'Over there, boss.' Sara pointed at a chalet at the end of one row. The curtains were drawn, the car parking area outside empty. Drake parked, and they walked over to the chalet. They heard the sound of a door squeaking open and being slammed shut. Drake and Sara ran over and watched as Jamie Eaton vaulted over a nearby wall into an adjacent field.

'Get backup,' Drake said. 'I'm going after him.'

Drake clambered over the wall and by the time he regained his footfall the man was almost at the bottom of the field, reaching a gate leading down towards sand dunes and then onto the beach. Drake heard the urgency in Sara's voice as she made a telephone call and followed him. He took off at a gallop towards the gate, ignoring the pinching around the toes of his brogues.

Occasionally the running figure cast a brief glance over his shoulder, and each time, realising Drake was on his tail, he pulled further away. Drake couldn't risk losing Jamie Eaton again.

He negotiated the farm gate easily enough and saw Eaton hopping over the tufts of marram grass and sand dunes that divided the fields and chalets from the beach. Eaton made heavy progress and Drake sensed he was gaining on him even though his heart wanted to crack his ribs open. His breathing became ragged. He really did need to get into better shape.

Glancing over his shoulder Drake saw Sara nearing and it encouraged him to increase his pace. Eaton disappeared from view as he approached the edge of the dunes. For a moment Drake worried, but then he saw that Eaton had slipped on a piece of flotsam discarded by the high tide. Eaton set off again at a steady pace over the flat, hard sand, his arms flailing around, his head bobbing up and down. Eaton was tiring: too many beers last night, Drake hoped.

Eaton continued towards Blackrock, the name of the large rock that gave the beach its English name. With the tide so low it might even be possible for Eaton to make his way around the coast. Drake pressed on, trying to take deep, regular breaths, filling his lungs to power his legs.

Eaton looked around again. Drake was in shouting distance now, so he bellowed. 'Stop, police.'

Eaton turned to look over at Drake but as he did so failed to see the remains of a child's sandcastle a few yards ahead of him. After his feet had lost their secure footing he went headlong, his hands struggling to prevent him landing flat on his face.

Drake reached Eaton as he got to his feet.

Drake landed squarely on top of Eaton, hearing the wind being forced out of his lungs. Seconds later Sara arrived. She produced handcuffs that she securely attached to Eaton.

They turned Eaton over.

'You're under arrest,' Drake gasped between breaths.

Chapter 20

Sunday 31st March
7.58 pm

Drake recoiled when he entered Eaton's caravan. The place stank of stale food and unwashed clothes. Inside he waved a hand in front of his nose. Sara followed him and stifled a cough. 'This is disgusting. How can anyone live in such conditions?'

Magazines, an Xbox, and empty pizza boxes covered the seating area at one end of the caravan. Old newspapers littered the floor in a pile as though they had been brushed off the seats when Jamie wanted to watch the fifty-five-inch television perched precariously on a thin table.

Drake joined Sara at the kitchen area. There was little sign of any food preparation from the bin overflowing with plastic takeaway food containers, all reeking of fat.

The panels of the internal walls creaked as he pushed open the door of the first bedroom with his shoe. The smell inside was no better and a duvet lay crumpled over the pillows.

'I can't imagine how anyone could sleep in such a place.' Drake tried to fathom out how a double bed could have been squeezed into the narrow space.

Sara stood at the door to the other bedroom. 'You need to see this, boss.'

Drake joined her and looked inside. The bed had been slept in recently judging by the duvet and clothes discarded in a heap in one corner. After snapping on latex gloves he picked up a pair of old jeans. He rummaged through the pockets, fingering loose change and a petrol receipt from services on the M56. He dropped the trousers on the mattress and shuffled towards the bottom of the bed. Drake kneeled to pick up a navy striped shirt lying on the floor. From the breast pocket he pulled out a sheet of folded paper.

'Bloody hell,' Drake said after reading the contents. He stretched out his hand for Sara to read the details. 'It's the discharge grant notification from David Eaton's time in prison.'

'So he's arrived in north Wales.'

'And we need to find him. Let's get a search team here and then we interview Jamie Eaton.'

Three hours later Drake sat in an interview room at Pwllheli police station. His shirt was damp, his suit crumpled, and his brogues scratched. Taking off his shoes and socks and shaking them hadn't been enough to extract all the grains of sand. They tickled his skin and it made him feel that the only thing he wanted to do was have a long, hot shower and change his clothes.

But he had Jamie Eaton to interview. The search team's progress in Eaton's caravan had delayed the process long enough. Drake ignored Eaton's lawyer's whingeing remarks about his own ruined bank holiday family plans.

A one-piece white paper suit crinkled every time Jamie moved. The forensic investigators were processing the polo shirt and jeans he wore when arrested along with all his clothes and possessions from the caravan.

'I'm investigating the murder of Nicholas Wixley and Tom Levine,' Drake said. 'We understand you had an argument with Nicholas Wixley the day before he was killed. Why did you try and abscond this morning?'

'You lot would do anything to stitch me up.'

'We wanted to talk to you about the death of Nicholas Wixley.'

Eaton folded his arms, dragging them close to his body. 'You can't pin that on me.'

'Is it true your argument with Nicholas Wixley got violent?'

'He wanted to do me over. I'd worked on the engine of his yacht. Then he made up some shit complaint about the engine not working.'

'Where were you on the night after you argued with Nicholas Wixley?'

Eaton shrugged.

Drake hesitated for a moment. He had seen this edgy, contemptuous attitude so many times and it never worked. He had every reason to detain Eaton in custody for at least twenty-four hours and absconding that morning would probably give him more than enough grounds to seek an extension that would see this arrogant youngster behind bars for another forty-eight.

'I'm sure it's in your best interest if you cooperate.' Drake looked over at the lawyer, who made no response. 'Have you been in touch with your father recently?'

Drake kept his eye contact with Eaton direct, watching for his response, gauging exactly the reaction. Eaton glanced at his lawyer, who raised an ambiguous eyebrow.

'Are you trying to fix my dad up for Wixley's death, now?' Eaton sounded shrill.

'I asked you a simple question about contact with your father. When did you last see him?'

'Go to hell.'

Drake flicked back through some of his papers on the table, hoping the pause would encourage a reply. It didn't.

'A search team has been busy going through the possessions in your caravan today. So, I'll ask you again – when did you see your father last?'

Eaton moving in his chair made a scratching sound and he jerked himself forward. He gave his lawyer a panicked glance before facing Drake. He tightened his jaw and flared his nostrils. 'You filth will stop at nothing.'

Drake took a moment and kept his eye contact direct. 'For the record we have evidence that your dad was staying in your caravan. Is that true?'

'Fuck off.'

'We need to speak to him in order to eliminate him from our inquiry.'

Jamie guffawed. 'Yeah, as if.'

'Where is he now, Jamie?'

Jamie shook his head again very slowly.

'Did you know Tom Levine?'

More shaking of the head.

'He was found murdered in his yacht in Pwllheli marina on Saturday morning. CCTV footage records you arriving at the marina and going down onto the pontoons early that morning. Can you explain to me what you were doing there?'

Eaton stood up abruptly and leaned on the table towards Drake. He'd caught everyone in the room by surprise. 'I was fucking working. You can't stitch me up for Levine's death.'

'Sit down,' Drake demanded.

For the next half an hour Jamie made no reply to any further questions. A sense of frustration made Drake tell the custody sergeant he shouldn't release Eaton at all and that they were going to charge him with assault on Nicholas Wixley. When Sara reminded him that they had no formal complaint, he relented and agreed to let the CPS decide Eaton's fate.

It was late in the evening by the time they watched Eaton leave the police station on bail.

At least they had his address.

Chapter 21

Bank Holiday Monday 1st April
9.00 am

Drake read an email from HMP Marchfield explaining that staff shortages meant the first available time for him to see Cornwell would be Thursday. It annoyed him that the prison authorities had ignored the urgency in his request. Complaining wouldn't get him far so he curbed his anger, left the car and headed for the Pwllheli marina building.

Tired faces looked at Drake once he arrived in the room on the first floor – he had promised them the day off after all. Eaton's arrest meant a change of plan and new priorities but the last thing he wanted was his team burning out. 'We get as much done by lunchtime. We all take this afternoon off. This week is going to be busy.'

Jaded faces brightened at the news.

Drake sat by a desk laden with boxes of paperwork and records. 'We need to know the names of everyone who was sleeping on their yachts or boats overnight Friday and we need a database of the names of everyone who owns yachts in the marina. But first we trawl through the CCTV records. We cross-check everyone on the footage against the names of boat owners.'

He shared a glance with the team. 'Get the CCTV footage up onto the laptop screens while I find the harbour master.' Luned fiddled with one of the laptops on the table. Winder nodded his understanding and reached for the second laptop.

Drake stood up and made his way to the control room where a stony-faced Mervyn Phillips sat with Joe. Drake had called Phillips the day before, making clear he and his assistant would be needed that morning.

'Sorry, we're both on holiday,' Phillips had replied.

'It's not a request,' Drake had retorted. 'I expect you there by nine.' He had finished the call without waiting to hear the response.

Drake jerked his hand at them and they followed him. He pointed at one of the chairs with Winder and Luned and turned to Phillips. 'You're with Detective Constables Winder and Thomas. We need names to match faces. The sooner we get finished the sooner we can all go home.'

Winder and Luned were allocated Good Friday while Drake sat with Sara and Joe watching the footage from Saturday.

They watched as sailors carried kit bags, laughing and joking as they trudged their way down to the pontoons. Sara recorded the names of sailors Joe recognised. He hesitated over others and shook his head for those who were strangers. Every unfamiliar face would need to be tracked down and their movements identified for Friday evening and Saturday morning. It was tedious and time consuming and the process only raised more queries. But someone might have seen something.

The footage for Saturday morning had far more people milling around the ramp waiting to enter the marina. Once the crime scene had been discovered it had meant the marina had been cordoned off and owners had been trapped in their boats and yachts until the crime scene manager had narrowed the perimeter to the pontoons around Levine's yacht.

A crowd gathered and streamed through the gate.

It was difficult to see every face and Joe struggled with the identification. 'I cannot possibly be expected to recognise all these faces.'

'Do the best you can,' Drake said.

'Stop it there,' Joe said as a group of a dozen sailors squeezed past the gate. He named three but didn't recognise the others. Drake peered at the screen. A face looked familiar. Someone involved in the inquiry, and for a second he couldn't place him.

'I know that face.'

Sara shuffled her chair nearer to him. Joe moved to one side.

Suddenly Drake recognised the face. 'That's David Eaton.'

Sara leaned forward and squinted at the screen. 'You're right, boss.'

'I wonder what he was doing there?'

Rationalising how he felt as he drove over to Felinheli that evening made him realise that more than anything he wanted his relationship with Annie to work. It didn't dispel completely the rituals and obsessions that could dominate his mind, but it had helped. Had it not been for her parents visiting that weekend Drake would have been staying at Annie's home: waking up by her side in the morning, enjoying breakfast around her kitchen table, sharing a joke, looking forward to life.

Annie's original plans were for them to spend the day with her parents. He had really hoped to have taken the day off and despite her reassuring him that she realised how important the case was, he still felt guilty.

His daughters, Helen and Megan, had met Annie twice. On the first occasion, Helen, the oldest, had been frosty, offhand-ish with her, and although Megan had been a more laid-back, she had taken the lead from her older sister. By the end of their afternoon bowling and then eating pizza at the girls' favourite restaurant, his daughters had relaxed. Annie had been sensitive, and when Helen asked Annie about her family, he knew his daughters would enjoy her company. The intervening winter months and Annie's encouragement that he needed to take things slowly meant contact with his daughters had been confined to trips to the cinema and meals.

Often Drake mulled over what Helen and Megan thought of Annie. He dismissed seeking out the girls' approval and dreaded the prospect of Helen, in particular, asking him intimate questions.

He tried to dismiss the knot of apprehension curling in his stomach as an immature teenage approach to meeting Annie's parents. He hadn't done this for years, but he was in his forties, he chided himself. Cancelling the arrangements to see Helen and Megan on Good Friday meant he felt guilty for spending the evening with Annie and her family.

Drake parked behind a ten-year-old BMW and glanced up at Annie's house. He looked in the rear-view mirror and with no tie to adjust, he drew a hand through his hair. There were bags under his eyes and he contemplated what he'd look like in ten years. Policing was ageing him prematurely. Leaving the car, he made his way over to the door and rang the bell.

Annie answered and kissed him lightly on the

cheek. 'I missed you last night.'

Drake really wanted to pull her close, but she went indoors, and Drake followed her to the sitting room on the second floor. Roland Jenkins had thin wisps of silvery hair still clinging on to life. He had an average paunch for man in his late sixties and a kindly, warm face that smiled as he shook Drake energetically by the hand. Rebecca, Annie's mother, was an older version of Annie – her face more lined, the hair a little thinner, more brittle, but she had the same engaging smile.

Sitting outside in Annie's garden overlooking the Menai Strait, Drake opened a bottle of wine and distributed four glasses. The sun began its slow descent, turning the sky a brilliant red. Two yachts passed each other, motoring on engines along the Strait; another slowed as it approached the harbour nearby.

'This is the most magical place,' Rebecca said. 'We should retire here.' There was a semi-serious tone to her voice.

'It is lovely,' Roland said.

When the temperatures fell, they sat inside.

Small talk came easily to Roland and Rebecca Jenkins. They were polite and interested in Drake and his family, although Drake guessed Annie had shared a lot of the details already. It led onto a conversation about his family and how long his parents and grandparents had lived in the foothills of Snowdonia. Drake didn't feel on edge with Roland and Rebecca, as he had with Sian's mother. He made polite enquiries about Roland's family, knowing Annie had mentioned his farming background in west Wales. Farmers always have things in common, Drake thought, as Roland recalled his own upbringing.

Annie made them dinner and they sat around the kitchen table until Drake's eyes burned. He had another full day ahead of him, a full week. He made excuses, shook Roland by the hand and warmly kissed Rebecca on the cheek, and Annie followed him outside to his car.

By the front door he pulled her close and kissed her lips. He had been wanting to do that all evening.

'I think my parents like you,' Annie said.

Drake willed himself to believe that everything would be all right between Annie and himself. A feeling of breathlessness made him realise he would miss her badly that evening.

Chapter 22

Tuesday 2nd April
11.30 am

Drake sat in his car at headquarters after attending Tom Levine's post-mortem and mulled over the pathologist's conclusion that the absence of defensive wounds suggested Levine hadn't struggled. It wasn't a surprise given Levine's drunken state.

He left the car and when he reached the Incident Room, Winder was pinning two photographs to the board. Luned and Sara, sitting at their desks, turned to face Drake.

'Morning, boss,' both women said in unison. Winder nodded an acknowledgement.

Even an afternoon off had revitalized the team: there was a clear-eyed determination on their faces.

'Any results for David Eaton?' Drake said.

Eaton's photograph had been circulated to every police officer and every community support officer in Northern Division area as well as the neighbouring police forces in England.

'Nothing yet,' Sara said.

'I found a picture of Sir Ivan Banks, the high court judge and Hector Murren, the journalist,' Winder announced.

'Any progress with establishing their whereabouts?'

Winder shook his head.

'The countrywide alert for Sir Ivan's car hasn't produced any results. I spoke to one of the Met officers this morning who told me a neighbour believed he owned a garage near his home so for all we know his car could be safely locked up,' Sara added.

Drake joined Winder, staring at the photographs of Sir Ivan and Murren. 'Let's hope there's an innocent explanation for both men being out of touch. Otherwise …' Contemplating the possibility that either were being sliced up by Zavier Cornwell's accomplice made him shiver.

'We need to find them,' Drake announced before turning and looking over at Luned. 'Call Murren's partner and organise a time for us to see him tomorrow.' The young officer nodded. He turned back to face the board again and took a couple of minutes to rearrange the images into a neat and precise order. The photographs of Levine's murder scene were placed alongside similar images from Nicholas Wixley's bedroom – the similarities unmistakeable. Drake stood back for a moment.

Drake turned to face Luned and Sara as Winder returned to his desk. 'We need to finalise the list of the owners of the yachts, boats, dinghies and everyone connected to the marina. And establish who was sleeping on their yachts or boats the night Tom Levine was killed.'

Luned again. 'That could be a long list, sir.'

'I still haven't finished the CCTV footage from the various garages and supermarkets, trying to track down the red car,' Winder said.

Winder and Luned scribbled on their legal pads. Winder's comments about the red car reminded Drake that the buyer of the pink gilet still needed to be traced. Turning back to the board, he tapped a finger against the image of the expensive piece of clothing. 'And I want progress made today on the gilet.'

Back in his office Drake spent an hour calling Sir Ivan Banks's clerk in the Lord Chancellor's department, talking again to the judge's neighbours, hoping that Sir Ivan had made contact. But they had nothing new to contribute. Drake reread the emails from Sir Ivan's brother, a retired teacher living in Vancouver, who hadn't heard from his brother for three months and, apart from an email address and his mobile and a landline number, had no other way of contacting him. Activity on all three was being monitored in any event. Drake ignored the tightening in his chest as he contemplated the possibility the high court judge was a target for the alphabet killer.

If Sir Ivan's body was found in some dingy, out-of-the-way location, the publicity would dwarf the press attention Nicholas Wixley's murder had received. But they already knew the judge had taken that week as holiday, so they couldn't demonstrate he was actually *missing*. Maybe 'unaccounted for' was the right description, Drake thought, or 'whereabouts uncertain'. The longer his absence continued the more Drake realised he would have to seek authorisation to enter the judge's home. A vivid image of Sir Ivan huddled over his desk in the study of his Chelsea home, his throat slit open and letters written in blood over expensive wallpaper suddenly invaded Drake's mind. It made him feel nauseous. One more day and he'd speak to Wyndham Price.

Silently he chided himself for not feeling as serious about Murren. He was a journalist of course, and not a high court judge or a circuit judge. He scolded himself.

Every death was just as important as another. There would be loved ones left bereft, a grieving family. Drake blanked out the noise from the Incident Room beyond the threshold of his office door and quickly read about Hector Murren. The home address was a village in Cheshire, convenient enough for a reasonable commute into the newspaper's offices on the outskirts of Manchester. Background checks on Murren had told Drake he had covered various trials and celebrity events and Drake worried that he was fretting unnecessarily about the prospect that Murren might be a target. The random nature of the alphabet killings made it impossible to figure out who might be the next victim. Sir Ivan Banks was a more likely candidate, but they had nothing to link Zavier Cornwell to Tom Levine. It persuaded him to believe there was more to Tom Levine's relationship with Nicholas Wixley than their shared membership of the Pwllheli Sailing Club.

Drake glanced at his watch; he and Sara had to leave soon. The telephone rang and interrupted his train of thought as he pondered the likelihood of delays to their journey along the A55.

'I've got some preliminary results on the forensics from Tom Levine's yacht.' Drake recognised Mike Foulds' voice.

'Anything?'

'There are dozens of partial fingerprints. And lots of possible DNA samples. It's no more than I would have expected from a yacht used by different people.'

'Any positive leads?'

Drake heard Foulds groan. 'We're doing a search, but I wouldn't hold your breath. I discovered a fingerprint on the whisky bottle and the glass but they both belonged to Tom Levine. The killer would have been covered in blood. My guess is that Tom Levine had already passed out on the bunk when someone slit his throat. There wasn't any sign of a struggle, no scuff marks or blood anywhere other than the cabin where you found the body.'

Sara appeared at Drake's door, tapping a finger on her watch to remind him that time was short.

'Send me the report, Mike.'

Drake finished the call, replaced the handset and, once satisfied his desk was neat and tidy, got to his feet and joined Sara.

The journey took an hour and a half, a good twenty minutes more than Drake anticipated. A white transit van, its rear doors open, stood on the drive of Dorothy Levine's bungalow behind an Audi SUV. Drake parked a little distance away. He and Sara made their way past men carrying furniture from the property and shouted a greeting at the front door. Moments later Dot Levine appeared.

'Come in, come in.' Levine sounded businesslike.

After directing a tall, lanky youngster holding a box precariously, she led Drake and Sara into a sitting room. The furniture was functional: practical sofas, coffee-ring stained table, no personal knickknacks or ornaments, a television and sound bar in one corner.

'I cannot wait to leave this place.' Levine sank into an armchair, obviously expecting Sara and Drake to sit down.

'We want to ask you about your husband's movements the night he was killed.'

Levine nodded, and her unwavering eye contact unsettled Drake.

'We arrived at the club at about seven pm. All the usual crowd were there. Tom started drinking with Colin Horton, Marcus Abbott and his sailing buddies. Later that evening, about eight-thirty, the club laid on a buffet. I spent my time talking with some of the other wives.'

'Who else did he talk to?'

'Lots of people I guess. I didn't pay that much attention.'

'Did he always plan on sleeping on the yacht?'

'Not really. He has done in the past when he's been drinking, and he can't be bothered to get a cab home.'

'Did you see your husband arguing with anybody?'

Levine contemplated the question for a few seconds. Then she shook her head. 'Not that I can recall.'

'When did you leave, Mrs Levine?'

Again, she paused for thought. 'It must have been about ten-thirty. I couldn't stand another minute of the place. I'd been drinking orange juice, so I was safe to drive home. By then Tom was deep in conversation with Michael Kennedy and Pamela.'

'Did he know them well?' Drake asked; her reference to Tom Levine knowing Michael Kennedy piqued his interest.

'Tom was brought up on a council estate in Manchester, so he thought he'd made it by mixing with people like Nicholas Wixley and the other barristers and people with families that have owned properties around this area for years and years.' She waved a hand limply in the air.

'When you say "deep in conversation"...' Sara made her first contribution. 'What exactly do you think they were talking about?'

'Tom persuaded Wixley to be his *general counsel*,' she gave the title with a snide tone. 'He thought it would add something to his businesses having some hotshot lawyer giving him some kudos.'

'We'll need more details about your husband's business interests.'

'Whatever.' Dot Levine gave a world-weary shrug.

Drake left Levine and headed back to his car with Sara, reflecting that the link between Nicholas Wixley and Tom Levine seemed improbable. What did Wixley gain? Drake suspected it was money and power, and now all he had to do was find the connection.

Chapter 23

Wednesday 3rd April
8.30 am

Drake ate breakfast watching a TV news item that featured a reporter in Pwllheli standing near the marina, describing how the police investigation was difficult and protracted. Several locals and yacht owners were interviewed at length about how frightened they felt after two murders in their 'close-knit community'. Finishing his Americano, Drake watched on his mobile the snippet of footage of David Eaton leaving the marina. He was the only person directly linked to Zavier Cornwell. Drake could see the motive for killing Nicholas Wixley, not that Zavier Cornwell needed a motive; that much was clear from the alphabet killings. But Drake struggled to find a motive for the death of Tom Levine and he resolved to focus his attention on Tom Levine's background.

The previous evening two uniformed officers had visited Jamie, making certain he was abiding by the curfew on his bail, which required him to stay in the chalet from eight pm to eight am. Managing to persuade him to allow them access inside satisfied them he was alone. Jamie had blanked out their questions about his father's whereabouts.

Drake tapped out a message for Winder to ensure that uniformed officers from Pwllheli would interview all the staff at the sailing club in the hope someone would recall seeing David Eaton there on the night in question.

He had time to spare before collecting Sara, so he

called Annie. It lightened his spirit to hear her voice as it soothed his mind and it kept him smiling to himself after their conversation had finished.

Half an hour later he collected Sara in the car park at headquarters; they drove down to the A55 and he powered the Mondeo eastwards towards the border with England. Hector Murren and his partner Oliver Barkley owned a terraced property in a quaint village with a pub and a church surrounding a small green with a stream running through the centre.

Barkley darted a nervous glance between Sara and Drake as he stood on the threshold. Barkley frowned over both warrant cards before relaxing and ushering them into his home. Two heavily bloodshot eyes gazed over the kitchen table at Drake once they sat down. Drake put him at forty-five, give or take a couple of years.

'Do you have any idea where Hector may have gone?' Sara took the lead, as they had agreed on the journey that morning.

He replied with a brisk shake of his head.

'Does he have family, apart from you, of course?'

'His parents are still alive. They live in Taunton.' He bowed his head. 'Hector hasn't been in touch with them for some time.'

'Some time?'

'They took it badly.' Barkley shared a glance with Drake and Sara, clearly hoping they would understand his meaning, but he explained it in any event. 'When Hector came out there was quite a row.'

'Does Hector have any siblings?'

'As I told you, things haven't been right with his family. They simply couldn't accept that he had decided to share his life with me.'

'Mr Barkley.' Using the surname was a sure sign he was getting under Sara's skin, Drake thought. 'Does he have a brother or sister he might visit or contact?'

Barkley blurted out a response. 'Without telling me, hardly.' Then he pouted. 'He has a sister who lives in Middlesbrough. She ... sends a Christmas card.'

'Can you find her contact details please?'

Barkley scrambled to his feet and left the room. Sara raised a dubious eyebrow at Drake, obviously sharing his discomfort at Barkley's attitude. Moments later he reappeared, a yellow Post-it note in hand.

'I've written down the addresses for his parents and his sister. And there are telephone numbers, but I can't tell you if they are still current.'

'Can you think of any reason that could account for Hector's whereabouts?' Drake could tell Sara wanted to say 'disappearance', but good sense prevailed.

'No, I cannot, Detective Sergeant.'

Sara paused. 'Does he have any friends that he might be staying with?'

'All his friends are my friends too. And I have spoken to them all. Nobody has seen him.'

'And tell us about his work colleagues,' Drake said.

Barkley scowled. 'I never liked any of them.'

'Do you recall the alphabet killings?'

'Yes, of course. Hector was working long hours then.'

'How did he feel about the case?'

'He really thought it would make his reputation.'

'And did it?'

Barkley's eye contact drifted away as he stared out

of the kitchen window. 'It was a dreadful case. I couldn't possibly have dealt with it.'

Sara butted in. 'Can you think of anything – a favourite holiday destination or—'

'We did everything together.'

'I'm sure you did.' Sara lowered her voice a fraction. 'But presumably Hector had friends or relationships *before* you met him. Can you tell us about those?'

Barkley gave her an incredulous glare, as though the mere suggestion was inconceivable.

'My life started when we fell in love and he felt the same.' Another disbelieving, pained expression crossed Barkley's face. Then he threaded the fingers of both hands together and leaned on the table. 'We always did things as a couple,' Barkley continued. 'Have you been able to trace his mobile telephone?'

'It's not switched on as otherwise we could triangulate the signal,' Drake said, injecting a degree of firmness into his voice. 'And we have issued an alert for his car.'

'How could Cornwell be directing these murders from prison, for goodness sake.'

'We're pursuing several lines of inquiry. Making certain Hector was aware of the potential risks is uppermost in our mind.'

Drake doubted Barkley had understood exactly what he was saying from the confused look on his face. But Drake had had enough of Oliver Barkley. 'Thank you for your help, Mr Barkley.' Drake nodded at Sara and stood up, finding a business card from his suit pocket, which he pushed over the table. 'If Hector contacts you or any of your friends or his work colleagues, do please get in touch.'

The card merited another bewildered face. 'What happens next?'

Drake made for the front door. 'I suggest you formally report him missing to the Cheshire police force. I'm sure they will be able to help.'

Barkley blinked furiously. Drake and Sara left and retraced their steps to the car.

'If I were Hector Murren I wouldn't want to go back to living with that sort of man,' Sara said as Drake fired the Mondeo's engine into life. 'And he didn't even offer coffee or tea.'

'We passed a tea shop in the village.' Drake nodded out of the windscreen. 'I'm parched.'

Drake pulled into a layby near a small cluster of shops. The Village Teashop nestled between an old-fashioned greengrocers and the local post office. A bell rang when Drake pushed the door open. Lace curtains hung on the bottom half of the window and starched white cotton tablecloths gave the place an old-world charm. They found a table and sat down.

A surly looking woman in her fifties took their orders.

'Do you believe all that stuff about their lives starting when they met each other?' Sara said.

Drake shrugged. 'We'd better contact the parents – they might know where he's gone. He might even be staying with them.'

'He's probably sick to the back teeth of Barkley.'

Tea and coffee arrived. Drake checked his drink, satisfied that it looked strong enough, having made clear he wanted two shots of espresso.

'And we talk to his work colleagues.' Drake turned

a spoon noisily around the china cup. 'I'll make contact with the newspaper.' Drake reached for his mobile and it rang as he pulled it out of his jacket pocket. He didn't recognise the number.

'Detective Inspector Drake.'

The voice was deep, educated and very confident. 'This is Sir Ivan Banks speaking. You left a garbled message on my mobile telephone for me to contact you. What the hell is this all about?'

Chapter 24

Wednesday 3rd April
12.30 am

Drake stumbled a greeting.

'M'Lud ... Sir Ivan ..., thank you for contacting me. We've been trying to reach you for several days.'

'I've been fly fishing in Scotland. I always go this time of the year. I switch my mobile off. It is the only way I can get any peace and quiet.'

Drake had left the café and stood outside, away from other customers, as he explained about the inquiries into the deaths of Wixley and Levine. Sir Ivan recognised Zavier Cornwell's name and assured Drake he would take his personal safety more seriously. He rang off, and a renewed determination filled Drake as he returned to the café, slurped a mouthful of the now tepid coffee and turned to Sara. 'Let's go.'

The journey back to north Wales felt shorter than the drive that morning.

Sara called Murren's family. Once she had finished she glanced at Drake. 'Looks like Barkley was right. They haven't heard from Hector.'

Drake nodded. 'Try his employers and then track down the officer in Cheshire who deals with missing persons and send his details to Barkley. At least he won't be able to complain about us being unhelpful.'

Sara had finished the various calls by the time they neared headquarters.

Drake barged straight into the Incident Room, letting the door crash against the wall behind it as he stalked over to the board. 'Sir Ivan Banks is safe and well.' He removed the judge's image and dropped it onto a desk. 'But Murren's partner has no idea where he might be.'

Drake turned to face his team. 'We need to track down David Eaton and later I want updates on Levine's movements the night he died.'

Drake's computer was booting up when Winder appeared on the threshold of his door. 'I've been doing some background searches on Tom Levine, boss.'

Drake motioned for him to enter.

'It looks as though he's got a lot of business interests. He's also got several limited companies; all of them seem to be connected in some way. I've sent you the link.'

Winder left and Drake scrolled down through some emails in his inbox. He scanned the more important ones and jotted down a reminder, on one of the orange Post-it notes, to read the updated policy from the Wales Police Service on gender balance.

Once he found Winder's email he clicked it open and read an article written by Norman Turnbull of the *Stockport Times*. It portrayed Tom Levine as a modern-day Al Capone, intimidating business associates, hounding tenants and threatening competitors. Even if half of it were true, Tom Levine was undeniably a gangster. It meant he had enemies, lots of them.

Who would want Tom Levine dead? His wife certainly wasn't grieving.

A few clicks of his mouse gave Drake the contact number for the *Stockport Times* and he reached for his telephone. After being passed from one journalist to another, he eventually spoke to a Patricia – the principal news desk editor. She made her title very clear by announcing it slowly.

'May I speak to Norman Turnbull?'

'Norman, is ...'Patricia said his name as though he had recently died and that everyone was desperately sad. 'He's freelance, but ... I'm not certain if I ...'

'This is a police inquiry.' Drake hoped the emphasis he got into his voice underlined the seriousness of the request. 'You must be able to contact him?'

'After his last piece about Tom Levine there was a lot of flak. His lawyers threatened hell and damnation. The editor became nervous about using Norman again.'

'Are you aware that Tom Levine was killed three days ago?'

'Jesus Christ. I hadn't heard. How did it happen? Has it got anything to do with that lawyer who was murdered?'

'I really need to contact Norman Turnbull.'

'Surely you don't think he's involved?'

'Do you have the telephone number, or do I need to speak to your editor?'

'There is no need to get aggressive.'

'Patricia, the number, please.'

Drake heard the fumbling as she clicked on her mouse, presumably accessing a database. Then she dictated the details and Drake scribbled down the number.

'Has there been a press release?' Patricia was now clearly in journalistic mode as she shrugged off her shock at Levine's death.

'I suggest you ring public relations.' Drake could have offered to put her through, but he finished the call.

What exactly did Turnbull know about Tom

Levine?

Rather than using his mobile Drake decided to use the headquarters landline. A businesslike message invited him to leave a name and contact number. Drake left his details, resolving to call Turnbull back again later that afternoon.

Returning to the *Stockport Times* article, Drake saw the smiling face of Tom Levine and his wife, less engaged, less smiling, standing in a group of dignitaries examining a building site and then another, with Mr and Mrs Levine at a black-tie event. They looked prosperous, successful, the very essence of a power couple. Another had images of Tom Levine addressing an audience of would-be property millionaires, all with ambitious-looking faces. He spotted another with Pamela and Michael Kennedy sharing a joke with a group including Levine at a cocktail party attended by the Lord Mayor of Manchester.

The telephone on his desk rang and he hoped it was Norman Turnbull returning his call – at least he was prompt, Drake thought.

Instead he heard the voice of Assistant Chief Constable Neary. He stiffened in his chair. 'Detective Inspector Drake, ACC Neary. The chief constable asked me to contact you about the minutes of the appointment panel when DCC Wixley was a candidate.'

'Yes, ma'am.' Drake recalled the pained expression on the chief constable's face from their first meeting when he mentioned the minutes to Drake.

'As we speak they are in transit. I wasn't going to transmit them electronically for obvious reasons. I'm sure you can appreciate they are *highly* confidential.'

'Of course.'

'Circulation is limited to yourself and Superintendent Price. Do I make myself clear?'

'Yes, ma'am.'

'In this day and age of utter and complete transparency I don't want any suggestion we haven't considered, and, of course, dismissed, the possibility that a senior police officer was responsible for the death of Nicholas Wixley.'

Drake analysed her remarks. Completely contradictory of course but it left him with a clear impression ACC Neary and the chief constable were covering their asses. If he messed up it would be down to him alone.

'I understand there was another murder this weekend?'

'The body of a Tom Levine was found in his yacht.'

'Is the death linked to the murder of Nicholas Wixley?'

'They were known to each other and the MOs are similar.'

'Does DCC Wixley have an alibi for Levine's murder?'

'We haven't spoken to her yet.

'Keep me posted.' Neary rang off.

Neary's abrupt response made Drake think she knew far more than she wanted to share. He replaced the handset and deliberated what the minutes might disclose.

He didn't have to wait long until reception requested his presence. A tall road traffic officer waited for Drake. 'I was given strict instructions to ensure this parcel was only delivered to you, sir.' He held up

Drake's warrant card, checking the picture against the live version. Assistant Chief Constable Neary wasn't taking any chances. Drake scribbled his signature acknowledging receipt. The traffic officer relaxed, announcing he was heading off to the canteen before restarting his journey back to Cardiff.

Drake retraced his steps to his office. Sara didn't look up from her desk; Winder stared at the computer screen, as did Luned. Drake sliced open the package with a pair of scissors he retrieved from the drawer of his desk.

Drake found the interview notes from the final round of the appointment process. Laura Wixley had been a strong contender. He read about her confident manner and impressive history of multidisciplinary policing. Glowing reports from stakeholder organisations praised her invaluable contributions in developing new strategies for investigating sexual abuse allegations. She had progressed effortlessly from constable to assistant chief constable in her early fifties and Drake guessed it must have been challenging having a career and being married to a high-flying barrister.

After Drake read the summary of the appointments panel recommendations he tried to fix in his mind the consequences. The intelligence reports about Nicholas Wixley's activities had a clear impact on Laura Wixley's career. Had she asked for feedback? The appointments secretary would be hardly likely to share with her the intelligence made known to the committee. Perhaps someone had had a quiet word in her ear – *'the committee is a bit concerned about Nicholas, perhaps you should reconsider your current ambitions.'*

How many other unsuccessful promotion applications had there been?

A series of discreet and confidential telephone calls took up most of the morning as he rang the three police forces in northern England where DCC Wixley had applied for the post of chief constable. Each telephone call was met with initial suspicion and reluctance to cooperate.

'I can't possibly discuss this with you over the telephone' was the least offensive response.

He decided on a different approach and, knowing that the chief constable of each force would have a personal liaison officer, usually an officer of inspector rank, he tracked down the respective individuals. It would be an easier and more effective way than trying to speak to each chief constable whose daily routine would be set in stone weeks, if not months, in advance. The calls were brief and professional, and Drake sat back and waited.

The tactic yielded dividends when a chief constable rang.

'On a fishing expedition, aren't you, lad?' The voice had a thick Yorkshire accent.

'I'm pursuing certain lines of inquiry, sir,' Drake retorted.

'Are you the senior investigating officer?'

'I am, sir,'

'And is this an authorised line of inquiry?'

'That's correct, sir.'

'Hmm.' The chief constable paused. 'I've met Laura Wixley a couple of times. I'll contact the appointments panel clerk and authorise the release of the files you need.'

Drake got the distinct impression the chief constable wanted to add. *'And it's got nothing to do with me.'* As though the mere process of suspecting a senior police officer was anathema to him.

He rang off and Drake blew out a lungful of breath.

Before late afternoon, the chairmen of one appointment panel had interrogated Drake, wanting information Drake wasn't able to share with him. Drake emphasised the urgency and, buoyed up by confirmation from each that they would provide the files, he headed for the kitchen to organise coffee. Annie had been pulling his leg about the fastidiousness he adopted when fussing over making coffee. He smiled as he recalled the last time she had teased him. He always used a blend of expensive ground coffee and allowed the water to come off the boil for no more than a minute and a half before letting the coffee brew in the cafetière.

The telephone on his desk rang. An unfamiliar voice introduced himself as the chair of the appointment panels for the North Lancashire Police Authority. His voice was gruff, and he got straight to the point. 'That Laura Wixley was something else. I didn't take to her at all. I couldn't get over the fact she rang for feedback after the interview.'

'What did you tell her?' Drake cut across.

'I told her straight that she needed to sort out her husband. That his name had been linked to some villains and that she'd never get promotion.'

'I see.'

'I always call a spade a spade. None of this political correctness. She were out of touch with the way we do things.'

Once the chair rang off Drake sat back wondering what sort of impact his feedback had had on Laura Wixley. Her whole life had been focused on being appointed a chief constable and being told that her husband had been the impediment to her promotion would have appalled her.

A nasty smell inevitably followed Laura Wixley. Insinuations and half-truths could be the most destructive. Assistant Chief Constable Neary had said 'utterly and completely transparent' on the telephone. But did she really mean it? The next task would be to contact the other forces she had applied to for vacant chief constableships.

The telephone rang again, interrupting Drake.

'Detective Inspector Drake.'

'Norman Turnbull.' The voice sounded abrupt, as though he were in a mad rush. 'What do you want?'

Drake took a breath. 'I need to speak to you about Tom Levine. You've written an article about his business dealings—'

'That was only the half of it.'

'I'm sorry?'

'It was only what the editor would allow me to print at the time. And who gave you my telephone number?'

'I rang the paper.'

'My number is private. I want your assurance you'll keep it confidential. I don't want any of Levine's cronies knowing how to contact me.'

'I need to speak to you.'

'I'm not getting involved. It's more than my life's worth. And I had nothing to do with his death.'

Drake decided to go on a fishing expedition. 'Do you know if Tom Levine was associated with Nicholas Wixley?'

All Drake heard was heavy breathing.

Drake continued. 'What have you got?'

Again, no reply.

'I think we should meet to discuss.'

Drake paused. 'You're aware presumably that Nicholas Wixley was married to Deputy Chief Constable Laura Wixley.'

Before the phone went dead Turnbull said, 'You have no idea what these people are like.'

Superintendent Price read the latest email from Assistant Chief Constable Neary asking for an update briefing memorandum as well as confirming she had sent Drake the papers from the appointment panel. Idly he considered what she would have been like as the senior police officer in Wales. She had worked in Cardiff but that would be a world away from policing in north Wales or west Wales – the people were different, their expectations and priorities a world away from those of a big city.

Although he had replied to HR, he had made excuses telling them that the recent case had taken all his time. It sounded plausible, but he knew there would be a reminder in his inbox soon. He surveyed his room. Retirement would mean never sitting at his desk again. Perhaps he and his wife should move. But where to? Penarth or Barry maybe – somewhere near a good golf course at the very least.

Hannah interrupted his rumination. He smiled as she entered his room after a discreet knock on the door, realising that he would miss her too. 'Ian Drake is on his way over.'

Price frowned. It was unscheduled, and he brooded over what was on Drake's mind.

He didn't have to wait too long.

Price ushered Drake into his room. Drake sat down and Price made him himself comfortable at his desk. He scratched his bald head; he needed to give it a shave that evening.

'We are going to interview Zavier Cornwell tomorrow, sir,' Drake said.

Price nodded.

'We've established a link between Zavier Cornwell and a David Eaton who was recently released from prison.'

'Good. That makes it easy. I love a straightforward case. One villain inside, another outside conspiring with him. Find the evidence, Ian and lock him up.'

Price could tell that there was more to come.

'I want to pursue a couple of other lines of inquiry. I've read the papers from the appointment panel in Cardiff and I've spoken to the chair of one of the authorities where Laura Wixley applied for the chief constable position. When she called for feedback he told her they had reports of her husband's link to "villains".'

Price sat back in his chair, and glared at Drake. 'You're not *seriously* suggesting …?'

'And we need more background on the relationship between Laura Wixley and Justin Selston, who was the other candidate for appointment as a circuit judge.'

Price threw the ballpoint pen he had been clutching onto the desk. 'Christ, Ian, one is a deputy chief constable and another is likely to be a circuit judge.'

'I'd like you to authorise a full financial search and background checks against both.'

Price glared at Drake.

'You should be concentrating everything on Eaton being Zavier Cornwell's accomplice. There *must* be a link.'

'I appreciate that, sir. But we need to look at all the lines of enquiry. And one of the team is looking into the staff members of chambers and business links Nicholas Wixley might have had to Tom Levine. I've read the original file of the case involving Zavier Cornwell. The original SIO had no evidence to suggest there was an accomplice apart from his gut feeling.'

'Okay, I get the message. And there's nothing wrong with gut feelings sometimes. I'll authorise the searches you need. I just hope they will all be worthwhile.'

Chapter 25

Thursday 4th April
1.30 pm

Visitors thronged around the main reception area of HMP Marchfield. A notice screwed to a wall indicated that the afternoon visiting slots started in half an hour. The woman behind the desk gave Drake and Sara a blank, lifeless look as she checked their warrant cards. Then she made a display of re-reading various forms in front of her.

Self-important people like her always irritated Drake. The prearranged meeting and their warrant cards would surely have been enough to smooth the process. He leaned down towards the glass partition. 'We don't have much time.'

The woman looked up at him and tilted her head, making it clear she was in charge.

'And we need our warrant cards back.'

'When I'm finished, Inspector.'

The harsh Scouse accent grated on Drake, who chewed his lip: it was all he could do to stop himself from raising his voice.

Eventually she shoved the warrant cards back through a trough-like opening at the bottom of the glass partition and pointed to a door. They scooped up their cards and stepped towards it. It opened, and a burly prison officer spoke to them. 'Follow me, sir.'

He led them through a corridor to a door that he unlocked using a key on a chain dangling by his waist. It led through into the prison area. The place had a cool, antiseptic feel; muted voices filtered down the corridor, alternating with the jangling sound of keys inserted into locks. An office window in front of a metal gate slid open as Drake and Sara approached. A broad Liverpool accent boomed out. 'Please leave all your personal possessions and valuables in these trays. And that includes your mobiles.'

Drake and Sara did as they were told. The legal notepad and file of papers under Drake's arm went unchallenged. A different officer, shaved head and tattoos on his forearm, produced another set of keys that unlocked a gate. A jerk of his head encouraged Drake and Sara to pass through.

They followed the officer down a passageway until they reached another gate. Beyond it more prison officers gathered by an office door, laughing and joking. The officer who accompanied them exchanged a few words with another officer.

The original officer left them in the company of a man with 'Harries' printed on a name badge. 'You've come to interview Zavier Cornwell.' It could be a question or a statement, Drake wasn't certain.

'That's right.'

'Follow me.'

After another gate was opened and locked by Harries he pushed open the door of a room with 'Interview Suite 1' printed on a metal plate screwed underneath an aperture filled with dull Perspex. Glass would definitely not be used.

'We'll organise to bring Zavier Cornwell down as soon as we can.'

Drake drew his finger across one corner of the table, checking for dust. He dropped his papers on the surface. Three hard, uncomfortable plastic chairs stood by a table screwed to the floor. Lights built into the ceiling filled the place with a pale yellow light. The atmosphere was clawing and stale – no air conditioning here. Lawyers like Nicholas Wixley or Justin Selston used rooms like this to interview their clients.

They didn't have to wait long as two officers escorted Zavier Cornwell into the room. They released him from handcuffs and pointed to a chair.

'We'll be waiting outside,' one of the officers said.

They left, and Drake saw both men staring in blankly through the Perspex. A risk assessment had probably determined that the officers should stay near at hand.

Both sides of Zavier Cornwell's head had been shaved. It left him with a piece of auburn hair perched on the top of his scalp. Most prisoners Drake had met always looked undernourished and badly in need of sunshine, and from Cornwell's pasty appearance he was no exception. It made him look older than fifty-four. His gaze settled a second too long on Sara's face before scanning her figure. He turned to face Drake. There was an intense, unsettling expression on his face. Was it more than simply being excited at a trip away from his cell?

'I'm Detective Inspector Ian Drake and this is Detective Sergeant Sara Morgan.'

Zavier grinned.

'I'm investigating the murder of Nicholas Wixley. He was a well-known barrister.'

Zavier leaned forward, placing the threaded fingers of both hands on the table. 'Nicholas Wixley, of course. I was very sad to hear of his demise.'

Drake paused for a beat. 'You do remember Mr

Wixley?'

'How could I forget? He was the barrister who prosecuted my case. How did he die?' He managed a salacious, voyeuristic tone to his answer.

Drake hesitated. 'The letter 'E' had been stencilled into his chest. It was exactly like the circumstances of the murders for which you were convicted. The press called you the alphabet killer at the time.'

'I remember that very well.' Zavier preened himself. Drake hesitated, uncertain whether Zavier was going to say any more.

'You carved the letters A, B, C and D onto your victim's bodies.'

He gave Drake another grin. 'And how do you possibly think I could be responsible for murdering Nicholas Wixley when I'm stuck here behind bars?' Zavier raised an eyebrow. 'I know, I know,' he added in a rush. 'I've got a time machine in my cell. A Tardis, like Dr Who.' He waved his arms in the air like an orchestra conductor. 'I transported myself to north Wales and sliced up Wixley.'

His voice taunted Drake.

'The City of Manchester police force couldn't satisfactorily explain the circumstances of the various murders. The senior investigating officer at the time—'

'Ramsbottom.' Zavier made him sound like a long-lost friend.

'… believed you had an accomplice. Someone who assisted you in perpetrating the murders.'

'And why the hell would he think that?' Zavier snapped. 'Why would I need someone to help me? It was nothing to do with anybody else. He had a hell of a cheek to think I needed assistance. It was all my own work.'

'Are you protecting someone?'

Zavier guffawed. 'It was all my own work.' His voice drifted off, as though he couldn't believe anyone would suggest otherwise. 'Ramsbottom went on and on about it.'

Drake fumbled with the folder in front of him and removed the photographs of Nicholas Wixley and the crime scene. He set them out methodically, facing Zavier who leaned forward.

He beamed in appreciation and dragged them nearer to himself.

'The socks are a nice touch. After all, red and white are a good colour. Dad played for Rotherham for a couple of years.' He stood up and rearranged the images like a curator assessing the best arrangement to exhibit them. Seeing that the photographs hadn't shocked Zavier, that they had entertained him, emboldened him, Drake was sickened by Zavier's performance.

An intense frown creased Cornwell's forehead as he examined the funeral orders of services. Examining each in turn, he dwelled on the letters written on the inside in Wixley's blood. 'One of them French art films gave me the inspiration for the funeral material – shame the press never mentioned them at my trial.'

After glancing at Sara, who stared intently at Zavier, Drake turned to face him. 'It would help our inquiry—'

Zavier chortled. 'Help your inquiry?'

'You've been sentenced to several life sentences. And a minimum term of thirty years. If you cooperate there is every possibility the parole board would smooth your path to early release.'

Zavier leaned on the table. 'I know your tricks. I didn't need anybody to help me, Inspector. An artist doesn't need help. Did van Gogh have someone to help him when he painted them pictures?'

Sara straightened in her chair. Zavier continued. 'I don't know why you think I had somebody with me.'

Sara made her first contribution. 'Have you discussed the circumstances of your crimes with anybody here? For example, you might have told a cell-mate how you perpetrated the murders.'

Zavier shook his head very slowly and gave Sara a pitiful glance. 'You don't understand anything do you?'

'I've got a list of the prisoners that shared a cell with you.' Drake announced, adopting a businesslike tone, although he doubted it would have much impact on Zavier. 'A David Eaton was one.'

Surprise and confusion crossed Zavier's face. Drake had expected him to have shown contempt, a scornful derisive look, but instead he saw surprise.

'Did you tell Eaton about the murders?'

Zavier sat back in the chair, folded his arms in front of him and pulled them tightly to his chest.

'In the long hours you were banged up together you must have talked about your exploits. Boasted about your achievements.'

'Nice try, Inspector. It won't work. I don't even remember Eaton.'

Offering a sweetener, something to ease his time in prison, was the only option Drake had left.

'We are also investigating the murder of a Tom Levine.'

Zavier grinned wildly again.

'Don't tell me – F was printed on his chest.' He made an exaggerated movement with his right-hand, mimicking marking out the letter. He focused intently on staring at Drake, who continued. 'If you did provide information about your accomplice that leads to a satisfactory outcome, we could make certain your cooperation didn't go unnoticed. A formal report could be made to the prison service and the parole board. It might accelerate your transfer to an open prison and improve your privileges.'

It was Drake's last throw of the dice. Zavier sat impassively.

'You still don't get it, do you?' Zavier glared at Drake. 'Are we done?'

Drake walked over to the door, nodded at the officers to enter and turned to Zavier.

'We are finished, for now.'

Zavier smirked as he pushed out his wrists, inviting handcuffs to be snapped in place. Seconds later Drake and Sara were alone.

'What did you make of that, boss?'

Drake gathered his thoughts. 'He is one sick individual. But somehow I don't think he had an accomplice.'

Drake recalled Zavier's disappointment that the press hadn't printed details of the funeral orders of service. Perhaps they had been his calling card, like an artist's signature. Perhaps he was offended that a copycat was faking his work. Or was he simply a psychopath like the press described with a sick and twisted mentality?

'So, do you think it could be a copycat? Maybe Jamie Eaton and his dad?'

'We need to talk to David Eaton. But I can't help feeling that Zavier is a waste of time.'

Chapter 26

Friday 4th April
7.45 am

'Bore da, Dad.'

Drake loved to hear Helen's voice with her good morning greeting and it lifted his spirits when she spoke to him in Welsh. She sounded so grown-up, too grown-up, Drake feared, realising he still missed seeing his daughters every day. Sian had warned him in a brusque tone not to be long and, determined that he and his ex-wife had to make the best of their situation, he agreed. He kept his conversation brief, asking Helen about one of her school projects. Megan sounded tired, disinterested, with no more than a monosyllabic exchange; he tried to sound upbeat, unaffected by her tone. He reminded both his girls that he was seeing them over the weekend.

Drake tidied away his breakfast dishes, made certain the dishcloths hung neatly from the oven handle and walked through into the hall. He pulled at the fold of skin under his eyes, hoping he didn't look as tired as he had felt last night. He drew a comb through his hair, fastened his jacket and left the apartment.

He was walking down to the Mondeo when his mobile rang.

He didn't recognise the number. 'It's Norman Turnbull.'

Drake paused for a moment and pitched his head up towards the early spring sunshine.

'I'll meet you in the Plaza Café in ten minutes.'

The line went dead before Drake had an

opportunity to respond. Bloody journalists, who did he think he was – Jason Bourne?

The Plaza Café had a corner slot on the outskirts of the main street in Colwyn Bay. He pulled up a little distance away and scanned the cars parked nearby: all empty.

He crossed the road and over to the café. The greasy smell of frying bacon filled the air, with the loud conversations from a group of men in high-visibility vests sitting at one table, heavy work boots indicating a busy day on a building site.

He sat down. When a waitress came over he shooed her away with an excuse about waiting for someone to join him. He read the time from his watch, deciding he'd give Norman Turnbull ten minutes; after that he'd head over to headquarters.

Surreptitiously he scanned the customers. Two men sat alone, both busy reading a red- topped newspaper and supping enormous mugs of tea or coffee. Neither of them looked like a journalist, not that Drake knew what to expect.

On the other side of the café three women enjoyed their early-morning tea, taking turns to stare out of the window. When a minibus arrived, they trundled out. It reminded Drake of the excursions his mother would make for shopping in Chester or one of the outlet malls.

None of the other customers paid him any attention.

The waitress came back a second time. Drake offered the same excuse and glanced at his watch again. Ten minutes were almost up. Norman Turnbull would have to stop this cloak-and-dagger stuff if he wanted to be serious.

Drake made to leave as his mobile rang.

It was the same number again. 'What the hell are you playing at?'

'Seashore Café in ten minutes.'

Drake protested but it was pointless. The line was dead. He left the café and got back to his car. The Seashore Café occupied a small booth, no more than a kiosk really, on the seafront. His irritation with Norman Turnbull built to the point that unless the journalist appeared immediately Drake wasn't going to wait around.

He passed the Seashore Café, staring at every stationary car along the promenade. Turnbull had sounded tense, so Drake searched for somebody who looked hunted, troubled by the weight of the world. He parked a little distance away and took his time to walk over to the café. The proprietor was setting out metal tables and chairs outside, clearly hoping to encourage custom. Drake tapped out a message on his mobile to Turnbull's number. 'You've got two minutes to arrive.'

The café was empty. A woman behind the counter smiled at him, encouraging him to order. He trotted out his explanation about waiting for someone. He pulled out a stool from under a bench near the window and waited.

Moments later Norman Turnbull appeared, a disturbed, agitated look on his face, his eyes darting back and forth. His round, open face hadn't seen a razor recently; his clothes were dishevelled, as though he had slept in them. A battered canvas satchel hung over his shoulder.

'Have you ordered?' Turnbull said after demanding to inspect Drake's warrant card.

Drake shook his head and asked for a two-shot Americano. Turnbull rejoined Drake after ordering.

'What *are* you playing at?' Drake said.

'I wanted to be certain.'

'Of what?'

'I had to be certain you'd be alone. I don't trust anyone.'

'So why trust me?'

The question floored Turnbull. He sagged. 'I don't have a choice.'

Their coffees arrived, and Turnbull took a hungry mouthful. The caffeine hit settled the journalist.

'I've been investigating Tom Levine and his business dealings over the years. He was a gangster, a thoroughly disreputable evil person.'

'So, you won't shed a tear at his passing?'

Turnbull gave Drake a sharp, reproachful glance. 'You've got no idea.'

Drake needed an explanation. 'What do you mean?'

Turnbull ran the back of his hand over his mouth. He gave the staff in the café a glance, ensuring that none of them were paying them any attention.

'Tom Levine has dabbled in various nefarious activities for years.' Turnbull's quiet voice trailed off. 'He got into property development using a Midas touch to buy up tenanted homes cheaply. He then gives the tenants notice to quit and if they become awkward; he has a legion of unsavoury thugs to make life difficult for them. Eventually they decide to give up and leave.'

'Was he ever reported to the police or local authorities for that sort of intimidation?'

Turnbull raised a finger. 'That's where it gets

interesting. The local authorities were in his back pocket, or certainly the officers involved in enforcing the regulations he broke. And he was always on very good terms with police officers, in particular one Laura Wixley.'

Drake didn't respond. Reference to Deputy Chief Constable Wixley made it more compelling to hear Turnbull out.

'Levine owns a string of nightclubs and I'm convinced Nicholas Wixley was involved as an investor in Levine's business.'

Now he had Drake's complete attention.

Turnbull continued. 'There was a case a few years ago when the vice squad in Manchester were looking into a prostitution ring being organised by Tom Levine through one of his nightclubs. The rumour was that Levine brought in girls from Eastern Europe.'

'Do you mean he was trafficking women into Manchester?' Drake gave his voice a steely tone.

'I never got that far with my investigation. The vice squad inquiry never got anywhere. The whole thing was closed down because of operational priorities, resources having to be reallocated. Tom Levine was in the clear and from the intelligence I gathered he cleaned up his act. It helped of course that Laura Wixley was the officer in charge. She made it go away, she made certain that any possible embarrassment from her husband being involved with Tom Levine would never see the light of day.'

'Can you substantiate any of this?'

Turnbull reached down for the satchel. It had a large canvas flap that he unbuckled to produce a green folder. He held it tightly by both hands.

'This is part of the file I have. There are details of the companies Tom Levine owns. Nicholas Wixley was involved directly in one as a 'general counsel'. Go after the money – there'll be cash coming into Nicholas Wixley's bank accounts from Levine.'

'If Tom Levine is dead why are you so worried?'

'The Levine family have lots of friends, lots of associates and no doubt plenty of reasons to avoid me printing stories about them.'

Turnbull pushed the folder over at Drake. 'I made copies of everything on a memory stick. I don't trust computers. They could easily hack into my computer and destroy everything.'

'There's no way I can use any of this information unless I can get evidence.'

Turnbull nodded, as though he had been prepared for this question. 'There is a detective sergeant, former detective sergeant I should say; he's retired.'

He reached for his mobile and, finding a number, scribbled on a Post-it note from his satchel. 'His name is Jack Warmbrunn. He's expecting your call. And you should be aware that it's one of Tom Levine's limited companies that owns the office building occupied by Britannia Chambers.'

'Why would Mrs Wixley want to kill Tom Levine?'

'He was the last person that could have embarrassed her. You probably know that she wants to be a chief constable more than anything else in the world. It consumes her; it's her mission in life not to take orders from anyone. And with her husband out of the way any embarrassment he causes has disappeared. I'm guessing Tom Levine has a detailed folder on all the Wixley family shenanigans.'

Drake nodded. Turnbull had anticipated the question.

'All you have to do is extract a confession from her.'

It amazed Drake that Turnbull could contemplate such a possibility. When Turnbull left, Drake sat for a moment, a heavy shadow dragging its way into his mind, that Laura Wixley was involved somehow.

Chapter 27

Friday 4th April
9.30 am

Drake arrived back at headquarters, his mind on edge. He made straight for the board, ignoring the greetings that followed him from the team.

'I've just spoken to Norman Turnbull. He's the journalist on the *Stockport Times* who ran a story on Levine.'

'Did he have anything useful?' Sara said.

Drake tapped Nicholas Wixley's photograph. 'We need to trace the person in the red car urgently. She was with him the night he died. She could be the killer and perhaps she even killed Levine too.'

'I've spoken to all of the shops who stock the Michael Jason brand,' Luned said. 'No luck so far but there are members of staff that I haven't been able to contact. They should be available on Monday.'

Drake responded, still gazing at the board. 'Make it a priority.'

He turned his attention to the image of Levine next to Wixley. Both men were connected through the business Levine ran selling courses to aspiring property millionaires.

Drake sat down at the nearest desk and scanned the team's faces, bringing to mind his meeting with Cornwell the previous afternoon. 'I think Cornwell was a loner despite what Ramsbottom thought. He looked surprised when we mentioned David Eaton, and the suggestion he needed an accomplice riled him.'

'So do we ignore the Zavier Cornwell link? Do you

think it was a copycat killing?'

It seemed the likeliest solution. 'We put the Cornwell link to one side.' Drake got up and moved Cornwell's image to the far side of the board. He was still part of the investigation but for now he'd be in the shadows.

Drake's gaze drifted down to the face of Laura Wixley before he retook his seat at the desk.

'We don't know where Laura Wixley was on the night her husband died.'

'Or the night Levine was killed,' Luned added.

'So, we need to know why she was evasive about her whereabouts. Turnbull suggested she covered up her husband's involvement with Levine and that she would do anything for promotion. I'm going to requisition the City of Manchester force's file. It might make interesting reading.'

Drake turned to face the other images on the board. 'Selston was in the sailing club the night Levine was murdered and we know that he hated Wixley, who was appointed ahead of him as a judge. He is an odd character ...' Drake glanced at the image of Wixley and his university friends that Mrs Thorpe cherished. 'I wonder what went on between them at university. We didn't get to the bottom of their relationship.'

Drake left the Incident Room, dumped Turnbull's folder on the desk and rang the operational support department of the City of Manchester police force, who raised little objection to Drake's request for the Levine file. As SIO he could requisition any file from any police force. Asking for it to be available that morning met with a sharp intake of breath and initial prevarication.

'This is a murder inquiry,' Drake reprimanded the person at the other end of the telephone. The real reason for the urgency was to ensure that nobody had the opportunity to warn Deputy Chief Constable Wixley that the WPS was poking around into the Levine file. 'I'm sure I won't have to take it up with Detective Chief Superintendent Roxburgh.' Drake quoted the name of the senior officer in charge of the department whose identity an initial telephone enquiry had given him.

Drake bellowed through the door of his office into the Incident Room once a time had been arranged. 'Gareth, get in here.'

Seconds later Winder stood on the threshold. 'I need you and Luned to collect a file from the City of Manchester police force headquarters. And call this former officer.' He held up a scribbled note with the number for Warmbrunn, Turnbull's contact. See if you can track him down and find out what he has to say.'

Winder turned on his heels and raised his voice at Luned as he made for the door. A telephone call to Superintendent Price's secretary organised a briefing meeting later that afternoon. 'And you'd better invite Andy Thorsen, the senior Crown prosecutor,' Drake said to Price's secretary.

Drake sat back in his chair. Turnbull had certainly made him think. Clearly, something frightened Turnbull. Was it Laura Wixley? She came across as a tough, uncompromising senior manager. But was that really enough to justify making her a suspect and not merely a person of interest?

Before starting, he adjusted the photograph of Helen and Megan a few millimetres, tidied the columns of Post-it notes, reminding him of telephone calls he had to make. Drake began with a pile of photographs. He flicked through dozens of different images of strangers in the street, sitting at table in cafés and talking around restaurant tables, and there was even a set of a man feeding birds in a leafy square. Drake examined the back, but Turnbull hadn't been as fastidious as Mrs Thorpe with noting names. All Drake had was the date stencilled in one corner of the front of the image.

Discarding the images to one side, Drake thumbed his way through various newspaper clippings and financial reports from Companies House. Turnbull had made spider diagrams on sheets of paper, marking sections in yellow and pink highlighting. It was impossible to make sense of all the interconnecting information – only Turnbull could explain the detail.

In a plastic envelope Drake found a portable memory stick and he plugged it into his computer. He found more photographs. Hundreds of them. And then he noticed a folder entitled 'Wixleys'. He clicked it open and found dozens more images of Nicholas and Laura Wixley. Some featured both of them in meetings and there was one with Wixley alongside Levine on a stage with a large poster behind them advertising the company, promising the secrets of making a million by investing in property.

A second folder was called 'Kennedy'. Michael and Pamela Kennedy had been snapped from afar in similar locations to the Wixleys. The images that caught Drake's attention were a set with Holly Thatcher at a table near the window of a café. It wasn't one of the main chains and all but the bottom of the letters had been obliterated making it difficult to identify it.

A Google search against Tom Levine quickly showed Drake a dozen entries, all relating to individuals with that name, including several with Facebook pages. One man with the same name was a conductor based in a town in Germany, another was a basketball player in an unfamiliar American city. Dismissing most proved easy enough. Drake bookmarked those relating to Tom Levine. Nearly all related to his activities in the sailing fraternity. Tom Levine even had his photograph taken in a prestigious yacht club on the south coast of England. How many other high-flying barristers and judges had Tom Levine met, Drake pondered.

Drake found the website of the various nightclubs Tom Levine ran. The company that owned them was called The Happy Hour Chain. It promised the visitor an unparalleled experience to relax and unwind in superlative circumstances away from the hustle and bustle of daily life. It sounded ideal; Drake was almost tempted to visit.

Mrs Levine struck him as an uncomplicated woman reluctantly drawn into a lifestyle alien to her. The stiff, awkward look on her face in the photographs from the newspapers, when they attended official functions, only underlined how uncomfortable she appeared. She would probably have been more at home in front of the television watching a soap opera quietly sipping on a gin and tonic.

Norman Turnbull's articles in the folder painted Levine as a slum landlord who took advantage of his tenants. Several reported cases, where Levine had sued tenants, featured Nicholas Wixley as his lawyer, and

Drake sifted out the images, deciding to add them to the board in the Incident Room. Tom Levine's face smiled out at Drake from a YouTube video offering to make people property millionaires within five years. It gave them several lines of inquiry – the mystery woman in the red car; David Eaton, who would have known all about the alphabet killings from Zavier Cornwell; Laura Wixley driven by her naked ambition; and perhaps even Selston. Drake suspected they had a lot more to learn about Levine and the way the tentacles of his business empire interlinked. Michael Kennedy and his wife needed to be talked to again. And now Holly Thatcher's image had surfaced.

Sara rapping her knuckles on his door interrupted his thoughts.

'After Cornwell mentioned the orders of service I checked the prosecution file and a decision was made not to mention them at trial to avoid any hurt to the bereaved families.'

'So the killer knew some of the details that hadn't been made public?' Drake waved her to chair.

'Looks that way, sir. And the bank statements and financial background details on Nicholas Wixley and DCC Wixley arrived this morning.'

'Excellent, you get started on Laura Wixley's and I'll deal with her dead husband, as soon as I've finished this.' Drake patted Turnbull's folder on his desk. 'Turnbull had taken dozens of photographs of Michael Kennedy and his wife and of Laura Wixley. Some have them in restaurants and cafés with Tom Levine, and he took several in the sailing club. I also found others of Holly Thatcher.'

Sara gave him a puzzled look. 'Why did he keep

them?'

Drake shrugged. 'Another thing that's been on my mind is how the killer overpowered Wixley. A woman he knew might have tricked him into bed and then ...' Drake mimicked a slashing motion with his hand.

'But it might have been a man.'

'Yes, I know ... The evidence doesn't point to a struggle.'

'I don't think you can assume it was a woman. Do you think Holly Thatcher could be involved? She was quick enough getting us to listen to her in Nant Gwrtheyrn.'

Drake nodded. 'And we need to know what links Laura Wixley to Tom Levine. We'll review again once we've finished the bank statements.'

Chapter 28

Friday 4th April
9.23 am

Laura Wixley hadn't been able to account for her movements on the day before her husband was murdered or on the day he was killed. It convinced Sara that Laura Wixley was hiding something even though every part of her mind told her to be wary of suspecting a senior police officer. Tom Levine's links to Nicholas Wixley certainly added a new dimension to the inquiry. But enough to notch up the pace of the investigation into Laura Wixley?

Laura Wixley had several accounts with a high street bank in her own name and others jointly with Nicholas Wixley. Sums of money were transferred regularly between the accounts and Sara gawped at the amounts involved. How could anyone spend so much? Sara found herself daydreaming about her prospects of promotion and how far up the hierarchical chain of command she might aspire to. Detective inspector sounded very attractive, chief inspector even better, but she doubted many women made it as far as superintendent. Even with an inspector's salary, she could afford a new car and a decent holiday every year, provided they didn't clash with an inconvenient murder.

For the first couple of hours she fell into a routine of identifying the monies paid into Laura Wixley's bank account and the sums paid out. Quickly Sara realised that Laura Wixley didn't spend a substantial portion of her income. The monthly transfers into various savings pots were more than Sara's gross salary. There were direct debits to a wine company, regular purchases at a clothing shop in Manchester, as well as evidence of frequent visits to a restaurant Sara discovered had two Michelin stars and a waiting list of at least six months. Its fixed menu cost as much as Sara spent on food in a fortnight.

Payments over a two-week period the previous summer at various destinations in Cape Town suggested South Africa had been her last holiday destination. What surprised Sara were the regular cash withdrawals. There could be as many as three a week. She built a spreadsheet establishing that Laura Wixley withdrew £4,500 in cash from her account over the last three months.

In the age of contactless debit cards and Apple Pay on smartphones, it was difficult to imagine why she needed cash. By lunchtime, Sara focused all her attention on establishing a pattern to Laura Wixley's cash withdrawals. In the last twelve months they totalled £16,250 and in the two years prior £18,350. Sara had ten pounds in her purse. Everywhere she went took electronic payments and she had read that Sweden had decided to ban cash transactions at some point in the near future.

So, what had Laura Wixley done with all this money?

By early afternoon Sara finished building a spreadsheet that gave her an accurate picture of Mrs Wixley's withdrawals over the past three years. She scribbled a list of the financial records she'd need to requisition in due course. It read like a Who's Who of the main investment fund managers in the United Kingdom.

She had to speak to Drake, and, for the second time that day, she rapped her knuckles on the edge of his office door and stepped in. He was poring over papers on his desk, neat piles of Post-it notes indicating various different tasks in hand. She admired the neatness but knew that behind the rituals lay a dedicated and thorough detective. But having everything just so got on her nerves. Living with a man like this might be trying, and Sara guessed the fastidiousness had contributed to his marriage break-up.

'I've made some progress, boss,' Sara said.

Drake looked up. 'Good, so have I.'

Sara sat down.

Drake began. 'Apart from having a substantial income he was a real heavy spender. I found a regular pattern of substantial cash withdrawals.'

'It's exactly the same in Laura Wixley's bank account.'

Drake stared at Sara. 'How much money are you talking about?'

As Sara recounted the details Drake double-checked his notes before butting in. 'In the same periods of time Wixley withdrew £15,425 and £14,725.'

'That's almost £60,000 between them, boss.'

Sara guessed Drake was thinking exactly the same as her.

He cleared his throat and announced in a soft tone. 'What did they do with all that money?'

Drake frowned and when he said nothing, Sara continued. 'Somebody might be blackmailing them – perhaps Jamie Eaton or his dad? Nicholas and Laura Wixley tell him they are not making any more

payments. They demand more money. Wixley refuses –
there's an argument and they decide to finish him off.'

'But that doesn't match the premeditated nature of
the offence.' Drake ran a hand over his face as though
doing so rebooted his mind. Drake fingered the file of
papers on his desk. 'These are the documents Norman
Turnbull left. He got really paranoid and told me he
never stored documentation on his computer in case it
was hacked. One of Tom Levine's companies
specialised in property development. Nicholas Wixley
gave him the nod about a property being sold by one of
Wixley's clients. Levine turned a massive profit he
shared with Wixley.'

Sara whistled under her breath.

'There's a substantial chunk of money that comes
into his bank account at about the same time as the sale
of the property takes place.' Drake added 'And he
receives a quarterly payment from Levine's business –
presumably for his work as *general counsel.*'

'Is it enough to interview Deputy Chief Constable
Wixley?'

The door to the Incident Room swung open noisily.
Sara recognised Winder's voice as he approached
Drake's office door. He appeared with a box in his
hand, Luned behind him.

'We've got the papers you wanted.'

Sara followed Winder to his desk, Drake trailing
behind them. The first box was dumped onto Winder's
desk and the second on to Luned's. Both full of
paperwork, all needing hours of work. Drake glanced at
his watch.

'Did you track down Warmbrunn?'

Winder nodded.

Luned responded. 'He's a washed-up drunk with a jaded attitude. I don't think he'll be of any help.'

Winder continued. 'He wasn't that bad.'

Luned again. 'Yes, he was—'

Drake raised a hand. 'A quick summary only, please.'

Winder stiffened. 'He's got an axe to grind against Mrs Wixley all right. He hates her and most of the senior officers. He thought she interfered in their case. Destroyed a perfectly good inquiry.'

'Okay.' Drake turned to the boxes. 'Let's see how much we can do before my meeting with Superintendent Price.'

Two hours flew past. Telephone calls were ignored. Coffee and tea were left undrunk as they ploughed through statements, case summaries and opinions from Crown prosecution lawyers. A few minutes before Drake's meeting he summoned everyone into his room.

'Updates please.'

'The whole thing stinks, boss,' Sara said. 'They had enough to prosecute Levine and some of his cronies for people-trafficking. There was enough corroborative evidence from mobile phone tracking and from number plate recognition.'

Standing by her side she could sense Winder and Luned nodding slowly.

Luned was the first to respond. 'I found a memorandum on the file from Sergeant Warmbrunn. He recorded formally that he didn't agree with the decision not to prosecute.'

Winder added, 'I couldn't understand why Deputy Chief Constable Wixley got involved at such an operational level. It struck me as unusual. Was she protecting Tom Levine, boss?'

Sara gazed over at Drake, who hesitated. 'I came to the same conclusion from the papers I read.'

Drake stood up. 'I'm going to talk to the super.' He nodded at Sara. 'And you too.'

Wyndham Price spent the afternoon ignoring the email from the director of human resources at headquarters in Cardiff inviting him to telephone for a discussion about retirement planning and 'transitional arrangements', which Price assumed meant handing over his responsibilities to another officer. The reality of not arriving at work each morning opened up a bottomless chasm in his mind. Imagining someone else staring over his desk as he explained who did what and how things ran would be a torment, too much to bear. It would be easier to leave on a Friday afternoon, Price thought, and face a life of cruising with other retired couples. The prospect made him feel nauseous.

He shrugged off his rumination. The investigation into Nicholas Wixley's murder was the most challenging inquiry in Northern Division since two officers were killed on duty several years previously. Planning for his retirement could wait until this case was finished.

Ian Drake's request for a meeting meant he needed Price's support and requesting Andy Thorsen, the Crown prosecutor attend, suggested he was making progress. Having a deputy chief constable in the mix as a person of interest complicated things. He knew it shouldn't. Every person of interest, every suspect, needed to be treated the same, but it was never that simple. Negative headlines about the lack of transparency and fair play were the last thing he wanted as his legacy on retirement.

The daily emails from the chief constable or one of his assistants meant more pressure. Drake better have something positive to report, Price thought.

Andy Thorsen was one person Price wouldn't miss when and if he retired. The Crown prosecutor had the personality of a dead fish, and often in meetings Price had suppressed the desire to shout at him. Invariably Thorsen got the law right, which grudgingly earned him Price's respect. Drake, on the other hand, would be missed. He could be earnest and finicky but deep down Price liked him and trusted him too. He had worked with too many officers where lingering doubts over their trustworthiness had tugged at his mind.

The telephone rang on his desk and Hannah announced Thorsen's arrival. Early as usual. Price jerked his head at Thorsen after opening the door, inviting him into his office

'What's this about?' Thorsen settled himself into a chair around the conference table.

'Ian Drake wants to brief us on the Wixley murder case.'

Thorsen gave his watch a bored glance. Hannah knocked on the door. 'Detective Inspector Drake is here.'

Drake and Sara appeared behind her. Price waved them in and pointed to chairs before smiling acknowledgements. Thorsen sat expressionless. Sara deployed an enthusiastic expression ambitious officers used to impress senior colleagues.

Drake got straight to the point. 'I want authority to interview Deputy Chief Constable Laura Wixley. I need to ask her about her finances, which may have a material bearing on the investigation.'

Thorsen grimaced, ran his thumb and forefinger along his bottom lip and almost snarled. 'You do realise what you're suggesting?'

Price butted in. 'Of course he does. Detective Inspector Drake has been the senior investigating officer on several murders. You know that better than anybody, Andy.' Price turned to face Drake. 'Let's hear you out.'

Price sat and listened although occasionally Thorsen jotted some notes in a legal pad. Drake methodically worked his way through the questions he wanted to ask Mrs Wixley. Lying about her husband's family made Thorsen scribble furiously and kept Price's eyebrow raised.

'I'm still not convinced we have a motive,' Thorsen said. 'Are you suggesting she killed her husband to further her career and that she killed Tom Levine to shut him up, again to further her career?' Price looked over at Thorsen. It was exactly what Drake was suggesting. He continued. 'Because if you are it is very serious indeed. She's a senior police officer and Nicholas Wixley was a circuit judge. The public put their faith in the police, judges have to be respected. It beggars belief to think …'

'That's exactly why we've got to get to the bottom of what the relationship was between Tom Levine and Nicholas Wixley and his wife.' Price said. 'The public have a right to know that everyone is equal under the law.'

For another half an hour they reviewed all the evidence again. Price drilled down into every option. He wanted every argument rehearsed, every eventuality examined. Was he avoiding a decision? He wasn't going to rush.

Thorsen added, 'Have you consulted Assistant Chief Constable Neary at headquarters?'

Price turned to the prosecutor. 'I'll be notifying her of my decision in a conference call later.' Then he turned to Drake, sharing a glance with Sara at the same time. 'In the meantime, both of you have got a lot of preparation to do before an important interview.'

Chapter 29

Saturday 4th April
9.41 am

After arriving promptly at the senior management suite of the City of Manchester police force headquarters, Drake detoured into the bathroom and cleaned his hands, a ritual that soothed his mind. Then he drew a comb through his hair after adjusting the blue striped tie against his white shirt. Expensive furniture filled reception and there was a quiet, settled atmosphere Drake associated with clear thinking, and high-level decisions.

He wore his best suit, the one he reserved for meetings with the chief constable of the Wales Police Service or occasions where a good impression was called for.

On the journey that morning Drake read aloud several times a summary of their notes from the evening before. It hadn't relieved the tension gripping his chest like a vice. Even his pulse had settled into a sporadic spiking pattern.

Wyndham Price had telephoned Drake as they reached the outskirts of the city. His comments were meant to settle Drake's nerves, but they only made him feel uneasy.

A long corridor led off the waiting area where Drake sat with Sara. He imagined the chief constable and the assistant chief constables all with palatial offices. Behind one of the doors was Deputy Chief Constable Laura Wixley. She wasn't a suspect in her husband's murder, yet, but as a person of interest there were too many loose threads for Drake's liking. He wanted to tie them off neatly. Superintendent Price and Assistant Chief Constable Neary wanted Laura Wixley's involvement in the investigation to end, quickly. Comments implying the preposterousness of suspecting her dominated his mind, mixing with the harsh reality that policing imperatives dictated she assist with their inquiry.

Vases of freshly cut flowers had been strategically positioned on various spotless surfaces. They weren't the variety available in the nearest supermarket garage.

When a civilian walked down the corridor towards them, Drake's mouth dried until his lips stuck together. 'Detective Inspector Ian Drake?' The accent was cultured, educated. Drake looked up and nodded. 'This is Detective Sergeant Sara Morgan.'

The woman gave Sara a brief, noncommittal smile without opening her mouth. 'Please follow me.' She turned on her heels and Drake and Sara followed her over the glistening solid-wood floor to a door with a brass plaque – the name on it read Deputy Chief Constable Laura Wixley. A voice from inside invited them to enter after the woman knocked. Drake straightened, took a deep breath and walked in.

Laura Wixley stood up as Drake and Sara entered and she directed them to the visitor chairs. Two glistening monitors clinging to metal brackets were positioned at eye level. The size of Superintendent Price's desk always impressed Drake and he assumed that the further an officer was promoted the larger their workspace became. Papers might even get lost on Laura Wixley's desk, Drake judged.

She gave Drake and Sara a perfunctory shake of

the hand and sat down.

The black rim to the folds of skin under each eye suggested little sleep. Her lips still had that lifeless quality Drake had noticed when they first met.

'How is your investigation proceeding?'

'We've made one arrest of a man seen arguing with your late husband the day before he was killed. It transpired he was the son of a convicted killer your husband prosecuted.'

'I am assuming from your comments that he was released.'

'On bail.' Drake took a moment; he wasn't here for small talk or to discuss the confidential mechanics of his inquiry. After all, Laura Wixley wasn't an officer in his police force. But treating her like a civilian wasn't on the cards.

'How can I help?'

Drake ran his tongue over his lips. He would have given anything for a glass of water.

'Forensics discovered an amount of a Class A drug at your property. Was your husband a regular user of cocaine?'

The silence was sharper than any finely honed steel. Laura Wixley dipped her head slightly and stared at Drake.

'Although the man we arrested denied supplying your husband. It suggests Mr Wixley had a supplier in the Manchester area. We need to identify that person and eliminate him from our inquiry.'

'I cannot help you, Detective Inspector.' Her voice was measured and exact. But was she being truthful?

'Did you ever suspect your husband used Class A drugs?'

'Never.' The reply too quick, too emphatic.

Drake gripped the folder on his lap tightly. No surprises so far. He had expected a denial. How she'd react to his next questions would be interesting.

'Did you know whether your husband was expecting to see anyone the night he was killed?'

'He didn't mention anyone.'

Interviewing Laura Wixley was like walking into a cul-de-sac repeatedly.

'We found an item of clothing that we cannot identify.' He pulled a photograph of the pink gilet from the folder on his lap and pushed it over the desk. 'Do you recognise this?'

'No, I don't.'

'It's a woman's size 10.'

'Is that relevant?'

'We thought it might belong to a *friend* of your husband's?'

Wixley paused, narrowing her eyes. 'What are you implying?'

'We need to trace this woman and we hope you can help.'

She gave the image one final glance. 'I don't know who owns this gilet.'

Drake took a slow breath. 'A suggestion has emerged that your husband had links to nightclubs frequented by escorts.' Laura Wixley was a person of interest and he wasn't going to sugar-coat these questions. 'Did your husband use escorts?'

'If you're going to hurl that sort of allegation around about Nicholas you'll need more than innuendos.'

It made him sound like a Sunday School teacher.

Drake paused. He had to tread carefully.

'We're also investigating the murder of Tom Levine.'

Laura Wixley nodded.

'His body was found on Easter Sunday on his yacht.'

'I saw the news reports.'

'I understand you knew Tom Levine?'

Wixley stiffened, her face taking on a granite-like expression. Drake continued. 'I was hoping you might be able to assist us with identifying any possible links between your late husband and Tom Levine. Did your husband have any business dealings with him?'

'My late husband made a number of successful investments.'

Smoke and mirrors were not going to fly, Drake wanted to tell her. He decided to get straight to the point.

'Did you ever meet Tom Levine?'

Wixley paused. Was she calculating whether to lie? Working her way up through the ranks, she would have conducted this sort of interview dozens of times. Surely she would assume they had done their detective work.

'I believe I did on one occasion. He was being interviewed here at the central custody suite in relation to various allegations of fraud and intimidation of witnesses.'

Drake tightened his grip on the folder with photographs of Laura Wixley meeting Tom Levine. Only one way to find out how she'd react.

'So, it was only on that one occasion you met Tom Levine?' Before Drake reached inside the folder he saw the frown on her face. He pushed the photograph over the desk towards her. Her frown deepened.

'Do you recall this meeting with Tom Levine?'

'Where the hell did you get this photograph?' Surprise and aggression combined as Wixley raised her voice.

She stared at it, puzzled by it. Was she taking time to find an excuse? To find a rational explanation? 'It must have been at a restaurant. I can't recollect the name.' Vagueness, a sure sign of prevarication. Drake mellowed to the task of questioning Laura Wixley.

'What did you discuss?'

Wixley shook her head.

'What did you make of your husband's connections with someone like Tom Levine?'

'Tom Levine was never convicted of any offence. He ran various businesses. And my husband dealt with a lot of successful businessmen in his life.'

Another reply that didn't answer the question. Drake paused. 'But Tom Levine was investigated several times by your force in relation to money-laundering and people-trafficking. It must have been embarrassing when those investigations were taking place.'

Wixley took a moment to compose herself. 'Tom Levine was never prosecuted.'

Drake stared over at her. Did a shadow of uncertainty cross her face? 'We are aware of the case where Tom Levine was investigated in relation to people-trafficking, involving a prostitution ring at one of his nightclubs. Do you recall the inquiry?'

Wixley raised a challenging eyebrow before she drawled a reply. 'Of course.'

'A decision was made not to proceed with the

investigation. A decision you made. Can you remember how that came about?'

'I'm sure, Inspector, you realise I have dealt with dozens, probably hundreds, of complex cases over a thirty-year career. I'd need to see the file of papers to be able to give you a properly considered reply.'

Drake cleared his throat. 'We need to formally ask you to confirm your whereabouts on the night Mr Levine was killed.'

Wixley didn't blink or miss a beat. 'I was staying in our holiday home and I went out to Portmeirion for dinner. I got back home at about midnight. So, Detective Inspector, that doesn't give me an alibi for the small hours of Sunday morning.'

'I want to ask you about your unsuccessful applications for promotion. Have you received any feedback from the appointment panels?' No turning back now.

Wixley's jaw tightened. 'What the *hell* are you implying?'

'Being appointed as a chief constable must be a clear ambition, Mrs Wixley.'

'Ma'am,' Wixley snapped. 'You still respect my rank whatever you're trying to do.'

Drake took a moment to consider. She wasn't his ranking officer. He was the senior investigating officer. 'Has your husband's choice of friends and associates played a part in your unsuccessful applications?' Drake added after a pause, 'Ma'am.'

'Don't be absurd, Detective Inspector.' Wixley threaded the fingers of her hands together and steepled them on the table in front of her.

'That's not correct is it, ma'am?' Drake said

slowly.

She glared at him, forcing away an awkward swallow.

Drake continued. 'It was made clear to you by the chair of the North Lancashire appointment panel that your husband's links to organised crime groups was an impediment to your promotion.'

'I do recall him mentioning something.'

Drake kept her eye contact: obfuscation – her only choice really.

Drake moved on. 'When we spoke to you about your husband's family you told us they had died when he was a teenager.'

'Yes, that is what I told you.' Wixley's tone suggested her patience was running out.

'That's not true, is it?'

Wixley took a double take, leering at Drake as though he were mad. 'What the hell do you mean?'

'We've interviewed both his parents. So why did you lie to us?'

Wixley sagged back into her chair. 'I had no idea.'

Drake watched Wixley digesting the news – her shock genuine. Now he had the advantage.

'Nicholas told me … told everyone … they had been killed in a car accident. I shall have to contact them. Where do they live?'

'One of my team will ask them if they're happy for you to contact them.'

Wixley nodded.

Drake reached into the buff folder again and found the spreadsheet of cash withdrawn from Nicholas Wixley's account. 'We've completed financial inquiries into your husband's bank accounts.' Wixley stared at

Drake. Surely she'd have assumed that they'd scrutinise her finances too. 'One of the things we would like to understand is why there were substantial cash withdrawals in the two years prior to his death.'

He pushed the printed sheet over the desk. Drake couldn't read her reaction. 'Were you aware of the cash withdrawals?'

'Tell me exactly where you are going with this line of inquiry. Am I a person of interest?'

Drake hesitated. 'Can you explain the substantial cash withdrawals?' Drake reiterated, firmly determined not to be goaded by Deputy Chief Constable Wixley. He'd ask the questions.

'Because unless you are prepared to tell me if I am a person of interest I think this interview is at an end.'

Drake had expected her to stonewall him. It left him with no alternative. He took out from the folder a second spreadsheet, detailing the cash withdrawals from her account.

'You must appreciate, ma'am,' Drake began, 'we need to look at every possible line of inquiry. A substantial cash withdrawal from an account raises questions. We need answers. And ...' He pushed over the second spreadsheet. 'This is a list of cash withdrawals from your accounts. There is a combined total of over £60,000 in the last two years.'

Wixley gawped at the information in front of her. It surprised Drake she hadn't assumed they'd requisition her financial details.

'I need an explanation behind the withdrawals.'

Wixley pushed the two pieces of paper back at Drake with a defiant jerk. 'If you're going to treat me as a suspect then you'd better bloody well arrest me. See how far that gets you, Detective Inspector.'

Drake had hoped for a degree more cooperation but her belligerence wasn't unexpected.

'You were formally asked to clarify your whereabouts on the day before your husband's death. But you haven't been able to provide us with any details. As you can appreciate, ma'am, we need to know your movements.'

After a few seconds she nodded and the defiant edge to her face mellowed to resignation. She let out a breath.

'I was visiting my sister.' There was a serious tone to her voice. Drake shared a glance with Sara, busy scribbling in her pocketbook.

'Where does your sister live?'

Wixley looked up at Drake and stared at him for a moment. 'She's in prison.'

Now it was Drake's turn to be surprised.

'She was convicted of causing death by dangerous driving and she was sentenced to five years.'

Wixley never averted her eyes from Drake as she explained her sister's circumstances. After her husband had deserted her she drove home one evening after drowning her sorrows in a pub. But an accident had resulted in a cyclist being killed. A guilty plea quickly followed but prison was inevitable. Arrangements were put in place for carers to look after her two disabled children. Twenty-four-hour care came at a price that needed to be paid in cash. Sara jotted down the contact telephone numbers for everyone involved: all would be contacted in due course, the details checked, the prison visitor record analysed.

As Laura Wixley explained all the circumstances,

Drake could see how it had caused her such pain. A sister convicted of such an offence would be embarrassing, the sort of embarrassment an aspiring chief constable didn't want. No wonder she wanted to conceal the details surrounding the cash payments.

Wixley's face settled back into a defiant mould once she had finished. She was challenging Drake to challenge her back – as though she were goading him to find fault with her for looking after her family.

'Thank you for all the details.' He even thought of adding how he understood how hard it must have been for her but decided Wixley would judge it to be far too patronising. 'We shall need to speak to the various individuals involved.'

Wixley stood up, announcing that their meeting was at an end. 'And if I am no longer a suspect, you can both fuck off back to Wales.'

Chapter 30

Saturday 6th April
3.30 pm

Driving back to Northern Division headquarters, Drake dictated instructions to a detective sergeant based in Skipton for him to visit Laura Wixley's family. He had sounded less than enamoured with the possibility of spending Saturday evening travelling to an isolated farmhouse simply to establish that Laura Wixley's nephew and niece did exist and that a team of carers was needed.

'How long will you take to get back to me?' Drake asked after he had given the address.

Drake heard a groan. 'I guess it's a round-trip of an hour and a half.'

'Can't you call me on your mobile?' Now exasperation kicked in.

'There's no signal up there.'

Drake glanced at the clock on the dashboard. With any luck they'd be back at headquarters by then. 'Call me soon as you know anything.'

'It's got to be true, hasn't it boss?' Sara negotiated the late afternoon traffic on the outskirts of Manchester, heading for the motorway and the A55 back to Colwyn Bay. 'She's hardly likely to make all that stuff up when we can so easily check.'

Grudgingly Drake had to accept Sara might be right. 'I'm still not convinced she's telling us the truth about what she knew about Nicholas Wixley's family.'

'I agree that is very odd. After all, who disowns their family? It's not natural.'

Drake cast a glance down at the stream of lorries and cars as they passed over the M6 motorway linking Birmingham to Manchester and Liverpool and beyond to Scotland when an email reached his mobile. He read the results of his search of the police national computer.

'It's the result of the PNC check against Laura Wixley's sister. It checks out all right.'

Sara pulled into the same services they had used on the first return journey from Manchester and they ate another greasy burger and chips without saying very much. Drake could feel the tiredness nagging at the bottom of his back. His hands felt greasy, his shirt and clothes laden with sweat and the muck and grime from a full day in Manchester. The sergeant in Skipton had still not contacted Drake by the time they were back on the A55.

'What the hell is keeping him?' Drake said.

'I've been to Skipton once. I went with a boyfriend who wanted to go on the train that goes from Settle to Carlisle over the Ribblehead viaduct. He was dead keen on steam trains at the time.'

Drake glanced over at Sara. It had been the first time he had heard her mention a boyfriend even in the past tense. It made him realise that he needed to get to know Sara better. Annie had even suggested inviting Sara to dinner one evening. Drake had deflected her enthusiasm, but perhaps it wasn't a bad idea after all.

'What happened? I mean, between you and your boyfriend – not on the train journey.'

'He went to work in Poland on a big electricity plant. It sort of fizzled out after that.'

Sara pulled into the almost empty car park at headquarters and found a spot near the entrance. In the distance Drake noticed Superintendent Price's Jaguar. His spirits sagged, realising that he couldn't delay explaining the outcome of his meeting with Laura Wixley as a small part of his mind had hoped might be the case. No time like the present, Drake scolded himself.

As Drake reached the corridor leading to the Incident Room his mobile rang. He noticed the number he had used to speak to the Skipton police station earlier. Sara gestured she was going to make coffee and Drake nodded his encouragement.

'DI Drake.'

'It's exactly as you described, Inspector. There are two disabled children living in the property. There are carers there around the clock and all are paid in cash by Mrs Laura Wixley when she travels to see them. Laura Wixley stayed that Saturday you asked me to double-check. Apparently, she left some time Sunday morning.'

Drake reached his office and sat down. Why the hell hadn't Laura Wixley told them where she had been when they first enquired? It would have saved a lot of time, a lot of hassle. As a senior officer she should have known better.

'Thanks, send me a report when you can.'

Drake turned to think about Laura Wixley again. She had looked genuinely surprised when they had confronted her with details about Nicholas Wixley's family. Her amazement sounded authentic enough. He made a mental note to call them and ask if she could contact them. It was another part of the picture that told them Nicholas Wixley was a particularly odd individual.

Sara arrived with a coffee each. 'Sorry boss, no coffee grounds left in the kitchen.'

Superintendent Wyndham Price appeared on the threshold of Drake's office. Sara jumped to her feet. Price sat himself down in one of the chairs, waving for her to do likewise. 'Let's have the details then.'

By the time Drake had finished, a pained look had crossed Price's face.

'Why the bloody hell didn't she tell us that at the start?'

'Exactly what I was thinking, sir. She has an alibi for the night of Nicholas Wixley's murder, which means we can rule her out, and the night of Tom Levine's murder she was in her family holiday home having been out to Portmeirion for dinner.'

Price gave his skull a comprehensive scratch. It was an affectation Drake had seen often enough when the superintendent was flummoxed. 'I suppose it's not beyond the realms of possibility that she had an accomplice who conveniently does away with her husband while she has a gold-plated alibi.'

'Someone like Jamie Eaton?' Sara said.

Both men looked up at her. Clutching at straws often happened after a setback.

Price stood up. 'I'll talk to ACC Neary in the morning. You did well, Ian, and you Sara. There was nothing wrong in treating her as a person of interest. She should have cooperated much earlier. She should have known we'd take an interest in her. Someone like that doesn't deserve to be a chief constable.'

He made to leave but turned to face them. 'It's been a long day for both of you. Don't hang around, go home.'

Drake ambled with Sara through headquarters, intent on doing exactly as Price suggested. Sara turned to him as they reached the stairs for the ground floor. 'What do we do now, boss?'

'A good night's sleep and a day off tomorrow. On Monday we'll look again at Selston and the cases Nicholas Wixley was involved in and what links him to Tom Levine.'

'Somebody must have hated him badly enough.'

Drake's mobile rang. He heard Winder's voice. 'We've found Hector Murren's car.'

Chapter 31

Saturday 6th April
6.30 pm

Drake glimpsed the glistening beach at Trearddur Bay as he listened to Sara's directions. He passed a RNLI inshore rescue station on his left that dominated the small promenade and a whitewashed hotel on his right-hand side. Uniformed officers had discovered Murren's car parked behind the hotel, and Drake turned the Mondeo into a dusty, gravel-surfaced area. Two young officers sat in a marked police car alongside the Volkswagen Golf.

Drake parked, and Sara followed him as they joined both officers. Two large information hoardings had details of local attractions and walks around the island of Anglesey.

Force of habit made him peer into the car even though it was clearly empty.

'We were called to a domestic disturbance in a house nearby,' the taller of the two officers began.

'We spotted the vehicle and it rang a bell,' the young female officer said. 'We ran the number plates through the system and we were told to wait for you, sir.'

'Well done.'

Portakabins in one corner provided a makeshift office and reception centre for a company offering kayaking holidays. The place looked empty, shutters over the windows, the door locked. From the far end, the warm smell of baking and garlic drifted in the early evening air from a mobile pizza van.

'We need to find out how long his car has been here.'

Single-storey bungalows dotted the surrounding area. Drake expected Winder and Luned to arrive any second, so with Sara, himself and the two uniforms there were six officers available.

'Why the hell did he park his car here?' Drake said, not expecting an answer.

In the distance he could see the silhouette of a foreboding property built on a small promontory. It reminded him of the houses in villages of the Llŷn Peninsula – popular with the holiday home owners from Liverpool and Manchester. Drake turned to Sara. 'Call Murren's partner and ask him if there is any connection with this side of Anglesey. There must be a reason why he's here.'

Sara fished her mobile out of a pocket. Drake walked over to the pizza van. The two men running the food stall, a fit, active-looking pair, stared at the image of Hector Murren on Drake's mobile.

He gestured over to the Volkswagen Golf. 'He owns that car. We need to trace him urgently. Have you seen him?'

Both men shook their heads. 'There are dozens of cars that come in and out of this car park every day. We don't keep track of them.'

He pushed a business card towards one of them. 'If anyone comes anywhere near it – call me.'

Drake gave their pizzas a hungry look, deciding he didn't have time to eat. He paid for a bottle of water for Sara and himself and rejoined her as she finished on the telephone. She nodded at the hotel. 'They stayed here for a few nights last year. But otherwise he hasn't got a clue why Murren left his car here.'

Sara took a mouthful of her drink after thanking Drake.

Winder's car turned into the car park and after parking he and Luned joined Drake and Sara. Drake gestured to the two uniformed officers to do likewise.

'We need to establish if anybody in any of the nearby houses remembers anything that might link us to Hector Murren. And we need to do that this evening.' Drake forced into a dark corner of his mind the possibility that he would have to work tomorrow. He had determined to spend the day with Annie and his daughters. Nothing was going to prevent him, so tonight they had to find Hector Murren.

Both uniformed officers were tasked with visiting every house along the coast road. 'There's a big holiday chalet complex nearby,' the young woman officer said, clearly emphasising the scale of the potential task Drake was requesting. He ignored her.

He pointed towards the far end of the beach and then at Luned and Winder. 'Both of you get to the opposite end of the beach. Visit as many of the houses as you can.'

'Yes, boss,' Winder said with faint enthusiasm. Luned nodded seriously.

'Message me as soon as you know anything. Sara and I will visit the hotel and the restaurant nearby.'

Winder and Luned drove off.

En route Drake and Sara detoured into half a dozen properties; three were obviously empty and three more had owners who had recently arrived for the weekend and knew nothing about the Volkswagen Golf. Murren's image on their mobile telephones elicited blank responses.

Reception staff at the hotel beamed at Drake and Sara as though they were guests to be offered the best suite. The smiles became serious as Drake and Sara produced their warrant cards. The manager appeared.

'We need to trace a Hector Murren, whose car was left in the car park behind your hotel.'

'It is nothing to do with us,' the manager responded quickly. 'It belongs to the local authority.'

Drake produced the image of Murren. 'Apparently, this man was a guest some time last year. Has he been staying here the last few days?'

'We have hundreds of guests every year,' the manager started. 'It would be impossible to remember everyone.' He glanced at the face again. 'But I'm fairly certain he's not a guest at the moment nor in the recent past.'

Two women by his side squinted at Drake's phone, foreheads creased in concentration. Both shook their heads simultaneously.

'I'll send you the image. I'd like to speak to your bar staff.'

'Yes, of course,' the manager replied. 'Anything we can do to help.'

Drake followed him through into a bar area teeming with people eating and drinking. Luckily, the bar was reasonably quiet, and the manager motioned for the staff in turn to gather at the end. It took a few minutes for Drake and Sara to show the photograph to each of them.

After more shaking of heads Drake and Sara stood on the hotel car park in the evening gloom as the last of the sun disappeared over the horizon. Near the beach and next to the RNLI lifeboat station was another restaurant. 'Let's go.' Drake pointed in its direction.

After twenty minutes they had drawn another blank and they stopped to enjoy the view overlooking the sand as the tide lapped at the stone-clad promenade. Drake messaged Winder – *Anything to report?* He replied quickly – *nothing yet boss.* Uniformed officers gave him a similar reply. He heard a vehicle slowing at a speed bump and turned as he saw a van with the livery 'Anglesey Walking Holidays' hauling a trolley of kayaks behind it.

It caught Drake's eye and he thought about the information board near where he'd parked the Mondeo. It had details of the popular circular walk around Anglesey.

Drake watched as the van indicated into the car park where the Golf was parked.

And then he knew he had to talk to the driver. His mind leaped ahead, thinking that Hector Murren was walking around the island. His mobile telephone switched off, out of contact, especially from his overbearing partner.

'We need to speak to that van driver.' Drake announced, breaking into a jog. Sara ran ahead of him and she reached the van as the driver was busy uncoupling the trolley of kayaks.

'We need a word,' Drake gasped.

Sara showed him Murren's photograph. She didn't even sound breathless. 'Have you seen this man recently?'

'Yeah, why do you ask?'

Drake's heart drummed in his chest. He had to believe they had found Hector Murren before the alphabet killer.

'When did you see him?' Drake blurted out.

'He's doing the round-the-island walk. He was going to do the first half camping, so I've moved his bags to one of the bed-and-breakfast places we use. That was a few days ago.'

'We'll need the address,' Sara said.

The man reached for his mobile and scrolled through his contacts. Sara dictated a number and once it had been tapped in, he messaged her with the contact number.

In the meantime, Drake spoke to Winder. 'Get back here, Gareth. We know where he is.' Drake called both uniforms telling them to get back to their normal duties.

Sara called the guesthouse where Murren was staying. Drake's apprehension turned into real worry at her one-sided conversation.

'When did he leave?' Sara paused, sharing a grimace with Drake.

'So, you are expecting him back?' Sara nodded.

Winder pulled into the car park.

'He's staying in a village called Benllech and he's gone out for something to eat.'

'Does she does know where?'

Sara shook her head.

'For Christ sake. Let's get over there. He can't be far.'

Drake ignored all the speed limits along the A55 as he made towards the Llangefni junction that would take them through the countryside to Benllech. At this rate a journey of forty minutes would take significantly less. After negotiating his way through the town of Llangefni he kept the Mondeo in third gear as he tore through the country lanes.

He rarely saw Gareth Winder in his rear-view mirror and when he parked on the pavement outside the Bryngwyn Bed-And-Breakfast he didn't bother locking the car. He thumped on the front door, Sara standing by his side. He got straight to the point with the proprietor when she opened the door, not bothering to show her his warrant card.

'Where could he have gone for something to eat?'

His tone startled Mrs Wood, who stammered the names of three possible venues. Sara jotted the details in her pocket book. Winder drew up outside as Drake gave Mrs Wood his business card demanding she call him if Murren returned.

'He's probably at one of these three places.' Drake nodded at Sara, who announced the locations as they reached the car.

Winder looked jaded and Luned stared at Drake, an expectant look on her face.

'Sara and myself will visit the pub in the centre of the village – both of you get started on the other venues.'

On his way into the village Drake rammed the brakes on when he saw someone resembling Murren. Jumping out of the car, he ran over and called out to the man. When he turned to Drake, a puzzled look on his face, Drake apologised and dashed back to his car. 'Murren has shorter hair,' Drake said.

After an hour they drew a blank. No one had seen anyone looking remotely like Murren and Drake's increasingly irritable mood had earned him several brusque replies and dismissive comments. Murren was nearby and he had to be found that evening. Tomorrow Drake was spending time with his children no matter what, and the unproductive search become an obstacle in his mind preventing clear thinking.

Winder called Drake as he stood outside a café wondering where to try next. 'Someone has mentioned the Tavern on the Bay in a holiday park, boss.'

If he wasn't there the best they could do was park outside Bryngwyn B&B and wait. Unless the killer had found Murren first.

'Send me the details. We'll meet you there.'

After driving past chalets and static caravans they reached a public house and restaurant with panoramic views over the shoreline and the bay beyond. Drake gave the view a fleeting glance. Inside Drake and Sara made for the diners by the windows as Gareth and Luned searched the bar area.

Fearing the worse sickened Drake and he doubted that he'd enjoy his day off tomorrow unless he found Murren. The possibility the journalist might be sliced open would crowd into his mind.

Then he saw a man sitting alone preoccupied with an e-reader, a glass of wine on the table.

'Jesus, that's him,' Drake hissed as he barged past a waitress.

Sara joined him as they reached the table.

'Hector Murren?' Drake said, the sense of relief almost making him want to sit down.

Murren gave Drake a troubled look. 'And who are you?'

Chapter 32

Sunday 6th April

Drake ate breakfast that morning, recalling Hector Murren's comments that he needed time away from Barkley. It didn't come as a surprise. 'I should have left a long time ago,' Murren had said. How many people persevered with a failing relationship, Drake thought, reflecting on whether he'd been guilty of the same with Sian.

Drake had eavesdropped Murren's call to Barkley telling him he was safe. His voice sounded determined as though he was certain it was the right thing to do. After finishing he assured Drake he would travel to stay with his parents that morning.

Drake left the flat after breakfast to collect Helen and Megan. Sian gave him a suspicious look, honed over many years to a sharp edge, combining criticism with annoyance. 'You'd better come in. The girls aren't quite ready yet.'

Drake followed her into the hallway and cast a glance up the stairs as he heard the sound of activity. In the kitchen he sat by a chair near a pine table. Sian sat opposite him, a businesslike look to her face as she placed one hand over another on the table top between them.

'I wanted to tell you something. I'm seeing somebody.'

It didn't come as a surprise and Drake found himself unaffected by the announcement. Encouraging Sian to be less protective of Helen and Megan had been difficult, especially about meeting his half-brother and his family. Both his daughters were resilient enough to change, having experienced their family break up.

'I thought so.' Drake's admission might make it easier for Sian to share the details, lessen the impact somehow.

A mysterious trip to Berlin a few months previously and a recent weekend away suggested she was sharing her time with somebody new.

'It's Robin ...' Sian said and avoided eye contact.

Drake hadn't seen Robin Miles for how long? He recalled boozy evenings at Robin's home when the accountant would boast about the expensive wines he'd buy and his successful investments. Calling him a friend was a stretch but, even so, Drake was surprised.

'What about his wife?'

Sian looked up and reconnected with his gaze. 'They separated some time ago. She went back to live in Coventry.'

Sian being in a new relationship was one thing, but knowing it was with somebody they knew, had socialised with, was quite different. Robin was Sian's practice accountant. What did they talk about? The latest Bordeaux vintage and his net worth? For a moment, Drake hoped Robin's ex-wife had expert divorce lawyers that would made a serious dent in his finances.

'I see.' It sounded lame and ineffectual, but he couldn't think of anything else to say. How did Robin tolerate Sian's mother? He decided to leave that for another day.

'He wanted me to tell you. He was concerned you didn't hear it second-hand.'

Was Robin worried about his personal reputation,

Drake thought?

'How are things between you and Annie? Does she put up with all your little foibles? I'm surprised it doesn't annoy her.'

Just because Sian couldn't tolerate his obsessions and rituals didn't mean another woman couldn't. He was tempted to tell her that Annie was a completely different personality to her. Words like understanding, kinder, tolerant came to his mind but all implied a criticism of Sian. Even so, was Sian jealous? That prospect surprised him.

The sound of footsteps descending the staircase interrupted the developing awkwardness. When Helen and Megan walked in he stood up and hugged both his daughters. He ushered them out towards the car, promising Sian he wouldn't be late back.

Resisting the temptation to cross-examine the girls about whether Robin Miles was a presence in the house, he resolved to focus on making certain they developed their relationship with Annie – he wanted her to be a fixture for the future.

Reaching Annie's house exactly on time, he sensed the girls' apprehension as they gazed up at the property.

'There's a wonderful view of the Menai Strait from Annie's garden.'

Annie opened the door as they approached and smiled broadly. She showed them the small garden that looked over the Strait: it was a clear, crisp spring morning; the water glistened and the sound of halyards clattering against masts filled the air. Upstairs, standing on the balcony looking out over the water, Helen became more talkative and Drake felt pleased his eldest daughter seemed comfortable in Annie's company.

Megan maintained a slight aloofness. Like her maternal grandmother, Drake thought. After drinking Annie's fresh lemonade and eating a large flapjack each, Drake's confidence grew, that the day would be a success.

They left and an hour later were indicating for the entrance to Portmeirion. Annie engaged both girls in small talk, cracking the occasional joke, and Drake was glad that she pitched her conversation exactly right.

Driving down towards the hotel reminded him of his first meeting with Selston and Kennedy when both men had described Nicholas Wixley as well liked. It had been far from the truth. In fact, apart from Pamela and Michael Kennedy, all the employees and barristers disliked him.

'You're miles away,' Annie scolded him with a brief whisper.

'Sorry.' Drake smiled back.

Each building of the Italianate village built by Clough Williams-Ellis in the 1920s and immortalised by the fantasy series *The Prisoner* in the 1960s was separately painted a strong, vibrant colour. An ice cream mid-morning helped to maintain his daughters' interests as they strolled around gazing at the wonderful architecture. After a meal at lunchtime Drake relaxed as the inquiry and Laura Wixley and her late husband dissipated from his mind. Helen and Megan smiled as they enjoyed Annie's company and it chased away the last of his worries about his daughters and Annie getting along.

They reached the terrace overlooking the estuary and sat and watched as boats pottered around in front of them. A boat made its way towards a pontoon nearby, fishing rods hanging over the side. A group of men clambered aboard.

Drake thought about the pontoons in the marina in Pwllheli. The only direct access was through the gate guarded by a keypad entry system monitored by CCTV. But what if the killer had approached from the sea?

Annie's elbow digging into his ribs painfully reminded him he was having a day off. She gave him an angry look this time and he hoped the puppy-dog response would be enough of an apology.

'There's one more thing I want to show you,' Drake said.

He stood up and ushered them back towards the centre of the village.

'I remember *nain* and *taid* bringing me to this place years ago and taking me to the Hercules Hall. It's got this wonderful roof showing the Labours of Hercules.'

'What's the Labours of Hercules, Dad?' Helen frowned.

'It's from ancient Greek mythology. It's a story about Hercules, who had to complete twelve labours as a penance.'

'Penance?' Helen again.

'He had done something wrong, so he had to make it right. Like saying sorry.'

Opposite the entrance was a café that took the attention of both girls. 'It won't take long and afterwards we'll have something to eat.'

Inside they craned to take in the vaulted plaster ceiling rescued from a country house demolished in the 1930s. 'It really is quite spectacular,' Annie said.

'The ceiling was constructed in 1720.' Drake was pleased that a little bit of research beforehand made him sound knowledgeable.

Even Helen and Megan were impressed. But they were more impressed by the enormous cakes available in the café near the Hercules Hall.

Drake was disappointed when the day came to an end.

It had certainly recharged his batteries, refocused his mind. His daughters had taken all of his attention and, Annie, of course, but he should have been more prepared over the years to dedicate time for his children. Now, like Hercules, he had to make amends too.

Chapter 33

Monday 6th April
9.47 am

'I don't believe it.' Holly Thatcher stared at the photographs that Drake set out on the table in front of the young barrister.

'Do you know where the photographs were taken?' Sara said.

Thatcher didn't answer directly. 'This is all cloak-and-dagger stuff – like something out of *Midsomer Murders*. Who took these?' She shared a glance with Drake and Sara.

Drake doubted the fictional county in the popular television series was a good comparison, although he had never seen an episode. Wallander and Harry Bosch were more his taste. The café near Thatcher's apartment in Manchester bustled with men in open-necked shirts and laptops perched on small tables. Nobody paid them the slightest attention.

'We acquired them as part of the inquiry,' Drake said.

Thatcher gave the images another long glance. 'But who took them? And why?'

'Do you know *where* they were taken?'

Thatcher gave him a questioning look.

'Am I being stalked? Because it could be a serious matter. Do you have any more photographs of me?'

'We have no reason to believe your personal safety is at risk. We can't disclose any more details. Can you tell us where you were?'

Thatcher's frown made clear she wasn't happy

with the reply.

'It's a café in Salford. I take my uncle to meetings of Gamblers Anonymous – he lost his driving licence last year. You still haven't told me why these photographs were taken.'

'How often do you take your uncle?'

She shrugged. 'I suppose I could check my diary. Maybe once a month. Sometimes less often. It depends.'

Sara butted in. 'How long do the visits take?'

'An hour or so. I usually take some papers with me so that I can catch up with work.'

Drake fumbled for the photograph of Michael Kennedy in the same café and showed it to Thatcher. 'Have you ever seen Michael Kennedy in the café?'

She squinted at the image. 'No, I haven't … although I had heard a rumour that he liked a flutter. Who gave you these photographs?'

'I'm sorry, I can't give you any more information.'

Thatcher pouted and then finished the dregs of her latte before expressing surprise at the time and leaving Drake and Sara.

'That didn't take us anywhere,' Sara said.

Drake contemplated another coffee; after all, it was going to be a long day.

'We should get going, sir,' Sara said. 'We don't want to be late for Julia Griffiths.'

Their meeting with the head of Britannia Chambers was the second of the morning. His mind turned to Turnbull. A natural scepticism from years of policing had taught him to be suspicious of the journalist. His paranoia contributed to Drake's cynicism, but he couldn't simply ignore the link between Britannia

Chambers and Tom Levine. And Laura Wixley's shock at discovering a photograph of her with Tom Levine lingered in his thoughts. What had really happened?

Drake parked in a multistorey car park convenient for Britannia Chambers after the short journey from seeing Holly Thatcher.

Julia Griffiths wore a glistening, starched white blouse under the ink-black jacket that complemented the scattering of grey in her hair.

'We need to identify whether the murders of Tom Levine and Nicholas Wixley are linked in any way other than by the killer's modus operandi,' Drake said.

Griffiths turned a fountain pen with a blotched barrel through her fingers while keeping direct eye contact. Drake continued. 'Your chambers have a lease for this building.' Griffiths frowned now. 'And the landlord is a company owned directly by Tom Levine.' The annoyance morphed into outright astonishment as her mouth fell open.

'I don't know what you're talking about. We paid a substantial premium.'

'Your landlord is a limited company whose shares are owned indirectly through a series of other companies belonging to Tom Levine.'

Griffiths discarded the fountain pen and drew her chair nearer the desk. The telephone rang. She didn't give the caller any time. 'I know I have a conference, but this is more important. Tell them to wait.'

She turned to look at Drake. 'We paid £50,000 as an initial payment to secure the lease. I can't remember the exact terms of the rent but there is an escalating clause for the rents to increase every year. Our chief clerk dealt with all the negotiations.'

'Is it usual for such large payments to be made in advance?' Sara said.

'It was the basis of our commercial arrangement. We considered it sound business and we took independent advice about the rental payment.'

'When exactly was the payment made?'

Griffiths frowned. She reached for her mouse and let her eyes dart around the screen. 'We took occupation in September two years ago. So, at a guess I would say the payment of the premium was made a month or two before. Why do you need to know?'

'We still have loose ends with the inquiry into Tom Levine's death. His financial and business affairs were complex.' Drake hoped his reply deterred further questions.

Griffiths returned to fidgeting with her pen.

'Mrs Griffiths,' Drake started formally. 'The initial impression given to us by your colleagues made us believe Nicholas Wixley was well respected and valued in chambers. The picture we've built subsequently contradicts that. Were there any issues between Nicholas Wixley and the other professional members of chambers or the administration staff?'

Griffiths chided him. 'I hope you're not relying on idle tittle-tattle.'

Drake gave himself a moment to recall Holly Thatcher's comments that anyone in chambers would have been capable of killing Nicholas Wixley. He doubted a jury would call her evidence tattle-tattle. A natural defence mechanism kicked in for Griffiths, protecting her own, defending the integrity of her barristers' chambers.

'We may need to speak to you again.'

No outstretched hand now: only a simple, courteous nod dismissing Drake and Sara.

'Obnoxious bitch,' Sara said under her breath as they made for the administration department.

A red polka dot handkerchief was draped from the breast pocket of Michael Kennedy's suit at a rakish angle. He gave them an oleaginous smile and waved a hand towards his office.

'May I offer you some coffee? We've got this wonderful machine that produces the best cappuccino.'

'Americano, reasonably strong,' Drake said.

Sara added. 'Cappuccino will be fine.'

Kennedy scooped up the telephone with a flourish and dictated the orders.

'How did you get on with Mrs Griffiths?'

Drake tried to detect an attitude. Was Kennedy implying she could be difficult?

Before leaving headquarters, Drake had taken the opportunity to print off a list of Nicholas Wixley's most prolific and significant clients. He intended to check off every name and establish whether any of the convicted criminals had threatened Wixley or anyone else in chambers. And Drake calculated that while he needed this information, Turnbull's photographs and the financial details of the property arrangements were the real reason for speaking to Kennedy.

'We want to go through the list of Nicholas Wixley's clients we've identified as possible persons of interest who might have a grudge against him.'

Kennedy gave him another version of his unctuous smile. Coffees arrived, and Drake worked his way through the list. Kennedy pointed out names he thought might be capable of murder and others who were regular criminals.

Then Drake turned his attention to the photographs and the property transaction.

'Were you aware that the landlord of this building is a company indirectly owned by Tom Levine?'

Kennedy had made an exaggerated gesture of surprise. It seemed out of place, forced. 'I had no idea.' Kennedy wouldn't admit chambers had entered into a lease with a company owned by Levine, Drake thought.

'I understand all the negotiations for the lease were handled by you.'

'With the full consent of chambers management, of course.' Kennedy forced a tight-lipped smile. 'All these sorts of matters are dealt with by me. The barristers prefer not to get involved with the nitty-gritty day-to-day running of chambers.'

'We'll need to see the full file of papers relating to the property transaction.'

'Whatever for?'

Kennedy should have realised that any link with Tom Levine needed to be investigated. Before Drake could reply, Kennedy continued. 'The file is in storage; it has been for several months. It will take me a few days to be able to recover it.'

Drake stared back at Kennedy realising that he was being deliberately obstructive.

'Yes, please make arrangements.'

Kennedy gave a smile that died at birth.

'Did you know Tom Levine well?'

'Hardly at all.'

'How often did you meet him?'

'In the Pwllheli Sailing Club occasionally but otherwise I can't say our paths crossed that often.'

'I see.' Drake reached for the photographs of Levine and Kennedy in the folder on his lap. 'These photographs came into our possession recently.' Drake noticed Kennedy's lips tighten.

How would he react? Suggest the images had been doctored in some way? Bluff his way out of it?

His voice trembled a fraction and he caught his breath. 'Of course, I forgot. There was some charity event he wanted chambers to sponsor and I was discussing the details with him.'

'How often did you meet?'

'I cannot possibly remember.'

Good move – covering his back.

'More than once?'

'I'm sorry, Inspector, I simply cannot recall.'

Drake allowed a pause to hang in the air. Kennedy blinked away his discomfort.

'When we initially spoke to you, it was made clear to us that Nicholas Wixley was a well-liked and valued member of chambers, but that's not true, is it?'

Kennedy made a flouncy attempt at looking offended. 'There were never any complaints about him. I always got on well with him.'

'Again, that's not strictly true either, is it, Mr Kennedy? Several members of chambers have complained to us about Wixley's behaviour, describing him as obnoxious and odious. Were you glad to see him appointed as a circuit judge?'

The door to the office opened after a brisk businesslike tap and Pamela Kennedy swept in before Kennedy could reply. She gave Drake and Sara an inquisitive glare as though she were surprised to see them, which Drake found hard to believe.

'Good morning.' She gave Drake and Sara a brief nod.

'DI Drake was asking about any of Nicholas' clients that may have been likely killers.'

'Where do you start?' Pamela drew up a chair. 'He defended so many of the crème de la crème of the Manchester underworld it could be a long list.'

Her husband nodded. 'We could go through the list for you if that might help.'

Pamela added. 'Do send it to me and I'll see if I could suggest any likely culprits. And we could ask our colleagues.' She even smiled.

'I was telling Inspector Drake that I'd completely forgotten that I'd met Tom Levine to discuss the charity fundraiser.' Kennedy fingered the photographs on his desk.

Pamela gave them a cursory glance. 'I remember that – it was a great evening – very successful.'

'When did you both see Tom Levine last?'

Kennedy and his wife shared a glance and shrugged.

'I can't remember,' Kennedy said.

'Did you see him at the sailing club the night he was killed?'

'Oh, yes, come to think of it he was there ...'

More half-truths Drake thought as he recalled Dot Levine telling them she had seen the Kennedys deep in conversation on the night her husband was killed. Why did he have a feeling the Kennedy's were hiding something ...?

It was early afternoon when Drake and Sara found themselves outside Britannia Chambers. 'Let's find somewhere to eat,' Drake said.

'Michael Kennedy was lying through his teeth, boss.'

Drake nodded his agreement. He was hungry, and he needed to spend time computing everything they had learned that day. 'These barristers live in a world where covering your back is commonplace; it makes it tough to see who's telling the truth. We need to get to the bottom of the connection between Levine and Britannia Chambers.'

Chapter 34

Monday 6th April
10.45 am

Mid-morning arrived, Winder organised coffee for Luned and himself and got back to researching Tom Levine. Wixley had been foolish to associate with Levine and, returning to his desk, he settled down to more Google searches.

On the second page the name Euan Levine appeared. Intrigued, Winder clicked it open. Euan Levine was being prosecuted for a complex VAT fraud and Winder's interest was sharpened; he blanked out the noise from the Incident Room. He was about to bookmark the page as another small cog in the bigger picture of Tom Levine's life when he read 'prosecuting barrister, Justin Selston'. The rest of the article disappeared into a blur. He needed to find out what exactly this case was about. And more importantly, how Justin Selston fitted into Tom Levine's life.

Winder took an hour to track down Joe Young, the senior Crown prosecutor responsible for the case against Euan Levine.

'I'm investigating the death of Tom Levine. A barrister called Nicholas Wixley was murdered a few days before him and there's a possibility both deaths may be connected. Was Tom Levine involved in your case?'

'He doesn't feature at all. It's his nephew who's in the frame. It's a complicated cross-border fraud involving mobile telephones.'

'I understand the prosecuting barrister is Justin

Selston.'

Young took it as a question.

'He's a stuffy old character, real old-school but he's got great attention to detail. Having said that, the defence lawyers are extremely well organised.'

'What do you mean?' Winder didn't like the sound of the last remark.

'We've been preparing the case for months. Euan Levine has been interviewed several times and every time we thought we had all the bases covered he outmanoeuvred us, offering an explanation that suggested he knew exactly what we were doing.'

'Are you suggesting some sort of leak?'

'I can't say. It certainly felt like that. It was frustrating because Euan Levine was prepared for us at each stage.'

Winder finished the call but the sense there was far more to the relationship between Tom Levine and Nicholas Wixley lingered. Something made him decide to call Dot Levine. She might be able to offer more information.

'What do you want?' Dot Levine said after he had been as polite as possible.

'I need some background and I hope you might assist. Did your husband know a Justin Selston?'

'He's the barrister prosecuting Tom's nephew, Euan, isn't he?'

'And did Tom ever talk about him?'

'What do you mean? Like they were best buddies or something? You people never stop do you?'

Winder needed to sound helpful and he wasn't doing a good job at the moment. 'Mrs Levine, I do appreciate this is a difficult time, but we believe the death of your husband and Nicholas Wixley are linked. Is there anything you can tell us about comments your husband made about the case against Euan?'

She sniggered. 'Just that Euan didn't have to worry.'

Luned found the whole investigation daunting, intimidating even. She had been brought up to believe that police officers and judges should be completely above reproach. They were all pillars of society, people her parents and their generation looked up to. It was inconceivable they were contemplating treating a deputy chief constable as a person of interest. Being a senior police officer and a judge surely meant certain values had to be maintained.

Luned had made few contributions during the various team meetings. The implications of what had taken place, who had been murdered and the possible suspects frightened her. Her parents were a quiet, law-abiding couple with a deep commitment to doing things properly, treating everyone with dignity. Her father nearly always turned off television programmes in which swearwords were used. And her mother always treated Sunday as a day of little activity. Sharing the most basic details with them about the inquiry was awkward – she knew how it would have shocked them.

She had spent hours contacting the shops that stocked the Michael Jason brand and hours more talking to staff members, hoping she could track down the shop that had sold the item and its buyer.

DNA results from the fibres and strands of hair recovered had proved inconclusive. It simply meant the owner wasn't known to the police. Luned read the DNA test result again, imagining what the person looked like. The recommended retail price was over £150, which suggested someone with deep pockets, and a good dress sense with a figure to match.

Since Nicholas Wixley's murder each of the outlets on a list of stores in Manchester had been contacted and, frustratingly, several gilets had been sold. Luned had a list of customers from half of the shops. She had spent hours the previous week calling each in turn, prepared with a standard list of questions.

Had they purchased a pink gilet?

Did they know a Nicholas Wixley?

Could they provide their whereabouts for the day of his death?

Over half of the list still had their gilets hanging in wardrobes. Three had been given as gifts, one had been chewed by an angry Alsatian and one had been stolen. Luned hoped that morning she would have better luck with the stores in Liverpool. She found the list of stores in the Liverpool area as well as a store in Altrincham, Chester and Knutsford that were still left to contact. All of the stores had been supplied with stock in the previous two months and all had received preliminary emails inquiring about sales of the pink gilet.

The shop in Chester was first on the list. The store manager became dismissive when Luned asked if she had a list of customers.

'I haven't thought about it. We haven't got time to do that sort of thing.'

'This is a murder inquiry, madam.'

'Yes, I understand that, but we get hundreds of people in here every week – we can't possibly keep track of everybody.'

'Please make certain you remind all your staff.'

Grudgingly the woman confirmed her agreement, but it sounded half-hearted. This really was needle-in-a-very-large-haystack time. After she typed out an email attaching to it a photograph of the garment, Luned made a note in the calendar on her computer to call again in two days. Then she changed her mind and set a reminder for the following day.

The shop manager in the Altrincham store had a far more cultured drawl than her counterpart in Chester. She spun various platitudes that annoyed Luned. The outcome was the same – the staff couldn't identify any customer who bought the item. Next was a shop in Knutsford.

Luned recalled a visit to the small, well-to-do town a few months previously with her mother, and promising themselves to return for a longer visit. A friendly-sounding voice at the other end of the telephone interrupted her daydreaming.

'I need to speak to Joan Baker,' Luned said, reading from the details on her monitor.

'Yes, dear, that's me.'

Luned made the appropriate introductions, and reminded Baker that someone had spoken to her previously and that she had received an email inquiry about the pink gilet.

'Of course, I remember. We're a small, bespoke outfitters here. We don't stock many of those items. I did ask the staff if they could remember who bought it. They were very popular.'

Luned's enthusiasm sagged. Another dead end like the Chester and Altrincham stores.

'One of the girls thought she remembered who might have purchased one of the gilets. A lot of our customers are visitors, but Jeanette was convinced she had seen a woman who bought one with her husband or boyfriend walking past the shop last week.'

'Last week?' Luned's pulse missed a beat but she kept her voice calm. 'Is Jeanette with you now?'

'Yes, she's just finishing with a customer.'

Luned could barely contain her enthusiasm. There was the sound of movement down the telephone and an exchange of words. Finally, she heard her name being mentioned.

A young woman's voice spoke down the phone. 'It's Jeanette here.'

'Detective Constable Thomas.' Luned forced a serious note into her voice.

'I saw one of the customers who bought a gilet. And when Joan mentioned the email, well, it sort of lodged in my mind. I've got a good memory for faces and they were such a nice garment. I wish I could have afforded one myself.'

'Yes, thank you, Jeanette. What can you tell me?'

'I've seen her twice since she was in the shop. The first time she was with her husband walking into the hotel opposite. They do this special lunchtime meal. I know it's expensive, but it is lovely food.'

'And the second time?' Luned's lips ran dry.

'I saw her getting into her car. It was one of those Mercedes sports cars. There are lots of them around the town. It was a lovely red colour.'

'Do you know if she went into any of the other

shops?'

'I can't tell you.'

'Do you recall seeing her in the shop before?'

'No.'

Luned sensed this lead was busy fizzling out.

'And I don't suppose you know her name?' Luned added, without any real hope of a positive reply.

'No, sorry. But I did make a note of the number plate.'

Chapter 35

Monday 6th April
3.35 pm

'Good work, Luned,' Drake said, after listening to her update. 'What's her name?'

'Mandy Forsyth.'

'Email me the address and contact details. Do you have a telephone number?'

'No, sir.'

'We'll pay her a visit this afternoon. Do we know anything about her?'

'Nothing on the PNC, sir and I'm waiting intelligence from the City of Manchester police force.'

'Thanks, Luned.'

Moments later an email reached his mobile with an attachment: Mandy Forsyth's driving licence. Finding and interviewing her was a priority. Drake glanced at his watch. He would text Annie before leaving the café, telling her he wouldn't be able to Skype that evening. A sense of loss that he wouldn't speak to her and see her face and warm to her smile made him realise how much he valued the relationship. How much he hoped things would develop in the future.

Ten minutes later, texting completed, he settled the bill and returned to his Mondeo with Sara. His mother had persuaded him he needed something more practical *than* ~~them~~ the Alfa GT to ferry his daughters around on the weekends he saw them. Even so, a Mondeo was boring, and he missed the buzz and simple enjoyment the sports car gave him.

Sara punched the postcode into the satnav. Drake

cursed as he realised he hadn't listened to the disembodied voice telling him where to indicate. At one point he took a wrong turn and listened to the announcement that a route recalculation was underway. But it meant negotiating a convoluted journey around a one-way system that eventually brought them back onto the main road they had just left.

Drake glanced at the screen of the satnav as though by sheer willpower it would direct him to Lakeland Towers. The name implied a rural location, but nothing suggested a country setting from the rows of tower blocks that lined an old industrial canal. Raised beds constructed from lengths of recycled railway sleepers had been planted with spring flowers.

Window boxes hung from the occasional balcony. Faux wooden panels added colour and texture to the bland external concrete render. Drake toured around the car park for any sign of the Mercedes coupe. Eventually he drew the car onto the grass verge and called the Incident Room.

Luned answered the call. 'We've been able to trace Mandy Forsyth to the address you've got, boss. She has owned the flat for five years. Paid for it in cash.'

'And is there anything known about her through the City of Manchester force?'

'Gareth is still chasing.'

Drake thanked Luned and rang off. He turned to Sara. 'She paid cash for her flat a few years ago.'

Sara raised a quizzical eyebrow. 'So, what do you think Mandy Forsyth does for a living, boss?' There was enough insinuation to make clear Sara knew the answer.

'Flat bought for cash. Mercedes coupe. It all

suggests she's a high-end escort.'

Sara nodded. They left the car. The numbering system at Lakeland Towers soon vexed Drake. The first block they approached was Block A with flats one to ten. Logically Drake hoped the next block would be B with flats 1 to 10 but it was H with flats 15 to 25. They were looking for Block C, flat 12.

While Drake made for the next apartment block, Sara spoke to a tall, thin man walking towards a car. Sara joined Drake as he stood outside Block L, despairing of the lettering and numbering system.

'The man I spoke to had no idea where Block C could be.'

'Bloody annoying numbering system. How the hell do people find their way around?'

The absence of residents irritated Drake as well. 'Is everyone at work?'

He took the initiative and paced through a covered alleyway, deciding it was sheer potluck if he could find Block C.

Luckily they found a plan of the estate screwed to a wall. Drake heaved a sigh of relief as he saw Block C nearby. 'Let's go. I hope she's at home.'

A couple deep in conversation left Block C before the door closed behind them and Drake and Sara slipped inside without having to trouble the video entry system. It was quiet apart from the dull hum of televisions and the occasional sound of muted conversation. They took the stairs to the second floor.

They stood outside the door of flat 12 for a moment, listening. Drake turned his head and put his right ear nearer the door; he heard a television inside. He pressed the doorbell. A discreet jingle played.

Instantly the sound inside muted. Drake sensed the presence of a body on the other side of the door looking at him.

'Who is it?' It was a woman's voice.

Drake took a step back and held up his warrant card, hoping the person behind the door could see it clearly. He kept his voice low. 'My name is Detective Inspector Drake from the Wales Police Service. We'd like to speak to you, Mandy.'

Silence.

Was Mandy Forsyth thinking how the hell they'd tracked her down? Could I lie? Do I really want to be involved in a murder investigation?

A security chain was pulled into place before the door eased open. Drake and Sara held their warrant cards aloft long enough for the woman on the threshold to read them carefully. 'Are you Mandy Forsyth?' Drake said.

She nodded. Obviously satisfied, she unfastened the safety chain that clattered against the rear of the door.

'Come in.'

Sara followed Drake into the hallway and Mandy closed the door behind them.

She led them into a sitting room with a small balcony occupied by a plastic chair and two expensive-looking ornamental trees. Forsyth waved a hand to comfortable leather sofas. She sat on a recliner nearby. She wore no make-up, her hair needed attention and her baggy tracksuit bottoms and white T-shirt suggested she wasn't going out that evening.

'We're investigating the death of Nicholas Wixley.'

'How did you find me?'

Drake paused and Sara offered the explanation. 'We tracked you down through the shop where you bought the gilet.'

Forsyth nodded politely. 'Of course.'

'Why haven't you come forward to tell us you were with Nicholas Wixley on the night he died?'

Forsyth sagged into the chair as though Drake had punched her in the solar plexus.

'He was one of my regulars.' Her gaze drifted towards a large, modern, abstract painting hanging on the wall.

'I take it you're an escort. And how often did you see Nicholas Wixley?'

Forsyth nodded. 'By appointment only of course. And I'd see him once a month. He was generous. And very … energetic.' Although she had chosen her words carefully, it still sounded deadpan.

'And had you been to his holiday home previously?'

She shook her head. 'He had … an interest in … having sex in different places. It was a big turn-on for him. And I thought it would be nice to have a day in Wales.'

'Why didn't you stay overnight?'

She gave Drake a quizzical look. 'I never stay overnight.'

'So why didn't you contact us when you learned that Nicholas Wixley had been murdered?' Drake detected an edge to Sara's voice.

Forsyth threaded the fingers of both hands together and clasped them tightly. 'I didn't want to get involved.'

'Involved?' Now Sara sounded incredulous. 'A man has been killed and you were there on the night.'

'It's not that easy.'

It never is, Drake thought. 'Look, Mandy, if you're not going to cooperate with us and tell us exactly what you know then we'll treat you as a suspect. We can interview under caution in our area control custody suite. And before we leave we'll need a DNA sample.'

She blinked at the realisation of the seriousness of her position. 'I heard him talking on the telephone. I only heard one side of the conversation. He told the other person to be very careful and he had all the information he needed safely stored away. If that other person did anything stupid then he'd share all the personal details. He made it sound ominous.'

Drake frowned. Without knowing who Wixley was talking to it would be impossible to identify the caller. Drake wracked his recollection for details of any calls received on Wixley's mobile: an untraceable pay-as-you-go number called him on the evening he was killed.

'Could you tell whether it was a man or woman he was talking to?'

Forsyth shook her head.

'What time was that call?'

Forsyth looked over at him blankly, clearly unable to recall.

'What was Wixley like after this telephone conversation?'

'Hyped up. I've noticed an aggressive streak in him before.' Forsyth breathed out deeply before continuing. 'I've seen Nicholas with other girls when he was in some nightclubs. And he was friends with a man called Tom Levine.' She let the name hang in the air while staring at Drake and Sara. 'So, when I learned what had happened to Tom Levine it was too much of a coincidence. I got scared.'

Her voice trembled, and Drake read the concern on her face.

'I knew I'd left the gilet. That's why I went back to look for it.'

'You went back?' Sara said.

Drake butted in. 'But you left it there.'

'I didn't go in. Somebody was standing by the front door. So, I left.'

Drake's hands felt clammy: Mandy might be their only eyewitness.

'Can you describe this person?'

Forsyth gave them a detailed description of the man she had seen. Before she finished Drake frantically tapped into his mobile telephone the details of where exactly an image of the man she described could be found. He tapped on the website of Britannia Chambers scrawling through to the face of Justin Selston.

'Is this the man you saw in Nicholas Wixley's home on the night he was killed?'

Forsyth nodded.

Chapter 36

Tuesday 7th April
5.56 am

Drake woke before six, his mind racing. The dream that ruined his sleep had Justin Selston and Nicholas Wixley in a Crown Court, arguing about some point of law. When their argument intensified, both barristers lashed out at each other. The lawyers' wigs went flying as fists connected with cheeks before they crashed around the benches where they stood.

Drake swung his legs out of the bed and sat for a moment chasing the dream into the abyss. Convinced sleep would elude him, he got up. Dragging on a pair of jeans, a sweater and some old trainers he set off, tramping the streets, hoping the fresh air and the morning activity would focus his thoughts. Delivery trucks and vans were parked on pavements replenishing stock for the shops and cafés. Early-morning dog-walkers passed him as well as a lone jogger.

When he reached the promenade, he stopped and watched the sea lapping against the shingle. Selston and Wixley returned to his thoughts. Both men studied at university together. Both men had practised from the same chambers. Why had Selston lied about seeing Wixley the night he was killed? Had his jealousy boiled over into something much worse?

A man appointed as a circuit judge should have been more liked, even respected, Drake thought. But personableness wasn't in the job description. His conversation with Mr and Mrs Thorpe, telling them Laura Wixley knew nothing of their existence, was made more depressing by their numb reaction. They had become immune to the harsh bullets life could shoot at them. Reluctantly they had agreed to meet her, and Drake wondered what they'd find to talk about. Bearing the loss of a child challenged the natural order of things but at least they could meet their son's widow and it might give them some closure, perhaps also a degree of reconciliation.

He picked up a handful of small stones and hurled them one at a time into the still surface of the Irish sea. The death of a circuit judge had certainly created headlines although the initial news frenzy had died down. The press would go into meltdown if they knew Deputy Chief Constable Wixley was a person of interest. Once Superintendent Price and the Crown prosecutor knew an eyewitness existed, Drake fully expected them to agree that Selston be arrested.

Back in his flat he showered and breakfasted and left for headquarters.

The Incident Room was empty when he arrived. He leaned against a desk, deciding Laura Wixley needed to be moved from her prominent position and relegated to one side. A grainy image from Mandy's driving licence replaced the A4 sheet with 'mystery woman' written on it. The faded photograph of Wixley and his university friends took his attention and he wondered what they could tell the inquiry about Selston and Wixley.

Sara was the first to arrive. She looked healthy, healthier than he felt despite his early-morning exertions. She dumped her bag on the desk and sat down.

'Morning, sir.'

'We need to fill in a lot more of Selston's

background before we can contemplate an arrest. See if you can find out more about Selston and Wixley from their student days.'

Drake had settled back at his desk, intending to call Phillips, the harbour master, at Pwllheli, wanting to satisfy himself that the killer could have got access to the marina from the sea without the harbour master noticing. He found the telephone number and as he spoke to Phillips, he heard Winder and Luned entering the Incident Room. Questioning Phillips only made Drake realise how easy it would be for a rib to approach the marina at night undetected. And Selston owned a rib. It was another piece of the jigsaw.

Winder appeared at his door before he had finished the call, a flushed look on his face.

Drake looked up at him as he ended the call.

'We've found David Eaton in Blaenau Ffestiniog, boss.'

Drake stood up, grabbing his car keys and jacket. 'You're with me Gareth.' As he passed Sara he said, 'And get that background on Selston finished. I need to speak to the super later.'

Drake accelerated along the A55 to the Black Cat roundabout near the main junction for Llandudno where he indicated left for the Conwy Valley. As he powered towards Llanrwst, Winder shared with Drake the details of his work from the day before.

'Tom Levine's nephew, a Euan Levine, is being prosecuted for a VAT fraud. And guess who the prosecuting barrister is?' Winder didn't wait for Drake to reply. 'Justin Selston.'

'What!'

'And there's more, boss. The CPS lawyer I spoke to told me the defence is so well prepared he reckoned they might have inside knowledge.'

'You mean he thought there was a leak?'

Winder nodded. 'And when I spoke to Dot Levine she said that Tom Levine had said that Euan had nothing to worry about. I couldn't believe it.'

'What the hell links Selston and Wixley to Levine?'

They reached the junction with the main road to Betws-y-Coed and Drake indicated south towards Dolwyddelan and the Crimea Pass. Soon they would pass the spot where two road traffic officers had been killed in the middle of the night. Although not recent, it had been one of Drake's first cases and the journey reminded him about that terrible night.

They reached Blaenau Ffestiniog in good time. The town nestled underneath mountains littered with slate waste, a legacy of its history at the centre of the Welsh slate industry. The satnav guided them through the streets, past terraces of houses with slate roofs and slate windowsills.

Winder pointed through the windscreen into the distance. 'There's the patrol car.'

It was parked outside a row of closed shops. Drake pulled up behind. He and Winder got out and joined the uniformed officer who left his car. 'Eaton's car is at the bottom of a dead end. It's tucked out of sight, but I spotted it because I was calling at the house next door.'

'Do you know who lives there?'

The officer shook his head.

'Is there a back gate?'

'No, sir. All the properties have a small backyard.'

Drake turned to Winder. 'Let's go and visit David Eaton.'

The uniformed officer followed them down towards Eaton's property, a two-storey end terrace, and stood a little distance away as Drake rang the doorbell. Moments later David Eaton opened the door and looked at Drake and Winder as though he were expecting them.

'David Eaton?' Drake said.

'Yeah, who's asking?'

Drake pushed his warrant card at Eaton. 'Detective Inspector Drake and this is Detective Constable Gareth Winder. We need to speak to you.'

Eaton's lips formed a cynical grimace. 'You people never give up, do you? Is it you that gave Jamie a hard time?'

Not waiting for an answer, he turned his back on Drake, who took it as an invitation to step inside. Winder followed him through into the kitchen at the rear. Foil containers from a Chinese takeaway littered the table alongside two empty beer cans.

'Do want some chow mein?' Eaton raised an eyebrow.

'We're investigating the murders of Nicholas Wixley and Tom Levine.'

He nodded.

'Last Saturday you were recorded on CCTV leaving Pwllheli marina.'

'What's wrong with that?'

'It was the day we found Tom Levine's body.'

'And what's that got to do with me?'

'You shared a cell with Zavier Cornwell when you were in prison.'

'He was a fucking nutter. I told the screws he should have been in a cell on his own.'

'What did you talk about with Zavier Cornwell?'

'Football. He was mad about Rotherham. I heard the name of every manager they've had in the past twenty years, every team captain and all I can remember is that they've been up and down from the Championship to league one repeatedly.'

From the hallway Drake heard the sound of footsteps descending the staircase, and a woman in her mid-forties wearing a cheap dress clinging to her thin frame entered the kitchen.

'This is Beth,' Eaton said.

She gave Drake and Winder an inquisitive, open look. 'Do you want a *paned*?' She used the Welsh word for cup of tea in a broad local accent.

'I was staying with a mate who has a boat on the marina. We caught the tide first thing that morning to go fishing. We must have left about four o'clock in the morning. He's a mad-keen fisherman and thought it would be good for me to get out onto the water.'

'What time did you get back?'

'Once we came back into the marina we tidied the boat and then left. We didn't realise until we reached the security ramp what had happened.'

Eaton's explanation sounded plausible and his friend needed to be contacted. 'What's your friend's name?'

'Darren – I suppose you want his number?' Eaton reached for a mobile near the electric kettle. He dictated the number to Winder, who left the house, already punching the number into his mobile.

'What else did Zavier Cornwell talk about when

you shared a cell? He must have told you about how he killed those people. He's the sort of bloke to boast about his achievements.'

'It was all over the newspaper, for Christ sake. If there's someone copying Zavier Cornwell – it's not me. And, yes, he did tell me all about his '*modus operandi*'. But he had a ready supply of drugs inside and was completely off his head most the time.'

Standing in the kitchen with the smell of stale Chinese food playing on his nostrils Drake judged that Eaton had been candid. His replies hadn't made him suspicious, but he still needed to ask about Nicholas Wixley's death.

'I need to ask you where you were the weekend before Tom Levine was killed. It was the weekend before the Easter bank holiday.'

'That's easy enough.' Beth reached for her smartphone. 'We were in Blackpool.' She tapped the screen and then thumbed her way until she found the page she was looking for. She pushed the telephone at Drake. 'I took lots of photographs. We went to a concert.' Beth mentioned the name of a well-known Welsh singing duo that owned a hotel in the seaside resort.

The first thing Drake noticed was the date. It corresponded to the weekend of Wixley's death. Then he noticed David Eaton grinning for the camera.

'You're welcome to check with the hotel,' Eaton said.

Drake gave them a simple nod. One of the team could check as they'd have to check Beth's Facebook page. 'Is this your permanent address?'

Eaton nodded.

'I'll need your telephone number. And don't move home without notifying me.'

Once Drake jotted down the details he rejoined Winder as he finished a telephone call. 'His alibi stacks up, sir.'

'And I've checked the photographs on his partner's Facebook page confirming they were in Blackpool the night Wixley was killed.'

'Doesn't look like David Eaton then.'

Even in daylight the town was gloomy – the mountains towering above it suffocating the atmosphere. Now they had to focus on a killer who knew all about the alphabet killings and not on Zavier Cornwell's elusive, possibly imaginary, accomplice.

Chapter 37

Tuesday 7th April
9.56 am

Sara read the names of the university friends added by Mrs Thorpe in a neat hand on the back of the photograph. Had they all become lawyers? Sara searched the Law Society's records of solicitors in England and Wales with the name Roger Brown. Depressingly, there were twenty-four. If Roger Brown qualified as a lawyer three years after graduating, then a starting point would be 1986 and onwards for a maximum of three years. It narrowed her search to four individuals. She spent far too long tracking each of them down to the various law firms where they worked. After two hours she established that none of them read law at the same university as Nicholas Wixley. It left her with one likely candidate, who worked in Newcastle upon Tyne.

She called the number, and the voice of a receptionist announced the practice name.

'My name is Detective Sergeant Sara Morgan of the Wales Police Service,' Sara said. 'I'd like to speak to Roger Brown.'

Seconds later she listened to a mystified voice. 'This is Roger Brown; what's this about?'

It took her a few moments to outline how Roger could help her, and he made the occasional mumbled sound of recognition. He sounded shocked when she shared the news about Wixley. 'I need background on his relationship with Justin Selston.'

'Justin was a formal stuffed shirt. I think he came

from a long line of lawyers and judges. He had a sense of destiny about his career. Most of our group of friends enjoyed being undergraduates. We'd work hard and play hard, but Justin Selston was the serious one.'

'What was his relationship like with Nicholas Wixley?'

Brown chortled. 'There was this girl ... Jennifer ... she and Justin went out together and he was infatuated with her, he thought she was the one for him. But Nicholas ... took an interest in her and when Justin caught him having sex with Jennifer in his car outside a rugby club following some college do there was an almighty argument.'

Sara was scribbling notes. 'We have a photograph of you with Nicholas Wixley and Justin Selston with two other girls, one called Jennifer, the other Mary.'

Their conversation filled out valuable background about Selston and Wixley. Had the student antics been enough for Selston to harbour a grudge?

'Mary died in a car accident a few years ago.' Brown sounded pensive. 'She left two young daughters. It was all very sad. I think Jennifer lives up in the Highlands of Scotland somewhere.'

'How did you get on with Nicholas Wixley?'

'He was always selfish and egotistical, but he could be fun. Were Nicholas and Justin still working in the same chambers?'

'Yes.'

'That surprised me. I never thought Justin would want anything to do with Nicholas again. He was the sort of man not to forgive and forget. He could carry a grudge forever.'

Sara thanked Brown and rang off. It had took her

far more time than she anticipated to find Jennifer Blackburn on Facebook. It amazed her how many people shared their surname with the industrial town in the heart of Lancashire and how many Jennifers there were.

Luckily, not many lived in Scotland.

Sara started with the faces that looked similar to the grainy image open on her monitor. The hair might be shorter, grey with age, and the face would have filled out but the basic features would remain the same, Sara concluded. There was an outside possibility that the Jennifer Blackburn she was looking for didn't have a Facebook page. She found two women with a passing resemblance to the young student of the photograph, her arm hitched around Selston's.

Sara found addresses for both women and numbers from the telephone directory. She dialled the first. A woman with a broad Scottish accent answered – 'Avonmouth Bed-and-Breakfast.'

Cheerily, the woman told Sara she had never been to university before embarking on a summary of her life story, recounting how she'd inherited the business from her mother who unsurprisingly came from near Bristol.

The second Jennifer Blackburn picked up the call after five rings just as Sara had decided to try later.

'Mrs Blackburn?'

'Yes, who's calling?'

Sara couldn't make out the accent; it definitely wasn't Scottish, more the English Midlands.

'My name is Detective Sergeant Sara Morgan of the Wales Police Service. We're investigating the murder of Nicholas Wixley.'

Sara was convinced she had a gasp.

'How ... I mean ... I haven't seen Nicholas Wixley for ... A long time.'

'I understand that whilst you were at university you had a relationship with another student, Justin Selston?'

'Yes, briefly. Look, is this going to take long? My husband is going to be back shortly. I don't want him to know anything about this.'

'Can you tell me about your relationship with Justin Selston?'

Sara heard Blackburn draw breath. 'We were students. He was urbane, came from a wealthy family. I'd never met anyone like him. But he got too serious. He kept talking about our life together in the future as though he had everything planned out in detail. Surely you don't think he's involved?'

'I've spoken with Roger Brown.' Sara decided to barge right into this woman's private life. 'He recounted an incident when you had a brief fling with Nicholas Wixley at the same time as you were going out with Justin Selston. How did Mr Selston react?'

All Sara could hear was the sound of regular breathing down the telephone.

'That was long ago.' The voice trembled slightly.

'Every murder inquiry means we have to dig into people's backgrounds.'

Blackburn sighed heavily.

'Justin lost his mind. He brought our relationship to an end. But after we finished at university he wrote to me. And before you ask, I haven't got any of the letters. I read two or three, but they were filled with bile as though he couldn't get over what had happened. I threw the rest unopened in the bin.'

If Selston had reacted like this as an undergraduate,

how much deeper would his enmity be towards the same man who had now beaten him to the one thing he cherished – being a judge?

'Did you ever hear from him again?'

'No, and I don't want to. And I don't want to hear from you again either.' She slammed the phone down.

Sara sat back in her chair. From university to the barristers' chambers and now the recent judicial appointment, the lives of Nicholas Wixley and Justin Selston were intertwined. How much more had they to learn about Selston?

Drake returned to headquarters with Winder, who made straight for the canteen and a late lunch. Drake had little appetite. He sat at his desk nursing a bottle of water when Sara appeared in his door.

'Any luck, boss?'

Drake blew out a lungful of air. 'David Eaton has an alibi for the nights that Wixley and Levine were both killed. Any progress with Selston?'

Sara sat down and summarised her conversations with Blackburn and Brown. 'It's not giving us evidence, sir.' She added forcibly.

Drake grimaced. She was right, of course, and he feared that Superintendent Price and Thorsen would dismiss out of hand the prospect of even interviewing Selston for Wixley's death. The decision to interview Laura Wixley and its consequences festered to the point of poisoning his mind. He had to banish this uncertainty.

'I spoke to the harbour master this morning and he confirmed it would be easy for a cuddy or day boat or small rib to slip in late at night and leave without having to report to the office. And there's no CCTV on the pontoons. So Selston could have left that landing stage near his home for the marina.'

'But we've got no evidence and no motive.'

Drake took a mouthful of water. 'We've got enough to arrest him on suspicion of Wixley's death.'

Sara gave him an unconvinced look and finished her tea.

An hour later Drake sat monitoring Andy Thorsen's facial expressions. It was like watching a fish swimming around in a tank. Thorsen was breathing but he remained expressionless as he listened to Drake.

Eventually Thorsen cut in. 'I am exercised about the value of the evidence regarding his relationship with Nicholas Wixley from his undergraduate days.'

Drake had prepared for this. 'You know as well as I do, Andy, any relevant details relating to the defendant's past gives the opportunity for a jury to form a clear picture. Their history of animosity is surely relevant.'

Drake half expected Thorsen to challenge his assertion, but the Crown prosecutor simply sat impassively. Drake was prepared to remind Thorsen that a recent case involving the prosecution of a man in his sixties for murder offered evidence about his military past forty years earlier.

It was Superintendent Price's body language that really unnerved Drake. He rubbed his hands vigorously over his face as though he couldn't quite believe what he was hearing. 'So, for thirty-odd years Selston has a festering hatred of Nicholas Wixley because he slept with his one and only true love?'

'Selston is the sort of character to take that personally.' Drake hoped he didn't sound too pleading.

Price replied. 'Even so, it beggars belief. And you're saying that because he was passed over as a circuit judge it tipped him over into becoming a murderer.'

Drake sensed Price wanted to continue.

'This is a man from a fine, upstanding family. His father was a judge and his grandfather too, for Christ's sake. It's inconceivable …'

Thorsen added in his measured tone. 'A jury isn't going to be swayed by all that family stuff. They'll be more interested in the history of conflict between both men. It could be a persuasive argument to suggest the disappointment of failing to become a judge and seeing his nemesis appointed in his place would be enough to make him murder. We've all seen these sorts of barristers, pompous idiots, but very clever and very good at what they do. And then we have the eyewitness evidence—'

'She's a fucking escort.' Price raised his voice.

For the first time Drake noticed a grin playing on Andy Thorsen's lips.

'She has no possible axe to grind, nothing to gain and she was terrified of coming forward because of Nicholas Wixley's choice of friends.'

Drake paused before continuing. 'Selston was one of the defending barristers in the case of Zavier Cornwell. He knew all the details of Cornwell's MO. The person who killed Nicholas Wixley knew all about the alphabet case. And Selston is the prosecuting barrister in a case involving Euan Levine, Tom's nephew. The prosecutor in that case is convinced someone is leaking information to the defence lawyers.'

Price threw a silver Cross ballpoint he had been playing with onto the desk in a huff. 'That's a stretch. It could be anyone. And you haven't given us any single link between Justin Selston and Tom Levine.' Before Drake replied, Price held up a hand. 'And all you've done is suggest he could have accessed the marina at Pwllheli undetected because he has a boat. Anybody could do that. There must be dozens of people with boats along the coast.'

Drake didn't reply. The superintendent was correct. Everything about the inquiry suggested the death of Tom Levine and Nicholas Wixley were linked. They just hadn't found what linked them so far.

Price persisted. 'There could be two killers.'

'Two copycats is pretty unlikely, Wyndham,' Thorsen said.

Price glared at the prosecutor.

Andy Thorsen announced in a serious voice. 'The eyewitness evidence changes everything. It turns Justin Selston from a person of interest to a suspect. And we all know that must mean his arrest. When you interview him, you could take the opportunity to ask him about Tom Levine.'

A panic-stricken look crossed Wyndham Price's face.

Drake nodded. 'And it means we can execute a search warrant.'

Thorsen added in a pleased tone, 'Of course.'

Chapter 38

Wednesday 7th April
7.45 am

Drake arrived in the leafy suburb where Selston lived and parked the Mondeo. Sara had said little on the journey from north Wales and Drake guessed she was still worried about the impending arrest. A few minutes passed before a marked police car pulled up behind them followed closely by an anonymous van with a search team of six officers. Later that morning another team would arrive at Selston's holiday home. The pavement was litter-free and discreet signs promoted the neighbourhood watch group. Drake left the car and nodded briefly to the officers who'd accompany Selston.

A woman wearing an immaculate housecoat opened the door once Drake had rung the bell, which chimed impressively through the building. Colour drained from her cheeks when she saw the two police officers standing behind Drake.

'May we speak to Mr Selston?'

She scampered back into the house and a troubled-looking Selston emerged, the creases on his forehead deepening as he reached the door.

'What the hell are you doing? I'm due in Crown Court for a remand hearing this morning. Whatever it is you want, it will have to wait.'

'Justin Selston. I am arresting you on suspicion of the murder of Nicholas Wixley.'

The housekeeper gasped. Selston took a deep breath and leered at Drake.

'You are making a terrible mistake.'

Once Drake had cautioned Selston, he said, 'These officers will escort you back to the area custody suite at Northern Division headquarters of the Wales Police Service. We're likely to be in a position to interview later today. Can we contact a solicitor to represent you?'

Drake packed Selston off with the two uniformed officers and stood on the threshold of the barrister's substantial home. Moments later a search team filed in. It had been difficult assembling officers with sufficient training at short notice and a number of the constables present were on rest days. The overtime on offer had been the sweetener in persuading them to agree to take part.

Drake and Sara walked through the house. The sitting room was cold, uninviting, the sort of room a bachelor with few friends or visitors would maintain. The kitchen had a similarly old-world feel with a tired-looking Belfast sink surrounded by a wooden draining board that badly needing re-varnishing. Pots and pans hung from butchers' hooks suspended from a cage above an oak table. It was easy to imagine Justin Selston sitting here alone eating scrambled eggs for breakfast.

'Sad old place, isn't it, boss?'

Drake couldn't agree more. 'I wonder whether this was the lifestyle he chose? Did he blame Nicholas Wixley for not having another girlfriend?'

'That would be dead weird.'

From the kitchen they took the staircase and found the first search team working their way through various bedrooms. It would have surprised Drake had Selston ever entertained guests. Why did he need such a large house? It reminded Drake that living a lonely, sad existence wasn't something he wanted to contemplate.

They retraced their steps downstairs, knowing that by now Gareth Winder and Luned Thomas were in Selston's room at Britannia Chambers. Another barrister would no doubt be in the Crown Court advising the defendant about his bail application while trying to ignore the shattering news about a senior colleague.

Drake turned to Sara. 'Let's get back. We've got a suspect to interview.'

Drake worked his way through half a round of a soggy ham sandwich, sitting at a desk in the Incident Room, listening to Sara ticking off the questions on the interview plan between mouthfuls of her cheese salad.

The custody sergeant had already notified them that a solicitor from Manchester was on his way. A quick Google search told Drake he was from one of the prestigious firms. He checked in with Gareth Winder, who was still busy gathering Selston's documents and paperwork from Britannia Chambers. They expected to be back later that afternoon. The search team supervisors at Selston's home and his holiday home had little to report.

Arriving at the area custody suite Drake detoured into a bathroom where he scrubbed his hands and dowsed his face with water. The rituals soothed his mind. He drew a comb through his hair and straightened his tie. He stared at himself in the mirror – were they treating Selston any differently from any other potential suspect? He was a highly experienced barrister, so of course they were.

The interview suite was the only one at area custody control able to record on tape and video simultaneously. Before starting, he had spoken briefly with Superintendent Price, who was going to sit and monitor the recording live. Price said little; after all, Drake was the senior investigating officer; he was in charge of the interview. Drake collected the tapes from the custody sergeant and shared one last encouraging look with Sara.

Justin Selston looked exactly as he did earlier. He wore a navy three-piece suit with a shirt with a detachable collar, favoured by barristers. He looked completely unperturbed at the prospect of being interviewed. Drake expected nothing less. He had probably read hundreds of interview notes, cross-examined dozens of detective inspectors, represented murderers and rapists, so he wouldn't be intimidated.

Price's last words rang in Drake's ears. 'Treat him as you would any other suspect. Don't give him any quarter. You've got a job to do.'

Aiden Turner sat alongside Justin Selston. Drake guessed he was early forties; his hair was immaculately tidy and he had clear, intelligent, probing eyes.

Formalities completed, Drake clicked on the tape machine and everyone in the room identified themselves. Drake took a moment to compose himself, sipping slowly from the bottle of water on the table in front of him.

'How would you describe your relationship with Nicholas Wixley?'

Selston stared back hard, his head slightly lowered, his eyes hooded. 'We were professional colleagues.'

'Would you call him a friend?'

'It's depends on how you define "friend".'

'I was asking if *you* described him as a friend. I repeat the question.'

Drake noticed a nervous twitch at the back of Selston's jaw.

'We never socialised, apart from events relating to chambers.'

'Did you know his wife, Mrs Laura Wixley?'

'I met her a few times.'

'How long have you known Nicholas Wixley?' Drake fixed Selston with a steady gaze. Would Selston take the risk of assuming they hadn't investigated his background before the arrest was justified?

'We went to the same university.'

Another indirect answer that satisfied the question, just.

'Were you friends as undergraduates?'

Selston paused; again Drake read the calculation going through Selston's mind. He must be assessing how much they had discovered.

'No, we weren't.'

From the folder in front of him Drake drew out the photograph given to them by Mr and Mrs Thorpe. He pushed it over the table at Selston. 'This is a picture of you at university with a group of friends. One of those present was Nicholas Wixley.'

Selston's eyes bulged. It convinced Drake he hadn't seen it before.

'Yes, that's me.'

'And Nicholas Wixley?'

'Yes.'

'Do you know the names of the others?' Surely he

wouldn't lie now; surely he would realise they knew their identities.

'No, I'm sorry. I don't recall their names.' Selston fidgeted with the nail of the forefinger of his right hand. He pushed the photograph away.

'You don't remember their names.'

Turner butted in. 'That's not a question, Inspector. Do please move on. Are you going to show my client more photographs from decades ago? I thought you were dealing with a current murder inquiry.'

Drake gave him a narrow, cold smile.

'Let me help you, Mr Selston. Mary died a few years ago and Jennifer now lives in Scotland. The other man in the photograph is Roger Brown. Did you have a relationship with either of these women?'

Selston raised an eyebrow a fraction and let it rest before a contemptuous shadow filtered across his eyes.

'Would you like to reconsider your previous answer to my question about remembering the names of these fellow students?'

Selston shook his head briefly.

Drake gave Aiden Turner a brief nod as though he were warning him that he was taking the interview up a notch. 'We've spoken to Jennifer Blackburn. She confirms that while you were at university you had a relationship with her. An intimate relationship. Is that correct?'

Selston threaded the fingers of both hands together and placed them slowly on the table between him and Drake. Then he proceeded to turn each thumb around the other.

Drake stared at Selston. 'For the purposes of the tape, Justin Selston makes no reply.'

From the folder Drake produced the notes from the interview with Jennifer. 'Mrs Blackburn was very frank. During her relationship with you she had a brief liaison with Nicholas Wixley. She describes it as having a devastating effect on you.'

'Really, Inspector,' said Turner again. 'This is ancient history.'

Drake ignored him. 'You see, Mr Selston, I think you bore a grudge against Nicholas Wixley from that moment on. Do you blame him for destroying your relationship with Jennifer?'

Selston gave Aiden Turner a tired sort of look as though it was beneath his dignity to respond. 'No comment.'

Drake paused. 'Let's move on to something else. I understand you represented Zavier Cornwell. The press called him the alphabet killer.'

Drake's new line of questioning took Selston and Turner by surprise. Turner scribbled something in his notebook that he passed over to Selston. The barrister shared a scornful look with his lawyer.

Drake continued, deciding it was a decent enough attempt at mind games. 'The letter E was tattooed into Nicholas Wixley's chest. Exactly the same modus operandi as Zavier Cornwell.'

'Then I suggest you should be looking for a copycat killer,' Selston blurted out.

'Or someone with an intimate knowledge of the original case. At Cornwell's trial no mention was made of the orders of service daubed in the victim's blood. A copycat killer would never have known those details. But you knew them all. Do you agree?'

Drake noticed Selston taking a long, hard swallow.

'I can't possibly remember all the details ... of every case I have handled.'

Drake took a moment to allow the implication of his last questions to sink in. Then he spent time questioning Selston about the prosecution of Zavier Cornwell, pushing over images of Nicholas Wixley's corpse, comparing them to the bodies Cornwell had carved up on his killing spree. They would have caused revulsion for most people but Selston appeared unaffected. Professional immunity, Drake thought. Selston said little, made the occasional response, and glanced over at his lawyer, who sometimes interjected, all of which Drake ignored.

A message reached Drake's mobile and he scolded himself for not having turned the thing off. He saw the name of Michael Foulds, the crime scene manager, asking him to make contact urgently.

'I need to suspend this interview,' Drake announced. He got up and motioned for Sara to follow him.

He found an empty interview room and called Foulds.

'We found a bloodied knife at Selston's holiday home,' Foulds said.

The implication didn't sink in for a few seconds. 'What?' Drake sounded throaty and disbelieving.

'It was in a drawer in the garage. It had been given a cursory wipe. There are no fingerprints on the shaft but the blood residuals are enough for a DNA test.'

'Send me a photograph.'

'On its way.'

'And Mike, get the DNA done urgently.'

'Of course.'

Drake let out a long breath. Interviewing Selston was demanding and he could feel his energy sagging. Now the possibility they had evidence made him want to punch the air. His telephone bleeped, and an image reached the screen. He showed it to Sara. 'They found this knife with blood residuals at Selston's holiday home.'

She whistled under breath. 'That changes things.'

'You bet.' Drake headed back for the interview room once he had calmed.

They retook their seats and Drake restarted exactly where he had left off. They had time at the end to ask about the knife. Drake opened the folder again, shielding its contents from Selston by propping it at an angle on the table. He took out an email from the judicial appointments board. He read the text, conscious of two pairs of eyes boring into him. Then he handed it to Sara, prodding at the middle of the page, pretending to draw her attention to something. She gave him a conspiratorial nod.

'Nicholas Wixley was favoured over you for the best cases. How did that make you feel?'

'Don't be an idiot.'

'He got all the major murder trials and he garnered a very high reputation. Did that annoy you?'

'This is beneath contempt.'

'Would you describe yourself as ambitious?'

Selston rolled his eyes.

'Your father was a circuit judge and also your grandfather. Is that correct?'

'I don't see what my family background has to do with this.'

'It must have come as a blow when Nicholas

Wixley was appointed as a circuit judge.'

Selston's complexion faded.

'It must have been galling to see the person that you blamed for ruining your chance of happiness with Jennifer being more successful in your chosen profession and then being appointed as a judge.'

'I can't believe this interview is being conducted.' Selston struck a high, cultured tone to his voice.

Drake pulled out from the folder the images from Tom Levine's yacht. Slowly he set them out on the table facing Selston. 'These were taken at the scene of Tom Levine's murder. The circumstances of his death are similar to Nicholas Wixley's. The letter F was written in blood near the door.'

Selston raised his eyes after checking each image and gave Drake an incredulous look.

Drake continued. 'You are the prosecuting barrister in a case involving Euan Levine, Tom's nephew.'

'And do you think that gives you a basis to link me to Tom Levine's death?'

'The Crown prosecution lawyers strongly suspect that Euan Levine's defence team is being leaked information.'

Selston almost shrieked his disbelief. 'This is absurd. Pam worked on that case as well as my pupil.'

Turner raised his voice too. 'Detective Inspector. There isn't a shred of evidence to connect my client to Tom Levine's death.'

Just wait until what comes next.

'Please take a look at this photograph.' Drake showed Selston and Turner the screen of his mobile. 'This knife was found in your garage. Is it yours?'

Drake searched for a spasm of fear passing over

Selston's eyes, but they remained unaffected.

'I've never seen it before.'

'The forensic team believes there are blood traces on the blade. DNA tests are currently being conducted. Now is your chance to offer an explanation for the knife.'

Selston shook his head but fixed Drake with his eyes.

'Where were you on the night Nicholas Wixley was killed?'

'I was staying in the Portmeirion Hotel. You know that well enough.'

'Did you leave at any point that evening?'

'Of course not.'

Drake sat back for a moment. It had been the one lie he was waiting for.

'We have an eyewitness that saw you at Nicholas Wixley's holiday home in the early hours of the morning. Is that correct?'

Panic threatened to overwhelm Selston. He made an odd grunting sound and stammered a reply.

'I ... I ... knocked the door, but nobody replied. I had some urgent chambers business to discuss.'

'Why did you lie to me about leaving the Portmeirion Hotel?'

Colour seemed to drain from Selston's face. Drake could see that he realised he had stepped over into the abyss.

'I believe you killed Nicholas Wixley as a result of your deep-seated jealousy that turned into pure hatred.'

Selston shook his head slowly.

Chapter 39
Wednesday 8th of April
6.36 pm

Drake sipped a coffee that Sara had organised. It was a weak and insipid concoction, but Drake was beyond caring. Selston's interview had drained him. He wanted to sit in a dark room for hours, saying nothing, doing nothing.

Instead he was watching the television screen with Superintendent Price standing by his side. Drake recognised the face of the reporter outside Northern Division headquarters.

'I believe that the Wales Police Service has this morning arrested a man on suspicion of the recent murder of Nicholas Wixley. He's being held at a secure police station in north Wales. The police haven't as yet formally confirmed his identity, but I understand from sources in Manchester that one of Mr Wixley's colleagues has been arrested.

This is now a fast-moving inquiry and the police have asked for any eyewitnesses or any members of the public who may have anything to contribute to contact the helpline. The murder of Nicholas Wixley caused considerable shock and revulsion in legal circles and the wider community as he had recently been appointed a circuit judge and he was a well-respected and well-known lawyer in Manchester with family connections to north Wales. It is understood that his widow, a senior police officer in the

*City of Manchester force, has been kept fully
informed of all the latest developments.'*

'Typical load of bollocks,' Price said.

'Have you made contact with Laura Wixley?'
Drake said, finishing the last of his drink and dropping
the plastic cup into a metal bin.

Price nodded. 'I spoke to her this afternoon. I
thought it was only right she should be informed –
professional courtesy and all that.'

'How did she react?'

'Hard to tell. She sounded businesslike. It took me
a while to track her down. She's been ordered by the
chief constable to take a week off so she's staying at
her holiday home. She's planning on selling up – too
many bad memories so she's getting the house ready to
be sold.'

It was easy to imagine Laura Wixley coordinating
the necessary work to have the house professionally
deep cleaned, making sure that all the walls and floors
were scrubbed clean. But once the house was on the
market it would probably attract a few voyeuristic
rubberneckers keen to know exactly where Nicholas
Wixley had been killed.

Price sat down at the desk, and Drake and Sara
pulled up two chairs.

'Bring me up to date on the searches of his various
properties.'

Drake took a long breath. 'Progress is slow. Gareth
Winder and Luned Thomas are working through boxes
of papers from his chambers, and both search teams are
still at his home and the holiday home. I'll need to go
through all the paperwork in the morning and see if we

can establish a link to Tom Levine.'

'Do we have enough to charge Justin Selston with the murder of Nicholas Wixley?'

Drake hesitated. It wasn't solely his decision to make, surely? Superintendent Price was involved, as was Andy Thorsen and Assistant Chief Constable Neary. A suspicion Price was covering his back needled its way into Drake's mind.

'Selston lied to us. At first, he denied having been at Nicholas Wixley's home on the night he was murdered but then he offered a lame excuse that he called to discuss something about chambers business. It didn't strike me as anything to justify him turning up at Wixley's place late at night.'

Price grunted a reply. Drake continued. 'Selston has a long history of a fractious and disjointed relationship with Nicholas Wixley. He bears grudges and the latest and ultimate insult would be Nicholas Wixley's appointment as a circuit judge. Everything about Selston's background suggests he coveted that role as a personal family fiefdom.'

A contemplative silence filled the space between the officers. The consequences of what they were discussing challenged everything they valued, respect for the rule of law, the importance of judges. Little wonder Superintendent Price hesitated.

'We review again in the morning. I'll organise a video conference call with ACC Neary first thing.'

Price loosened his tie and shared a glance with Drake and Sara. 'You've both done well.'

'Thank you, sir.'

Drake and Sara left Price staring at the television that carried reports about the derby game between

Swansea and Cardiff in the Premier League.

The same match was playing on a big screen in the public house where Winder had suggested they meet. Winder scrambled to his feet when he saw Drake and Sara approaching the table he shared with Luned. 'What's your poison, boss?'

Drake rarely socialised with the rest of his team. Other detective inspectors were comfortable mixing with the constables and the sergeant on their teams, but Drake knew little about Winder's social life apart from the occasional comment about his girlfriend. Perhaps a better man-manager than him would know whether the detective constable on his team drank lager or beer or spirits or nothing at all.

He joined Sara in opting for a soft drink. Winder padded over to the bar and Drake sat by Luned. Winder wasn't long, returning with a pint of fizzy-looking lager for himself and orange juice and soda for Drake and Sara.

'The barristers in the chambers are a poncey bunch,' Winder said. 'They looked at us as though *we* were the criminals. Have the search teams found anything of value?' Winder took another long slug of his drink. Drake guessed it was his second, perhaps even his third. No driving home tonight for Detective Constable Winder, Drake thought.

'They haven't finished yet.'

Luned added quietly, 'Will Selston be charged?'

The seriousness in Luned's tone made Drake realise the inquiry had taken its toll on her. 'We've got a video-link organised with the assistant chief constable tomorrow morning when a final decision will be made but it looks as though he will be charged with the murder of Nicholas Wixley and, depending on the result of forensics, Tom Levine.'

Winder reached for the laminated menu propped in a plastic container on the nearby table. 'I'm starving.'

Drake realised he, too, was hungry and he couldn't recall when he had last eaten. He decided there was little point going home to an empty flat or even travelling over to see Annie. Justin Selston was going to be charged with murder in the morning and that was a result. It was worth taking an opportunity to share the team's success. He should have done something like this years ago, shown how much he appreciated them, how much he valued their input.

When Winder handed him one of the menus, he smiled. 'The curry is bloody good here.'

By the end of the evening Winder and Luned had both relaxed. She shared how much her parents had been shocked by the death of Nicholas Wixley. A friend of her mother's knew the housekeeper who found his body. Luned didn't need to share the details – her mother knew them all. 'They don't realise what we have to do.'

Winder and Sara both nodded.

Luned's eyes took on a glazed expression and Drake realised she'd drunk a glass of lager too many. Sara saved her embarrassment. 'I've got a spare bedroom you can use tonight.' Luned gave her a bleary-eyed look of thanks.

Winder regaled them all with his hopes for the Liverpool football team. Being second in the Premier League gave them a great chance at being the champions. Perhaps he had underestimated Gareth Winder in the past, Drake thought. Every team needs a detective constable like Winder, determined, focused, never going to progress up the ranks of CID but invaluable nevertheless.

Drake listened to Sara as she told them about her running and then that her friends had been to Dublin for the Easter bank holiday and that one of her girlfriends overindulged on Guinness. A return trip, with Sara, was planned over the summer.

An uneasiness crept into Drake's mind when he realised that he wasn't sharing any personal details. He had always found it awkward. He hadn't expected anyone to be quite as blunt as Sara when she asked him, 'And how is Annie?' She accompanied the question with a smile that lit up her face.

His defences penetrated, he had no choice and actually enjoyed telling them about his girlfriend.

Drake dropped Winder off outside his home, and he thanked Drake for the lift and staggered away from the car. Drake parked on the street near his apartment, wondering how Sara was getting on with Luned. It had been the sort of evening he should have arranged before, should have encouraged before, should have participated in before. Regrets were useless, Drake thought: it was what he did in the future that was important.

Chapter 40

Thursday 9th of April
7.25 am

Not talking to Annie the day before had made Drake feel his day was incomplete, as though an essential part was missing. After separating from Sian he had felt the same about his contact with Helen and Megan.

Although his conversation that morning with Annie was brief, by the end it restored equilibrium to his mind. He even contemplated the possibility of skipping his daily routine of starting the Sudoku puzzle from the morning newspaper. A step too far, Drake thought as he left the apartment and headed for his car, the first stop the newsagent nearby.

The ritual was less a necessity now and more of a habit. He completed a few squares easily enough and drove away towards headquarters, his mind settled.

He parked and clocked the Jaguar belonging to Superintendent Price. One morning, Drake concluded, he would arrive before his senior officer. Arriving at his office he hung his jacket on the coat stand before booting up his computer.

Foulds appeared in his room before he could gather his thoughts.

'I've got the DNA results.' Foulds paused. 'The knife had blood from Wixley and Levine. It's the murder weapon, Ian.'

It took a few seconds for the full impact to sink in. Drake almost said, *Are you sure?*

'Send me the report as soon as you can.'

'It'll be tomorrow – I'm going back to the house

now.' Foulds stifled a yawn. 'And by the way – this is academic now, but the partial fingerprint on the champagne flute in Wixley's house isn't Mandy Forsyth or Justin Selston, but the pubic hair does have her DNA.'

'Thanks.'

Foulds nodded his acknowledgement and left.

Drake filled a page of a notepad with comments and jottings intended to fix in his mind what he needed to tell Assistant Chief Constable Neary. Assistant chief constables occupied a rarefied atmosphere with little hands-on involvement in a day-to-day inquiry. Nicholas Wixley and Deputy Chief Constable Wixley made this investigation different from any other case he had conducted.

Drake reached the video conference suite in good time, where Andy Thorsen and Price were waiting. He wasted no time.

'I've had the DNA results on a knife found at Selston's home. There were traces of Wixley's and Levine's blood.'

Thorsen straightened in his chair.

'Bloody great result.' Price fisted the desk. 'We've got the bastard.'

A civilian fiddled around with the controls of the video-link equipment and soon the image of the three men appeared in a rectangular box at the bottom of the screen.

Bang on time Assistant Chief Constable Neary entered the empty room at force headquarters in Cardiff and spread out some papers on the desk in front of her. She looked up. 'Good morning, gentlemen.'

Price and Drake replied in unison. 'Ma'am.'

'Bring me up to date.'

Drake glanced at his list. 'We've had the results of forensic tests on a knife found in Selston's home. It had traces of Wixley's and Levine's blood.'

'That's excellent news. And how did Selston's interview pan out?'

'Justin Selston lied to us about being at Wixley's home on the night he was killed. When I put to him there was an eyewitness, he came up with a convoluted explanation about visiting Wixley to discuss business involving the barristers' chambers. He denied all knowledge of the knife.'

'Do you think the eyewitness is reliable?'

Price butted in. 'Although the woman is an escort she has no motive to implicate Selston, and she didn't come forward because she was frightened about the links between Tom Levine and Nicholas Wixley.'

Neary pondered. 'I guess it will be a matter for a jury to decide whether Justin Selston's explanation is to be believed. Andy, what do you think?'

'Applying the standard test: if a conviction is more likely than not then clearly there is enough evidence to justify charging Justin Selston. It has to be in the public interest to do so.'

'Good. And Ian, I know this case has attracted a lot of attention and scrutiny but I think your team has done well.' Neary picked up her papers and left as the screen went dead.

Thorsen was the first to respond. 'I'll have the charges drafted by later this morning.' He paused, gazed over at Price and then Drake. 'What about bail?'

A defendant like Selston might well expect bail. It was a racing certainty Thorsen wanted to object to any possibility Selston be freed until his case was heard. It would take a very convincing barrister to persuade a court that a defendant charged with murder be released on bail. What was the risk of him absconding? Nothing suggested he would take the first plane to some exotic location that didn't have an extradition treaty with the United Kingdom. And they could prevent that by ensuring he surrendered his passport.

'We object of course,' Price said after a moment's contemplation. 'It would be sending the wrong signal if we agreed for him to be released.'

'There's a strong chance the court will release him on bail. After all, he's a fine, upstanding member of the community, no previous conviction, vehemently denies any involvement. And he has a settled address and is unlikely to leave the country.'

'That'll be a matter for the courts,' Price said.

Drake returned to a far busier Incident Room than when he left it. Winder appeared a bit sheepish, Luned gave Drake an embarrassed look and Sara was the only one that managed a normal greeting. 'Good morning, boss, how did you get on?'

'The knife the search team found in Selston's home has traces of Wixley's and Levine's blood.' The revelation changed the atmosphere in the Incident Room. Bodies straightened, and concentration sharpened. 'We proceed to charge him with the murders of Nicholas Wixley and Levine.'

Winder gave a brief huff of exhilaration. Luned pursed her lips and Sara nodded exuberantly. Drake walked over towards the board. He stood looking at the various images on it.

The mobile telephone rang in the pocket of his

jacket and he fished it out with two fingers.

Drake recognised the number for area control. 'DI Drake.'

'I've been asked to notify you about a car fire relating to a person of interest in your inquiry.'

'Car fire?' Drake said, failing to hide his irritation.

'A car belonging to a Norman Turnbull is ablaze in Hell's Mouth.'

'Hell's Mouth, do you mean the beach?'

'Yes, sir.'

A burnt-out vehicle was a job for uniformed lads, but Norman Turnbull's involvement made Drake wary. 'Has Mr Turnbull reported his car missing?'

'That's the problem, Inspector. There's a body inside the car.'

Chapter 41

Thursday 9th of April
9.25 am

Drake wished he had a helicopter for occasions like this. Something to get him to the crime scene in minutes rather than the one hour fifty-five the satnav predicted. Knowing the ongoing roadworks might delay the journey Drake even contemplated the possibility of driving down the Conwy Valley and then through the mountains towards Pwllheli. Fewer hold-ups, but the roads were narrow and unpredictable.

He switched on the blue flashing lights under the grill and then the siren's wailing noise filled the car. Vehicles drew into the inside lane and then onto the hard shoulder as he raced ahead. Drake swept past motorcycle outriders in high-visibility jackets standing at either end of the extended roadworks between Penmaenmawr and Bangor, ensuring an unimpeded journey.

The satnav quickly adjusted its estimated time of arrival. Drake kept badgering Sara to get updates from area control about the officers present at the scene and the likely arrival time of the scientific support vehicle and the CSIs.

After screaming along the A55 towards Bangor, Drake indicated for Caernarfon and his speed dropped but his annoyance increased. Avoiding the town centre, he used the back roads, negotiating ninety-degree bends and narrow, tight junctions. The flashing light and siren had little effect until he reached the other side of the town.

Now he was making progress as he floored the accelerator. The three peaks of Yr Eifl appeared in front of him and he skirted round them to cross the peninsula. Until then his mind had been concentrating on driving, getting to the scene. Now he started to think.

What on earth was Norman Turnbull doing at Hells Mouth at the end of the Llŷn Peninsula? Porth Neigwl, the Welsh name for the wide expanse of beach, didn't sound as dramatic as its English version. He knew the name but not the location.

Pwllheli felt familiar as he slowed to negotiate the centre of the town. Once clear, he powered towards Abersoch. After the village, popular with the Premier League footballers of England, Drake eventually saw two marked police cars and a fire engine in a car park.

He braked hard and the car jolted to a halt on the gravel.

A thin plume of smoke drifted off Turnbull's car. Two fireman stood nearby with handheld extinguishers blasting out the occasional puff, discouraging any more of the flames from rekindling.

'Let's get going,' Drake said.

They left the car and a uniformed officer approached them.

'Glad you've arrived, sir.' His name tag read Williams. 'Some campers in the adjacent field heard the explosion.'

'Where are they now?'

Williams nodded over Drake's shoulder. 'They're with Harry.'

Drake glanced behind him and noticed another uniformed officer with two civilians. 'We'll talk to them later.'

Drake moved towards the car. 'Don't get too close,' a firefighter nearby called out.

Even from a distance the smell of burning flesh lingered. It was a charcoal-like, sulphurous odour. Without looking at the firefighter, he asked, 'The CSI team are on their way. Will it be safe for them to complete their investigation?'

'I suppose so. I guess they know what they're doing.'

The sound of another vehicle slowing caught Drake's attention. He watched as a man broke into a run once he had left the car. Williams blocked his progress, but he became hysterical. 'That's his car, that's his fucking car. Where the hell is he?'

Drake and Sara walked over.

'I'm Detective Inspector Ian Drake, Wales Police Service, and this is Detective Sergeant Sara Morgan. Who are you?'

'I'm Alan Turnbull. I'm Norman's brother and that's his car.' The man doubled up in pain. 'Where's Norm? Jesus, he's not inside is he? Oh, for Christ's sake.'

'We don't know yet who is in the car.'

Alan gave Drake a pleading look. 'So, there's a chance he could be safe?'

'We are expecting the crime scene investigators and once they have completed their work we can get back to you. Are you on holiday?'

Alan nodded. 'Norm called us yesterday and announced he was coming down to see us. He got here last night and he was really agitated. He thought he was being followed. I told him he was getting paranoid and that he had to calm down.'

'When did he leave?'

'He left this morning really early saying he had to meet someone.'

Sara already had her pocketbook out. 'Can you tell me your brother's mobile number?'

Sara jotted down the details. Standard protocols meant a full search against the number he had called and, more importantly, every number that called him in the last twenty-four hours.

'I'll need your contact details, Mr Turnbull. As soon as I know anything I'll be in touch.'

Alan Turnbull sat in his car staring out at them. He left when the scientific support vehicle arrived. Mike Foulds got out and walked over towards Drake, grim-faced.

'I suppose you are looking for identification.' Foulds looked over at the smouldering remains.

'Top of the class,' Drake said.

Foulds gave him a weary look. 'This might take some time.'

The fire officers kept watch while two crime scene investigators began their macabre work. Sara followed Drake as he circled around the car park taking the footpath down towards the beach. Hell's Mouth stretched out in front of Drake for what he guessed was a mile, maybe more. It had a narrow band of sand and shingle, and being in the teeth of the south-westerly gales made it unappealing for a family beach outing.

'What was he doing here?' Sara said.

Drake shivered. Windsurfers on the bay skimmed over the surface of the sea; the wind was fresh and salty against his face.

Drake turned on his heels and retraced his steps

towards the car park.

Mike Foulds kneeled by the driver's side open door. The investigator with him was standing nearby, a hand over his mask shrouding his face. Inside the car Drake could see the remains of a body sitting upright. He wasn't going to venture any further. The smell of burning hair could linger in the nostrils for days. He could make out that most of the skin around the face was charred. Identification might only be possible from dental records. Mike Foulds was rummaging around in the man's jacket. Without warning the investigator standing behind him hurried away towards some nearby shrubs and promptly puked.

Foulds walked over to Drake and Sara, holding something in his hand. 'He's got a weak stomach.' Foulds nodded towards his colleague who drew the sleeve of his one-piece white suit over his mouth.

Foulds opened the leather wallet held in his left hand. The material was scorched, its threads unravelling. The first bank card Foulds removed had melted so badly none of the numbers or names were visible. He read aloud the first six digits from the second card. 'The name?' Drake said.

Foulds shook his head. From the inside pocket underneath a flap Foulds pulled out gingerly a semi-melted driving licence. He looked up at Drake and gave a nod of accomplishment. 'Norman Turnbull. Does that match the person who owns the car?'

Drake nodded.

Behind him Drake's name was called, and he turned to see the second uniformed officer waving at him. Two civilians stood by his side. Drake strode over, relieved to be leaving the putrid smell.

'This is Byron Green,' Constable Harry Pritchard said.

Green had a long chin that matched his thin frame.

'I witnessed the explosion.'

Sara reached for her pocketbook as Drake spoke to Green. 'Tell us what you recall.'

'I'd already been up for an hour. I'd done my early-morning constitutional along the beach. This place is so beautiful and tranquil ... until this morning that is.'

'Time,' Drake said too sharply. 'Do you know the time when the car exploded?'

'Of course.' Green gave them a pleased look. 'It was just before the eight am news headlines on the *Today* programme on Radio 4. I never miss it no matter what. I can even remember which politician was being interviewed. They were discussing—'

Drake raised a hand to stop Green. 'We'll need your details. One of the inquiry team will contact you for a full statement.'

Chapter 42

Thursday 9th of April
11.35 am

A ball bounced its way towards Drake and Sara as they neared the static caravan. Alan Turnbull's three small children were completely oblivious to the catastrophic events unfolding a few miles away.

The flimsy metal door squeaked open and Alan Turnbull's gaze darted between Drake and Sara. 'It's him, isn't it?' His voice sounded desperate.

'Can we talk in private?' Drake said.

He gasped and held a fist to his mouth. 'Oh, Jesus Christ.'

Children's clothes and toys strewn all over the caravan created a scene of organised chaos. Drake and Sara pushed some possessions out of the way and sat down on a sofa, looking at Alan Turnbull as the colour drained from his cheeks.

'We recovered a driving licence from the car belonging to your brother. We'll organise formal identification through dental records in due course.'

Alan Turnbull stared at Drake and then at Sara. It was the stare of a man unable to take in what he was being told.

'Mr Turnbull, can you tell us why Norman was in this area?'

'He was going to spend the weekend with us. He's been under a lot of stress recently.'

Sara used her most sympathetic tone. 'What kind of stress?'

'He was always highly strung. He argued with the

editor of the newspaper where he did some freelancing about an article he had written, about a Tom Levine and his business dealings. The man had taken over his life – he had become completely obsessed with him. He thought he was going to break a big story that would build his reputation and get him a job with one of the national newspapers.'

'Did he tell you where he was going this morning? Or who he was meeting?'

'He left first thing. I should have warned him, told him to be careful.' Turnbull's gaze drifted out of the window into the far distance, ignoring the sound of a child crying outside. After a moment, he added, 'He said he was going into Abersoch to that Italian café on the main street.'

'Did he tell you who he was meeting?'

Turnbull shook his head. 'I should have stopped him from going.'

'We may need to see you again,' Drake said as he got to his feet.

Outside they made their way back to the car. 'We need to get house-to-house organised around Porth Neigwl. And get the usual search done on Norman Turnbull's phone.'

Sara nodded.

'Let's go and see if anyone in the café can tell us anything.'

Abersoch was certainly bucking the trend for shop closures in rural areas: an Italian café, a fish-and-chip shop, a fancy-looking ice cream parlour and various convenience stores. Property prices in the village, driven skywards by wealthy families from England, made it a fashionable all-year-round destination resort.

Drake passed half a dozen metal tables and chairs on a narrow terrace in front of Sergio's café, as described by Alan Turnbull, and reached the counter. Drake pushed his warrant card at the owner.

'I'm investigating the murder of a man who might have been here this morning.' Drake thrust his mobile into the man's face: it had a copy of the image from Turnbull's driving licence.

The man nodded. Drake expected a singsong accent from Sicily or Naples but he guessed the man had travelled no further than Blackburn.

'He was here with Dot Levine. Really sad about her husband. They were regulars every weekend when they were down. I hear she's selling up.'

'How long were they here? Where did they sit?' Drake asked, stunned at this revelation.

A puzzled look passed over the man's face. He jerked his head towards a table by the window. Drake hurried over and looked straight out over a terrace onto the main road. Gliding past were high-end SUVs driven by glamorous women with glistening hair. He noticed the CCTV camera under the eaves: it would have recorded all the activity outside.

'Have you got the CCTV footage from earlier?'

'I'm busy right now. I've got a delivery to collect.'

'This is a murder inquiry.' Drake pointed an angry finger at the restaurateur. 'I need to see your CCTV footage. Now.'

Drake and Sara were led through a stale-smelling kitchen towards a room at the rear with a desk and piles of folders and papers. Sitting down, the owner fiddled with a mouse until the screen came to life.

It took a few minutes for him to find the right footage. Drake leaned over his shoulder, making sure the man knew they had little time to waste. Drake read the time; the CSIs would be finished, he would need to report to Superintendent Price, and he had to prepare for the remand hearing in the magistrates' court the following morning. Time was scarce.

Price would probably decide Turnbull's death should be transferred to a new detective inspector.

The owner stopped at the image of Dot Levine entering the restaurant. He paused the footage. The clock on the screen read 7.15. Drake nodded for him to move the footage on. They saw Norman Turnbull marching across the road, his head turning in all directions: the time said 7.26.

'Do you want to see the footage of when they left?'

The owner ran the footage on until Turnbull left. The time said 7.46. Mrs Levine was still sitting by the window; they watched her wordless instructions to a waitress. Traffic drove past the café, occasionally stopping at the pedestrian crossing outside. Drake thought he recognised a driver of a car that pulled to a halt as three teenagers meandered over the road. The footage carried on running until Drake realised who he had seen driving the car moments earlier. 'Go back.'

'How far?'

'Back to when Mrs Levine speaks to the waitress.'

The man sighed his frustration. Drake listened to the mouse being clicked and when the youngsters appeared he raised his voice. 'Stop there.'

Sara joined him as they looked at the screen. Michael Kennedy, the chief clerk of Britannia Chambers, was sat drumming his fingers on the steering wheel of his BMW.

Dot Levine opened the door of her bungalow and the sound of Celine Dion drooling out a love song far too loudly followed behind her. The expensive-looking, crisp white blouse gave her a healthy, summery look.

'May we come in, Mrs Levine?' Drake said.

She shrugged her agreement, pushed the door open and let them enter. Behind him Drake heard the door being snapped shut by Sara. Boxes were lined up along the kitchen table, on every available space of the worktops.

Drake got straight to the point. 'Did you see Norman Turnbull this morning?'

'Yes, he is that damn fool journalist. He printed some articles about Tom a while ago. He was making a nuisance of himself and he wanted to ask some questions. I told him I'd agree to meet him on one condition – that he never contact me again and that if he did I'd report him to the police.'

'What did he want to ask you about?'

'He wanted to know if I knew anything about the betting shops in south Manchester Tom had bought a few years ago.'

'Betting shops?' Drake looked at Mrs Levine, but his mind frantically sorted threads from earlier in the investigation. Nicholas Wixley had a list of betting shops on his computer.

'He bought a small chain of bookmakers. He thought he might turn it into something successful.'

Successful at money-laundering, Drake thought.

'Anyway, I remember Tom telling me I'd be

surprised about who was in hock to the company.'

Mrs Levine put an ancient-looking liquidiser into the nearest box. 'So, I told Turnbull he'd be the last person I'd help.' She turned to face Drake. 'Why are you asking about Turnbull anyway?'

'He was killed a few minutes after seeing you.'

Chapter 43

Thursday 9th of April
3.35 pm

Wyndham Price kept his eyes fixed on Drake as he finished summarising the details from Hell's Mouth, adding. 'It's too early to formally confirm Turnbull was murdered. But I've—'

'Treat it as murder immediately.'

'Yes, sir.' Price hadn't waited to hear that Drake was doing just that.

Winder was coordinating house-to-house inquiries. Luned was taking a statement from Alan Turnbull and officers from Stockport were at his flat securing the property and removing computers and paperwork.

Until forensics had completed their work he couldn't rule out the possibility it was a freak accident. Cars do catch fire, Drake had observed to a sceptical Price.

'Selston's remand hearing is tomorrow morning. I need you in the magistrates' court with Andy Thorsen.' Price left no room for Drake to contemplate being anywhere else. 'If the magistrates refuse bail you can be certain there will be an appeal to a Crown Court judge. I'm not putting any money on him not getting bail.'

Selston would have the very best legal team. Arguments would have been researched, sureties already available, his passport ready to be surrendered to secure his release.

Price was right; Selston would probably be out on bail by Friday evening.

And it was only a matter of time until Price

allocated the Turnbull inquiry to another detective inspector. Drake left the senior management suite and returned to the Incident Room.

Since discovering Turnbull's body Drake had smothered a worm of doubt wiggling around in his mind about Selston's guilt. He hated the possibility he'd been responsible for deciding to charge a man who might be innocent. Miscarriages of justice did happen, but why had Selston lied to them?

Below the photographs of Selston and Wixley on the board was the list of Britannia Chambers' staff headed by Michael Kennedy.

'Why was Kennedy in Abersoch yesterday?' Drake swept his gaze around the images and details pinned to the board.

'We know about the telephone calls Turnbull made last night,' Sara said after joining him. She handed Drake a list of the numbers on a printed sheet. Drake read them carefully. Two looked familiar. He strode back to his room, Sara following in his slipstream. 'I've seen these numbers before.'

Drake trawled through the details on his computer until he reached a list of persons of interest, witnesses, and people spoken to during the course of the inquiry. He found the number and turned to Sara.

'He called Laura Wixley last night. Can you believe that?' Drake recalled a comment from Price. 'She's staying at her holiday home.'

'You don't think she ...?'

Drake reached for his phone. Winder answered after two rings. 'I need you to go over to the Wixley home. I want to know exactly where Deputy Chief Constable Laura Wixley was last night.'

'What, me, boss?'

'Yes, Gareth, you and Luned.'

The second telephone number he recognised belonged to Michael Kennedy. The worm of doubt suddenly struggled to break free in his mind. Why had Norman Turnbull called Michael Kennedy?

'Norman Turnbull called Michael Kennedy last night.'

'I don't understand what the connection could be, boss.'

Drake fumbled for a clean sheet of A4 paper from a drawer in his desk. Then he carefully moved the columns of Post-it notes to one side. 'What do we know about Michael Kennedy?'

Sara began. 'He's the chief clerk of Britannia Chambers.'

'And he was regularly humiliated by Nicholas Wixley.'

He paused, allowing the cogs of the investigation to slot slowly into place. 'We've been told Nicholas Wixley got all the best cases. How did he manage that unless Michael Kennedy favoured him?'

Drake got into his stride.

'What if Wixley had something on Michael Kennedy? Something that gave him the ability to maximise his income.' A comment from Dot Levine the night before, about her husband being surprised at who owed the bookmakers money, made him turn his attention to the records from Nicholas Wixley's laptop.

'Come on, boss.' Sara sounded patronising. 'It wouldn't give him a motive to murder Nicholas Wixley.'

He ignored her, and after finding the list of debtors

he scrolled down to the surnames beginning with K. Nothing. 'Damn. He isn't on the debtors list from Wixley's computer.'

Sara paused, obviously unconvinced. 'I suppose the fact that he had an affair with Kennedy's wife adds to the mix.'

'There could be something else ...' Drake said. 'Nicholas Wixley threatens to share the details of what he knows about Kennedy with the other senior barristers. After all, he's been appointed a circuit judge. He doesn't need Kennedy any longer.'

Drake stood up and paced around the room before stopping to peer out of his office window. Trees were in bud and the grass on the wide expanse of parkland surrounding headquarters needed its first cut. The image of Laura Wixley's immaculate garden came to his mind. It was the first gardening activity he had seen that season. Then it struck him that she had mentioned Kennedy. He turned abruptly to Sara.

'What did Laura Wixley say about Kennedy?'

Sara left the room, returning moments later with her notebook. She flicked through the pages until she found the right notes. *"Funny little man from Nicholas's Chambers."*

Drake looked at Sara. A guilty silence enveloped the room. Drake didn't need to tell Sara: Michael Kennedy needed their immediate attention.

Drake sat down, fisted his right hand, and tapped the table. He added the name *Selston* in capitals on the top of the sheet in front of him. And alongside it the name *Michael Kennedy*. He gestured for Sara to sit down.

'We need to analyse everything again.' Drake said

through drying lips. 'Selston would have known about the funeral order of service. Kennedy could too, from access to the prosecution papers. The press didn't mention them, which means only someone on the inside knew that detail.'

'It could be anyone. Dozens of people in the Crown Prosecution Service, the defence lawyers and the courts had access to that information.'

Drake didn't let Sara's comments deflect him. 'We've assumed it was Selston because he was the defending barrister, but Michael Kennedy could have read the prosecution file.'

'And he was staying at the Portmeirion Hotel when Nicholas Wixley was killed.'

'Damn it.' Drake straightened in his chair, reached for the telephone and dialled Winder.

'I've arrived outside DCC Wixley's home,' Winder said.

'After you've seen her, call at the Portmeirion Hotel and identify the staff working the evening Nicholas Wixley was murdered. Find out if anybody ordered a taxi or if any of the staff can remember anybody leaving late at night. And see if they have any CCTV footage.'

Drake finished the call and turned to Sara, who shook her head. 'He'd never take the risk of leaving the hotel.'

In Drake's experience murderers and criminals always took risks. There was always something that let them down, some detail they hadn't considered, some possibility of detection that eluded them. It made his job worthwhile.

'I'll go through Nicholas Wixley's papers again.

You work on Tom Levine's death. We've missed something.'

Sara struck a serious note. 'And we still have the knife found at Selston's home.'

Drake rubbed his hands over his face. 'I know, I know.'

Drake barked instructions for reception to make certain he wasn't disturbed, and he got straight down to looking at everything again. Even if his fears were unfounded he had to prepare for the court appearance tomorrow. By the early evening his desk was a mass of papers and it unsettled him.

Drake heard Winder and Luned as they entered the Incident Room. By now he welcomed the interruption, so he left his office.

Winder stood by his desk. 'Nobody has seen anything.'

Luned nodded. 'Porth Neigwl is a very isolated spot.'

'Even so,' Winder continued. 'It's not every day that a body is burned to a crisp in a car.'

'And Mrs Wixley?' Drake said.

'She wasn't there, boss,' Winder said. 'And we spoke to a neighbour across the road that you'd spoken to previously. Funny old dear, she kept asking if we wanted tea and scones.'

'I think she's lonely,' Luned added.

Winder continued. 'She told us Laura Wixley had left the previous afternoon to go back to Manchester.'

Drake circled around the desks belonging to his team and reached the Incident Room board as Sara posed the question that was on his mind. 'So, I suppose that means she is not implicated in the murder of

Norman Turnbull?'

Drake sighed. 'So why did he call her?'

'That Portmeirion Hotel is a swanky place,' Winder announced after slurping on a bottle of Diet Coke he produced from a jacket. 'We spoke with two of the night staff working on the night of Nicholas Wixley's murder. They don't remember anyone leaving the hotel in the middle of the night or anything strange or unusual. Some of the younger barristers stayed in the bar until the early hours getting shit-faced.'

'We've got three more names to contact in the morning,' Luned contributed.

'Some of the guests were going fishing when we left. Catching the evening tide.'

Drake then knew exactly what he had missed about Kennedy. 'Christ, I've just remembered. Kennedy has a boat in Porthmadog.'

Three pairs of eyes gazed over at him, questioning.

'He could have got into the marina undetected.'

Sara sounded a note of caution. 'We still don't have a motive for Kennedy to kill Levine.'

Drake stared over at the image of Selston on the board. If he was innocent then a serious miscarriage of justice could be prevented. He had to satisfy himself, be certain, he had discharged his duty. Suddenly the priorities sharpened into clear focus. He turned to face his team.

'Gareth, speak to the night staff in the morning. Sara you contact the harbour master at Porthmadog and establish if there's any evidence of Kennedy's boat being moved the night Levine was killed.'

Drake paused. Concentration oozed from every pore of the officers present. 'I'm in court tomorrow so I want updates as soon as you have them.'

Back in his office he requisitioned an urgent financial search against Kennedy. The Incident Room had emptied by the time Drake had finished preparation for the court hearing the following morning. Evenings like this drove his obsessions, forcing him to check and recheck everything, guaranteeing he'd stay chained to his desk until something could free him. Annie's telephone call did just that.

'Are you still in the office?' She scolded.

'I've got a lot to do before tomorrow.'

'Ian, go home. There's nothing more you can do.'

Drake did as he was told, reluctantly. He could never fully dismiss the risk in his mind that he had done something wrong. But he listened and grabbed his jacket and left headquarters.

On the way out, he sneaked a look at the board. All the photographs were still there: the brutal record of each crime scene, the funeral order of services and list of persons of interest. He switched the light off as he left the Incident Room and went home.

Chapter 44

Friday 10th of April
6.35 am

Drake jolted into consciousness as his dream faded to a silhouette. He had been shaking hands with the mourners at his father's funeral. Earnest, intense faces expressed their condolences as they shook his hand, reminding him that his father had been well liked and loved. The sight of his grandfather's open casket had been a recurring theme of his dreams over the years, or were they nightmares? He sat on the edge of the bed interrogating his thoughts. Had the orders of service he had inspected before leaving the Incident Room been the catalyst for his disrupted sleep?

Andy Thorsen's text message the night before had reminded him he needed to be at the magistrates' court by nine-thirty at the latest. It meant he would have to leave headquarters by no later than eight-thirty. Listening to the news as he ate his breakfast, he half expected an item referring to Selston's court appearance, but the radio bulletin focused on the latest round of depressing trade figures with an analysis from an economist about the certainty of interest rate rises.

He detoured to the Incident Room at headquarters and perched on the side of a table gazing at the board. The criminal justice system would grind Justin Selston through its relentless mangle. He hadn't told Price about the doubts surfacing in his mind. Facing up to the possibility they had blundered would be painful. As police officers their first duty was to establish the truth. Personal reputations could go to hell. But was it always that simple? Reputations were hard earned and admitting a mistake could be the toughest thing to face.

Something made him stand up and remove one of the orders of service. After the image of the loved one on the front page there were the usual hymns inside with the prayers and readings. On the back were thanks to the staff of the care home that had looked after the family member. Donations were to be made to a well-known charity. None of the persons of interest had any links to the deceased or their families. The funeral undertaker didn't keep a register of mourners. The second order of service was similar, but the charity was different.

It reminded Drake that his mother had sent a cheque to the cancer ward of the local hospital for the donations collected at the time of his father's death. Then it struck him that there was one thing they hadn't checked.

He stood up abruptly, grabbed both orders of service and read the contact details of the funeral directors. Back in his room he picked up the telephone and rang the first number. Although it was still early, a voice answered. 'Sunnyside funeral undertakers.'

Someone with a dark sense of humour, Drake thought. He spelled out his request in clear terms. Then he repeated the same exercise for the other undertakers. He glanced at his watch, worried he might be late.

The magistrates' court shared a building with the Crown Court on the outskirts of Caernarfon. Drake saw the phalanx of reporters gathered by the main entrance after parking his car. He recognised two of the faces of journalists from the Welsh TV channels and another from the major UK-wide network. Selston's court appearance was at least generating substantial press coverage. With Selston in custody the cameras couldn't record the perp-walk favoured by the news. Drake gave them no more than a passing glance as he went inside.

Andy Thorsen paced around the conference room reserved for the prosecution.

'Good morning,' Drake said.

Thorsen grunted a reply. Moments later Rhodri Boyd, the barrister representing the Crown Prosecution Service, breezed in. He made Drake feel like the poor relation even though he had chosen his best suit, newest shirt and least-used tie. Boyd was immaculate, his suit clearly made to measure. A little over six-foot and flat-stomached with neatly trimmed auburn hair, it was difficult to make out his age – late forties at a guess, Drake thought.

'Good morning, gentlemen.' His accent flowed with the natural rhythms and confidence of a man accustomed to addressing a court and who expected his every word to be given the weight and importance it demanded. It was a sensible move by Thorsen to have a Welsh barrister from the capital working for the prosecution as Drake could hear the Welsh undertone to his accent. The magistrates would appreciate that, as well as the circuit judge who'd inevitably consider the appeal that afternoon.

'Good morning, Rhodri.' Thorsen's voice trembled slightly. 'This is Detective Inspector Ian Drake. He is the senior investigating officer on the case.'

Boyd reached out a hand and gave Drake's a firm, brisk shake. 'Pleased to meet you. Are we all ready?'

A part of Drake wanted this process to pause. Give him time to reconsider. But it was too late for that. After all, they had enough to satisfy the test for prosecuting Justin Selston. A bloodied knife had been found in his home. He had ample motive; he had been to Nicholas Wixley's property on the evening he was killed. He had lied to them. That was the biggest thing, Drake reminded himself.

Killing time at court hearings had wasted hours of Drake's career and it never got any better. Delays seemed to be an inherent part of the process. They waited around exchanging small talk; Boyd quizzed Drake about the interview with Zavier Cornwell. Drake surreptitiously checked his mobile, hoping that all the threads his team were working on would soon enough come to fruition. He wasn't going to second-guess what the outcome might be, but he needed to be convinced Justin Selston had rightly been charged.

A few minutes to ten Selston's barrister appeared at the door of the conference room followed by a team of lawyers. Introductions made, Selston's barrister turned to Rhodri Boyd. 'A word, please.'

Both barristers left and the defence team did the same.

'Do you know Selston's barrister?'

Thorsen nodded. 'Howard Allport is a Queen's Counsel from London. One of the youngest ever appointed as I recall and he sits as a deputy high court judge and has a reputation for being utterly ruthless.'

'A QC?' Drake said, thinking it was highly unusual for a senior barrister to appear in a magistrates' court. 'No pressure then.'

Thorsen made a grunting sound.

When Rhodri Boyd returned, Drake searched his face and body language for some tell-tale disclosure, some comments from Selston's barrister that would make them rethink. 'They've organised for the local circuit judge to deal with the appeal this afternoon. On the assumption the magistrates refuse to grant Selston bail.'

'That's what we expected,' Thorsen said.

'Allport made some very uncomplimentary remarks about the investigation. I basically told him to go to hell.' Boyd grinned. 'And it's Dewi Richards sitting as the judge today so Allport's accent will be enough to persuade him to deny Selston bail any day of the week.' Boyd chortled now.

Another agonising hour drifted past as the magistrates heard two drink-driving cases.

Drake checked his emails repeatedly for any sign of the financial reports on Michael Kennedy. Thorsen and Boyd gave him suspicious glances. He returned weak smiles that he hoped and prayed wouldn't give them any inkling of how his nerves were torn to shreds. Sweat soaked through his armpits.

Another half an hour passed before he texted Luned. *Check all team emails for Kennedy finances.*

A text to Sara and Winder asking for updates followed. Both men in the room with Drake gave him a guarded look when he finished. A court clerk appeared at the door and Drake's pulse quickened. 'The magistrates will hear the case at midday.'

Chapter 45

Friday 10th of April
9.37 am

Winder knew not to challenge the logic of Inspector Drake's orders. But that morning he felt like he was being sent on a fool's errand. They had a defendant in the dock and enough evidence to get a conviction. He regretted not saying anything in the last team briefing. After all, Luned had grown in confidence and secretly he admired her determination even if she was probably the most boring person he had worked with.

Winder reached the first address on his list and banged on the door of the terrace in Porthmadog but his efforts went unrewarded. He had a mobile number for Iwan, employed part-time at Portmeirion, and Winder dialled it, but it went straight to a voice message asking him to leave his details; he didn't bother. He gazed up at the curtained first floor windows. No movement or any sign of life.

He got back in his car and punched in the postcode for the second address. Conveniently, it was close to the third; Winder was confident he'd be the first to report progress to Drake.

Gwel y Mynydd was a detached house overlooking Penrhyndeudraeth and near enough to Portmeirion for Hywel Parry to walk to work. A woman in her fifties opened the door.

'I need to speak to Hywel. Is he in?' Winder gave her little time to inspect his warrant card.

She ushered him into a sitting room at the front of the property and then yelled Hywel's name. A display of Toby jugs and Moorcroft pottery adorned a shelf above the picture rail.

Hywel looked flushed when he entered. 'Sorry, I was in the back of the garden.'

'I'm investigating the death of Nicholas Wixley.'

Hywel nodded. 'Is that the judge who was killed?'

'I understand you were working at the Portmeirion Hotel on the night he was killed.'

'Yes. I was helping in the bar and reception. There isn't a lot to do at night.'

'Do you remember anyone leaving in the middle of the night? One of the guests?'

Hywel crumpled his forehead. 'I wasn't paying attention to who left.'

Winder had Hywel explain his evening, where he worked, and who he was with until he was satisfied that he could learn nothing more. His interrogation of Hywel would satisfy Drake and his own conscience when he'd reassure the inspector he had thoroughly quizzed the witness.

Winder left soon after and drove to the next address.

Fred Williams led him into a sitting room, announcing as he did so that he needed to get to bed soon. Winder repeated his request for information about the night Wixley was killed.

'That was the night a crowd of lawyers stayed up late. Jesus, they drank a lot. I've never seen so many champagne bottles ordered in one night.'

It suggested Williams had been busy, so Winder decided to wrap up the interview and get back to headquarters. 'Did you see anyone leaving the hotel that night?'

He shook his head.

Winder made to leave when Williams added, 'But when I was having my break and a smoke outside, I did see a car arrive. It must have been after twelve.'

It grabbed Winder's attention. 'Did you recognise who was driving it?'

'No.'

Nothing to help us, Winder decided.

'But the car was a BMW. I noticed the colour – Le Mans blue. My father has a car in the same colour, and the car parked below one of the street lights.'

A message reached Drake's mobile as they filed into court. Selston stood in the dock staring straight ahead, flanked by a security guard. Drake settled into a bench behind Thorsen, who sat behind Boyd. There was a definite pecking order to barristers, solicitors and police officers.

The magistrates entered and the sound of a collective shuffle filled the courtroom as the lawyers, court staff and journalists stood up. Drake's mobile vibrated on silent in his pocket. Surreptitiously he reached into his pocket as Boyd got to his feet.

'Bore da, Your Worships.'

Opening in Welsh was inspired, Drake thought as he looked over at Allport, who had an eyebrow raised.

He read the bland, neutral language of the email with the results of the financial search on Kennedy. He let out a slow breath as he opened the attachment, hoping he could concentrate on Rhodri Boyd's opening remarks to the magistrates and read from the screen of his mobile simultaneously. He scrolled through the attachments until he found the relevant statement.

He glanced up, hoping that no one paid him any attention.

Boyd's voice filled the court. 'The prosecution's case is that the defendant had been driven to murder because of deep-seated resentment and hatred of Nicholas Wixley nurtured over many years. And ...'

Drake blanked out the rest of Boyd's comments as he read the date of Kennedy receiving the sum of £50,000 into his bank account. He fisted a hand and tapped his knee – it was the first part of the information he needed.

He tapped out a message for Luned.

She might give him the second part of the jigsaw.

Chapter 46

Friday 10th of April
10.35 am

'I don't work nights, love.'

The Porthmadog harbour master had a corpulent face, a massive paunch and the most annoyingly dismissive attitude to Sara's questions.

'Is there anyone who works nights?'

'Why do you want to know?'

Sara counted mentally to ten. Drake would have been rude by now. She adopted a softer tone. She had to get this man's cooperation.

'I need to establish any boat movements for a certain evening.' She gave him the date. 'It was the night a Tom Levine was murdered in Pwllheli marina. We want to eliminate as many people from our inquiry as we can.'

The harbour master shrugged. Then he waddled around in his chair, adjusting his seating position. 'I'll dig out the details of every vessel that requested access. It is not going to be a long list.' He found a large bound volume from the drawer of his desk and flicked through the pages. 'You might try some of the local fishermen. They have small boats that come in and out all the time.' She jotted down two names in her pocketbook.

Sara sighed to herself. This was supposed to have been a simple exercise: identify if anyone could confirm Michael Kennedy had left Porthmadog harbour on the evening Tom Levine had been killed. A few minutes later she had a scribbled note confirming the names of each boat entering the harbour the night Tom

Levine had his throat cut. It didn't help, as it recorded only vessels over 1.5m draft, which excluded Michael Kennedy's fishing cuddy. Glancing at her watch, she realised by now the magistrates' court would be well underway.

She enjoyed going to court, listening to the lawyers summarising in cold, objective terms the evidence taken hours to assemble. It made their job sound easy. She skirted around the quayside to the public house the harbour master had recommended as a haunt for the fishermen he'd mentioned. It was still early, and a cleaner was busy vacuuming the floor while a woman with a severe blue rinse stacked the shelves of the bar.

After showing her warrant card, Sara asked, 'I'm looking for Harry Austin and David Jones.'

The woman glanced at an old clock on the wall behind her. 'They should be here in half an hour.'

'I'll wait.'

'Do you want something to drink?'

Sara shook her head, sat down and waited.

Half an hour turned into forty-five minutes. The woman was still busy behind the bar and she rolled her eyes at Sara. 'Trust them to be late.'

Sara accepted her offer of a cappuccino into which she stirred two teaspoons of sugar. A text from Drake asked for an update. She replied – *Nothing yet.*

Sara waited over an hour before two men arrived. They sat down on bar stools and the landlady nodded at Sara before tipping her head at both men.

Grabbing her warrant card, she gave each an opportunity for a cursory glance. 'Which one of you is Harry Austin?'

The blonde-haired youngster replied. 'That's me.'

'I've spoken with the harbour master and he tells me you fish regularly. I want to know if either of you can remember seeing any boat leaving on Friday night, 29th March. We're investigating the murder of Tom Levine, whose body was found in Pwllheli marina the following morning. We want to eliminate anybody using their boat that night.'

Austin turned to Jones by his side. '*Ti'n cofio noson honno, wyt? Parti Jack 'te.*'

Sara caught something about 'evening' and 'party'.

'Sorry, we can't help you. We were at a mate's party. We didn't surface until Saturday afternoon.' Austin smiled at the recollection.

Jones beamed his agreement.

Sara shrugged on her coat, grabbed her bag, reached for enough change to pay for her cappuccino and made for the door.

'It was a Friday night, wasn't it?' Jones said.

'That's right.'

'You need to talk to Peter Foster. He always goes fishing on a Friday night. He comes down from Bolton, regular as clockwork. He says it's the only thing that keeps him sane.'

Sara wanted to believe it was going to be a sensible use of her time to speak to Peter Foster.

'He'll be here in a couple of hours,' Jones added.

The three magistrates looked terrified. It must have been intimidating having a Queen's Counsel from London and a senior barrister from Cardiff appearing in their court arguing about bail for another eminent lawyer. Inevitably, it meant they would play safe, refuse bail and that the appeal process would take its course, allowing the circuit judge in the Crown Court nearby to make a decision. Drake could see the clerk mentally twiddling his thumbs, knowing that everybody was going through the motions.

Rhodri Boyd was using the opportunity to practise and hone his address to the circuit judge later that afternoon. He could assess, too, the arguments Howard Allport would advance to secure his client's release. No doubt the defence would accuse the Wales Police Service of incompetence, citing Selston's previous unblemished character, his upstanding place in society. Drake consoled himself with knowing they had an eyewitness and the bloodied knife.

Luned's next message to Drake's mobile arrived as Rhodri Boyd sat down.

He read the details and his chest tightened; momentarily he felt winded. Tom Levine had sent £50,000 to Kennedy within a few days of Britannia Chambers completing the lease on their offices. Like a rabbit in a headlight Drake sat rigid. He couldn't tell Thorsen and definitely not Boyd. He needed to get back to headquarters, talk to Price.

But Howard Allport hadn't finished.

He had barely started. The accent was far back, but authoritative and persuasive, even if it sounded out of place.

'The charges will be contested with the utmost vigour.'

Drake glanced over at Thorsen, who was staring at Allport, a hurt, pained expression on his face.

'I should make it clear that we assert that the investigation has been riddled with inconsistencies and irregularities, and the decision to prosecute has been made on the basis of the flimsiest and most compromised eyewitness imaginable.' He gave Boyd a sideways glance that almost stretched to Thorsen and Drake. 'And the discovery of a bloodied knife is laughable – it does not belong to Mr Selston and the prosecution has nothing to link him to it. The characters of all those involved will be subject to the most intense scrutiny.'

Had they made the right decision? In the harsh light of legal scrutiny, it was easy for a defence team to score points.

A message from Winder reached his mobile.

Eyewitness saw blue BMW return to Portmeirion in middle of night when NW killed. Have checked records. Kennedy owns vehicle with same colour.

Drake instinctively glanced around at everyone in the courtroom as though Winder had been there sharing secrets with him in a loud voice. He ran a finger over his lips.

Allport's peroration sounded utterly convincing. He tried to read the faces of the magistrates. He threaded the fingers of both hands together and squeezed tightly. There were probably a dozen BMWs in Portmeirion the night Nicholas Wixley was killed and perhaps more than one in Le Mans blue. But it was a coincidence too far. Drake needed to hear from Sara and more than anything he wanted to hear back from the undertakers he had spoken to first thing that morning.

He didn't even notice when Allport sat down. Then the chairman of the magistrates stood up, announcing they would retire to make a decision.

As soon as they left the courtroom, tension dissipated and a quiet hum of conversation and rustling of papers took over. Thorsen walked over to Drake.

'How did you think it went?' Drake said.

'Difficult to say. I still think they will refuse bail. I don't think they'll be long.'

Thorsen went back to his seat, restarting his conversation with Rhodri Boyd.

Drake frantically scrolled through his emails, hoping he hadn't missed the message he had been waiting for all morning. Suddenly the screen filled with a series of emails with various attachments that he clicked open in turn. He used his thumb and finger to enlarge the attached lists and focused so hard that the sound in the courtroom faded to a whisper. The lights above him shone more brightly; he could hear his own breathing, sense his throbbing pulse. Finally, he found the surname *Kennedy* on each list. It was like a knockout punch from a heavyweight boxer. Drake couldn't work out whether to feel elation or panic or despair.

He did not have time to rationalise his thoughts as the magistrates returned.

Everyone in the courts stood up. Drake struggled to his feet, gripping his mobile tightly.

'In view of the seriousness of the charge we are denying bail. The defendant will be remanded in custody,' The chairman announced.

The magistrates left immediately afterwards, the security guards returning Selston to the cells.

Thorsen and Boyd stood by Drake's side. 'There will be an appeal hearing this afternoon of course,' Boyd said.

Drake barely nodded, his whole body stiff with tension. 'I need to get back to headquarters.'

Thorsen now. 'What the hell do you mean?'

'I need to check some papers.' Drake wasn't going to share the growing suspicion they had charged the wrong man. The prospect made his insides quiver. He had to double-check and triple-check everything to be certain.

Boyd frowned. Thorsen scowled. 'Be back here by four at the latest.'

Chapter 47

Friday 10th of April
1.05 pm

Drake crunched the Mondeo into first gear and hurtled towards the junction of the side street near the Crown Court building before turning onto the main road out of the town. He convinced himself he didn't need to be back by four pm. Andy Thorsen and Rhodri Boyd could manage perfectly well without him. A possibility existed that Michael Kennedy had killed Tom Levine – it meant he needed to reassess everything. The evidence that linked both men suggested Kennedy had taken a bribe to secure a lucrative lease for the barristers' chambers. Had Turnbull somehow discovered a link between Kennedy and Levine and decided to challenge Kennedy, confront him face-to-face?

Drake broke every speed limit. Once clear of Caernarfon, he floored the accelerator, weaving in and out of the traffic until he reached the dual carriageway that by-passed Felinheli. Within a few minutes he was in the outside lane of the A55 making for headquarters.

Kennedy's image on the CCTV footage from the restaurant in Abersoch dominated Drake's thoughts. The man was even drumming his fingers impatiently on the steering wheel. What could he be impatient about? Was he late for his appointment to kill another human being?

Drake flashed the headlights of his car, blasting the car horn and gesticulating wildly at various motorists idling in the outside lane. He called headquarters via the hands-free connection. Luned was in the Incident

Room; she told him Winder was due to arrive any minute, but she hadn't heard from Sara.

Drake dialled her number.

She answered promptly. 'I'm waiting to speak to the fisherman who goes out from Porthmadog every Friday night. I hope he might be able to help.'

Drake braked violently as a car pulled out in front of him. Another blast of the horn reverberated around the cabin. 'Get back to me as soon as you can.'

Next Drake rang Price's office. 'I'm on my way to see the superintendent.'

'I thought you were in court, Ian?' Hannah replied. 'He's very busy this afternoon—'

Drake ended the call abruptly.

It was a little before two pm when Drake pulled into headquarters and dashed into reception, bounding up the stairs to the Incident Room. Winder slurped on a can of soda.

'My office, now, both of you,' Drake announced.

He turned to look at Luned standing with Winder. 'Are you absolutely certain about the bank that paid Kennedy and Wixley?'

'I double-checked, boss. I rang the branch to check the sort codes and account numbers.'

'Get a list of all the guests staying at the Portmeirion Hotel the night before Nicholas Wixley was killed. I want them all cross-referenced with the database of car registrations. Find out if any of them own a Le Mans blue BMW.'

'On to it, boss.'

'Have you heard from Sara?' Luned said.

'She is waiting to speak to a possible eyewitness.' Drake read the time on his computer monitor – 14.30.

There was no way he would be back in court for the appeal hearing. He'd have to live with Thorsen's anger.

He booted up his computer and after clicking into his emails, he printed off the sheets he had read earlier. He drew a yellow highlighter through the name *Pamela Kennedy* on each.

He scooped up the papers and threaded his way over to the senior management suite. Instinctively he knew what the right decision was going to be.

It would be painful, even embarrassing, but immensely better than facing the possibility of an innocent man being held in custody. His job was to get to the truth, and miscarriages of justice often happened, but Drake didn't want his police career tainted by such an eventuality.

He stood and waited while Hannah buzzed Superintendent Price. He appeared at the door of his office seconds later.

'What the hell are you doing here?'

'There is something we need to discuss.'

Price turned to Hannah. 'No interruptions.' She nodded back.

Drake sat in the visitor chair looking over at Price. 'This looks serious, Ian.'

'One of the similarities between Nicholas Wixley and the alphabet killings is the funeral order of services the killer left. Zavier Cornwell had written in blood the letters of the word 'death' on each. When his case came to court it was decided not to make mention of that feature to avoid distress to the families of the bereaved.'

'I remember.'

'Cornwell collected the orders of service by simply pretending to be a mourner at his local crematorium.'

'Where is this taking you?'

'Only someone with an intimate knowledge of the case could have known about them.'

'That included Selston.'

'And Michael Kennedy could easily have read the prosecution file and learned the details.'

Drake passed Price the orders of service found in Nicholas Wixley's bedroom. 'The bereaved families asked for donations to be made to various charities. I called the undertakers this morning. They emailed me a list.'

Drake produced another sheet with the yellow highlighting. 'Michael Kennedy's wife gifted to each of the charities named.'

'She knew all the families?'

'It means he easily got hold of copies of these orders of service.'

Drake's mobile rang in his pocket and he read Sara's name on the screen. Price gave him a critical glare, obviously surprised Drake hadn't switched off his mobile. 'I need to take this call, sir.'

Drake heard Sara's voice. 'I've spoken to Peter Foster. He went out fishing early the Friday evening that Tom Levine was killed and when he returned he saw Michael Kennedy scrambling to get off his boat. He hadn't tied it in his usual place, which struck Foster as unusual at the time. It looks like you are right, boss.'

'Get back here now.'

Drake turned to Price, who spoke first. 'Good news?'

'We have an eyewitness who can place Michael Kennedy in Cardigan Bay on the night Tom Levine was murdered. And another thing, sir. Kennedy received a substantial sum of money from Tom Levine just after Britannia Chambers agreed a new lease for property. It was exactly the same as the premium they paid.'

'Jesus Christ, you mean he took a bribe?'

'It looks that way. And Levine and Wixley are close. So Kennedy doesn't want to risk chambers finding out so he kills Levine. And we know that Kennedy's car left the Portmeirion Hotel on the night Wixley was killed – we have an eyewitness who saw it arrive back in the early hours.'

Price used an eerily neutral tone. 'Did you mention any of this to Andy Thorsen?'

'Of course not.'

Price nodded.

'They're expecting me back at court for Selston's appeal at four pm.'

'To hell with that. We need to decide what we're going to do.'

Drake took a long breath. He had thought of little else for the last two hours. 'We have enough to justify the arrest of Michael Kennedy on suspicion of Tom Levine's murder.'

Price whistled under his breath.

Drake added, 'And the possibility must exist that he was responsible for Nicholas Wixley's killing too. He was treated badly by Wixley, who'd had a relationship with Kennedy's wife some time ago.'

Price blew out a lungful of breath. 'You're overlooking the knife found at Selston's property.'

Drake heard the superintendent's comment and his mind focused on something else lurking in the back of his mind. The first time he had learned about Britannia Chambers had been from Holly Thatcher. Then he remembered her comments about attending a chambers party at Selston's home. Kennedy would have been there too.

'Perhaps somebody planted the knife to implicate Selston.'

Heavy silence filled the space between both men.

Drake stared at Price, who stared back. Price spoke first. 'What do you suggest?'

'We withdraw our objection to Justin Selston being bailed.'

Price reached for the telephone on his desk and grabbed the handset. 'I agree. I'll call Andy Thorsen. Go and arrest that fucking bastard Michael Kennedy.'

Chapter 48

Friday 10th of April
3.00 pm

Drake made two telephone calls. During the first he dictated clear instructions to an inspector at the City of Manchester police force headquarters. For the second he adopted an emollient tone.

'Is Mr Kennedy in chambers?'

'He's in a training event this afternoon and cannot be disturbed. May I ask who is calling?'

'I'll call back later.'

He turned to Sara, who was sitting in the visitor chair. Her eyebrows were drawn together tightly, and she pinched the skin at her throat before half choking a comment. 'What are we going to do about Justin Selston?'

'Superintendent Price will be calling Andy Thorsen before the appeal is heard, indicating that we have no objections to him being bailed. Until we've had time to interview Michael Kennedy, execute a search warrant at his home and the chalet he owns in Porthmadog, we're not going to make any decisions.'

Sara nodded weakly.

'In the meantime, we arrest Michael Kennedy and bring him back for questioning tonight.'

'Tonight?' Incredulity laced Sara's voice.

'We haven't got time to waste. If he is involved, the sooner we interview him the better.' Drake stood up, grabbed the keys to his car and, collecting his jacket from the coat stand, gestured to Sara that they had to get going.

During their journey to Britannia Chambers, the marked police car from the City of Manchester police force, sitting outside the premises, kept them regularly informed. Michael Kennedy hadn't moved from the building.

Driving on the A55 and then the motorway through Cheshire to the centre of Manchester gave Drake the opportunity to order his thoughts and prepare questions for the interview later that evening. Kennedy must be preening himself, Drake thought. The case against Selston appeared to be strong. He had admitted lying to the police about travelling to see Nicholas Wixley on the night of his death. Planting the knife with Wixley's and Levine's blood at Selston's property had been the masterstroke of Kennedy's plan.

By late in the afternoon Drake parked behind the marked police car. Both officers inside jumped out and joined Drake and Sara on the pavement. 'We're here to arrest a Michael Kennedy on suspicion of murder.'

'Are you taking him back to Wales tonight?' one of the officers asked.

Drake nodded. 'I don't expect any trouble.'

The reception staff at Britannia Chambers gawped as Drake and Sara marched in with the two uniformed officers. Drake asked politely for Michael Kennedy's whereabouts. A young girl stammered a reply, pointing down one of the corridors that led off the main reception.

'He's in our training suite. He wasn't to be disturbed.' The last few words died on her lips as Drake ignored her.

As Drake and Sara and the uniformed officers entered the room, a dozen inquisitive faces turned to look at them. Questioning expressions soon changed into gasps and mouths fell open. 'Will everyone please leave except Michael Kennedy.'

Drake engaged Kennedy directly with his eye contact. He shuffled back a step or two and then his pose stiffened. An exodus of staff filed out of the room past Drake and Sara in absolute silence.

He stepped towards Kennedy. 'Michael Kennedy I'm arresting you on suspicion of murder. You do not have to say anything …'

Arranging a solicitor, processing the paperwork and protecting Kennedy's rights as a prisoner were all done in double-quick time. Drake was determined he would be interviewed that evening. He ignored telephone calls from Andy Thorsen.

By eight pm Drake sat on a hard plastic chair in the windowless cork-lined interview room staring over at Michael Kennedy. He had expected Kennedy to have opted for a lawyer from one of the firms in Manchester to represent him but had raised no objection to the local duty solicitor being called.

'This is most irregular,' Penny Hughes complained. 'I haven't had nearly enough time to consult with my client. I want to formally record my objection.'

Drake brushed her comments aside. 'Objection noted. We proceed.'

Hughes fell into a sullen mood. Kennedy stared over at Drake, a plastic mug of coffee in front of him. Kennedy's expensive silk tie was knotted neatly against the collar of a white shirt and his suit jacket was draped over the rear of the plastic chair, the same sort that would give Drake a stiff back by the end of the evening.

'Michael Kennedy, you have been arrested on suspicion of having murdered Tom Levine.'

'I know. I killed him.'

For a split second, Drake thought he imagined the admission. He glanced over at Sara, who had a dazed look on her face. He squinted over at Kennedy, sharpened his gaze. The next obvious question was to ask him for confirmation. 'Can you repeat that for the tape once again?'

'Yes, I killed him.'

Drake sat back and looked over at Penny Hughes, wondering exactly what was going through her mind.

The interview textbook suggested that an interview should always start with that simple question – did you kill the victim? But Drake hadn't even asked that question. Kennedy had admitted his involvement without prompting. This looked likely to be the easiest interview Drake had ever conducted.

Drake placed his arms on the table and then forward slightly. 'Mr Kennedy, perhaps you could tell us exactly the circumstances of why you committed this crime?'

'Tom Levine had threatened to tell chambers that I had taken a substantial bribe from him to secure the lease of the premises from the company he controlled. I had debts I was struggling to pay off. There was a house in Spain and credit cards and I couldn't manage financially. I saw the chance of making some money.'

'What did Tom Levine threaten?'

'He was going to tell Julia Griffiths, the head of chambers, that I had demanded payment of £50,000, which chambers paid as a premium. He was an evil, vicious bastard.'

'Explain the circumstances of how you got access to his yacht.'

'He'd been drinking heavily in the sailing club.'

'Did you spike his drinks?'

'I didn't need to. I could see that he was going to be comatose before the end of the evening. So when I got back to the chalet I took my boat over to the marina. It was easy to get alongside the pontoons and he was there in the forward berth, crashed out. I took my chance and sliced him up.'

This wasn't going to be a cat-and-mouse sort of interview with Michael Kennedy. Drake had his admission. He would be charged, bail would be refused, and he would be remanded in custody.

'The knife used to kill Tom Levine also had traces of Nicholas Wixley's blood.'

For a second Kennedy frowned.

'I couldn't stand working for the man a moment longer. It was a living hell, a daily nightmare having to tolerate the ritual humiliations. If ever there was a man deserved to die it was Wixley.' Kennedy barely paused for breath. 'I left the Portmeirion Hotel where I was staying and drove to his home. I could tell he'd been entertaining some expensive escort again. The man sickened me.'

'Describe how you were able to get Wixley onto the bed.'

'I overpowered him with chloroform and after that it was easy to drag him into the bedroom.'

Drake took a moment to rearrange the papers on his desk. Kennedy's frankness had wrong-footed him; it meant the interview notes were redundant. All they now

needed was a confession to the killing of Norman
Turnbull and Drake could confirm that no further action
be taken against Justin Selston, bring Kennedy to court
and live with the consequences that an innocent man
had been caught up in the case.

'Yesterday Norman Turnbull was killed in his car
at Porth Neigwl near Abersoch.'

Kennedy nodded. 'He'd been scratching around for
a story for so long. He knew all about Tom Levine. He
was threatening to speak to Dorothy Levine, so I drove
over to see him. He had all the evidence he needed. I
had no alternative. He knew too much.'

Once Kennedy was safely back in his cell Drake
sat nursing a coffee in a nondescript mug in the
canteen, Sara sitting opposite him, working her way
through a chocolate bar. Doubts about prosecuting
Selston had been replaced by relief that they had a
confession from Kennedy to multiple murders.

'I have never seen anything like that,' Drake said.

'It was almost too easy,' Sara said.

Drake agreed, and that worried him.

'Andy Thorsen and Rhodri Boyd weren't pleased,'
Wyndham Price announced in an I-don't- give-a-damn
tone. 'Justin Selston's defence team had a collective fit,
demanding to know if there was any evidence or details
we hadn't disclosed to them.'

Price sat across from Drake and Sara in a
conference room at area custody centre. Three empty
plastic cups stood on the table between them. Drake
couldn't remember whether the taste of the coffee was
acceptable or not. It was late and he was tired but at

least they had a confession.

'When will we formally discontinue the charges against Justin Selston?' Sara said.

'We'll formally conduct a review tomorrow afternoon with Andy Thorsen. He can formally notify Selston and his lawyers that he won't face further action. We shall have to deal with any fallout, but we did the right thing.'

For a few seconds nobody responded. Exhaustion seeped into every part of Drake's body. His thoughts were a jumble of contradictions. Had they been justified in interviewing and arresting Justin Selston? The man's reputation was in tatters. Should they have done something differently? But they had the forensic evidence, and had Selston been honest would they have made the same decision?

'There's nothing more we can do tonight,' Price said. 'Go home.'

Annie was waiting for Drake when he arrived back at his apartment. 'You look tired.' He held her close in a tight embrace. He had returned to the apartment to spend a lonely evening by himself far too often and he had been looking forward all day to seeing her smiling face and her presence next to him.

He took a bottle of chilled lager from the kitchen fridge and slumped onto the sofa in the sitting room, Annie by his side. He took a long slug of the drink. His eyes burned, his back ached and more than anything he wanted to have a long, hot shower.

'Is the case finished?'

Drake nodded. 'Thank God for that.'

Chapter 49

Saturday 10th April
8.47 am

Drake woke from a dreamless sleep, sensing that he hadn't moved in bed all night. Sunshine filtered into the bedroom and he moved a hand to touch Annie, but the bed was empty next to him. The sound of activity from the kitchen filtered into the bedroom. He couldn't remember going to sleep last night – but he could recall her telling him he needed to take some time off now the case had been finalised. Had she mentioned going to Cardiff for a long weekend?

Getting up, he pulled on an old T-shirt and padded out into the kitchen.

Annie smiled. He wrapped his arms around her waist and kissed her on the lips. 'It's wonderful having you here.'

'How do you feel?'

'Tired.' Drake sat down by the kitchen table.

Annie produced a perfect cup of coffee for him.

'You need to have a break, Ian. There's this wonderful walk through the forests near Dolgellau. Perhaps we could go tomorrow?'

'How far is that?'

Annie shrugged. 'Somebody at work told me about it and gave me the details of a website. It's so easy to work out how long a car journey will take these days. I don't think it's far. We could stop for a meal on the way back.'

That afternoon Drake had a difficult meeting with Andy Thorsen and Price, and he hoped he would be able to relax with Annie on Sunday. 'I may not be the best company.'

'I won't take no for an answer; you have to unwind.'

Drake's mobile rang from the cradle where it had been charging overnight near the bed. He answered the call after striding from the kitchen. He recognised Mike Foulds' number.

'I hear there have been developments,' Foulds said. 'I don't suppose this will make any difference, but we've had the toxicology report back on Tom Levine and there were traces of Rohypnol in his body.'

Drake thought of Michael Kennedy's denial during his interview that he had spiked Levine's drinks. Drake refocused his mind on Michael Kennedy's interview. Something made Drake ask: 'Was there any trace of chloroform in the toxicology report on Nicholas Wixley?'

'We didn't request a test for chloroform. But chloroform takes minutes to be effective –it's only in TV dramas that it has an instantaneous effect. Do you want me to organise a test?'

At that moment, his mind wanted to shake everything. But more than anything he wanted to know why Michael Kennedy hadn't admitted to using Rohypnol.

'Ian, are you still there?'

Drake shook off the troubled thoughts dominating his mind. 'Yes, get a toxicology report done on Nicholas Wixley.'

Foulds rang off and Drake turned his mobile through his fingers, desperately wanting to identify why he was feeling apprehensive. The smell of frying bacon tickled his nostrils and Annie calling that breakfast was ready disrupted his thought process. He parked it for the moment, something to mull over before his meeting with Andy Thorsen and Superintendent Price.

Returning to the kitchen, a plate of bacon and eggs and freshly toasted bread waited for him. Annie was tapping away on her tablet computer. 'It's only a drive of an hour and a half and that's assuming average traffic.'

Drake ate his breakfast and then organised a second cup of coffee. He listened to Annie as she planned their day out. But he paid her little attention: his mind was troubling him about the inquiry.

'What time could we start?' Annie said.

Drake returned to the chair by the table – the crema on the top of his coffee took his attention. Annie was still tapping on her tablet.

'Start?' Drake said.

'Yes, I've told you Ian. I've been able to check how long the journey will take.'

'The journey?'

Annoyance crept into her voice. 'I've checked the length of the journey.'

Drake stood up, abruptly realising the one thing he hadn't checked. 'I need to get to headquarters.'

Hurriedly he showered, found a pair of denims, a casual shirt and a half-zip top.

He stood in the hallway in front of the mirror drawing a comb through his hair. Annie gave him a troubled look. 'How long will you be?'

'I'll call you later.'

He could sense the worry on Annie's face. She squeezed his forearm. 'Be careful, Ian.'

He kissed her lightly and pulled the door closed behind him, already dialling Sara's number. 'Get over to headquarters immediately; we need to check something.'

He didn't bother calling at the newsagent for his daily fix of the Soduku from the morning paper. He made straight for headquarters. After parking he jogged over to reception, taking the stairs to the Incident Room two at a time. In his office, he scrambled to find the CCTV footage of Michael Kennedy passing the café on the morning of Turnbull's death.

The time on the screen said 7.57.

Quickly he googled the journey time from the middle of Abersoch to Porth Neigwl/Hell's Mouth. It would be at least eleven minutes. But these were country roads, unfamiliar to Kennedy. There might be tractors or a caravan – anything to impede Kennedy's journey.

Then it took a few minutes to find the statement from the eyewitness who had seen the fire take hold of Turnbull's car. Drake printed out a copy and read each line focusing carefully. He didn't hear Sara entering the Incident Room. He ignored the good morning greeting as she stood on the threshold of his office. It was only when she rapped her knuckles on the door that his concentration was interrupted.

He looked up, waved her in.

'We've missed something.'

Sara gave him a puzzled look.

'I've checked the timings for the morning Norman Turnbull was killed.'

'Timings, sir?'

'Michael Kennedy didn't have time to reach Porth

Neigwl.'

Sara frowned. Drake knew he wasn't making any sense.

'We've got Kennedy on the CCTV footage passing the café at 7.57. It would have taken at least eleven minutes to reach the car park where Norman Turnbull was killed in his car. That takes us to at least 8:08. But it's probably going to take longer.' Drake's voice had become louder at the implication of what he was about to say. 'But even so, the eyewitness we have says that the car started burning at eight o'clock. Just before the news headlines on the *Today* programme.'

'That means he can't have been the perpetrator.'

Drake flopped back into his chair.

Sara continued. 'So why the hell did he admit to murdering Norman Turnbull?'

Drake tried to measure his breathing. Foulds' initial conversation with him that morning had created a jumble of thoughts. He had to sort them.

'Mike Foulds called me this morning. There was a trace of Rohypnol in Tom Levine's body.'

'But ...?'

'I know. Kennedy specifically denies he had spiked Levine's drinks.'

'So who did?'

'The killer had to overpower Nicholas Wixley somehow but there wasn't any trace of a struggle.'

'Was Wixley drugged?'

Drake shook his head. 'No suggestion in the toxicology report. And Kennedy's suggestion of using chloroform doesn't make sense. It would have taken far too long to have incapacitated Wixley. And do you remember yesterday in the interview he looked surprised when I told him about the blood on the knife.'

'What are you suggesting, boss?'

'Turnbull photographed him in the café near the meeting place of Gamblers Anonymous and Holly Thatcher mentioned she thought he liked a flutter. So if he was being honest, why not tell us he has a gambling problem?' Drake took a deep breath. 'It's someone else ... It must have been a woman. Someone Wixley went with willingly to the bedroom.'

Sara's mouth fell open. 'But ... Kennedy has admitted the murders. Who is he protecting?'

'Wixley had an affair with Pamela Kennedy.'

'That was no more than office gossip.'

Another recollection fell into place in Drake's mind and he cursed to himself as he realised he'd ignored it at the time. 'Selston told us that Pamela had access to the Euan Levine prosecution papers.'

Sara looked unconvinced.

'And what if it wasn't Michael Kennedy who went to the Gamblers Anonymous meeting, but his wife? And while she's in the meeting he visits the café where Turnbull takes the photographs.'

Sara raised a doubting eyebrow.

'Call that fisherman you spoke to. I want to double-check he was absolutely certain it was a man – he might have *assumed* he saw Michael Kennedy. I think we got the truth from Kennedy about his financial problems. But it was probably only half the truth. I've got to check the list of debtors that Tom Levine acquired when he bought the bookmakers.'

Sara left and within a couple of minutes he heard her voice on the telephone. He blanked it out as he clicked through the documentation on his computer until he found the list of debtors. A search against the K produced no links to Pamela Kennedy. What if she didn't use her married name? He clicked on the Britannia Chambers website and moments later he was rewarded with an entry for a Pamela Farley extolling her virtues as an experienced barrister.

Sara was still on the telephone, so he decided to check one further thing.

The bank statements of Michael Kennedy showed the receipt of £50,000 but it also showed that the money was paid out a week later. The name of the recipient said Mrs Pamela Kennedy. He focused on the details for a second or two until he noticed Sara standing in the doorway to his room. She nodded slowly. 'You were right, boss, the fisherman couldn't be certain it was a man.'

'Farley,' Drake said. 'It's her professional name and she was in hock to the bookmakers that Levine purchased to the sum of £180,000.'

Sara whistled under her breath. 'She could have placed the knife in Justin Selston's property on the day of the party.'

'Only one way we can check that. We need to talk to Selston's cleaner, Mildred.'

Drake grabbed his car keys and got up. 'Let's go.'

Chapter 50

Saturday 10th April
10.09 am

Drake listened to Sara's one-sided telephone call as they travelled west along the A55 through the tunnels towards Penmaenmawr and then on to Bangor.

'Do you have the contact telephone numbers for the owners of these two properties?' Another period of silence as Sara listened and ummed and ahhed occasionally.

'And do you have a mobile telephone number for Mildred?'

Now Sara jotted something in her pocketbook.

She turned to Drake once the call was finished. 'She's cleaning two holiday homes this morning ready for the changeover this afternoon. Her husband was a bit pissed off because he had only just got to bed. Apparently, he works nights.'

'Try her mobile number.'

Drake grabbed the steering wheel tightly as the call rang out. Sara punched the postcode of the first holiday home into the satnav. Drake didn't bother checking the details. He could see that it was in Pwllheli and he knew the route well.

By late morning Drake had pulled into a small estate of bungalows on the outskirts of Pwllheli. The property where Mildred was working appeared empty. Drake and Sara walked over and unlatched the gate but couldn't see any signs of life and there was no indication of Mildred's car so he gave the front door a cursory knock without waiting for a reply before hurrying back to the car.

The second address was on the opposite side of town. Traffic through the middle delayed their journey and Sara tried her mobile again. She turned to Drake and shook her head. 'It goes to voicemail straightaway.'

A mobile delivery van from one of the main supermarkets had drawn up outside the property next to the holiday home Mildred was cleaning and it obstructed their view initially until Drake was rewarded by seeing a silver Fiesta parked in the drive. He could see movement inside the house and he drew the car onto the pavement. They darted up the drive.

His mobile telephone rang as he reached the door. He didn't recognise the number and, giving it a cursory glance, he sent the message to voicemail. Reaching the front door, he banged on the frame of the glass-panelled door. Seconds later he saw movement inside and Mildred opened the door. His mobile bleeped a reminder that a recent caller had left a message. He'd pick it up later.

'We need a word, Mildred.'

She frowned. 'What's this about?'

'There's nothing for you to be worried about.' Drake and Sara entered the hallway.

'There was a party at Justin Selston's house on Easter bank holiday Monday. Were you there?'

She nodded. 'He likes me to be there for parties. I got some of my family to help with serving food and drinks. Is this about Mr Selston? I mean, how is he? It must be terrible ...' Her voice faded.

'We want to ask you about the guests present.' Drake used a serious, determined tone. 'Do you know Michael Kennedy, the chief clerk of the chambers where Mr Selston works?'

Mildred nodded. 'And his wife, Pamela. She was there too and she helped out. In the kitchen and with organising food for everyone. It was lucky she was there really. Most of the others expect us locals to do all the work.'

The tension Drake had been feeling all morning dissipated a notch. At least they had confirmation Pamela had the opportunity to leave the bloodied knife in Selston's property.

Drake and Sara left Mildred cleaning the holiday home and returned to the car. He took a moment to retrieve the mobile from his pocket and listened to Dot Levine's message.

'I won't be able to wait for your officer to call. I've got to go out. Can we rearrange?'

Drake turned to Sara. 'Did you send someone to see Dot Levine?'

Sara shook her head.

Drake's heart raced when he realised what could be happening. 'Let's get over to Dot Levine's place. Now.'

As Drake turned a corner approaching Dot Levine's property a Series 2 BMW was parked in a layby nearby. He jolted the car to a halt across the entrance. Drake had one hand on the car door when Sara said. 'I think we should wear stab jackets.'

'You're right.'

They left the car and seconds later dragged from the boot two stab jackets.

They walked up to the front door. It was ajar. Drake gave Sara a nervous look. They stepped inside.

Resisting the temptation to call out and warn Pamela Kennedy, Drake tiptoed past the empty sitting room.

They turned into the kitchen. At the far end of the room the noise of activity filtered through a door that Drake guessed led to the garage adjacent to the property itself. Drake's pulse pounded in his neck when he saw the prone body of Dot Levine on the floor by the kitchen table.

'Call for an ambulance and back-up immediately,' Drake hissed at Sara.

She kneeled by Mrs Levine, searching for a pulse. Drake made for the door into the garage. He pushed it open and in the far corner Pamela Kennedy was searching through the drawers of a metal filing cabinet, extracting documents, examining papers. She saw Drake and her features turned into outright hatred.

'Mrs Kennedy I'm arresting you on suspicion of ...'

Drake didn't have time to finish. Pamela picked up a length of timber and, taking three quick steps, launched herself at Drake, swinging the long piece of wood. He held up his right arm. She grunted as she poleaxed her weapon onto Drake's arm. He heard a crack and a shattering pain shot up through his arm. He fell to the floor as she prepared for a second blow.

He watched as she drew both hands behind herself, lifting the makeshift baton high over her head. But it didn't fall, he wasn't struck. He heard the crackle from the discharge of a Taser and saw Sara standing by the door to the garage, both hands pointing at Pamela Kennedy's body wincing as she convulsed into a heap on the ground.

Chapter 51

Sunday 10th April

Drake hadn't realised how painful a broken wrist could be. Despite regular painkillers and a padded splint, he had slept fitfully after Annie had collected him from the hospital. Under protest he had agreed not to take any telephone calls on Saturday evening but by Sunday morning he was restless. Annie gave him a scolding look as he announced he had to get into headquarters.

She pulled up in the car park outside headquarters and kissed him warmly. 'After this is finished we're going on holiday.'

'Of course.'

She was right. Once he had interviewed Pamela Kennedy he could relax. He would book time off and he and Annie would take that forest walk she had planned. He would leave his mobile at home and he would relax and forget about Nicholas Wixley and the holiday home owners of the Llŷn Peninsula. And they'd have a holiday – sitting on a beach in the Mediterranean sounded appealing.

He watched her drive away and turned and walked up to the Incident Room. Sara was the first to look up as Drake entered. She glanced at his wrist. 'How are you feeling?'

'I've been better.'

Winder and Luned gave him warm smiles.

'How's Dot Levine?'

'She's got concussion and a gash to the head. The hospital is keeping her for a few days,' Sara replied.

'Did you get that video footage I asked for? Drake

sat by one of the desks.

'On your computer, boss,' Winder said.

'Bring me up to date.'

'We recovered the document Pamela Kennedy was looking for, sir,' Sara said. 'It was a record of all her gambling debts. She must have got desperate once Levine decided to blackmail her over his nephew's case.'

'The search teams found a supply of Rohypnol in her car,' Winder added.

Drake wanted to punch his fist in the air but settled for feeling pleased that his first question to Pamela Kennedy would be to invite her to explain the presence of the date rape drug.

'We've taken her fingerprints and DNA,' Sara continued. 'The partial fingerprint on the champagne flute matches Mrs Kennedy's. She probably tried to clean the glass and was only partially successful in removing the print.'

Now they had two key pieces of incontrovertible evidence that Pamela Kennedy had actually been in Nicholas Wixley's home. 'We can organise to interview her later this afternoon.'

'Will you be fit enough, sir?'

'Of course I am.'

When Drake sat down by his desk he realised how tired he really was. But he wasn't going to miss the opportunity of interviewing Pamela Kennedy no matter how exhausted he might be. Sara wandered into his room and sat down uninvited. 'I have prepared some outline notes for the interview.' She pushed various sheets of paper over the desk.

'Thank you.' Drake realised Sara must have known

he wouldn't miss the interview.

'I also had a triangulation report completed on Pamela Kennedy's mobile. It places her near Porth Neigwl the morning Norman Turnbull was killed.'

'Let's see what she says about all this.'

Drake turned his attention to the CCTV footage from the Morfa Bychan holiday park near Porthmadog.

'It's easy to make out Pamela driving the car,' Sara said once Drake had finished.

'She probably hadn't noticed the camera.' Drake had almost missed it himself – it had become second nature checking for CCTV wherever he went. He and Sara spent the rest of the afternoon reviewing the interview plan she had prepared. It was late in the afternoon when they reached the area custody suite. He was fortified by coffee and one of Winder's flapjacks and a sense he had to see the investigation through to the end. He wasn't going to delegate the final stages to any other officer. He had been responsible for the investigation however flawed it might appear and he was going to take responsibility. The final piece of the evidence they needed was in the forensic report that arrived late that afternoon. He smiled broadly to himself when he read the conclusion.

Pamela Kennedy had to suffer the indignity of wearing a police issue paper one-piece boiler suit. It made a wrinkling sound whenever she moved, and it would chafe her skin. Drake thought it suited her very well, as, in due course, would standard prison attire. Her expensive designer clothes were already in the forensic lab.

Drake produced from the folder on the table in front of him a set of photographs showing the body of Nicholas Wixley and he turned them, so they faced Pamela. He pushed each in turn towards her.

'Did you call to see Nicholas Wixley on the night he was killed?'

Kennedy reached over a carefully manicured forefinger and moved one of the images to one side.

'Why did you kill him?'

Drake looked over at Kennedy. Her hair was matted, her make-up smudged and the well-groomed professional he had met at Britannia Chambers was a world away from the woman sitting across the table.

She raised her head slightly and looked up towards the corner of the ceiling as though the interview process was beneath her contempt.

'How well did you know Nicholas Wixley?'

She gave her eyebrows the faintest twitch.

How many of his questions would she ignore?

'Did you have an affair with Nicholas Wixley?'

She blinked enough to suggest it caught her unawares.

'We have an eyewitness who saw your car arriving back at Portmeirion Hotel in the early hours after Nicholas Wixley was killed. Were you driving?'

Very few defendants say nothing at all in a police interview. It was human nature to engage, respond to questions, defend oneself. And sooner or later he would get her to react.

'We recovered a champagne flute from the crime scene. And we found a bottle of Tattinger 96 vintage in the kitchen. It's a superb vintage apparently. Did you enjoy it?' Drake leaned over the table. He lowered his voice. 'We recovered a partial fingerprint on a glass that matches yours. Pamela, we can place you at the crime scene. You know better than anyone that this is your chance to tell us what happened.'

The barest hint of a smile wrinkled her mouth. It was almost complimentary.

Drake sat back and looked over at Sara, who squinted at Kennedy before turning and sharing a determined look with Drake. He flicked the paperwork and folders on the table while waiting for Kennedy to flinch – change her position in the chair, fidget with her hair. All she did was breathe out a long sigh.

He carried on thumbing through the paperwork until he found the image of Michael Kennedy taken by Norman Turnbull in the café. He showed it to Sara. She raised an eyebrow and nodded. Drake turned to Pamela.

'How long have you been going to Gamblers Anonymous?'

Her mouth fell open slightly, she squeezed her eyes shut and then tipped her head to one side. She might not say anything, but she couldn't hide the surprise in her body language. She reached for a plastic beaker of water and took a sip before resuming her sphinx-like pose.

'You owed Tom Levine over £180,000.' Drake tried the same trick again, leaning over the table, softening his tone; he even tried making his Welsh accent sound more pronounced, a little more sympathetic. 'That must have been humiliating. I can understand how you would have felt.' He kept his elbows on the table, giving her a sympathetic glance.

She smiled as though to say, 'nice try'.

'It must have sickened you when Tom Levine

blackmailed you into disclosing details of the prosecution's case against his nephew. Tell me how you felt.'

She barely took her gaze away from the same spot on the ceiling, but she forced back a swallow.

'I'd like to know where you bought the Rohypnol.' Drake sounded genuinely interested. 'I guess it must have been on the internet. One of my officers is doing a search at the moment through your laptop and your computer at home. You might like to tell us – it would assist with the inquiry.'

Kennedy folded her arms and pulled them closer to her chest.

'And the night of the party at the sailing club you spiked his drinks, making certain that by the time you arrived later he'd be completely comatose.'

Drake replaced the photographs of Nicholas Wixley with images from the cabin of Tom Levine's yacht. Then he reached for the laptop in the case behind his chair. Pamela gave him a longer glance this time.

'Modern technology is wonderful isn't it?' Drake smiled as he opened the laptop. It took him a few minutes to boot up the machine and then he clicked into the CCTV footage Winder had recovered.

'Did you know that the campsite has CCTV at the entrance?' Drake looked at Pamela, but her eyes never wavered from the ceiling. 'We have you recorded leaving the campsite at 12.30 am on the morning Levine was killed. Would you like to tell me where you were going?'

Drake ran the footage and Pamela glanced at it just long enough to see the car crossing the speed bump. Pamela shook her head for a moment but said nothing.

'I know what you're thinking. It's poor quality. A jury wouldn't be persuaded.'

Drake tilted his head, inviting her to agree. She didn't.

'You see, Pamela, I think you were going down into Porthmadog where you took the cuddy you and Michael own to the marina in Pwllheli. And that's where you killed Levine.'

Another brief shake of her head.

'There must have been a lot of blood. And you know that bloodstains can be very difficult to eradicate from clothes. I've got a forensic team going through the clothes from your wardrobe and combing your sailing cuddy.'

A confident defiance on Pamela's face told Drake she'd probably burned every item of clothing associated with both deaths.

Pamela sipped more water.

'It was clever leaving the knife in Selston's garage. I have to admit that. It was clear evidence that linked him to both murders and conveniently for you it appeared he had a motive to kill Nicholas Wixley.' Drake nodded his appreciation.

Drake continued using an exasperated tone. 'Forensic science is a wonderful thing, isn't it, Pamela. I'm sure you've defended cases where the prosecution has sought to establish guilt by establishing DNA from the flimsiest sample.' He made the contest between prosecution and defence sound like a tiresome board game.

'What colour is your nail varnish, Pamela?'

She gave him a sharp look before instinctively curling her fingers and hiding her nails. Now his voice took on a harder edge. 'The knife used to kill Nicholas Wixley and Tom Levine had small pieces of varnish on it.'

Drake looked over and the arrogance had disappeared, dissolved into a dawning realisation that she had no chance. She blinked lazily but she continued to gaze upwards.

He peered over at her. 'The DNA extracted from the nail varnish fragments matches your DNA. Pamela, we can link you to the murder weapon and to both men. Your husband has already told us that Nicholas Wixley held him to ransom about the monies that he had received from Tom Levine. And we know that all of that money was transferred to you.'

Drake took another moment to distribute photographs of Norman Turnbull's car from Porth Neigwl on the table. Looking at the charred upright remains of a human body sitting in a driver's seat was grotesque and foul but Pamela barely flinched.

'When we interviewed your husband, he admitted killing Norman Turnbull.'

Drake waited to see her response. Perhaps she'd be relieved to hear her husband had killed Norman Turnbull. Then she'd only face two murder charges instead of three.

But she said nothing, so Drake continued.

'But, Pamela, we can prove it wasn't your husband. We have CCTV footage of him in Abersoch that morning, so he didn't have time to reach the car park at Porth Neigwl. And we triangulated your mobile to that area on the morning Turnbull was killed.'

Pamela Kennedy took another sip of water. Drake paused. He could almost hear everyone's heartbeat; he could certainly hear his own thumping in his ear.

'Did you kill Nicholas Wixley, Tom Levine and Norman Turnbull?'

'Nicholas Wixley was the worst.' Pamela Kennedy turned to look at Drake. Then she spat a mouthful of saliva at Drake that dribbled over his face.

Chapter 52

The morning after Michael Kennedy and Pamela Kennedy appeared for sentencing in the Caernarfon Crown Court, Drake purchased a copy of *The Times*, *The Guardian* and *The Telegraph*. When he arrived at his office he opened *The Times* first and spread the paper out on his desk after moving a developing column of Post-it notes.

Once the accumulated evidence against Pamela Kennedy became overwhelming Michael Kennedy had broken down at subsequent interviews, sobbing confirmation that he had nothing to do with the three murders. Pamela Kennedy had remained aloof, stonewalling further questions from Drake. But she couldn't avoid the inevitable consequence of her husband withdrawing his admissions and she took advantage of the court system by pleading guilty at the first opportunity, hoping to lessen her time behind bars.

Drake read with interest a profile of DCC Wixley in *The Times*, and smiled as he thought to himself what the journalist would have made had he been aware that suspicion had initially fallen on her for her husband's death. The paper printed comments from her chief constable that 'she had been an exemplary police officer, holding the highest standards, an example to all young recruits', but what did he really think? Laura Wixley was taking up an appointment as a chief executive of a charity dealing with abused women. The newspaper included a photograph of her leaving the Crown Court building. She had grown her hair, lost some weight. Mr and Mrs Thorpe had agreed to meet her and Mr Thorpe had called Drake the day after the meeting. 'We can't turn the clock back. Nobody can, but we enjoyed meeting her. The missus cried.' Drake hoped that Laura Wixley's promise to keep in regular contact would be fulfilled.

Once Drake had finished *The Times* he folded it away and turned to *The Guardian*. It carried a critical section about the initial prosecution of Justin Selston, suggesting that the Wales Police Service had been precipitous in charging the barrister. There were several pictures of Selston and a quote from a press release issued by his solicitors. Drake had learned from Holly Thatcher that Selston was more in demand now than he'd ever been. The criminals of north-west England charged with serious offences were flocking to be represented by him.

The Telegraph reported accurately the prosecuting case. A high court judge had been allocated the case and had spent a week in Caernarfon dealing with burglars and minor assaults. The highlight of his week was obviously sentencing Pamela Kennedy and Michael Kennedy. The court had listened in stunned silence to all the details. Occasionally the judge had asked for clarification of some points.

Pamela Kennedy had sat silently gazing straight ahead without ever turning her head even to look at her husband sitting a few feet away from her. At least Michael Kennedy had taken in his surroundings. And he had scanned Drake and Sara without acknowledging their presence.

Pamela Kennedy's life sentences were automatic and the judge's recommendation that she serve a minimum of eighteen years had generated comments in *The Telegraph* that the sentence appeared too lenient.

Neither of the other newspapers on his desk had made any comment about the length of the minimum term. In reality, eighteen years meant at least twenty, possibly longer, once the parole system had ground its way through mountains of paperwork.

Michael Kennedy's four-year sentence for theft seemed unduly harsh in the circumstances. He had nodded grudgingly when the judge passed the sentence, and when he left the dock Drake was certain he had given him the faintest nod of acknowledgement, or was it thanks?

The Telegraph did at least have an article suggesting the system for the appointment of judges needed to be far more transparent, even handed. It suggested that the present system was shrouded in nepotism without any real accountability.

Drake finished reading *The Telegraph* as Superintendent Price walked in and sat down.

'We've had confirmation that Justin Selston isn't going to pursue any complaint about his arrest and charging.'

Drake gave a slow smile and bowed his head. It was the news he was waiting for. It meant they could have closure on the inquiry without the threat of Justin Selston's legal action against the Wales Police Service.

'Apparently he's more in demand now than he's ever been from the villains of Manchester,' Price said. 'He's been retained to appear in several murder cases already.'

'That's good news. I mean, Selston deciding not to sue the WPS.'

'I agree.'

Drake sensed that Wyndham Price had more to say.

Price paused again. 'I should tell you that HR in Cardiff have been lining me up for retirement.'

Drake sensed a feeling of loss. It would be difficult working with a new superintendent. Someone who didn't know how he worked or understood his background. And he would miss Price.

'Are you looking forward to retirement, sir?'

'You've still got me around for a few more months yet.'

Price got up and made to leave.

'Your team did well, Ian.'

Epilogue

Annie's insistence that Drake invite Sara for dinner couldn't be ignored any longer. Drake's stumbled excuses that he wasn't good at socialising with the others on his team had raised an eyebrow. 'You all work together. The least you can do is to invite her to dinner occasionally.'

It brought back memories of the wizened inspector Drake had worked for years ago holding forth in a pub on a Friday night about the value of teamwork when in reality what he expected was unquestioning loyalty and obedience.

Sara arrived promptly at Drake's apartment with a bottle of Rioja and a bouquet of flowers for Annie. Drake took Sara into the sitting room and Annie made excuses about finalising their meal of lasagne and salad and disappeared into the kitchen. A chilled bottle of Pino Grigio sat in a wine cooler.

'White wine okay?' Drake said.

Sara nodded. 'Thanks.'

Annie joined them soon after they had sat down. 'It won't be long.' She turned to Sara. 'Now tell me all about yourself. Ian is hopeless about telling me about his work colleagues.' She rolled her eyes. 'Men.'

Sara smiled. The ice had been broken. Only Annie could have achieved that, Drake thought. He listened as Sara shared with Annie details of her family background that he knew little about. Her parents were still alive, and she saw them regularly. They were a small family; she had some distant cousins but no siblings.

The conversation continued around the dining table

and Drake gradually relaxed into sharing his own family experiences and the conflicting emotions on discovering he had a half-brother. He smiled to himself as he watched Annie engaging with Sara in an uncomplicated natural conversation. He couldn't have imagined Sian, his former wife, ever agreeing to entertain the detective sergeant on his team, nor showing as much interest as Annie had done.

'It must be difficult having to deal with dead bodies and murderers,' Annie said as they drank coffee.

'I found my first case very difficult,' Sara said. 'I know we've all got to die but seeing a body sliced open makes you realise how evil people can be.'

'You get used to it,' Drake added. 'The important thing is not to think it's normal.'

'I'm sorry I mentioned work.' Annie grinned. 'Ian tells me you had to cancel a holiday in Dublin.'

Sara nodded. 'The friends I was supposed to be going to Dublin with have booked a house in the south of France in the summer. Because there are so many going it's going to be affordable.'

'All the extra overtime that both of you worked on the Nicholas Wixley case would justify a long holiday,' Annie said.

'We're taking Helen and Megan to EuroDisney over the summer,' Drake announced. 'I hope there won't be an urgent case.'

Annie struck a serious tone. 'If there is, somebody else will have to be responsible.'

Drake smiled.

They drank coffee in the sitting room and talked about nothing particular until Sara read the time and announced that it was late. She thanked Annie and

Drake for the hospitality and left soon afterwards. Drake stood with Annie by the door to his apartment.

He pulled her close and she looked up into his eyes.

'Thanks for organising tonight. I should have done that a long time ago.'

He kissed her, and the warmth of her body and the lingering touch of her lips reassured him how happy she made him feel.

33956617R00217

Made in the USA
Columbia, SC
11 November 2018